Veduci grabbed the trunk of a young tree and slingshot around it to plunge his sword all the way through the side of the startled Jokapcul. He lost precious seconds twisting and working his sword out of the dead man.

Haft stood alone, backed against a large tree, fighting like a madman as he swung the half-moon blade of his battle-axe in broad arcs that wrapped all the way around to protect his sides from flank attack. He'd shattered every lance thrust at him. Twice he knocked arrows aside and once ducked out of the way of a shaft. Another arrow had slit along his ribs; a lance had gouged his thigh before he could break it with his axe. He bled from numerous other nicks and cuts, but half a dozen Jokapcul bodies lay before him and most others now kept their distance. To the lancers, it truly looked like he and his axe were one. . . .

By David Sherman

The Night Fighters
KNIVES IN THE NIGHT
MAIN FORCE ASSAULT
OUT OF THE FIRE
A ROCK AND A HARD PLACE
A NGHU NIGHT FALLS
CHARLIE DON'T LIVE HERE ANYMORE

Demontech
ONSLAUGHT
RALLY POINT

THERE I WAS: THE WAR OF CORPORAL
　　　HENRY J. MORRIS, USMC

THE SQUAD

GULF RUN

BOOK III OF
DEMONTECH

DAVID SHERMAN

BALLANTINE BOOKS • NEW YORK

A Del Rey® Book
Published by The Random House Publishing Group
Copyright © 2004 by David Sherman

www.delreydigital.com

ISBN 0-345-44376-4

Manufactured in the United States of America

First Edition: January 2004

OPM   10   9   8   7   6   5   4   3   2   1

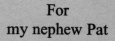

For
my nephew Pat

PROLOGUE

The coast huggers rounded the point of Land's Beginning in the dark of a moonless night. The orange glow from a tiny lamp mounted on the stern of each craft, shielded to be unseen from the front and sides, allowed the boat behind it to follow. One by one, each coxswain opened a second lamp to signal the furling of his boat's sails. When the sailors dipped oars to water to move against the westerly breeze, the coxswains lit a third lamp. Two hours after the first coast hugger rounded the point, it turned its bow shoreward and the men on each boat moved their oars only enough to keep it in place.

Eventually all the coast huggers were in line abreast, outside the sheltered bay that gave rise to the city state of Harfort, normally a welcome port for traders caught in storms where the Inner Ocean met the Great Southern Ocean, and Princedon Gulf mixed its waters with both. But the storm season was past and the only traders in Harfort port were the shallow-draft ships that plied Princedon Gulf. In another season the docks, taverns, and brothels would be abuzz with activity and jangling with coin, even so soon before dawn. In this season, solitary watchmen struggled to stay awake in the lonely quiet.

Now and again there was a soft plop as a blade reentered the water with the sound of a feeding fish taking a water skimmer. Muffled oarlocks made no noise that could be heard on shore. A bored dog's bark drifted over the bay from inland.

The first of the coast huggers formed a near solid line from one to the other of the sheltering arms of the bay. Later boats made a second line behind them, and still later boats a third. A fourth and a fifth line were in position by the time the eastern sky began to lighten. The oarsmen of the first line bent their backs and pulled forward to the docks and piers and the beaches in between. The second, third, fourth, and fifth followed sharply and closed the gaps until, when the first was in place, the others were touching so a man could walk from boat to boat to land without getting his feet wet.

Magicians accompanying the commanding kamazai of the wings of the massed boats sent imbalurises flying to the Kamazai Commanding of the invasion force, telling him they were in place. The Kamazai Commanding had his magician send the imbalurises back with the order to attack.

The attack didn't come with screams and battle cries, the flash of blades or thunder of demon spitters. Instead, soldiers in the hundreds padded swiftly through the town to preassigned objectives. The only casualty in the streets was a nodding watchman. A half-troop of soldiers swarmed through the barracks of the city state's small off-season garrison and captured the weapons before the sleepy Harfort soldiers realized there was danger.

The Earl of Harfort was yanked, naked, from his bed and hauled away by strong soldiers. While struggling, he barely noticed the dead attendants in his bedchamber, or the dead guards outside the chamber door. Behind him, his wife screamed as soldiers ripped away the bedcovers and tore off her nightclothes before taking their turns in the earl's bed. The soldiers hauled the naked earl to his throne room, where two kicked at the backs of his knees to bring him down. The earl continued to roar and struggle until something heavy thudded wetly into his chest. Then he looked at the floor and saw on the cold paving stones the severed head of his Colonel of the Guard. He looked up and saw the Kamazai Commanding lounging on the Seat of Office—a chair upon which none but the reigning earl ever sat, under penalty of death.

The earl resumed his struggles, trying to break free, until something smashed into the back of his head. By the time his head was clear, his arms were painfully bound and his feet were hobbled.

The Kamazai Commanding barked an order. A knight approached, bearing the earl's crown. He slammed it onto the earl's head, upside down, and its jeweled points gouged into his brow and scalp and drew blood. The Kamazai Commanding growled another order. A different knight approached with the earl's ermine-lined velvet cloak of office. At a nod from the Kamazai Commanding, the knight held out the cloak, and another knight sliced it sideways below the shoulder and let the velvet slide to a mound on the floor. The knight holding the remains of the cloak top curled it and its golden closure into a circle and unceremoniously dropped it over the earl's head. It landed askew on his shoulders. The Kamazai Commanding barked again then waved a one-armed signal, rose, and led the way out of the throne room. The bound and humiliated earl was dragged, stumbling and tripping, close behind.

Bells began to peal, a signal to the rising populace to gather before the walls of the keep.

The curtain wall of the keep wasn't high, not even twenty feet to the tops of the spiked crenellations, but behind it the rampart was a broad boulevard rather than a mere walkway. The soldiers holding the earl stopped just inside a door giving access to the rampart; he shuddered when he saw the heads of the officers of the Harfort Guard impaled on the spikes. No one stood on the rampart, yet the bells continued to peal and the sound of voices raised in worried question began to grow beneath the wall.

In a moment, members of the court, men and women both, all obviously roused cruelly from bed—as many naked as in bedclothes—began stumbling onto the rampart. Soldiers with pikes and long spears followed, prodding and jabbing them to stand in a rank along the crenellations, though the soldiers remained out of sight of the gathering below. Gasps and cries rose as the people saw the disheveled or naked nobles and courtiers above.

A horn blew to signal that the citizens of Harfort were gathered.

The Kamazai Commanding drew his sword and slapped the

earl across his buttocks hard with the flat of his blade. Wincing with pain, the earl moved forward in the short steps that were all his hobbles allowed. The Kamazai Commanding slow-stepped directly behind him, the point of his sword nestled against the base of the earl's skull. A slave in cleric's robes trailed.

Louder gasps and cries arose as the people recognized their earl, and rose anew when the stranger appeared at the side of their bound, nude lord.

The Kamazai Commanding looked disdainfully down at the crowd, many of whom wore robes hastily thrown over nightclothes. He snarled, and the cleric-slave came to his side.

The Kamazai Commanding roared unintelligible words that might have been growls from a very large and deep-chested dog. The cleric-slave fluttered nervous fingers about his throat and translated:

"People of Harfort, you have new masters now. Your nobles and their sycophants are no more!"

As one, the soldiers behind the nobles and courtiers thrust their weapons forward, piercing their hostages. Spraying blood, the doomed highborn screamed and gurgled and clutched at their wounds, to no avail. The soldiers stepped briskly forward while tipping the butts of their weapons upward, forcing their victims to bend over the top of the curtain wall. The soldiers then worked the blades free, put their weapons down, grabbed their victims' ankles, and threw them over the wall, where they landed with sickening crunches and snaps on the cobbled street below. Most were dead; a sturdier few whimpered or moved feebly.

The Kamazai Commanding roared.

"Do not touch them!" the cleric-slave shouted the translation. "Any who are still alive must be allowed to die on their own. Anyone who touches them will die."

A line of archers appeared at the top of the wall, their bows drawn, arrows aimed downward. People who had started forward to aid or to rob the fallen scampered back.

The Kamazai Commanding yanked the inverted crown

from the earl's head gouging another wound in the royal brow. He looked at the headpiece for a moment as though wondering what it was. Then a grin split his face and he jammed it onto the nearest impaled head. He nodded. A knight stepped forward, grasped the earl's hair with both hands and pulled up. The Kamazai Commanding's sword flashed in the morning sun, and the earl's body fell away from his head.

The conquest of Harfort was complete. Now it was only a matter of organizing the people into their new occupation as slaves.

A galleon dropped anchor at the mouth of Harfort Bay. On its quarterdeck stood Lord Lackland, self-styled the Dark Prince, half bastard third son of Good King Honritu of Matilda. He looked to the west, farther into Princedon Gulf. Just two more city states remained to be reduced, the two smallest and least important of the Princedons. Then the way would be clear to Dartmutt, where he would finally deal with those infernal Frangerian sea soldiers and their motley army.

I
CROSSING
THE SPINE

CHAPTER
ONE

"This is a good place; we'll pull off there," Haft said softly. He used hand signals to show his men where to leave the road and where to go.

"Here" was where the winding road made a narrow cut through a spur of the Princedon Mountains, the range that formed the spine of the Princedon Peninsula. The ridge was heavily wooded on both sides of the cut, boulders barely visible among the trees on the right, upland, side of the cut. Haft's nine men, eight of them in the mottled green of the Zobran Border Warders, continued fifty yards beyond the cut to where Haft had indicated before carefully climbing the far side of the ridge and back to its top, leaving no sign that they'd left the road. The first man off the road clambered up a tree to watch their back trail. The other eight men filtered through the trees, seeking places where they would be hidden from the road and protected by stones or stout tree trunks while being able to observe where it climbed the ridge. They strung their bows and readied arrows, drew their swords or axes and lay them near to hand.

Haft moved from man to man, checking his position and view. The road ran straight for nearly a hundred yards from this vantage point before turning sharply left. Its farthest reaches were deeply shadowed. He moved two of his men to positions offering better fields of vision and fire.

"One," he said to the first man, clasping his shoulder. "Wait for me."

The former Border Warder nodded.

"Two," he said to the second, who grunted in reply. "Wait for me," he repeated.

9

"Three," to another.

And so he went along his thin line, assigning to each his target in the enemy's line of march. The eighth man—the one not in the Border Warders mottled green garb—was Jatke, a hunter from the town of Eikby. When all were in position, he took his own place in the middle of the line and lay his broadaxe and crossbow ready to hand. From there, through a break in the trees, he had a clear if shadowed view of the bend in the road.

Haft hadn't picked the best fighters for this squad—those were probably the Skraglander Bloody Axes who had sworn fealty to him. This was the rear point of the large band of refugees he and Spinner, his fellow Frangerian Marine, were trying to lead to a safe place away from the Jokapcul invaders overrunning the Princedon Peninsula. More important than the best fighting ability on the exposed rear point was the ability to move quietly and stealthily. The Border Warders were adept at stealthy movement and quicker than the Bloody Axes to spot followers. They also needed clear and quick communications; the Border Warders all spoke Zobran and the Eikby hunter spoke a dialect of it—he could understand the Border Warders well enough, and they him. Haft's own harbor Zobran, picked up during several port calls at Zobra City and sharpened by travel with the refugees over many weeks, was easily intelligible to these men, and he understood them as well—provided they didn't talk too fast or use words he didn't know. And not to be underestimated, they all carried the longbow, which shot its arrows with enough force to penetrate the metal-studded leather of Jokapcul armor.

He looked at the demon spitter he carried and cautiously tapped on the small door on the side of the tube. The door popped open, nearly catching his fingers, and the small, naked demon poked its head out.

"Wazzu whanns?" the tiny demon piped at him.

"See the road?" Haft whispered.

The demon looked down the length of the demon spitter tube. *"Yss. Whatch abou id?"*

"Look to the left. See the break in the trees? And the road through it?"

"Yss. Zo?"

"Can you spit through that break and hit horsemen on the road?"

The demon clambered all the way out to the top of the tube and peered intently for a moment, then said, *"Nawzwetz."*

"How should I aim?"

The gnarly little demon, hardly taller than Haft's hand was long, craned its head, side to side, up and down, for a few seconds, then pointed with a lumpy arm. *"Aam lik ziz."*

Haft shifted his head to look along the demon's arm and got smacked on the head—the demon hit surprisingly hard for so small a creature. He jerked back.

"Naw winnige," the demon sneered, *"vazion!"*

Wishing he could rub the sore spot on the side of his head, Haft drew back and looked at the angle of the demon's arm. The demon had told him not windage—the side-to-side aim of the weapon—but elevation, how high to aim.

"Like this?" he asked, pointing a finger at the same upward angle as the demon's arm.

"Thass righ," the demon said, then dove back into the tube, slamming the door behind it. Before Haft could settle the tube into its firing position on his shoulder, the door popped open again and the demon piteously piped, *"Veedmee!"*

Using his thumb and two fingers, Haft opened a pouch on his belt, withdrew a raisin-size pellet and held it out. The demon snatched the pellet and disappeared back into the tube. Crunching echoed hollowly from inside it.

A leaf rustled nearby and a dark form settled next to Haft, peering along the road they watched.

"Ulgh," the dark form said softly, and nodded.

Haft flinched, and looked askance at the wolf. "Wolf, you're supposed to be tracking them." Haft wasn't sure which bothered him more, the wolf who had attached himself to the original group months earlier, or the spitting demon that had taken a liking to him a week or so ago on the night he, Spinner, and a few others had conducted a raid on the Jokapcul encampment at the ruins of Eikby. Now the demon wouldn't spit for anyone else.

"Ulgh!" Wolf grunted, and hunkered lower behind the boulder—clearly, the trailing Jokapcul patrol was near, so he didn't need to track them anymore.

A bit of unsecured tack jangled somewhere out of sight.

Haft glanced at Wolf. He didn't trust the beast—men and wolves were natural enemies, and Wolf had no business traveling with people and aiding them. Still, "Watch my flank," he said.

Wolf looked up at him for a second, tongue lolling. Then, faster than the man could react, he stretched out his neck and lapped Haft's cheek.

Haft jerked away and swatted at him, but Wolf had already darted away to face the side. Before Haft could do anything else, he heard feet scrabbling on bark and the snap of a twig. He turned to see Birdwhistle, the man who'd climbed the tree, scooting toward him.

"They're less than two hundred yards away," Birdwhistle said quietly. "Still in one group, fifteen of them."

"Good," Haft replied. He pointed to his right, to the last open spot on the line. "You're four. Wait for me. Pass the word and bring it back." He then gave Tracker, the man to his left, the same order.

"Fourth man in line," Birdwhistle repeated, and went to the place Haft pointed to.

Haft told the next man in line where the Jokapcul were and readied his crossbow, arrows, and sword. Less than a minute later he turned to Haft and signaled—all nine men in the ambush had their assigned targets, leaving the last six men in the Jokapcul column unmarked. Those last six were the responsibility of Haft and the demon spitter. If the officer was still up, Haft knew he'd use the second spit to take him out—if he could see him from his position. They had to get the officer fast; the Jokapcul fell apart without an officer to give orders.

Haft checked the angle of the demon spitter's tube on his shoulder and sighted toward the section of transverse road visible through the trees. He looped his fingers lightly across the signaling lever. Shortly, he heard the faint clop of a hoof striking a rock, followed by a horse's wet snort. Soon he heard more faint sounds of horsemen on the road. Then the first Jokapcul appeared.

The Jokapcul horseman held his short bow in his hands, arrow nocked, string half drawn. A lance was tucked beneath his right thigh. He wore a gold-tinted leather armor jerkin, with shields that spread wide over his shoulders. A short skirt the same color as the jacket dropped from his waist over the top of brown leather trousers. His gauntlets had cuffs that reached to his elbows. A conical leather helmet sat on his head, a leather flap hung from its back and wrapped around to the front, protecting his throat. All of his leathern garments were studded with metal rectangles, save for his boots. He leaned forward in the saddle and peered intently to his front and sides as he trotted ahead to the road's bend, searching for any sign of the people he was following.

The point rider disappeared for a moment, then reappeared on the straight of the road; others soldiers began crossing the break. The second Jokapcul followed thirty yards to his rear. The remainder were at five-yard intervals. The point man stopped halfway to the cut and signaled for the officer to come forward. The officer was easy to spot when he appeared—his helmet was topped by a golden plume, and the polished metal rectangles on his armor glittered where shafts of sunlight struck them. He stopped alongside the second man in the column and examined the cut. After a moment he quietly ordered the second man to join the point and for the two to scout ahead. The second man readied his bow as he trotted forward. When he was nearly on the first, the first advanced his horse at a walk.

Haft looked to his right. He couldn't see all of his men. Those he could see looked like they were well-concealed from view from the road. It wasn't long before the scouts disappeared from his sight, hidden by the cut's rising bank. He listened carefully and heard the soft clops of their horses walking through it. His breath caught when the clopping didn't stop right away—would they go far enough to see where his squad had left the road? The Jokapcul outnumbered his men, and not enough of them were within range for his men to turn the odds in their favor with their first arrows.

No. It sounded to him as though the scouts had stopped about halfway from the top of the cut, where he and his men had left the road. He hardly dared breathe as he heard them return. They stopped before he could see them again. Evidently they had signaled "all clear," because the officer now signaled the column to move out.

But the officer didn't move when Haft expected him to. In every small Jokapcul cavalry patrol he'd ever seen, the officer was positioned near the front of the column, no farther back than the fifth man, often closer to the front. Haft counted: the two scouts, then a third, fourth, fifth, and sixth man. The officer remained at the far side of the road, watching his men troop by.

Haft straightened his fingers, moving them away from the demon spitter's trigger. Move! he thought. You're supposed to be up near the front of the column, where my men can kill you, not at the rear. He wanted the patrol's leader taken out with the opening shot, but the officer was far enough back that even a broadhead arrow from a long bow might not kill him, and horsemen were passing between him and the ambushers.

The fifth man in the column was a sergeant. Against soldiers from another army, he'd settle for shooting the sergeant first. But the Jokapcul weren't like other armies—their sergeants were little more than disciplinarians and relayers of officers' orders; they had no leadership function. Taking out the sergeant first would do little more than setting off the ambush by shooting a private. Haft glanced to his right. The first soldier behind the two scouts was already nearing the place where the cut would take him out of his sight. In only a moment or two the front third of the column would be beyond the ambush. The last men were passing through the transverse section of road, and he knew he had to have the demon spit now if he wanted to hit the rear of the column.

He lightly tapped the side of the tube near the demon's door to let it know he was ready, carefully aimed at a horseman passing his front, then squeezed the lever.

The demon spat with a thunderous crack. A second later a Jokapcul and his mount vanished in a burst of fire and smoke. To his sides, Haft was aware of arrows zipping through the air. He heard thunks as they struck leather, and the pings of arrowheads striking and glancing off the metal plates that studded the Jokapcul armor. He swiveled to aim at the officer—but couldn't see him; someone must have shot him.

In seconds half a dozen Jokapcul were down, arrows sunk into chests, bellies, thighs. As Haft looked back to the transverse section of road, a horse staggered and went down on its hindquarters with an arrow sticking out of its chest. Another, struck by an arrow that glanced off its hip, reared violently and threw its rider. The tossed Jokapcul rolled over and started to rise, then dropped back down when three arrows hit him—one glanced off, another pierced his armor over his chest, and the third found its way between the protective neck flaps of his helmet.

A roaring voice drew Haft's attention, and he saw the plumed officer's head alongside a standing horse that strained against its tightly held reins—the officer had dismounted and was hiding behind his mount. Before he could aim the demon spitter, its door popped open and the demon gave him a sharp rap just below his eye.

"Hey!"

"*'Ey oozeph! Ook!*" The demon pointed a gnarly arm at the road where it came from the trees.

Haft looked and swallowed a gasp as he swiveled the demon spitter away from the officer—the demon had spotted a dismounted Jokapcul aiming a demon spitter at the ambush! The other demon spat even as Haft was sighting. Thunder erupted fifteen yards to his right and twigs and clods of dirt rained at him through the brush. The Jokapcul with the magical weapon darted to another position, but Haft followed his route and was able to fire before the other could begin to take aim once more. The enemy with the demon spitter disappeared in a thunderous gout of flame.

Haft gave the field a quick glance but didn't see any other demon weapons, then looked again for the officer. The tall golden plume was right where he'd last seen it, sticking up behind the shoulder of a struggling horse. Haft sighted on the horse's shoulder and fired the demon spitter again. The horse erupted in blood and gore; when the smoke cleared, the officer wasn't anywhere to be seen, but his plumed helmet hung from a nearby tree branch. Then yells and the clatter of galloping horses came up the road. The few remaining Jokapcul were fleeing.

"REPORT!" Haft bellowed.

"One, got mine!" called Hunter from the first position.

"Two, mine's dead." That was Archer in the second position.

"That was too close, but I'm all right," someone called out—the Jokapcul demon spitter hadn't caused any casualties.

In seconds all of the ambushers reported they were all right and that each had shot a Jokapcul. The enemy hadn't had a chance to fight back.

"There are two more down farther back," reported the former Border Warder named Tracker.

Haft looked to his left. Wolf wasn't there. "The beast probably ran away when the fighting started," he muttered. He breathed deeply. Not bad. They'd taken down thirteen of the fifteen Jokapcul in less than a minute and suffered no casualties of their own. The remaining enemy was in flight.

"Let's secure the bodies, see if any of them are still alive."

Hunter and Archer went down the back side of the ridge to check on the scouts, while Haft and the rest went down the front. He shouted orders as they went, and five of his men ran ahead beyond the farthest Jokapcul body for security while he and the others checked the bodies. Not all of them were dead yet, though only three were likely to survive their wounds.

"Bandage them," Haft said of the three who had a chance. "Gather all weapons and any horses that haven't run off."

He looked up at the sound of men and horses screaming in the distance. "Hurry up!" He didn't know why men and horses were screaming on their back trail—might there be bandits attacking the Jokapcul survivors? If there were, he didn't want his small band caught in the open were the bandits to come this way.

Haft looked up and down the road and saw that his men had collected weapons and six horses along with other supplies. Someone brought him the demon spitter used against them. Its tube was split along most of its length and the signaling mechanism was badly bent. The demon's door was missing and the demon itself was nowhere to be found. He tossed the broken tube aside.

"Let's move out," he ordered, pointing his right arm up then swinging it forward in their direction of march.

Even though they now had horses, they went on foot. They left the wounded and dying in place. They'd barely made it through the cut before Wolf broke out of the trees beside the road to walk next to Haft. He looked up at the man.

"*Ulgh!*" Wolf's muzzle and chest were bloody.

"Did you get all of them?" Haft asked, not believing the wolf could actually understand his question.

"*Ulgh!*" Wolf nodded vigorously twice and gnashed his jaws together with each nod.

Haft shuddered.

CHAPTER TWO

Wheels rumbled on the road. Overladen wagons and carts creaked and groaned as they dipped and yawed over the rutted, uneven surface. Weary feet tramped and thudded alongside and between the wagons and carts. Curses and shouts came as people urged recalcitrant draft animals to haul when they wanted to stop, or dealt with dangerously shifting cargoes. Children shouted in play, or sobbed in fear and were hushed by fearful, tired, or exasperated parents. Babes cried until given breast. An infrequent echo reverberated, shocking in the confines of the forest that muffled and dulled most sounds. Sunlight splashed here and there, wherever it could break through the overarching foliage of trees that grew to the road's verge and made a tunnel of it. Flying insects buzzed about the human and animal banquet that moved through their territory; people waved and swatted at them, and horses and oxen twitched their ears and whisked their tails. Unmindful of its casualties, the insect horde continued to dine. Only the occasional eddy that made its way down to the surface from the breeze that ruffled the high leaves disturbed the massed fliers.

Spinner endlessly rode the two miles from the head of the column to its tail and back again, offering words of encouragement and an occasional helping hand, urging laggards to close growing gaps.

They'd started out from Eikby with more than two thousand people under his and Haft's protection. Most of them were the remnants of the town's once-thriving population. Close to two hundred others were refugees from elsewhere in the Princedons, Zobra, Skragland, Bostia, or other countries in the conquered lands. Few more than one hundred were trained soldiers from a variety of armies, and a few hundred more were hastily trained soldiers who, a couple of weeks earlier, had been farmers, apprentices, tradesmen, or craftsmen. These disparate people all had two things in common: they were refugees, fleeing the invading Jokapcul, with nowhere to go, and they would go wherever Spinner and Haft led them.

Many of the trained soldiers were deserters, men who had run from the field of battle or fled the approach of the Jokapcul. Others had moved purposefully in small units in search of their own armies, their own command, to continue the fight or flight, or to surrender, as ordered by their generals. Whether they had fled ignominiously, remained cohesive, or were newly trained and still uncertain about themselves as soldiers, they had fought and defeated two Jokapcul forces that outnumbered them just days earlier, and they would follow Spinner and Haft into whatever battle came.

A couple hundred more refugees had joined them during the march northward, nearly eighty of whom were soldiers or former soldiers. A score of the soldiers were Conquestors from Penston under the command of a lieutenant. The officer of the Conquestors—a grandiose name for a military that was little more than a local militia—and his men as well, had been so demoralized by the ease with which the Jokapcul had invaded and conquered Penston on the ocean side of the Princedon Peninsula that he gratefully accepted Spinner and Haft's command—even though he knew they were low-ranking enlisted men. Spinner and Haft seemed to know what they were doing. And the soldiers already with the two Frangerians told him that they'd never lost a battle against the Jokapcul.

Spinner, however, if not Haft, didn't see all of their encounters with the enemy as victories.

They were three days gone from the charred ruins of Eikby, traveling north across the Princedon Peninsula, headed for the city state of Dartmutt. There, the people hoped for refuge. For Spinner and Haft, the salvation they sought was shipping that

would take them down the length of Princedon Gulf, across
the Inner Ocean, and around the southeast corner of the eastern continent, Arpalonia, to the archipelago nation of Frangeria, where they would report to Headquarters Marine Corps
for debriefing and reassignment.

"Debriefing." Yes, Spinner was sure he and Haft would be
quizzed at length about how they escaped the Jokapcul invasion of New Bally, and their transcontinental trek across
Nunimar to the Inner Ocean. Headquarters would want to
know everything they knew about the Jokapcul, and probably
ask for everything they thought or could guess. He was sure
that under the circumstances they wouldn't be court-
martialed for desertion in the face of the enemy.

Fairly sure. After all, they were the only Frangerians not
killed or captured when the Jokapcul surprise attack swarmed
over New Bally.

As for the refugees, Alyline, the Golden Girl, would go with
them, of course. Silent, the giant nomad from the steppes, had
said he'd like to cross the ocean to see a new land. Maybe Haft
would take Maid Marigold with him, the young woman he'd
hooked up with in Eikby. The others? Perhaps they could find
safety in Dartmutt. Not that Spinner thought Dartmutt was
strong enough to resist the Jokapcul. He'd never visited the
Gulfside city states of the Princedons, but from all he'd heard,
they were smaller and weaker than those on the shore of the
Southern Ocean. His hope was that Dartmutt, at the head of
Princedon Gulf and abutted against the bottom of the Low
Desert, was too insignificant for the Jokapcul to bother with.

That was something he didn't want to think about too hard.

He knew other refugees were streaming in large numbers
toward Dartmutt, and many of them were soldiers. With the
influx of new people and soldiers, the city state should be
stronger than it had ever hoped to be. If there was room to
hold everyone. If there was food enough to feed them. If there
was enough potable water. If—

Spinner cut off those thoughts. He and Haft were just very
junior Frangerian Marines. How could they possibly be responsible for so many people? They had to get the refugees to

Dartmutt and let the earl there take care of them. That's what princes and earls are for, isn't it? he thought.

Three days gone on a journey over and around the foot of a mountain range, a journey that wagons should be able to cover in a week or not much longer. But that was only a few wagons with an armed escort to protect them from bandits, not a caravan of nearly two and a half thousand people, most of them walking, many of them children or elders unable to maintain the pace for an entire day. And they were pursued by the Jokapcul—and likely flanked by bandits biding their time to strike, rob, and run. Did they even stand a chance of reaching Dartmutt without suffering serious losses?

He was three-quarters of the way to the rear of the column, headed to its end. He stopped and looked at the people plodding by. Some looked frightened, some too numb or defeated to do anything more than put one foot in front of another until someone told them to stop—or they fell from exhaustion. Yet others were warily aware of their surroundings. Only a few looked alert and determined. He vaguely recognized one of the latter and edged his gelding toward the man.

"Lord Spinner," the man greeted him.

"I'm not a lord," Spinner muttered with a grimace. But so many of the refugees insisted on calling him and Haft "lord" that he no longer objected as strongly as he once did. "I know you," he said in a normal voice.

"Yes, lord. I'm Postelmuz, I was an attendant at the inn where you and Lord Haft stayed the night after you defeated the bandits in their lair."

"Yes, Postelmuz, I remember you. And I'm just Spinner, I'm not 'Lord' anybody."

"Yes, of course, lord. How can I be of service?" Postelmuz's eyes sparkled with eagerness.

Spinner swallowed his groan. Postelmuz was obviously one of those who believed the Jokapcul would have killed all the people of Eikby if he and Haft hadn't led the town's defense. Spinner himself wasn't convinced the Jokapcul would have done any worse than enslave some of them if they hadn't been there to organize them to fight. Instead, more than half of Eikby's population died in the battles. "I'm leaving the road," he said. "If anyone comes looking for me, tell them I'm inspecting the left flank."

"You're inspecting the left flank. I'll tell them, lord."

Spinner swung his leg over the gelding's hindquarters and dismounted. "Will you hold my horse for my return?"

"I'd be most honored, lord," Postelmuz said, reaching for the reins.

"Thank you." Spinner spun about and headed into the trees before Postelmuz could "lord" him again.

There hadn't been much direct sun on the road; the trees to its side were tall and lush and threw boughs and branches across it, casting most of the road into shade.

There was no sunlight away from the road; except where an aged or lightning-wounded tree had fallen, the trees were too lushly foliated to allow the sun to see the ground. In the dimness, few weeds or bushes dotted the ground, and those were pale things that needed little sun. They were sickly looking, unappetizing, as though they held no nourishment for man or beast—yet most of them were nibbled or chomped, and nearly all were home to crawling insects that lived and survived on them. Despite the presence of numerous tracks, there were few animal sounds other than the *squees* and chitterings of treetop dwellers and the caws of forest birds. A short distance from the road, even the sound of the refugee parade was almost completely absorbed. The ground was soft and damp underfoot, coated with a layer of rotting leaves that gave uncertain footing.

In all, it reminded Spinner of the forest where Bostia came against Skragland, the forest where he and Haft were attacked by a gray tabur, a very large cat that had been imported for unknown reasons from his homeland of Apianghia.

The scar on his calf, the result of a swipe from the gray tabur's paw, twitched at the memory, and he limped for a few steps. His skin crawled at the thought of encountering another big cat. He looked closely at the ground but saw no pug marks, nor were any tree trunks marked by cats sharpening their claws; he forced himself to relax. The trees were closer together here than in the Bostia forest, and there were fewer treetop dwellers, and none of them threw slops down at him. Neither did anything slither through the mulch on which he trod. *This isn't like that forest at all*, he assured himself. He came close enough to believing his assurance that after a time the remembered pain in his leg faded away.

Distances were difficult to judge in the forest's half-light. He had to count paces to estimate when he was a hundred yards from the road—the flankers were supposed to be that distance out. Then he turned toward the head of the column and began walking parallel to the road. There were four flank patrols to each side of the road, each six-man patrol a mix of soldiers and Eikby hunters or woodsmen. The hunters and woodsmen had insisted to Spinner that they would easily be able to maintain the proper distance from the road and not get lost. The road disappeared from view completely at less than a hundred yards into the trees. If necessary, a six-man patrol was large enough to spread out on line, so one man could be in sight of the road, the next man out in sight of him, and so on until the final two or three were a hundred yards out.

Spinner suddenly realized he had only the most tenuous grasp of direction in this forest. Was he paralleling the road? Angling toward it? Angling away? Was he even walking in a straight line?

He froze and listened carefully for a long moment. But he heard no sound of people or horses. He was alone in a strange forest and didn't know if he was facing in the right direction or in a direction that would take him far away from anywhere he wanted to go. And danger might lurk just out of sight and sound.

No, there was at least one known danger: there were bandits in the forest. And there were Jokapcul behind.

Got any other bright ideas, Grace? he asked himself. That was one of the peculiar expressions Lord Gunny had brought with him from—from—from wherever he had come.

Lord Gunny. Yes. What did *Lord Gunny Says* say about navigation in deep forest?

He didn't know. He was a Frangerian Marine—a *sea* soldier. Yes, he'd been trained to fight in all kinds of terrain, including dense forest, but he'd never expected to be *alone* in a trackless forest. He'd certainly never been alone in a forest and so far from sight or sound of a road. He looked in the direction he thought was parallel to the road. If he angled slightly to the right of that direction, he told himself, he should be all right. Shouldn't he? He knew enough about land navigation to be able to find his way—most of the time. Pick a point and walk to it. But the trees grew just close enough that he couldn't see any point to pick that was farther than, what? Fifty yards? And mostly less than that. *If* he was judging distance right in the dim light. Fifty yards wasn't far enough for an aiming point.

Why did he come out here by himself? he wondered. He didn't know, it had seemed like a good idea at the time.

All right, Spinner, don't get excited. You can do it. Remember Lord Gunny's admonition: "You're a Marine. When in doubt, act decisively."

So where were the flanking patrols? Unless they had gotten badly out of alignment, he'd entered the forest between the third and fourth patrols. All he had to do was stay in position and the trailing flanking patrol would come upon him in a few more minutes.

There, he heard a footstep. Here they came now, just a little farther out than they should be. Or maybe he hadn't gone a hundred yards from the road. If the last patrol hadn't already passed.

He shook his head. The deep forest was so confusing.

"Don't move or you're dead," a voice he didn't recognize growled in Zobran from nearby.

A twig snapped several yards to the side of the voice. Spinner moved only his eyes and saw the man who spoke, a stranger who held a bow with an arrow drawn and aimed directly at him. Five yards to his left another bowman stepped from behind a tree, also aiming at him. He thought they must be bandits, and wondered how far away that fourth flanking patrol was—or if it had already passed by.

"You with those people on the road?" asked another voice. Spinner couldn't see the speaker.

"Yes." His Zobran, like Haft's, had improved considerably during the previous couple of weeks.

"What you doing out here by yourself, fool?" asked the first man.

"Nature's call. He's shy, that's why he's so far from the road," another, unseen voice said with a snicker.

"Knock it off," the second voice snapped. Then to Spinner, "We mean you no harm. Just had to make sure you didn't start fighting before we could talk. You can move now—just remember, we have archers aiming at you."

Careful to keep his left hand away from the quarterstaff in his right, Spinner turned toward the one who sounded like he was in charge. He looked like he was in charge too. He was tall—not spectacularly so, but a couple of inches taller than Spinner, who was slightly taller than the average man—and broad across the shoulders. Mostly, he exuded the kind of confidence seen in men accustomed to giving orders and having them obeyed. Like the two bowmen Spinner had seen, this one was dressed in a mix of rude homespun and princely finery; an unbleached homespun shirt was gathered by a fine leather belt from which hung a scabbarded sword and knife, his boots were a dandy's tooled leather and his trousers deep green, ill-fitting but well made. The garb and weapons added to Spinner's suspicion that these men were bandits.

"Who are you?" he asked.

"Refugees," was the immediate reply. "Same as you. We're running from the Jokaps."

Spinner slowly looked the man up and down. "Looks like you've encountered some other refugees," he said in pointed reference to the man's garb.

The man shook his head; he knew what Spinner meant. "What we did or didn't do before is in the past. Now I figure we're all in this together. We aren't interested in robbing anyone. Not unless we find a lone Jokap. We'd be quite happy to kill and rob one of them."

"What do you want from me? I'm carrying little money."

He wanted to keep the bandit talking long enough for the bowmen to begin straining from holding their bows drawn and let their aim wander. Then he could act.

"We don't want your money. There's eighteen of us, not counting our womenfolk and children. That's not nearly enough to fight the Jokaps combing the woods." It was hard to see clearly in the deep shade, but the man seemed worried, maybe even frightened. "We've been following behind your last flanking patrol—you've got lots of flanking patrols, plus those men in your rear. You seem to know what you're up to. We've been waiting to find one of you alone, someone to take us in to meet your leaders for parley so we can join forces." He raised his hand and lowered it, palm down. "He's listening, put your weapons down."

Spinner swiveled his eyes and saw the nearer bowman lower his weapon. The man kept the arrow nocked, though.

"Will you do that?" There was a tone of supplication in the bandit leader's voice. "Take us to meet with your leaders?"

Spinner hesitated a moment. What if this was a trick to get the bandits into the column? They could do a lot of damage, kill or injure a lot of people, before they ran off with whatever booty they could carry.

He looked around and for the first time took in the number of men facing him. There were three he hadn't seen before. What should he do? *When in doubt, act decisively.*

"Bring two men with you, leave the others here." He turned in what he thought was the direction that would lead him back to the column near where he had left Postelmuz with his horse. "Follow me. What's your name?" he asked over his shoulder.

"Veduci. What's yours?"

Spinner picked up his pace and didn't answer.

Spinner's blind navigation was better than he had any reason to hope. When he reached the road, he saw Postelmuz leading the gelding only forty yards ahead. Spinner called out to him.

Postelmuz spun about. "Yes, Lord Spinner!"

Veduci looked at him sharply, surprised by the name. "You don't dress like any lord I've ever seen."

"I'm not a lord," Spinner growled.

Postelmuz trotted up, leading the gelding, and held the reins out for Spinner.

Spinner shook him off. "Ride forward. Get Fletcher, tell him I want him."

Postelmuz stood erect and grinned broadly. "Yes, Lord Spinner!"

"Stop calling me 'Lord'!"

"As you command, Lord Spinner!" He bounded into the saddle and heeled the gelding. It took off at a gallop toward the column's front.

Spinner grimaced, then looked about. He saw two men he vaguely recognized from Eikby. They were both armed with short swords. "You two," he ordered. "Go back and get Haft. Tell him I need him right now. Tell him it's an emergency."

"Yes, lord." They started back at a brisk walk.

"Run!"

The two men sprinted.

He turned to Veduci. The bandit leader was eyeing him speculatively.

"Your youth fooled me," the bandit said. "I didn't think you were the leader. In what army are you an officer? I can tell that's a uniform, but I don't recognize the emblems on your cloak."

"I'm not an officer in any army," Spinner said wearily. "I'm an enlisted Frangerian Marine. So is Haft."

Veduci nodded as though that explained everything. "I've heard of you Frangerian Marines," he said. "You're a long way from the sea. Tell me, is it true that a war god descended from heaven and molded you in his image?"

Spinner remembered the story of how Lord Gunny appeared from nowhere in front of the assembled priests of many religions when they were watching a demonstration of the summoning of demons. "I've never heard it said that way," he said slowly as he and the bandits kept pace with the column of curious refugees, "but it was something like that, yes."

Fletcher arrived in just a few minutes. Alyline was with him. It took Haft a little longer. He looked very displeased to be riding a captured Jokapcul horse.

"This better be good," Haft snarled as he dismounted. He shoved the reins at someone and hastily stepped away from the horse. "We just ambushed a Jokapcul patrol that was trailing us. There's probably more coming, and we have to be ready for them."

CHAPTER THREE

Haft looked at Veduci and his two companions with suspicion. Fletcher merely eyed them curiously. Alyline ignored the strangers in favor of glaring at Spinner—he hadn't called for her, and she was angry at what she saw as his attempt to leave her out of whatever was happening. Veduci briefly gave her an appraising look, then turned his attention back to Spinner and the newly arrived men. He gave the demon spitter slung over Haft's shoulder a curious glance. His two companions gaped more openly at the Golden Girl.

"What do we have here?" Haft demanded, giving Veduci a hard look. "They don't look like honest refugees to me."

Veduci looked at him levelly; the two bandits who accompanied him glanced sharply at Haft, then looked about nervously, as though spying out threats and seeking escape routes.

"Because we are three men? Because of how we are dressed?" Veduci snorted. "Our womenfolk and children are hidden from danger. We took what clothing we needed from victims of the Jokaps or banditry, they didn't need them anymore."

"What banditry were they victims of?" Haft, a bit shorter than the average man, moved in closer and jutted his face upward at Veduci's. "And what danger do your women and children need to hide from here? Do you think these refugees," he waved his arm at the caravan, "are a danger to them?"

Veduci leaned forward to tower over Haft. "Seems to me you're a danger," he growled.

"Enough, you two!" Spinner snapped. "Haft, this is Veduci. He's got eighteen armed men, plus women and children. They're running from the Jokapcul, just like us. You say they're getting close to us? If that's so, we'll need every fighting man we can get."

Haft nodded slowly. "If they *will* fight." He turned his face to Spinner. "Where are the women and children, have you even seen them? Has anybody?"

Spinner looked at the people who had stopped to look and listen. "Keep moving," he shouted at them. "Don't let the caravan break up. Move on!" While he waited for movement to resume, he thought about how he hadn't seen the women and children. Nor had he seen eighteen armed men, only six. And Haft might be right. "How *do* we know you won't break and run if the Jokapcul catch up with us?" he asked Veduci when the people began hurrying to catch up. "How do we know you'll stand and fight?"

The bandit leader spat to the side. "They're coming as fast as we're running. They're going to catch us sooner or later anyway. We're better off fighting them with a large group than by ourselves."

Veduci had a good point, but Haft didn't look convinced.

Alyline spoke up. "Your women and children, how many are there? What is their state? Have you any wagons to carry your injured or feeble?"

Veduci gave her a slight bow. "We have twenty-one women, lady." He had no idea who she was; her revealing vest and the translucent pantaloons that hung from low on her hips made her look more like a tavern entertainer than a lady, but her garments were a shimmering gold, and the gold coins that dangled from her necklace and girdle looked to be real. More, nobody objected when she spoke up. He thought it best to assume she had rank. "Four of them are with child. And there are children, two babes in arms and a handful of toddlers. And we got one crone." He sadly shook his head. "We've got no wagons and only seven horses to carry the infirm and supplies."

Alyline glared at Haft. "Two infants, half a dozen toddlers, and a crone, and you see a threat?"

"I haven't seen *any* infants, toddlers, or crones. And desperate people are always a threat," Haft answered.

"*We* are desperate people too," Fletcher interjected before Alyline and Haft could get started on an argument. To Veduci, "What supplies do you have? Food, medicines, trade goods?"

"Only what we can carry on our backs and three of the horses."

"Where are your women and children?" Alyline demanded angrily. "Why have you left them in the wilderness?"

"I didn't know how we'd be received," Veduci snapped. "So far, it looks like I was right to leave them hidden."

"Refugees with women and children," Spinner said firmly before anyone else could speak, "would be received better than the armed men who surrounded me."

"They ambushed you?" Haft stepped back to gain fighting room and reached for the axe at his side.

"They only surrounded me, Haft." Spinner's sharp voice stopped Haft before he could draw his weapon. "They didn't attack."

"We were simply ready to defend ourselves in case we were attacked," Veduci said calmly.

"You look like bandits to me," Haft said bluntly. He kept his hand near his axe.

Veduci's face twitched but showed no other reaction. His two companions began edging back to gain fighting room, and cast worried looks at Haft and the others.

Alyline suddenly interjected, "If you have women and children, bring them in. Let us see them. Then we will know if you are refugees."

"But—"

Alyline cut off Haft's protest with a sharp look. "Bring them in now," she commanded.

Veduci gave her another appraising look—yes, she did have rank here—then turned to Spinner and Haft.

"Leave your men here while you fetch your people," Spinner told him.

"Make sure your women and children are unarmed," Haft added with a wicked grin.

Veduci shot him a hard look and turned to the forest.

"Your weapons, please," Spinner said to the other two.

The two exchanged a wordless glance. One looked at the armed men around them; no one held a weapon in his hands, but all looked ready. He nodded to his companion, and they unbuckled their sword belts and handed them to Fletcher, along with their bows. Nobody demanded their quivers, so they kept their arrows.

"Keep moving," Haft shouted at a knot of people who had stopped to gawk. "Move along, you're getting too strung out." The caravan moved on.

The end of the refugee column was passing when Veduci emerged from the forest with a clot of women and children. They were as he had described.

"You, come with me," Alyline said to a young woman whose stomach was swollen with child. The young woman nervously took half a step back, then obeyed Alyline's peremptory gesture. The Golden Girl put her arm over the woman's shoulder and leaned her head toward her. She led her to the other side of the road and down it a bit, talking quietly as they went.

"Where are the rest of your men?" Spinner asked.

"Standing ready to rescue our people if need be."

"That's fair," Fletcher said before Spinner or Haft could reply. "We've given them no reason to trust us yet."

"We don't know who they are yet either," Spinner said.

"We know who you are," Veduci said.

The others looked at him, and Spinner gestured for him to continue.

Veduci nodded at the caravan now just past. "You're the Eikby people. You defeated the Rockhold Band when they attacked you, and you bested the Jokaps too. The Jokaps will catch and kill us if we remain by ourselves. They catch us when we're with you, maybe between us we'll kill so many of them they won't kill all of us."

Spinner didn't say so, but he agreed with Haft that Veduci and his people were bandits. Fletcher hadn't expressed an opinion. Alyline either didn't think so or didn't care. What should they do? Veduci gave a strong argument for the bandits being refugees seeking the protection of a larger group. But would they actually join the Eikby refugees, or would they wait for a chance to rob and run away? And what would they *really* do if the Jokapcul caught them on the road?

Alyline hustled back with the pregnant woman she had taken aside and broke his chain of thought.

"Spinner," she said preemptively, "we're taking these people with us. They need help and we can give it."

"But—"

That was as far as he got before galloping horses demanded his attention. He looked back along the road to see five horsemen racing toward them. He stepped through the group toward the approaching horsemen and waited. The lead horseman was Birdwhistle, who Haft had left in command of the rear point.

"A troop of Jokapcul lancers are coming at a canter," Birdwhistle said breathlessly as he leaped off his horse. "They'll be here in five minutes or less."

"Where's the rest of the rear point?" Haft asked. He had four more men back there someplace.

"In the trees, running this way."

Haft gave a disgusted grunt. The lancers would arrive first.

Somehow they had to stop the hundred lancers coming their way. Spinner took quick stock. They had himself and Haft, five of the men from the rear point, and Fletcher. Postelmuz had lingered; he was one of the partly trained men who'd fought the Jokapcul at Eikby. He was armed and looked ready to fight—nervous, but ready. The caravan was now too far ahead to get more men back before the Jokapcul arrived—nine men to stop a hundred. He turned to Veduci.

"You say you're willing to fight alongside us?" he asked.

"This is your chance to prove it. Get your men into an ambush position along the side of the road."

Veduci nodded sharply and darted back into the trees.

"Get those people out of here," Spinner ordered.

Fletcher put one able-bodied woman in charge and had her lead the women and children up the road as fast as they could go. He returned the weapons to the two of Veduci's men who'd stayed behind.

"Where's Xundoe?" Spinner muttered, suddenly sorry he hadn't sent for the mage. He glanced about; other than Haft's demon spitter, none of them were carrying demon weapons.

"Alyline, ride forward and get fighters." Spinner paused a second to think of who was where in the column. "Sergeant Phard and his men are near the rear. Get them."

The Golden Girl snorted; the Skraglander Bloody Axes alone wouldn't be enough to swing the battle in their favor. But she was already mounted and turning her stallion to ride for help before Spinner gave his order. She'd tell Phard, then she'd find demon weapons and bring them back. She galloped off, riding on the edge of the road to avoid forcing her way through the frightened racing women and children.

Veduci came back.

"Where are your men?" Spinner asked.

"They're in position."

Haft shot him a quick, hard look. "Yes, you would know how to lay an ambush, wouldn't you." It wasn't a question.

"I know even more," Veduci said, and hefted a thin, coiled rope.

Haft looked at it curiously.

Veduci ran across the road. He found a mid-size tree and tied one end of the rope around it near where its roots spread out. He ran back, uncoiling the rope to lay on the road.

"We don't have time to do this properly," he said. "Get your men into position."

Veduci grabbed a few handfuls of leaves and dirt from the edge of the road and tossed them along the rope. It wasn't effective camouflage, but it might be enough to keep the canter-

ing Jokapcul lancers from spotting the rope in time. He ran
into the trees.

Spinner and Haft quickly took in the situation under the
trees. Veduci's men were only a few yards off the road, far
enough to be hidden from a casual bypasser but not so far that
they didn't have clear shots with their bows. Short bows, Haft
noted, not powerful enough to be effective against the
Jokapcul armor. It was a well-set hasty ambush, even though
it had no rear security. It was as Haft had said: these men
knew how to set an ambush.

Haft went about quickly checking everyone's position.
Spinner ran from man to man saying, "Wait for my signal."
The lancers reached the killing zone before the two Franger-
ian Marines were settled in their own positions.

Veduci turned the end of the rope once around a slender
tree trunk a foot above the ground and waited for the first rank
of horses to get close enough.

Their armor was gray. Maybe it's supposed to be silver,
Haft thought. Unlike the trailing patrol he and the rear point
had ambushed a short while earlier, the lancers didn't have
scouts riding ahead. They were in a tight column of twos with
only enough space between ranks for the horses to avoid
bumping each other. The silver-plumed officer rode alongside the third rank. They carried their lances in their hands,
ready to drop the upheld points level with the ground and tuck
the butts under their arms. Short swords flapped from each
side of their belts.

As Haft thought they would, the lead lancers saw the rope
before Veduci could snap it taut at fetlock level to trip the
cantering horses. The men barked warning in their guttural
language and yanked hard on their reins, but it didn't matter:
they were already too close to stop in time.

Veduci pulled hard on the rope, snapping it off the ground,
and finished off the knot he'd started—the rope would stay up
without him holding it. He took up his bow and got ready.

The lead horses staggered, thrown off balance with their
heads jerked back and to the side. They hit the rope and tum-

bled, throwing their riders. The next rank wasn't able to stop in time either, and crashed into the downed pair. The snap of breaking bones was audible through the thudding of falling horses and thrown men, the neighing of frightened and injured animals, the shouts of thrown riders, and screams of the injured. The officer instantly saw that he was too close to stop or turn away from the trap and tried to jump his horse over the pileup, but one of the horses in the scrambling pile lurched upward into his horse and he was knocked off balance and fell from the saddle. The fourth rank tumbled into the horses at the rope and more bones broke; the screams of injured horses seemed to drown out other sounds. The fifth rank stopped short, but their horses were turned to opposite sides, prancing to keep their balance as the downed horses flailed near their legs and the horses behind jostled them. In seconds the entire column was stopped, packed close together near the front, the horses facing every which way. The soldiers were confused, waiting for orders from their officer, but he was dying, drowning in his own blood—Veduci had nocked an arrow and shot him through the throat as soon as he was down. The confused soldiers didn't immediately notice their ranks thinning from arrows that shot into them from their left flank.

But the confusion only lasted until Haft used his demon spitter. The weapon's thunder echoed and reverberated under the trees. Four Jokapcul milling uncertainly in the middle of the column were thrown away by the eruption of the demon's ejecta.

Half of the Jokapcul still mounted heard where the thunder came from; they spun their horses to charge into the forest. But they weren't in formation and couldn't see who they were charging until they got under the trees. Several more of them fell before they closed with their attackers. Then the forest was filled with thudding hoof beats, the harsh barks of Jokapcul war cries answering the battle cries of the ambushers, and it rang with the clangor of clashing weapons. Haft managed one more shot with the demon spitter before horsemen were on him and he had to drop it in favor of his axe. A cacophony of terrified squawks trailed birds fleeing to safer environs.

A lancer screamed a bloodcurdling war cry, leveled his lance, and turned his horse to charge Spinner. But the trees were too tight for the horse to maneuver easily and it smashed its rider's leg against a tree trunk, his war cry becoming a shriek of pain. Spinner let go of his crossbow and thrust his quarterstaff at the Jokapcul's throat. The soldier's screams abruptly cut off and he clutched his crushed larynx then slowly toppled off his horse, hitting the ground and spasming in his death throes.

Spinner didn't have time to finish him off, he had to swerve out of the way of another lance that darted at him from a Jokapcul whose horse galloped at him on a cleaner line. He swung his quarterstaff at the soldier as the horse went by, but was off balance and falling away, so the staff glanced off the horse's hindquarters. The rider threw back on his reins and his mount skidded into a spin. Turned about, the mounted man plunged back at Spinner. Spinner dodged behind a tree, and a shower of bark chips sprayed from the trunk where the lance's point struck it. This time Spinner was ready and jabbed with his quarterstaff as the rider and horse went by. He landed a solid blow on the lancer's short ribs, but the man's armor blunted the strike and he retained his seat. The Jokapcul dropped his lance and drew both short swords as he spun his horse for another charge. That was a mistake—Spinner's quarterstaff gave him a much longer reach. He thrust between the two threatening blades and caught the Jokapcul in the belly, catapulting him backward off his horse. Spinner jumped in before the Jokapcul could capture a breath and slit his throat.

A few yards away Haft ducked under a lance and swung his mighty battle-axe into the chest of a charging horse. The falling animal wrenched the weapon out of his hands as it threw its rider into a tree. The Jokapcul crashed into the trunk face first, his neck broke with a loud crack, and he crumpled to the ground, immobile and dying. Haft risked the dying horse's thrashing hooves to retrieve his axe, but it was buried too deeply and he couldn't quickly dislodge it. A lance caught his cloak and jerked him off his feet, but the lancer lost his grip on his weapon when its head stayed stuck in the cloak. He drew a sword and turned his mount about to finish his opponent. But Haft still had his knife. He drew it, dropped below the swing of the Jokapcul's sword, and swiped at the horse's hamstring, knicking it. The animal screamed and bucked, momentarily out of control. Haft jerked the lance from its hold on his cloak and slammed its point into the small of the Jokapcul's back as he struggled to regain control of his horse. Haft twisted the lance, the soldier fell from his mount, and Haft pinned him to the ground with his own lance.

Others among the refugees weren't as fortunate. Three of the fallen lancers from the head of the column scrambled to their feet and raced into the forest to confront Veduci and two nearby men. They were followed quickly by two other lancers—the remaining fallen Jokapcul were dead or dying. Three of the unhorsed Jokapcul went down, dead or badly wounded, but so did the two men with the bandit leader. Veduci managed to break away from the last two lancers before they could catch him in a pincer and ran to where two other of his men were fighting back-to-back, joining them in a defensive circle.

A Border Warder stayed down when he dove away from one charging horse into the path of another and was trampled. Another took a lance full in the back as he gutted a lancer he'd just unhorsed. Three more of Veduci's men were down, dead or dying. Postelmuz lay staring sightless into the treetops, the broken shaft of a lance sticking out of his chest.

In moments of fighting, thirty of the Jokapcul were down— as were eight of the twenty-seven ambushers. The lancers who'd continued to dance in confusion when the fight began turned into the forest to join battle.

Not all of them made it into the trees.

Panting from their run, the rest of Haft's Border Warder squad arrived to find enemy well within the range of their longbows. They toppled four of the lancers still on the road, then four drew their swords and raced at the Jokapcul flank. Wolf was with these last four Border Warders. He raced into the Jokapcul and quickly dispatched two of them by ripping out their throats.

Sergeant Phard turned around in his saddle and looked back when he heard galloping hooves approaching.

Alyline's stallion raised a dust cloud skidding to a stop when she hauled back on the reins.

"Golden Lady," Phard said and gave a half bow, more graceful than one might expect from so burly a mounted man.

"A troop of lancers behind," Alyline gasped. "Spinner and Haft need help. Go to them." She heeled the stallion and it bolted away, farther up the column.

"Axes!" Phard shouted. "With me!" He twisted his horse about and kicked its flanks. It galloped toward the end of the train of nervously hurrying people more than a hundred yards away. He didn't look for his men, he knew they'd follow with neither question nor hesitation—and once past the refugees and wagons clogging the road, they'd form up. As he neared the end of the caravan he heard the distant, muffled clash of weapons and shouts of fighting men. He swore under his breath, angry that the noises of the people and wagons behind him had blocked all sound of the conflict to the rear.

Well before the ten Bloody Axes reached the sound of fighting in the forest, they were riding two abreast on the sides of the road and had their battle-axes ready in their hands. Phard slowed to a trot and turned his short column under the trees. A wild sight met their eyes—close to three score gray-armored Jokapcul lancers, nearly half of them on foot, milled about in undisciplined packs, surrounding pairs and trios of defenders, fighting so closely that they interfered with each other's weapons.

Who are they? Sergeant Phard wondered, startled by the sight of strangers battling the gray-armored Jokapcul. He saw a Border Warder back-to-back with one of the strangers and knew whose side they were on.

At a one-word command from their leader, the Bloody Axes formed into two ranks, five abreast, facing the nearest fight, and broke into a canter—the trees were too dense to allow a gallop.

"GET THE GRAY!" Phard bellowed, and bent low to sideswing his axe into the neck of a dismounted lancer who was about to plunge his sword into the man backed against the Border Warder. His horse slammed loudly into a lancer's horse and staggered it, almost unhorsing its rider. The two Bloody Axes flanking him bowled over two more of the Jokapcul surrounding the Border Warder and the stranger, and bones snapped sharply under their trampling hooves. The following rank hacked at the lancers still upright. The two defenders took instant advantage of the Jokapcul confusion to skewer two lancers who'd been knocked down, cutting off their panicked barks. In seconds all but one of the lancers who had attacked the two were down. That one dropped his weapons and sped away, so disoriented that he fled deeper into the forest instead of toward the road. The Border Warder snatched up his bow and shot the man in the back.

"With us!" Phard ordered the two men he'd just rescued.

The Border Warder had enough Skraglandish to understand the command and ran behind the horses. The stranger didn't understand the words, but followed the Border Warder.

Bellowing battle cries, the mounted Bloody Axes crashed into the seven lancers swarming around a trio of defenders and scattered them. Phard swung his axe at a Jokapcul struggling to retain his seat on his staggering horse. The blade hewed off the man's arm, sank deep into his chest, and flung him to the ground. Another Skraglander swung his axe in a high overhead arc and brought it down on the helmet of a horseless Jokapcul, the force splitting it on a diagonal, half of the foe's head shooting away. The half-headless lancer remained on his feet for a long moment, jabbing automatically, aimlessly, with his sword, before he folded to the ground.

Two mounted lancers and one on foot broke away and sprinted to the next group while Phard and his squad finished off their two remaining companions. The three Jokapcul screamed warnings, and most of the lancers surrounding two Border Warders and a stranger wearing colorful clothes turned to face the new threat, which gave the others room to reach in and cut down the man in motley. The Border Warders shifted back-to-back and continued to fend off their attackers.

Eight lancers, five on horseback, faced the charging Bloody Axes. One of the dismounted lancers darted forward between two of his mounted mates and dropped to one knee with the butt of his lance planted on the ground at his knee. The horse his upraised lance point was pointed at saw the danger and shied violently to the left—but the animal saw the threat too late and its momentum slammed its shoulder into the weapon. It screamed as its right foreleg collapsed, and it rolled, throwing its rider onto the lancer and shattering the lance into kindling.

The thrown Bloody Axe rolled under the hooves of the Jokapcul horses flanking the lancer who'd taken his horse down—they reared and stomped down hard, crushing his pelvis and shattering his skull. His horse scrambled painfully to its feet and stomped the dismounted lancer to death. Then it lashed out with its head and viciously bit the throat of the nearest Jokapcul horse, which screamed and reared away, almost throwing its rider. Another Bloody Axe took advantage of that lancer's struggle to stay mounted and strike a blow that took off the man's leg at mid-thigh and split ribs on the horse.

The remaining horses crashed chest-to-chest, snapping and biting at each other. The Bloody Axes' horses had momentum behind them and staggered the Jokapcul mounts backward. The stranger on foot risked death by darting among the struggling horses and struck from below, gutting a lancer horse. The screaming animal stutter-stepped back for several yards with its steaming intestines spilling onto the ground. The footman grabbed the dying horse's bridle and went with it, stabbing up at its rider, who jumped off to face his antagonist. The footman twisted to his right, yanking hard on the bridle, and pulled the screaming horse over. The falling horse thudded into the Jokapcul, knocking him over and pinning his legs. Before the stranger could finish off the downed Jokapcul, another lancer swung his sword backhand at him and chopped deeply into his back.

Then, abruptly, this fight was over. Sergeant Phard and eight of his Bloody Axes remained on their horses; the Border Warder who came with them and one of the two to whose aid they'd rushed were still on their feet. All the Jokapcul were dead or dying.

"To the next!" Phard ordered, and they headed on line to the next struggling knot.

Veduci, who had escaped from the leading Jokapcul who lived long enough to pursue him, ran from fight to fight, back-stabbing a Jokapcul here and a Jokapcul there, evening the odds a bit at each confrontation, then running to the next fight and back-stabbing another Jokapcul. Only once was he chased by a lancer on foot. He grabbed the trunk of a young tree and slingshot around it to plunge his sword all the way through the side of the startled Jokapcul. He lost precious seconds twisting and working his sword out of the dead man.

Haft stood alone, backed against a large tree, fighting like a madman as he swung the half-moon blade of his battle-axe in broad arcs that wrapped all the way around to protect his sides from flank attack. He'd shattered every lance thrust at him. Twice he knocked arrows aside, and once ducked out of the way of a shaft. Another arrow had slit along his ribs, and a lance gouged his thigh before he could break it with his axe. He bled from numerous other nicks and cuts, but half a dozen Jokapcul bodies lay before him, and most others now kept their distance. To the lancers, it truly looked like he and his axe were one.

A short distance away, Spinner danced like a dervish, twirling his quarterstaff so fast it was a blurred shield before him. Whenever a Jokapcul came within the quarterstaff's reach, Spinner shot an end out to jab at a face or exposed throat, or to swing it to deflect a weapon or break an arm or leg or crack ribs. Dead and dying lancers sprawled on the ground beneath his dancing feet, injured Jokapcul shuffling away desiring nothing more than to escape with no more hurt.

Nearby, Fletcher and Birdwhistle fought back-to-back, fending off five Jokapcul. Three more lay dead around them.

They tried to move to where their attackers might trip over the bodies.

All about, the refugee fighters gave good account of themselves, killing more of the lancers than they lost. Wolf dashed about, harrying the horses, ripping at their hamstrings with his teeth, and brought several down, tumbling their riders. Seldom did the shaggy beast pause to finish off a fallen man, being too busy dodging the swords and lances that stabbed his way.

But there were too many Jokapcul and they were going to lose soon.

Thunder suddenly cracked under the trees. And again and again. One, two, three Jokapcul were flung to the ground, bleeding from mortal wounds. *Crack! Crack! Crack! Crack!* came more thunder bolts, and four more lancers were tossed aside.

Fighting paused as all heads snapped to the source of the thunder. Spinner and Haft and their men recovered almost immediately and fell on their foes with renewed vigor and violence. Veduci and his remaining men stood frozen at the sight that met their eyes. The Jokapcul saw an apparition in flowing robes heavily decorated with cabalistic symbols, holding a small demon spitter in his leveled hands, a large demon spitter slung across his back. They screamed in panic and ran. That broke Veduci and his men from their freeze and they joined the others in cutting the Jokapcul down.

"Yes, yes," Xundoe the mage cooed soothingly to the tiny demon that popped out of the handle of his demon weapon and piteously squeaked, *"Veedmee!"* "I'll feed you. Just a minute here." He fumbled open a pouch that hung from his belt and fingered out a pellet smaller than his fingertip. Gingerly, he held it out to the tiny demon, who snatched it away. The demon's mouth stretched open until it looked larger than its entire head and it shoved the pellet in. It closed its mouth, bulging huge around the pellet, and gulped. For an instant the demon's neck was almost as wide as its shoulders, then all sign of the pellet was gone. The demon let out a loud, contented burp and popped back inside the hand piece, slamming the door on its bottom behind itself.

Xundoe began to look up for more Jokapcul targets; his eyes jerked back to the demon weapon in his hands and his face blanched when he heard snoring come from inside it.

"Demon? Demon?" Xundoe squeaked, gaping at the hand piece and tapping it. "Don't go to sleep, we need to fight!"

"Xundoe." Alyline pulled on his arm. "It's all right, they ran. The fight's over."

"Eh?" Xundoe peeked up from under his brows, such as they were. "Oh!" he said brightly when he saw there was no more fighting going on. "Where'd they go?" he asked, looking cautiously around for more Jokapcul.

"They ran away when you used the demon spitter."

"Oh! Well!" The young mage stood erect and preened.

"Now get your healing demons out and get to work." Alyline strode onto the battlefield and began directing the survivors who were checking bodies, telling them where to gather the wounded for bandaging and treatment. She ordered Fletcher to take her stallion and ride to stop the caravan—and bring back more soldiers and all the healers.

Fletcher didn't object that she was out of line giving him orders, he merely said, "Tell Spinner where I've gone."

"Oh," Xundoe said softly when he saw how many wounded and dead littered the ground under the trees. He led his pack mule to the area where the wounded were being gathered and flung open the chest it carried, to rummage through it for the few healing demons it contained.

Nightbird, the healing witch who had been with them since before the original band descended into the Princedons, arrived and began helping with her potions and poultices. The Eikby healers were arriving by the time the last of the wounded were gathered in their makeshift, open-air hospital. So were more soldiers—Haft set them in a defensive perimeter to the south and sent a squad farther to scout for more approaching Jokapcul. Fletcher's wife, Zweepee, and several women who served with her as nurses arrived with the Eikby healers.

Once the wounded—including the Jokapcul—were gathered, Spinner set the survivors to collecting the dead; the

Jokapcul went into an unceremonious pile, the dead soldiers of the band were reverently laid in lines. They gathered all weapons and searched the corpses for anything usable.

Spinner looked at the wounded and the dead and sighed deeply. They had beaten the Jokapcul and taken many more lives than they gave up themselves. They held the ground at the end of the fight, which was the classic definition of victory in battle. But the victory was pyrrhic. Even though far more than half the lancer troop lay dead, and nearly a score more were in the makeshift hospital waiting their turns to be tended, half of the Zobran Border Warders who were in the fight were dead or seriously wounded, and a third of Veduci's men were down as well. Most of the remainder bore lesser wounds.

The Jokapcul could absorb such losses and replace every lost soldier with more, many more. The refugees couldn't replace any of their few fighting men without taking in more refugees, and most refugees were women, children, and oldsters; too many of the men had been killed defending their families and homes when the Jokapcul swept through their countries.

"We beat them again," Haft said, joining Spinner after seeing to the defense. His voice was weary.

"At what price?"

"Too great a price."

"*I* don't think so." Veduci limped up to them. His voice was hoarse, and blood seeped from a crude bandage on his leg and dripped slowly from his sword. "Had they," he nodded at the pile of Jokapcul bodies, "caught my people, they would have killed all of us. Instead, more than half of my men are mostly whole and all of our women and children are safe." He looked intently at them. "When word spreads that the Jokapcul can be beaten, they will begin to lose more often, and fewer people will die at their hands."

CHAPTER
FOUR

They dug a common grave and reverently buried their dead. A shallow trench sufficed for the Jokapcul. Nobody cared if scavengers dug them up later, they just wanted to prevent stench for the time they'd be in camp under the trees just over the ridge from the battleground.

Try as they might, it wasn't yet possible for the refugees to be silent in setting up camp; still, they were quiet enough that they sounded like only a few hundred refugees rather than the more than two thousand they were. It wasn't long before the men had a pavilion stretched over the wounded soldiers, tents pitched or lean-tos constructed for sleeping, and privy trenches dug away from the tents and water sources. That last was one of the innovations Lord Gunny had brought from wherever it was he'd come. Most people didn't understand the need at first, but they quickly enough came to learn that they had less illness with the remote privy trenches than they would have without them, so they dug them willingly enough.

Xundoe and the chief Eikby healing magician let loose their aralez, and the tiny, doglike healing demons scampered about, licking at the worst wounds, cleaning out what was bad and speeding healing. The healing magician was more careful in guiding his land trow; even though there were no young mothers or infants under the pavilion, there were a few nearby. While the land trow was a powerful healing demon, it was also a severe danger to nursing women and infants and had to be kept from them. It was waist high to the magician who controlled it and went about languidly on its business, never straining against its leash, from wounded man to wounded man. It stopped here and there when a wound interested it and probed deep inside with its long, slender fingers. Most of the time when it withdrew its fingers a greenish cloud came with them. The land trow examined each cloud curiously for a moment before dismissively flicking its fingers, dispersing the cloud into nothingness. Nightbird and the Eikby healing witches tended lesser wounds and bruises with unguents and poultices. At length, their wounded were all attended to and they turned to the wounded Jokapcul. The most severely wounded enemy soldiers were set aside and made comfortable during the short time they had left before they died. The lesser wounded were tended to and bound to prevent them from running away or causing mischief.

Meanwhile, older children collected dry wood and women got the cookfires burning. Middle-size children ran gaily to a nearby rill with buckets, struggling back just as gaily with water for the wounded and cooking. Haft busied himself setting quartets of soldiers in a sentry line south of the battleground and other watchers in the tops of high trees. Spinner tried to look like he was putting order to the camp while staying out of the way of Fletcher and Zweepee, who were really doing that job.

Soon water was boiling in pots into which chunks of meat, vegetables, and tubers were tossed, along with salt and what other spices were available. Cooking aromas began wafting under the trees.

Silent, the giant nomad from the steppes, came in more than an hour before sunset—he'd expected to arrive at dusk but the caravan had stopped early. The six Skragland Borderers who, like Silent, had been on distant patrols looking for a Jokapcul army that might be following, returned about the same time. Wolf greeted Silent with a yip and a bound to his chest. The giant ruffled the fur on Wolf's shoulders. Wolf then padded at the giant's side, brushing against his leg, occasionally lifting his head to be petted by the giant's dangling fingertips.

Silent, for a wonder, lived up to his name as he examined the battleground and looked at the wounded from both sides, seeing the extent of the graves.

Spinner, feeling mostly useless, finally stopped pretending to oversee the camp and joined him.

"I was too far from the road," Silent said quietly, "looking for bandits in the forest. I didn't see the Jokap sign until I checked the road before coming back. Then I saw a troop had passed. I followed fast to catch them, then to come ahead and warn you. I found the place where the rear guard ambushed the patrol trailing us. The lancer troop spent a short time there, then continued at speed. I didn't stop and try to question any of the wounded still alive, instead I got here as fast as I could. But the fight was already over." He shook his shaggy head. "If I'd been near the road all along I could have given you warning."

"No you couldn't," Spinner replied. "They were at a canter, you couldn't beat them, they would have reached us first no matter where you were."

Silent grunted. He thought he might have been able to reach the caravan in time if he'd seen the lancer troop. "How many did we lose?" He didn't need an answer, he knew within one or two how many were lost just from the length of the common grave.

"Three of ours dead, two seriously enough wounded they might not live. Seven of the others are dead and four more very badly wounded. I'm not sure how many wounded all told."

Silent looked toward the hospital pavilion. "They're bandits, you know."

Spinner nodded slowly. "Yes. But they're fleeing the Jokapcul, the same as us."

Silent's eyes narrowed as he looked at Veduci's wounded. "Can the snow leopard change its spots?"

"They fought alongside us, many of them died in the fight."

"I saw no other bandits," Silent said briskly, turning from the pavilion, but Spinner noticed the *other*. "There was a sign of bandits moving north, though. None of them coming to this road, it was like they wanted to keep to the deep forest. Like they think the Jokapcul can't follow them into the forest." He hawked into a bush that had been broken in the fight. "I think we'll be safe from bandits for a while, anyway." He glanced back at the pavilion. "At least until those are well enough. How many of them are left?"

"Twelve men, nearly all wounded."

Silent grunted again. He sniffed the air. "Something smells good, and I'm hungry." He turned and strode from the battlefield toward the encampment. Spinner had to scurry to keep up with the nomad's long strides.

Haft watched the middle-size children scamper off with the covered trenchers and waterskins for the pickets, amazed and delighted as always at their eagerness to fetch and carry and turn every chore into a game. The children seemed to think taking food and water to the sentries was a reward, a special treat, and performed that chore more eagerly than any other. Maybe it was: the soldiers and other men on sentry duty usually allowed the children to stay with them for a time and "help" watch. The children believed that by "helping watch" they were performing an important duty and being treated like grown-ups instead of children.

"Haft!"

He turned to the voice and smiled at Maid Marigold. She had been a serving girl at Eikby's Middle of the Forest Inn—when there'd been an Eikby and a Middle of the Forest Inn.

"It's your turn," she said, smiling at him and holding up a bowl.

His smile broadened and he joined the group gathering around the cookfire with its boiling pot.

Fletcher, Alyline, and Doli were already there, as was Maid Primrose, who had worked alongside Maid Marigold at the inn. Maid Marigold and Doli had worked with Maid Primrose to prepare dinner. Spinner and Silent joined the group right after Haft took his place on a log and accepted the steaming bowl of stew from his lover.

"Where's Zweepee?" Alyline asked.

"She said she'd be here once she saw all the wounded were fed," Fletcher replied.

Alyline nodded, Zweepee took her responsibilities seriously. Spinner and Haft had instituted a policy Lord Gunny had brought with him from—from—from wherever he'd come from: the leaders didn't eat until everybody else was served.

A proper commander always feeds his people before he eats himself. That makes sure the commander has provided enough food for his people, Lord Gunny wrote in the *Handbook for Sea Soldiers. Any commander who doesn't take care of his people will lose his war.*

The caravan carried enough food to last the trip to Dartmutt at the head of Princedon Gulf, enough and more. But what if Dartmutt didn't have enough food to feed the influx of refugees who must be congregating there? So caring for food and gathering more was necessary for the caravan. As they moved along the road, the women and older children who weren't needed to move animals and wagons along or tend to babies and oldsters often roamed under the trees in search of mushrooms, tubers, or other edibles. The point and flanking patrols kept watch for game as well as Jokapcul and bandits, and brought in what they could catch without neglecting their primary duties. Pairs of hunters prowled the forest beyond the flanks and point in search of game. They didn't find much; it seemed even the animals of the forest were fleeing the invaders.

For a few moments there were only the slurping and chewing sounds of eating around the fire. An occasional voice was raised elsewhere, mostly the cries of children happy to be traveling on what they thought was a grand adventure. Horses snorted in a nearby tether line, or pawed at the ground. The thin smoke from the fire kept most of the buzzing insects at a respectful distance. Wolf quietly gnawed on a bone; he'd dined earlier on one of the Jokapcul horses killed in the battle. But it wasn't polite to mention that—the people weren't anywhere near ready to eat horse meat.

Spinner kept looking to the south, though he couldn't see very far through the trees. Looking into trees that blocked his view was easier than looking where he'd have to see Doli and Maid Primrose pointedly ignoring him.

Once the edge was off his hunger, he asked Silent, "When do you think they'll come again?"

Silent swallowed loudly and belched before answering. "I saw or heard nothing but the Jokaps you dealt with on our back trail. Neither did the Borderers who scouted deep back." He looked south as though he could see through the trees. "They won't come at night, I think. If any more are following now, they're camped for the night. If we move out soon after dawn, no one should reach us before midday. But if there was more than one troop, I think they would have come together. I also think I would have seen sign."

"Why did they come faster after they saw their trailing patrol had been killed?" Spinner hadn't considered that earlier, he'd been too busy with other matters for it to occur to him. Now that he thought about it, it didn't seem to make sense.

Silent shrugged. "Who knows what a Jokap officer thinks? If they read the signs as well as I did, they knew their patrol was attacked by a small rear guard. Maybe they hoped to catch them and get revenge."

"That would have left them free to harry our rear," Fletcher said. "They could have done us a great deal of injury before we could organize a counterattack."

Haft snorted. "My rear point still would have beaten them," he growled.

"No," Spinner said. "You caught the first by surprise—and that lancer troop was much larger than the patrol you ambushed. If they didn't beat you immediately, the commander could have split his force, kept half of it back to deal with you, and sent the rest ahead to attack the caravan."

Silent nodded agreement with both. "We still would have beaten them, but at a much higher cost." He looked back into the trees. "But I don't think any more are following us now. What do you think, Wolf?"

Wolf looked up from the bone he was worrying and cocked his head at the steppe giant as though considering his answer.

"Ulgh!" he finally said with a vigorous shake of his head and shoulders.

"Do you want to backtrack tonight and make sure?" Silent asked.

Wolf growled and lowered his head and shoulders as though preparing to pounce.

"Good. We go in an hour."

"It's too dangerous to go back at night." Alyline spoke for the first time. "A patrol couldn't go far enough and have time to get back before we leave in the morning. Then the men would be tired and have to take up wagon space to sleep."

Silent chuckled, a bass rumble deep in his throat. "Just me and Wolf, we can do it and be back in time."

"If no one is behind us," Zweepee interjected, "we can stay here for a day or two. Our wounded need time to rest and heal. And we can use the time to gather more food. We *can* stop for a day or two if nobody's following, can't we, Spinner?"

"Maybe we can," Spinner replied in a voice that sounded like he didn't think they could.

Not long after that they finished their stew, wiping the bowls clean with bread old enough that it was turning stale and brittle.

Alyline and Zweepee, trailed by Doli, set out to check the encampment. Maid Primrose looked longingly after them before she turned to help Maid Marigold bank the fire and give the dishes a better cleaning. Silent stretched out for a short nap before he and Wolf left to check the back trail. Fletcher went to check on the horses.

Spinner stood. "Let's check the lines," he said to Haft.

Haft led the way because he'd placed the sentries and knew where they were.

It was night under the trees by the time they reached the first post. The four soldiers, Zobran Royal lancers, were nestled in a fall of tree trunks. If Haft hadn't remembered where he placed them, he and Spinner would have gone by without seeing the quartet. A stout tree had been felled by a lightning strike and dropped two lesser trees with it, the three forming a strong barrier the Zobrans were able to hide behind. Bushes behind them hid their silhouettes as they looked over the logs.

"Lord Haft, Lord Spinner," the Zobrans murmured greetings after signs and countersigns were exchanged.

"Don't call me 'Lord,'" Spinner muttered.

"Guma, Lyft, Ealu, Eaomod," Haft greeted them by name. "Hear anything out there?"

"Only the birds bedding down for the night," Guma replied.

"See anything?"

"Nothing moves."

Haft looked into the tree-night. "What's that?" he asked, pointing at a shadow that could be the head and shoulders of a lurking man.

Guma looked along Haft's arm to see what he meant. "That's a boysenberry bush," he murmured. "I knew it could be mistaken for a man when I watched night come."

"You memorized."

"Of course, Lord Haft. We all did. You taught us well."

"He's not a lord either," Spinner muttered.

Haft's grin went unseen in the dark and he ignored Spinner. He squeezed Guma's shoulder. "You learned well."

That was another of the lessons Lord Gunny had brought from—from wherever. Sentries on night watch should carefully examine their fronts as dusk faded to dark and memorize every shape and shadow as they changed, so when they looked out in the night they would know if they saw a shadow that hadn't been there in the light—and so they wouldn't mistake something that had been there as a threat.

They sat and watched and listened with the Zobrans for several more minutes. Nothing moved before their eyes. All they heard was the *whishing* of night fliers above, the buzzing of flying insects close by their ears, and the lightly skittering steps of small night browsers.

"Two up and two down," Spinner reminded them before they left; two men to watch while two slept. They visited the other posts, each in turn. Half of the men on watch were Zobran soldiers, the other half trained men from Eikby. All the watchers ignored Spinner's muttered objections to being called "lord."

When they got back to the camp and checked the hospital pavilion, they found all the wounded sleeping, some restlessly, most quietly. Nightbird, the healing witch from Bostia who joined them somewhere in southeastern Skragland or northeastern Zobra—nobody had been sure where they were at the time—sat watching quietly over them.

"Two are still in danger," Nightbird said softly. "The others mostly need time and rest."

"Time," Spinner repeated. Time was the one thing he thought they didn't have. Even if the Jokapcul weren't closely pursuing them, he felt an urgent need to get the refugees to Dartmutt as quickly as possible.

"Time," Nightbird confirmed. "Even a day or two will make a huge difference. If we move them too soon, some who aren't in danger now will be in danger then. The two who are now in danger could die if they are moved too soon."

"Can the healing demons heal them faster?"

Nightbird stiffened in the darkness; healing witches generally didn't trust healing magicians and their demons. They knew what their unguents and poultices could do. One could never predict with certainty what a demon might decide to do.

"I doubt it," she said with less heat than she felt. "They've already worked their magic. Now it is time the wounded need."

"We have to wait until Silent returns and gives his report," Haft said, stopping Spinner from saying anything else for the moment.

After a few more neutral remarks, they wandered through the camp.

All the fires were out or safely banked. Except for some of the older children and a few adults, everyone not on watch was asleep.

At their own fire they found Fletcher and Zweepee sitting close, Zweepee as usual tucked comfortably under her husband's protective arm. Alyline gave them a curious look. Maid Marigold seemed to glow in the fire's dim light when she saw Haft. There was no sign of Doli or Maid Primrose.

Zweepee disengaged herself from Fletcher to pour cups of water for them.

"All is secure in the camp," Fletcher said.

"We know; we saw," Spinner said as he took a seat on a log facing the fire. He accepted the cup with thanks.

"The sentries are alert," Haft said. He grinned at Maid Marigold, who took a cup from Zweepee and handed it to him. He sat cross-legged on the ground, she lowered herself and leaned against him. "All was quiet out there," he finished, and looped an arm around Maid Marigold to give her an affectionate squeeze.

"The healers all say we need to stay here for a day or two, to give the wounded a chance to mend," Alyline said.

"I'm not sure we can," Spinner told her.

"If no one's following we can," Fletcher said. "If the Jokapcul *are* closing on us, we're better off preparing defenses than trying to outrun them."

"We'll see what Silent says," Spinner said weakly. He thought this was an argument he was going to lose.

"We *have* to stop," Alyline insisted.

"We can *afford* to stop," Fletcher said with lesser insistence.

Zweepee said nothing. She lay her fingers along Fletcher's cheek and looked down at him. He returned her look, then rose.

"We'll see what Silent says in the morning," Fletcher said, then murmured good-nights as he and his wife headed for their small tent.

Haft had nothing to contribute to the discussion. He and Maid Marigold were cuddling perhaps more intimately than they should in front of the others.

Alyline looked at them and cleared her throat. "I'm for sleep," she said. "Perhaps we all should sleep now." She got to her feet and went to the small shelter she'd erected for herself.

Spinner ached to go with her but didn't move. He knew she'd rebuff him. He already felt everyone was against him on the matter of movement, and he didn't want to face a more personal rejection. He looked at Haft and Maid Marigold, who were now kissing passionately, and squeezed his eyes closed. Without a word, he rose and headed for his bedroll—he hadn't erected a shelter for himself.

A short while later Maid Marigold broke away from Haft and pushed a lock of hair back into place. "Not here, Haft," she murmured. "Let's go to our tent."

It was late morning by the time Silent and Wolf returned to the camp, which was already broken. Horses and oxen were hitched to wagons and dogs to carts. Riding horses were saddled, children, oldsters, the lame, and the worst wounded bided their time on wagons—the children restlessly. All was ready to go.

The giant steppe nomad went straight to where the command group's cookfire had burned the night before, Wolf padding at his heels. Once at the charred circle, he swiftly lay wood for a fire, then squatted and struck a spark to tinder. Flames quickly began to lick the twigs, then spread to the larger pieces of wood. Only when he was satisfied the fire was starting did he acknowledge Spinner and the others.

Spinner asked again, "What did you find?"

Silent didn't have to look very far up from his squat to look into Spinner's eyes. "I'm hungry, where's food?" he asked.

Spinner gaped at him. "You've been gone on a reconnaissance since last night's dusk and all you can say is 'where's food?'"

"And I haven't eaten since before then." He looked at Wolf, who lay contentedly at his side. "*He* ate, but he wouldn't share. *He* caught small rodents and chomped them down whole. But would he bring me a fawn? *No!*"

"*Ulgh!*" Wolf protested. There'd been no chance to hunt for a fawn; they were on a reconnaissance!

Silent laughed and briskly ruffled Wolf's neck and shoulders. "I'm just kidding, friend. I wasn't hungry enough for raw rodents, and we didn't have time to make a fire."

"Here's food." Doli approached with a loaf of not-too-stale bread. Maid Primrose carried a pot of leftover stew, which she set on the fire to warm up.

"My thanks, ladies." Silent took the bread and bit off a huge piece, which he quickly chewed and swallowed. He settled back and sat cross-legged on the ground. "Sit," he said to Spinner, with a gesture that included Haft, Fletcher, and Alyline. They sat on the log they'd used for a bench the night before. Zweepee squeezed in next to her husband, Doli shooed the two Eikby maids away, then knelt next to Spinner, facing the giant nomad. She either didn't see Maid Marigold and Maid Primrose come to kneel behind her or she ignored them. No one had called for Veduci, but he mirrored Silent at the opposite end of the log.

"We went fast," Silent began, keeping an eye on the stew pot, "all the way to where we could see into the valley that was our rally point after the Jokaps attacked Eikby. I went straight, paralleling the road. Wolf ranged the flanks. We saw no one. When I investigated the road for sign, all I could find was our own tracks and those of the Jokap troop that caught up with you yesterday. The tracks of the advance party that Haft's rear point ambushed were covered by the lancer troop's, but I saw where the ambush was—it was impossible to miss. The bodies were still there. It looked like when the survivors of your fight got back to them, they killed the wounded who weren't able to make it back on their own." He spat to the side in disgust at people who would kill their own wounded.

"No one is following us, at least not now." He looked away from the stew pot to the wagons. "Our wounded need rest. We can stay here for two days, maybe longer, and give them the rest they need to begin healing."

"Doli," Alyline snapped, "go to the healers, get the pavilion set back up for the wounded. You two," she added to Maid Marigold and Maid Primrose, "help her."

Doli shot her a resentful look, but got up to do as the Golden Girl said.

"Yes, ma'am!" the other two replied as they jumped to their feet and scurried to do her bidding. "Immediately, ma'am!" They had long been servants, and reacted automatically to the Golden Girl's commanding voice.

"But—" Spinner cut off his protest when Haft gripped his shoulder.

Zweepee saw the stew was now simmering and ladled it into a bowl that she handed to Silent. He gratefully took it and began spooning the savory stew into his mouth. Wolf looked up as though to say, *What about me?* Silent ignored him.

"I'll get men started on defensive works," Fletcher said, rising.

"I'll put out sentries," Haft said, and went to do so.

Around a mouthful of stew and bread, Silent said, "After I eat I'll get patrols out to our rear and flanks. They won't catch us by surprise."

"But—" Spinner started to object.

Alyline gave him a level look. "We have to do this, Spinner," was all she said before she got up and left.

Spinner turned to Zweepee, his last remaining hope for support. But before he could say anything, she said, "I'll see to the siting of new latrines. And I'll talk to Jatke about getting hunters out to find game for us."

Veduci, who had said nothing during the meeting, barely hid a smile as he left to find his own people. It was obvious to him the leadership here wasn't as firm as it might be. He needed to think about that; there could be advantage for him.

Silent had another bowl of stew, but when he was finished he left something in the bottom of the bowl for Wolf to lap up.

The defensive works weren't elaborate, little more than barricades to protect small teams of archers from opposing missiles, and limited fencing to channel attackers into better killing zones. Xundoe took the hodekin to the front of the defensive works to dig small pits to trip charging horses. He didn't set any Phoenix Egg traps, as he had during the final battle at Eikby; he doubted he'd be able to safely retrieve any unused eggs, and they were too precious to leave behind. He considered using the mezzullas to make a storm south of the encampment, but knew he didn't have the training to make a mezzulla do exactly what he wanted—it could just as well dump a storm on them and leave the weather clear for the Jokapcul.

Game was plentiful enough as the animals in the vicinity of Eikby moved north, away from the Jokapcul. But they were wary, and the hunters had trouble bringing any down. Still, they brought in more deer, boar, elk, and rabbits each day than was needed to feed the caravan. The meat was supplemented by fruits, tubers, mushrooms, and other forest edibles gathered by foraging women and children. Each day they spent giving the wounded time to heal, the refugees' store of food grew.

Reconnaissance patrols ranged far enough to see the ruins of Eikby in the distance, but they never saw sign of Jokapcul following them. They did see the Jokapcul constructing a base just outside Eikby's ruins, though.

The healers were pleased with the progress of the wounded. The land trow and aralez were tremendous aids in mending wounds. After two days, only half of the wounded were still unable to resume the march to Dartmutt under their own power—and all were out of danger.

Zweepee, backed by Jatke, wanted to stay another day or two in order to gather more food. Nightbird and the other healers—magicians and witches both—wanted to give the wounded more time to heal before stressing their healing injuries by moving them. But Haft and Silent threw their weight to Spinner in his insistence that even if the Jokapcul weren't coming directly at them from the south, the enemy was still on the move and they should move on as well. Alyline reluctantly conceded that Spinner, for once, was right.

They broke camp on the morning of the third day and resumed their slow progress north. To direct the scouts who were still out after they returned, Haft stayed behind with a rear guard.

The rest, brief as it was, was good for more than just the wounded. The people of Eikby had been in a state of high tension and activity since the arrival of Spinner and Haft and their company several weeks earlier: first with the Rockhold bandits who had attacked the town and had to be dealt with, then while preparing for another bandit attack, and finally the attack by the Jokapcul, which ended up destroying the town and imprisoning half its surviving population before the two Frangerian Marines and their fighting men rescued them and defeated the remaining Jokapcul. They then fled northward before more Jokapcul could arrive.

The two days in the encampment was the first respite the townspeople had had in all that time. Short as the rest was, it rejuvenated them and raised their morale—especially when it sunk in that they'd once more defeated the supposedly invincible Jokapcul. They started thinking of the Jokapcul as highly vincible.

Tramping or riding merrily along, on the fourth day after the rest, the van of the caravan topped a last rise and looked over the plain that led to the walled city of Dartmutt. They saw more smoke rising from the city environs and the harbor than could be accounted for by hearth fires alone.

II
FALLING WALLS

CHAPTER
FIVE

The ground sloped down to a broad plain that wrapped around the city of Dartmutt, which itself fronted the harbor. For almost a mile around the walls of Dartmutt, the plain was colorful chaos. Thousands upon thousands of people talked and cried and shouted in a score or more languages and dialects, and their garb was as varied as their tongues. The extravagance of smoke plumes that rose above the city was from the cookfires that lay at the center of many of the clusters of refugees. There was no order; each newly arriving group parked its wagons or pitched its tents wherever it could find space, and sometimes where it couldn't. Frequent fights broke out when one group decided a neighbor intruded on its space; blood was sometimes drawn or bones fractured, not infrequently a broken body was removed for burial.

The city itself was a square with thirty-foot-high stone walls nearly half a mile on a side. The tops of the walls had crenellations, barely seen from where the mountain road opened to the plain, and were cantilevered so they jutted out a man's length beyond the curtain wall. Towers situated at the corners of the walls and between the corners provided archers with angles to shoot at any attackers who attempted to gather under the overhang. Within the walls, only the towers of the central keep were higher than the curtain walls. In the past, before they turned to trade, raiders from the Low Desert north of Dartmutt had often attacked the city, and the city had built its defenses to hold them off. There was no moat, but the massive gates looked strong enough to withstand any but the mightiest siege engines.

Shallow-draft ships, the merchantmen of Princedon Gulf, were moored at the quays and piers; a few were off-loading cargo, none were boarding passengers or cargo for shipment east. Fishing craft and houseboats, strangers to that end of the Gulf, bobbed at anchor. Little more than half a mile from the shore, a thin screen of war galleys shielded the harbor's mouth, preventing other craft from entering its waters. In the distance, more craft, which appeared to be coast huggers, were approaching.

Companies of soldiers struggled to clear the roads the city needed to bring in provisions and goods from elsewhere—and to prevent starving refugees from assaulting the small supply caravans and looting them. Troops of cavalry patrolled the forest that edged the plain, other troops patrolling the farms to chase away refugees who would harvest the grains and vegetables for their own use.

One of those troops broke into a gallop when its commander spied the van of the column emerge from the Eikby road.

"Hold!" the captain shouted, reining up in front of the lead wagon. His men arrayed themselves in three ranks behind him, weapons at the ready—swords in the hands of the front rank, lowered lances behind them, nocked arrows in the bows to the rear. The light armor that protected the soldiers' chests and arms looked like it had seen battle; it was obvious even to the people in the column's van that these weren't ceremonial troops.

Esaulow, a stout, garrulous Eikbyer driving the lead wagon, stopped and looked fearfully at the cavalrymen. He hadn't expected to be greeted by the prince, but hostile soldiers were even further from any welcome he'd thought likely.

"Yes, lord," he said as he swept off his hat to bob his head and tug at his forelock.

"You must turn back," the captain announced in a strong voice. "None more may approach Dartmutt."

"Lord?" Esaulow asked. "I don't quite well understand

your words." He'd never been to Dartmutt and wasn't familiar with the local dialect.

"Are you deaf? I spoke clear enough. Turn back!" The captain put his hand on his sword hilt meaningfully.

"Stay, lord, stay!" Esaulow said quickly, holding up both hands as though to fend off a blow. "I'm sure someone else will gladly speak to you." He twisted around to look back down the column and huffed out in relief when he saw horsemen cantering forward. "Who can speak Dartmutter?" he called out, and wondered why *he* had to be driving the lead wagon, he who couldn't understand the way these Dartmutters mangled the tongue. Even as he asked the question, he saw Plotniko, the former master carpenter of Eikby, striding forward. Yes, Plotniko would understand the Dartmutt captain; he'd journeyed this way several times in quest for materials and tools. He watched Plotniko step aside for the horsemen—Spinner, Haft, and that harridan, Golden Girl.

"What's the problem, Esaulow," Spinner asked when he reached the van. He was proud of himself, he'd hardly had to pause before he remembered the man's name.

Haft pulled up alongside Spinner and graced the Dartmutt captain with a polite nod and a wolfish smile. He didn't put his hand on his axe, not quite, but it was obvious he could have it out as quickly as the captain could draw his sword. A sergeant murmured an order and half of the archers drew back their arrows and pointed their bows toward him.

Alyline shouldered her stallion forward and didn't stop until she was midway between them and the cavalry officer. Nearly all of the Dartmutters shifted their attention to her; the archers eased the tension on their bowstrings.

"What's going on here?" she snapped. Her meaning, if not her words, were clear.

The captain moved his hand from his sword and swept forward in a bow. "Lady," he said with a rueful smile, "I am distressed to say I cannot allow you passage."

"Can anybody understand him?" Alyline asked loudly enough for everyone nearby to hear.

"I can," Plotniko said as he came up. He looked at her, then turned back to Spinner and Haft. "He says we cannot pass." Turning to the captain, he said, "Sir, my name is Plotniko. I am Eikby's master carpenter—or I was until the Jokapcul came and destroyed our beautiful town. We are the survivors, along with strangers who came among us in flight from the Jokapcul. I can translate for our leaders."

The captain nodded brusquely. "Tell them my Lord Earl has decreed no more refugees are to approach the city. Your flight must take you elsewhere. I must demand that you turn back."

While this exchange was taking place, Spinner looked over the confusion surrounding the city and crowding the harbor. He could guess what the captain was saying though the Dartmutter dialect was unintelligible to him. He wondered if the galleys that screened the harbor would have to use force to stop the rapidly approaching coast huggers.

"We can't go back!" Alyline said when Plotniko translated the captain's orders. "The only thing back there is a destroyed town and the Jokapcul."

"We have fighting men," Haft said. "We can help defend the city while we are here."

The captain shook his head when Plotniko translated. "The army is full, we have no room for more deserters from other armies," he said harshly.

Haft's face went hard at the insult, but Spinner stopped him from doing anything by saying to Plotniko, "Ask him if there's another road we can take to the east. If we can go east, then we can completely avoid Dartmutt." He continued to watch the craft closing on the harbor.

There was a quick exchange during which the captain gave the wagons a doubtful look.

"There's a track about a mile back," Plotniko translated, "but he doubts it's wide enough for our wagons to pass. Maybe the dog carts can, he says."

Spinner remembered the track. It was narrow and looked like it had seen no recent use, he'd hardly taken note of it.

"I don't think we should go east," Haft said softly. "Look." He nodded toward the harbor.

Fifteen of the coast huggers Spinner had noted had broken from the mass of craft to form a line facing the galley screen and close to a couple of hundred yards from them. Puffs of smoke shot back from two of them, followed by sprays of water like whales' spouts splashing near the galleys. More puffs shot backward from the coast huggers and a galley staggered. Gnatlike specks flew from it, and other gnat-forms leaped from it to the water as flames began licking up its mast and spreading on its decks. The bangs of distant thunder reached them. There were more puffs from the coast huggers, and the galleys began to maneuver to dodge the geysers and close with the attacking craft. But the galleys turned too slowly, and several more were struck before any closed to grappling distance.

As soon as he realized the harbor was under attack, the cavalry captain forgot the Eikby refugee caravan and turned his troop to race to the city's defense—surely if the coast huggers broke through the screen they would land soldiers on the quays, or perhaps soldiers were already marching along the shore from the east.

"They've changed their tactics," Spinner murmured.

Haft nodded. "Must have," he agreed. "I thought they only attacked harbors before dawn."

"What are you going to do about it?" Alyline demanded. "Are you just going to sit here and let the Jokapcul take the port you led us to?"

Spinner wouldn't look at her. "That's a sea battle, we don't have a ship. So we *can't* do anything."

"You could go down to the harbor shore," she pointed at the side of the bay closest to the battle, "and use the demon spitters to even the odds."

Haft *did* look at her. "I don't know what those demon spitters are they're using. I *do* know ours don't have that much range. We don't have anything to hit them with until they get much closer to shore."

She muttered something unintelligible. Neither man asked her to repeat it. They watched the one-sided battle at the mouth of the harbor develop. A half-dozen galleys closed enough to grapple the smaller coast huggers. The others were shattered, burned, and sunk. A few crewmen managed to swim to the galleys still afloat and were hauled aboard to join in swarming onto the enemy craft. Others swam to shore. Too many went underwater and didn't resurface. The galleys were two and three times the size of the coast huggers; their much larger crews were able to overpower their antagonists, though with severe loss of life. The victories were short-lived, as the other attackers didn't hesitate to turn their demon spitters on the captured boats. The sea fight was over soon and the mass of coast huggers that gathered just beyond the fighting vessels advanced into the port.

"How many boats do you make out?" Spinner asked, peering through tubed hands.

Haft also had his hands curled into tubes held in front of his eyes to help focus his vision. "About a hundred," he said grimly. "Twenty men per boat."

"Two thousand men," Spinner said softly. "How many were in the landing force at New Bally?"

Haft shrugged. "Ten thousand? I wasn't counting."

"That was before dawn, in an undefended city. This is during the day, with the defenses alert. That's not a large enough force."

"No, it's not."

The two Marines lowered their hands and looked at each other.

"Where are the rest of them?" Spinner asked.

"I'll check that side trail." Haft spun about and galloped toward the rear of the train, bellowing out, "Bloody Axes, to me!"

Spinner looked back. A squad of Zobran Prince's Swords had edged forward. "Come with me," he ordered. He turned to Alyline. "Get Fletcher, tell him to see to defense from the east." He cantered east along the edge of the forest, looking for roads or foot paths. The Prince's Swords formed up behind him as they went.

Alyline sniffed. " 'Get Fletcher' indeed. As if I can't do it myself." Still, she went to get Fletcher. Between them they would organize the caravan into a defensive posture.

Two short lines of Prince's Swords rode with Spinner just inside the edge of the forest, almost invisible from the city and harbor. He hadn't told them what was happening, they saw for themselves when they reached the mouth of the road and looked across the farmland to the city and harbor. Half a mile ahead, the forest curved sharply north, almost to the waterline. Spinner slowed his gelding from a canter to a trot when he reached the bend and went partway toward the Gulf before turning into the wood. The trees grew close enough that he had to walk his horse. The Prince's Swords could have continued the trot, but he wasn't a good enough horseman to go through the forest at a faster pace. After a few hundred yards they began to hear the clash of arms to their front.

"I will go ahead, Lord Spinner," Wudu, the squad leader, offered. He heeled his horse and didn't hear Spinner's muttered response:

"Don't call me 'Lord.' "

Spinner and the others continued forward at a walk. Wudu rejoined them in five minutes.

"Several troops of Dartmutters are in the open, fighting a holding action against a large Jokapcul force, lord," he reported.

Spinner grimaced at the "Lord," but let it go for now.

"How far ahead?"

"The wood ends in a couple hundred yards. The battle is an equal distance beyond that."

"Let's take a look." Spinner risked a trot and managed to avoid being knocked off his horse by the branches he had to duck under.

They stayed far enough inside the trees that the combatants couldn't see them. From here the battle looked fierce but fairly even. Even enough that Spinner thought they might be able to turn the tide in favor of the defenders. But he couldn't be sure, and wasn't willing to risk so many of the refugees' defenders on someone else's battle. He looked about. Not far away was a tree with branches spaced for easy climbing. He rode to it and climbed high enough to see over the heads of the fighters. From that angle the fight didn't look as even as it had from ground level. Then he looked beyond it and saw more Jokapcul trotting forward. He clambered back to the ground and remounted his horse.

"They're going to be overrun shortly," he told the Zobrans. "We need to see to our people." He twisted his gelding around and followed Wudu back at a trot. Wudu carefully picked a line that avoided most of the branches that could unsaddle a horseman less skilled than his Prince's Swords.

Fletcher watched the Jokapcul swarming ashore from the coast huggers. "It's a feint," he told Alyline. "The main attack is going to come from the land side." He squinted and looked to the land on the north side of the harbor. Unlike on the south, vegetation was thin there, thin enough that he should be able to see any large troop formations if they were there. He saw none within a couple miles north of the city's walls. "They're coming from this direction, maybe through us. We have to move."

Alyline agreed. So did Jatke.

"If my memory is right," the former Eikby chief hunter said, "there is a place not far from here where we can have some protection."

"Can the wagons get there?" Alyline asked.

"I think so."

"Let's go."

Jatke led the way to the verge of the farmland and along the edge of the forest to the west. No Dartmutt cavalry troop attempted to stop them, they had all sped to defend their city. After three-quarters of a mile, a road cut southwest into the forest. Jatke turned onto it. The land rose and quickly became rocky, strewn with boulders, some the size of a small hut. Half a mile along he left the road in a treeless cut between two large boulders. Beyond was a maze of large boulders, with many paths between large enough to allow a wagon to pass.

He stopped and began directing traffic, different wagons into different paths of the maze. All but the two largest made it into the maze.

"We can use them to block the entrance if need be," he said.

By then Spinner and the Prince's Swords had rejoined the train.

"Where's Haft?" Spinner wanted to know.

Alyline sniffed and looked away.

"He's not back yet," Fletcher said.

Spinner grimaced. If Haft came across that battle, he was impetuous enough to have joined it. And the Bloody Axes would have joined him without question. *Damn!* He shouldn't have let Haft go without a cool-headed person along to keep him from doing things like that.

But he didn't have time to fret about what Haft might have done. A runner came from the end of the road.

"Lord Spinner," the runner gasped, "a large force of Jokapcul just came out of the forest and is attacking the refugees gathered south of the city!"

"Find a back way out," Spinner ordered Jatke before he sped to the mouth of the road.

"Dismount," Haft ordered when he reached the narrow trail leading east. He darted into the forest without looking to see how many of the Bloody Axes followed. He stopped fifty yards inside the trees and turned around. Fifteen Skraglanders gathered close.

"The Jokapcul are invading Dartmutt, but there aren't enough of them in the boats. They must also be invading from the land side. That's this way. This is a reconnaissance in force, to see if we can find them. If they're coming on this track, our people are in big trouble. Any questions?"

"If we find them, do we fight, Sir Haft?" Sergeant Phard, the Bloody Swords squad leader, asked.

"If we have to." Haft thought for a moment, then added, "If they're coming this way and we have time, we're better off going back to get our people out of their way." He heard the clopping of hooves and looked past the Bloody Axes.

"Where are we going?" Xundoe asked, panting, as he trotted up, leading a mule with two spell chests strapped to its back.

"Who sent for you?"

The mage drew himself up. "No one," he replied indignantly. "But when I saw you running off with the Bloody Axes like that, I thought there was trouble. I can help." He swept a hand at the spell boxes.

Haft nodded sharply. "I hope there isn't any trouble, but if there is, I'm glad you're here."

Xundoe preened.

"Just keep your mule quiet." Haft turned and led the way deeper into the forest.

Xundoe glared at Haft's back. As if he was a total greenhorn who needed to be told to keep his mule quiet!

They trotted along the track, fast enough to eat up distance, not fast enough to tire them. A mile along they heard the sounds of battle to their left front.

"On line," Haft said hoarsely, and used hand signals to tell his men exactly what he wanted them to do. He gave the Skraglanders a moment to spread to his sides facing the battle noise, then raised an arm and dropped it forward. They resumed trotting, but in line abreast instead of in a single file. Xundoe followed a few yards behind Haft.

The ground sloped gently down toward the unseen Gulf. The sounds of battle became louder and more widespread as they closed the distance. Haft stopped them when they reached a low rise—it sounded like the battle was right on the other side. He and Sergeant Phard lowered themselves and scrabbled up the rise to peer over its top. Haft wanted to back down soon after looking, but made himself stay and examine the scene before him. He knew the brush would hide him from eyes that merely glanced in his direction, but he still wished he had a Lalla Mkouma to make him invisible. It was too late now to check if Xundoe had one in his spell chests.

The land here was covered with scrub and had been set aside for goat pasturage. Bleating goats scampered about, trying to dodge the three or four troops of Dartmutter soldiers locked in desperate combat with legions of Jokapcul infantry.

Well, maybe not legions, Haft amended, but the Dartmutters were certainly badly outnumbered. They were giving good account of themselves; Jokapcul bodies lay piled in front of and around them. But many of the defenders were also down, sprawled atop enemy corpses. What looked like hundreds of goats were scattered about, red with blood, entrails spilled on the ground. A few butted indiscriminately at the men, more easily staggering or knocking over the smaller Jokapcul than the larger Dartmutters. To his right, Haft saw more Jokapcul infantry approaching the battle. An arm of the forest reached almost to the water's edge on the left. If any Dartmutter soldiers were coming to reinforce their compatriots, they hadn't yet reached its edge.

After watching for a few minutes, Haft slid back down. Sergeant Phard went with him and waited for orders. Haft briefly described to the others what was happening. The Bloody Axes gripped the hafts of their battle-axes and waited, ready to do anything he said, even if he led them over the rise to their deaths.

"We can't help them," he said. "There are simply too many Jokapcul for our number to make a difference. If they stay in the coastal flat, we're all right. But we still need to find out if anybody is using that track." He shuddered. He hated to leave those soldiers to their fate, but he knew if they tried to help, all they would accomplish was to increase the number killed by the Jokapcul—and reduce the number of fighters available to defend the thousands of refugees who had given themselves to his and Spinner's care. "We're going to follow the track for another mile, then head back."

The Skraglanders nodded; they understood. Little more than half an hour later they were back at the Eikby-Dartmutt road. The caravan wasn't there. Neither were the horses they'd left behind.

"Here, Sir Haft," Farkas said. "They went west."

Haft trotted to the mouth of the road and saw the wagon tracks and hoofprints that bent out of the road and headed west.

"Then we follow them," he said. He glanced toward Dartmutt. "But we stay inside the trees.

CHAPTER SIX

The thousands of people, men, women, children, oldsters, who were camped south of Dartmutt's walls were slow to realize the city was under attack from the Gulf. At first only those closest to the shore could see the sea battle raging at the harbor's mouth—and only a few of them happened to be looking in the right direction to see it. None of those who did look immediately realized what the pyrotechnics they saw were; signals perhaps. When they realized the growing flames were ships on fire, they became uneasy. They still didn't know it was a sea battle, they thought perhaps an accident had befallen a ship or two. Still, some of them began drifting away from the water's edge, either deeper into the masses of people or north or south into the farmland.

Those who went north or south at first thought they had to evade the patrols that were charging toward them, the patrols put out to protect the farms from the refugees. When the patrols passed by, the north- or southbound refugees became frightened and looked again at the harbor mouth. Now, frightened as they were, they saw a battle where before they had seen what they'd hoped were signals or an accident. Without thinking things through, they began running. Not running anywhere in particular, simply running from where they were. It didn't occur to any of the runners to wonder how or for how long they could survive without any of the things they left behind.

The refugees who went deeper into the mass of people were simply accepted by those they passed as elements of the constantly moving, milling mass and it caused no undue consternation, though a couple of fights broke out with other refugees

74

whose nerves were already frayed to the breaking point. Being densely surrounded by other nerve-frayed refugees calmed most of those who moved from the unsettling sight at the mouth of the harbor. When troops of cavalry rushing to the defense of the city forced their way through the crowds, well, rough treatment by rude soldiers was just something the refugees had learned to put up with, and most of them failed to realize anything was amiss.

It wasn't long before the sea battle was over and a hundred coast huggers sped to the piers and quays that lined the harbor before the city's sea wall and twenty Jokapcul swordsmen jumped from each. Most of the Jokapcul immediately assaulted the Dartmutter soldiers and refugee soldiers who were hastily assembling at the wall's foot. Two or three hundred Jokapcul raced to the northeast corner of the city walls to intercept reinforcing Dartmutter cavalry coming from that direction. An equal number headed directly to the southeast corner. Finally, the refugees closest to the shore realized what was happening and began a panicked flight. They fled the defenders as much as the attackers.

Arrows rained down on the Jokapcul from the cantilevered battlements above and from the towers at the wall's corners, while the defenders on the ground were protected by the overhang, but more of the arrows glanced off the Jokapcul armor or stuck in the stiff leather than penetrated to injure. The caldrons of boiling oil that were emptied onto the attackers had more effect. At the north- and southeast corners, the Jokapcul dispatched to intercept reinforcements crowded under the overhang and were mostly protected from boiling oil. However, they weren't protected from arrow fire from the towers. For a short while it looked like the assault was doomed to failure.

Ten of the coast huggers backed off from the quays and piers; they carried the large demon spitters that had sunk most of the galleys that screened the harbor mouth. The demon spitter crews positioned their weapons so the flanged back ends of the tubes were out over the water then angled the tubes to fire high, pelting the crenellations atop the walls. The merlons were weakened with each strike, until they burst, violently throwing chunks of rock about, injuring or killing the soldiers firing arrows or pouring oil onto the attackers. That gave the eight catapults on the sea wall's battlements and two to the north and two more to the west the angle they needed to fling rocks at the coast huggers—they sank two of the demon-spitter coast huggers before they were all knocked out. Half of the demon spitters returned their attention to the archers and oil-boilers, while the others blasted the wall just above the heads of the combatants on the ground.

Reinforcing cavalry troops began arriving at the north- and southeast corners, and the intercepting Jokapcul spread out to meet them. The cavalry was joined by some of the refugee soldiers who charged forward on foot. Most of the Jokapcul avoided the charging horses and chopped or thrust their swords at the cavalrymen or disemboweled their mounts. The surviving cavalrymen swung furiously, hewing off limbs and liberating large volumes of blood and gore. The first waves of cavalry were quickly dispatched, but many of the charging horses evaded the enemy weapons and slammed into the Jokapcul, knocking them down like ten pins and trampling them before falling themselves. When the second waves arrived, they faced fewer Jokapcul and killed a larger number before they were themselves killed. The third waves finished off the screening Jokapcul and waited for the fourth waves before they charged into the main force.

Most of the refugees were in panic. Some tried to climb the city walls, but found no purchase on the stone. Many huddled together, crying, seeking safety in mounds of protective bodies. A few hundred jumped into the harbor and attempted to swim to safety. Those who climbed aboard the Jokapcul craft were swiftly killed and thrown back to feed the fish and crabs. Several merchantmen and fishing boats capsized because too many swimmers scrabbled for their decks. But most of the refugees ran aimlessly hither and yon in wide-eyed panic. Few of the runners bothered to pick up more than a few random goods; a very few staggered under so much weight they couldn't advance faster than a stumbling shamble.

When the victorious army from the goat-field battle swarmed out of the forest, it fell upon the refugees in the farms south of the city. None of them survived, not even the refugee soldiers who tried to fight. Then the Jokapcul headed for the refugees fleeing west.

Spinner and the Prince's Swords who came with him skidded to a stop just shy of where the southwest road emptied into the farmland. The sound of running footsteps spun him to face the trees on his right and snapped his quarterstaff into position, ready to fight.

"Spinner!"

"Haft!"

Haft broke from the trees and stopped, facing Spinner. Spinner suddenly grinned and stepped forward to embrace his friend.

"Haft, I was afraid we'd lost you!"

"Lost me? Never! Why would you think that?"

"There was a fight beyond the trees. I was afraid you'd come across it and tried to help. But the Dartmutter cause was hopeless."

Haft pulled back and gave Spinner an odd look. "Yes, that fight was hopeless. We," he waved at the Bloody Axes with him, "couldn't help our people if we joined that fight and died. Anyway, we were a reconnaissance patrol, fighting wasn't our job. We had to find out if anyone was coming our way and bring back a report." He looked at the Jokapcul ravening the refugees on the farmland. "They missed us and got them."

Alyline joined them and, after a quick glance at Haft, studied the farmland. "We can't stay here," she announced.

They all looked at the slaughter beyond. Then a great gout of dust rose from the city's seaside wall, and about ten seconds later a growing rumble reached them.

"They've breached the wall," Spinner said softly.

The Jokapcul in the farmland had finished slaughtering the refugees. Now they raced toward the city's east wall, to pour through the broken wall and take the city. The surviving refugees to the west, and even more survivors to the north, continued to stream away from the city.

"What manner of demon spitter are they using?" Haft murmured. Whatever it was, it was far more powerful than the one he carried.

The two watched for a few moments longer, with the Prince's Swords arrayed behind Spinner and the Bloody Axes around Haft. They all ignored the Golden Girl's urgings to leave.

What Spinner and Haft watched differed from the invasion of the freeport of New Bally, where they'd had to escape a city held by the Jokapcul. In New Bally, the Jokapcul had killed all who resisted them, and hanged one out of ten soldiers and seamen of a score of nations to cow the rest. Here, they didn't have to escape from within Jokapcul lines, but find a way to lead more than two and a half thousand people safely away. However, the Jokapcul in Dartmutt engaged in wanton slaughter of civilians, which they hadn't in New Bally.

Spinner finally reacted to the insistent tugging on his arm and turned to Alyline. "Yes," he said absently. "We must leave. Let's see if Jatke has found a back way out. Or maybe Veduci knows this land and knows a way."

Jatke showed up a few minutes after they got back to the boulder-strewn area where the refugees were hidden.

"Lord Spinner, Lord Haft!" the chief hunter gleefully called to them. "Look what I found!"

Jatke strode rapidly toward them. Behind him two other hunters hustled along a richly garbed, obviously terrified man.

"Who is he?" both Marines asked.

"He babbled when we caught him, so I couldn't understand him. But the way he's dressed, I think he's some kind of functionary in the earl's court."

"Oh?"

Haft cocked his head at the man. "An important man?"

"Look at how he's dressed."

"Where's Plotniko?" Spinner asked.

"I'm here," the carpenter said, coming up.

"Ask him who he is and what he's doing out here."

Plotniko spoke to the frightened man, who indicated with gestures that he didn't understand, then Plotniko asked again. When the man still didn't reply, Haft caressed the spike that backed the half-moon blade of his axe and stepped close.

"If you don't need your tongue, I'm sure we've got a dog that would like it," he said in his best harbor Zobran.

Haft's best harbor Zobran was good enough. The man started talking so fast his words had trouble getting out past each other.

"Slow down," Plotniko said in the Dartmutter dialect, patting the air. "Take a deep breath and start again."

It took a couple of tries, but the man breathed deeply and began speaking less rapidly. Haft turned to hide a smile and moved a few steps away. "He understood me well enough," he said in an aside to Spinner.

Spinner nodded but didn't take his attention from the man.

Plotniko and the Dartmutter exchanged words, more from Plotniko, reluctantly from the man, then Plotniko said, "He says his name is bal Stanga, that he's a minor functionary in the castle." He looked back at the man. "As richly as he's dressed, I think he's more than a 'minor' functionary. He says he was just out for a ride, enjoying the fine day." He shook his head. "But he couldn't—or wouldn't—tell me where his horse is." He snorted. "Or explain why he's not dressed for riding." Indeed, the blue and red brocade robe the man wore hung like a dress and was far too stiff to allow him to straddle a horse.

"Ask him," Jatke interjected, "if he was riding with the wagons and soldiers we saw parked along the road a quarter mile north of here."

"Wagons?" Alyline exclaimed.

"Soldiers?" Haft yelped.

"What soldiers?" Spinner demanded.

"My apologies, Lord Spinner, Lord Haft." Jatke bowed. "He was just inside the forest, watching the Jokapcul enter the city, when we found him. But before that we followed a track north from here to where it met another road. Six heavily laden wagons were pulled under the trees and the horses tethered on a picket line. Several tents were set up. A small guard of soldiers, maybe twenty of them, guarded the wagons and people—they weren't very alert. We followed the road and found him alone at the edge of the trees."

"What people?" Alyline interrupted. "Tell me about them."

"I saw about a dozen, mostly women with a few children, but there may have been more in the tents. They wore travel cloaks and could have been any travelers, but flashes of fine garments under the hems of the robes made me think they are the families of wealthy merchants or, more likely, courtiers."

"How long have they been there?" Spinner asked.

"Not long," Jatke said. "Probably only a few hours. The ground wasn't as much disturbed as it would be had they camped there for long."

Spinner nodded and looked at Plotniko. "Ask him about them."

Before Plotniko finished his question, bal Stanga raised his hands and face to the sky and wailed. He dropped to his knees and nearly fell when the stiff brocade didn't fold as quickly as his knees did. He hid his face in his hands and burbled into them. Plotniko squatted, put a comforting hand on his shoulder and spoke in a reassuring tone. After a couple of moments bal Stanga lifted his tear-stained face from his hands and started talking.

Plotniko chuckled when the man finally stopped. "He asked if we were going to kill him. It took a bit to assure him, but then he started telling me about the travelers. He says they're the earl's family and a few retainers. The earl sent them out of the city this morning so they would have a chance to escape if the Jokapcul came."

Haft snorted. "Where did he think they could go to the southwest? The Jokapcul have everything in that direction."

Plotniko asked, then translated the answer. "They came this way so none of the refugees would think they were fleeing. Some miles to the west, that road intercepts a trade road between upper Zobra and the Low Desert. They are to follow it north. The earl has friends in the Low Desert who he believes will care for them."

Haft snorted. "Typical aristocrats. Sneak around to save themselves and leave the common folk to be slaughtered." Nobody replied; most agreed and didn't think it needed to be said.

Spinner thought for a moment. "I think we need to talk to them," he said abruptly. "Who is the highest ranking person in that party?"

Plotniko asked bal Stanga, then said, "He is."

"He's only a minor functionary, yet he's higher ranking than anyone in the earl's family?" Haft said in mock surprise.

The master carpenter gestured at the brocaded robe. "Chamberlain, majordomo. Someone important," he said dryly.

Spinner looked around. Fletcher stood nearby watching, as did the two groups of soldiers who had gone with them to the east.

"Haft, get the Royal Lancers and Blood Swords. We'll take them along with the Bloody Axes and Prince's Swords to visit these Dartmutters. I'm sure their wagons have things we can use. Fletcher, stay here and see to the defense."

"Turning bandit, are we?" Alyline asked acidly.

Spinner looked at her levelly. "The people are welcome to come with us. If they choose not to, they probably won't need their goods for very long anyway. Would you rather the Jokapcul took their possessions along with their lives, possessions we could put to good use?"

She turned her back on him and angrily crossed her arms under her breasts.

"Plotniko, you come too—and bring bal Stanga."

Haft quickly returned with the soldiers Spinner wanted and they moved out. Spinner knew better than to tell Alyline to stay behind.

Captain bal Ofursti of the Earl's Guard paced twenty yards along the road, spun about, paced back twenty yards, spun and paced again. His red cloak flopped out behind him, exposing a cerulean-blue jerkin and trousers and the bits of armor that covered his chest and shins; a saber with a finely wrought basket hilt banged in its filigreed scabbard against his thigh as he paced. His eyes were fixed on the ground a man's length before his feet, his hands clasped tightly behind his back under the cloak.

He muttered as he paced, cursing the fate that had him nursemaiding the earl's whores and their get. There were hundreds, maybe *thousands* of soldiers from broken armies among the refugee masses camped outside Dartmutt's walls. He and his men should be *there*, he thought, organizing those soldiers into a proper fighting force, able to take on the Jokapcul when they arrived—and they would arrive, no doubt of that. But *no*, the earl sent him away with his concubines and their sprats and maids-in-waiting and—and that *popinjay*, that court butler bal Stanga. That man was good for nothing but looking important and announcing the names of supplicants seeking audience with the earl. Why, he wasn't even significant enough to announce important visitors! Take them to Wuzzlefump, or whatever his name was, that Low Desert bandit chief the earl was foolish enough to count as friend. Fuzzlewump will care for them until I can send for them, the earl insisted.

Bal Ofursti snorted. As if Muzzlekrump would treat them as anything other than hostages to be held for ransom! Why, he had half a mind to leave the royal trollops here and take his guards in search of an army that was still resisting the invaders.

Hmm. Or . . . Actually, the women were pretty good looking, every one of them. Maybe he should parcel them out among his men and take them along. That bel Hrofa-Upp was *really* good looking, and she smiled so sweetly everytime she caught him looking at her. Yes, claim her for himself, *then* parcel the others out.

He had just about convinced himself to do that when bal Stanga called his name. What was that fool doing coming out of the trees on the east side of the road? And who were those two men who flanked him? And those other half doz . . . twenty, thir . . . How many men *were* there? All those *armed* men?

All of them soldiers—and of different armies! He recognized some of the uniforms. There were Skraglander Bloody Axes. Zobran Royal Lancers. And the two flanking bal Stanga—Frangerian Marines?—looking like nothing so much as prison guards, and the earl's butler their prisoner? He dismissed as a figment of his imagination the half-naked golden woman behind them.

He scanned quickly right to left—and saw no officer. Were these renegades, cut off from their own forces, fleeing the Jokapcul, turned to banditry? They must be! Where were his men? Were they in position to fight off these—gods, there were so many!—brigands? They had to protect the earl's consorts and their handmaidens! But he didn't have enough men to defend against this force. Could he bluff them?

Of course he could! He was an officer, and they had none. Captain bal Ofursti drew himself to attention and boomed in his best parade ground voice, "What is the meaning of this?" Behind him he heard the rustle of hurried movement and the clanking of weapons as his men suddenly realized the threat and formed up to fight, and squeals and running feet as the women and children ran in search of hiding places.

A man he hadn't noticed before, a townsman of some sort by his garb who stood behind bal Stanga, said something, and one of the Frangerians, the one with the wicked-looking axe, nudged the butler.

"Ah, Captain bal Ofursti," bal Stanga said in a voice far less self-important than the one he used to announce supplicants in the earl's court. He cleared his throat and resumed, though still not in his normal court voice. "I fear Dartmutt is taken. I saw with my own eyes the sea wall collapse under assault from demon weapons."

The Frangerian with the staff said something to the townsman, who in turn spoke to bal Stanga.

"Ah, yes." The butler cleared his throat again. "These— These soldiers are escorting a large refugee caravan. They, ah, they have need of our wagons." He swallowed and hung his head sheepishly. "They say we are welcome to join them, as Dartmutt is almost taken and t'would be folly for us to return thence."

Bal Ofursti's eyes widened. Was this, after all, a part of the resisting army he'd hoped for?

"I wish to speak to their commander. Where is he?" A feminine bark of laughter jerked his eyes a few yards to the side of the townsman and he almost missed what the butler said next because his eyes hadn't fooled him, there really *was* a beautiful, half-naked, golden woman standing there!

"Ah," bal Stanga shook his head, "these gentlemen are the commanders." He lifted his hands to indicate the Frangerians who flanked him like prison guards.

He forced his eyes away from the woman and, with an effort of will, pulled the dignity of his rank about himself. He leaned forward and peered at the two men flanking bal Stanga. Frangerian ships made port at Dartmutt infrequently, but often enough that he was vaguely familiar with their rank insignia. No, he had been right the first time, they weren't officers.

"They can't be the commanders," he snorted. "Look at them, they're junior enlisted men!"

Bal Stanga flinched as the townsman obviously translated the retort. The Frangerian with the axe looked across the butler to the one with the staff and said something in Frangerian. Bal Ofursti knew enough of that language to almost understand him. But, no, he couldn't *really* have said, "That's what you get when commissions are handed out according to *who* you know instead of *what* you know—really dumb officers." Could he?

The one with the staff touched bal Stanga on the arm, and that knot of four, including the townsman, came forward and stopped two paces in front of bal Ofursti. He blinked as the woman joined them. She was truly beautiful, and totally golden, wearing ballooned pants and a vest that didn't completely close between her breasts. The coins that dangled from her girdle looked like real gold.

"Captain," the townsman translated for the Frangerian with the staff, "we are Spinner and Haft, we command here. Your majordomo told you our requirements and terms. We require your wagons and goods. You will give them to us. You are welcome to join us or free to leave as you choose."

Bal Ofursti thought for a moment. Dartmutt had fallen, or was falling, if he could believe the butler—*majordomo*? If bal Stanga told them he was the majordomo, then everything he said was suspect. He looked to his left rear and almost stammered as he shouted out an order for two of the soldiers to run to the end of the road and report back what they saw—his soldiers were all gaping at the golden woman. Some of the soldiers opposite moved to stop them, but at sharply snapped orders in Frangerian and rough Zobran from—Spinner and Haft? What kind of names are those for commanders?—let them pass.

The scouts had barely disappeared beyond the first curve in the road when a half-dozen farmers came pelting along it. At sight of the soldiers they began screaming, "Jokapcul! The Jokapcul are here," and ran to hide behind the Earl's Guards and the Zobrans.

Bal Ofursti and all the soldiers turned to face the road, but neither Jokapcul nor the two scouts appeared. The Frangerian with the staff—Spinner?—gave an order in Zobran and two of the Royal Lancers ran to the bend in the road. They looked and reported the road was clear.

The scouts were back quickly, running at full speed.

"Sir," they reported, saluting bal Ofursti though their eyes were on the woman, "it is as the butler said. The Jokapcul have taken the city. The encamped refugees are being hunted down and killed in the fields."

Dartmutt had fallen! Now Captain bal Ofursti had a decision to make. Should he obey the earl's orders and take the women and children to Rak Adier for safekeeping? He seriously doubted the earl would be joining them—if the Jokapcul were inside the city, he would soon be dead. Going to that bandit Rak Adier seemed even less desirable an option than it had before. They had to go somewhere else. But where?

Just before bal Stanga had come with these soldiers, he'd been thinking of finding an army that was still resisting. Well, these soldiers seemed still to be resisting. They were a start. He was an officer, they would obey him. He could claim bel Hrofa-Upp and parcel out the other women tonight when they stopped for the day. His eyes flicked to the golden woman and wondered which of these men she belonged to. Perhaps he should claim her instead. Or why not both bel Hrofa-Upp and this golden woman? Commander's prerogative, of course, he could claim both.

"You men," he said, swinging a pointing finger to indicate the soldiers on the other side of the road—including the two Frangerians who claimed they were in command, "form up to protect the wagons and their passengers. We're moving out." He began to turn to order his men to harness the horses but was stopped by a finger that poked him in the base of his throat just above his breast plate. The finger belonged to the short Frangerian with the axe.

Haft said slowly and clearly in Zobran, "Did you understand what I said about officers and who you know and what you know?"

Bal Ofursti understood standard Zobran well enough. His jaws clenched and his face turned red. So he *had* heard right. "Yes, I did," he gritted.

"Were you born stupid, or did you have to learn it?" Haft roared inches from his face. "You don't give us orders. We're taking the wagons. You and the passengers can come with us or not, but we don't go with you."

He began to draw his saber. Haft didn't move a finger to defend himself, but forty men shifted their weapons, and bal Ofursti knew that if he drew, every one of them would do his utmost to kill him before his saber cleared its scabbard. He let go of the hilt and the blade slid back.

"Captain!" a voice said in very rough Zobran. Bal Ofursti looked at a sergeant of the Skragland Bloody Axes. The man looked like a barbarian in his fur cloak with its distinctive maroon stripes. "Sir Haft bears the rampant eagle. We follow him. You would be wise to do the same."

Sir Haft? Was the sergeant claiming the low-ranking Frangerian was a knight of some sort? And what was this about a rampant eagle? Haft could tell by his expression he didn't know what the eagle meant—he was glad he wasn't the only ignorant person on that score. Before bal Ofursti could ask about the rampant eagle, another voice demanded his attention.

"The Royal Lancers of Zobra obey Lord Spinner's commands," said a man wearing a royal-blue doublet and carrying a wicked-looking lance.

Lord Spinner? What was going on here?

Then two other men announced that the Zobran Prince's Swords and the Skraglander Blood Swords also followed Lords Spinner and Haft.

Lord Spinner, Lord—or was it Sir—Haft? Were they high-ranking officers in disguise? No, they couldn't be, they were too young! But—But—

Nobles, that was it! They had to be nobles. Younger sons of dukes or princes or something. They had the arrogance for it, especially that Haft. He'd straighten this out later. *He* was the officer here, the trained leader of men. These younger sons would have to learn the difference, that it took time to gain the experience to be real officers. The most important thing right now was to get away from Dartmutt before the Jokapcul extended their perimeter. He bowed, still wondering *why* these young lordlings chose to disguise themselves as such junior men.

"Lord Spinner, Lord Haft. I am at your command."

"Good." Spinner nodded curtly. "I'm glad you decided to join us. We need every fighting man we can get. You will stay in command of your troops, you know them better than anyone I might assign to them. We want to go north. Do you know a route that circles far enough west to avoid Jokapcul patrols?"

Yes, he did.

CHAPTER
SEVEN

It took nearly an hour for the caravan to wend its way from the boulder field to the other road and line up behind the six wagons from Dartmutt. This time, the Zobran Border Warders formed a mobile picket screen to the rear and Haft led the Bloody Axes between them and the caravan's tail as a strong rear guard. They had to be ready in case the Jokapcul sent a strong patrol in their direction. Half of the Earl's Guard and a squad of Zobran Royal Lancers rode ahead to scout the way. Silent and Wolf dogged them—to make sure the Dartmutters weren't leading the caravan into a trap.

There were twenty-three women in the Dartmutter party; bel Yfir, the Earl's favorite concubine, with five handmaids; three other concubines, each with four handmaids; and two wet nurses to care for the two babes among the six children. Captain bal Ofursti had twenty mounted soldiers of the Earl's Guard. The butler bal Stanga and six teamsters with their wives and five children filled out the royal party. Sixty-four people. The wagons and soldiers were the most welcome. As for the rest, well . . . The teamsters could be trained at arms—if they ever found time to stop and train them. The women were another matter. The concubines expected to be waited on and catered to. That didn't cause much problem, their handmaids dealt directly with that. The problem arose when the concubines expected the march to be run according to their whims.

Nobody in the caravan had time or energy to spare to taking care of the women Alyline had quickly dubbed "the royal bed toys." Certainly no one had the inclination.

"But we simply *must* stop now," bel Yfir insisted two hours after they set out. "I—I must attend to *private* matters. And I grow weary from sitting on this harsh bench. And my tent *must* be erected so I can refresh myself before we continue this journey." She waved a paper fan before her face. She had removed her travel gown because it "makes me perspire" too much. Her loose inner gown, finely stitched with delicate designs in gold and silver thread, clung in drapes to her body; a sheen of sweat turned the thin red material nearly transparent where the damp cloth clung to her flesh. One of her handmaids dabbed with a cloth at her neck and bare shoulders from just inside the body of the wagon behind her.

The wagon that carried her, her handmaids, and their goods was constructed like a small house, with a porch roof that extended over the driver's bench on which she sat. The wagon was exceptionally well sprung and, despite her complaints of its harshness, boasted nicely upholstered benches. Most of the wagons—and none of the dog carts—that had begun the journey in Eikby didn't have springs. Neither did any of them boast upholstered benches.

"Lady bel Yfir," Plotniko said with notably less patience than he'd had the previous dozen times he'd been called upon to respond to one of her complaints, "if your bottom is sore from sitting for so long, get down and walk awhile. If you have to make water, find a bush and squat, like everybody else." He strode off, leaving her gaping at him in shock at being so rudely spoken to, as though she was—was *like everybody else*!

She turned to Captain bal Ofursti, who was riding escort alongside her wagon, and sputtered indignantly. "Captain, chastise that man!" she finally said.

"Lady," he replied with a gallant bow, "I doubt the nobles for whom he serves as translator would take kindly to my chastising him without their permission."

She was nearly as shocked by that as by Plotniko's response to her oh so reasonable request. The instant she recovered, she thrust out her arm, poking her driver in the cheek with a sharp fingernail—he flinched away but voiced no protest—and shrilled, "Quit my company this instant! You are dismissed from the guard! The earl shall attend to you when he joins us!"

Bal Ofursti shook his head, thinking how glad he was he hadn't decided to claim this one for himself. "Lady, the Jokapcul took Dartmutt. I don't think the earl will be joining us." He wondered idly which of his men he disliked enough to give her to. It's probably a good thing bel Hrofa-Upp isn't one of her handmaids, he thought. He wondered again which of the nobles owned the golden woman. If neither did—or even if one of them did . . .

Bel Yfir brought him back to the present unpleasantness. "Of course he will," she insisted. "If those barbarians from the west have taken him, we will simply pay the ransom and get him back."

In pieces, he thought. If they haven't already killed him.

"Now quit my sight!"

He bowed again and drew his horse aside to let the wagon proceed without him.

Sergeant Afi, a grizzled veteran of the Skragland King's Outer Guards before he'd returned to Dartmutt to serve with the Earl's Guards, pulled up next to him. "She's beautiful to look at," he rumbled, "I grant you that. But what a shrew! I don't understand how the earl puts up with her."

Ofursti shrugged. "I guess if a man has enough power and wealth, a woman will be sweet to him and do whatever he wants."

"And think his power and wealth are hers so she can treat everyone else like chamber slops." Afi spat into the trees and watched the wagon trundle away, then asked, "Do you want me to move up and take your place next to her?"

"No, let her ride without a visible escort for a time." He shook his head. "I think tomorrow we'll have to trade off teamsters. It's cruel to have one man drive her every day." He idly noted one of bel Yfir's handmaids drop off the back of the wagon and walk boldly back along the column. Probably looking for one of the nobles, he thought.

*   *   *

The "noble" the handmaid bel Bra sought wasn't Spinner or Haft. Chief concubine bel Yfir thought a lady would be more sympathetic to her plight. That gilded woman might dress like a wanton houri, but she obviously had rank fully equal to the two noblemen who protected the mob of ragamuffin refugees.

There! The woman in the high-necked dress, she was one of the gilded lady's handmaids. The handmaid was quite lovely in her own right, though not as striking as the gilded lady. She was probably made to dress so plainly so as to not detract from her mistress's beauty—unlike the concubines' handmaids, who wore gowns that would be indistinguishable from their mistresses' except that they lacked the decorative filigree of gold and silver embroidery.

Bel Bra picked up her pace and headed directly to Doli.

"I don't understand you, I don't know that language," Doli replied in Bostian when bel Bra spoke to her. She said it again in Skraglandish, Frangerian, and a couple of other languages, but gave up when it became obvious bel Bra only understood Dartmutter. Doli looked around for anyone who might know Dartmutter and called out to Plotniko, who was walking briskly away, toward the head of the column.

The master carpenter had seen the Dartmutter woman, whom he recognized as one of the chief concubine's handmaids, and could guess why she had collared Doli. He didn't want anything to do with the matter and made haste to get out of Doli's sight before she could call on him to translate. When he heard his name, it felt like a stab between his shoulder blades, but he ignored the call and kept going. To no avail. A moment later a horseman cantered up to him and slowed his horse to a walk.

"Master Plotniko," the horseman said, it was Kovalev, one of the Eikby Guards, "Mistress Doli needs you to translate." He pointed in her direction.

Plotniko stifled a groan. "Can you tell her you couldn't find me?"

Kovalev shook his head. "She's looking at us."

Plotniko let out a sigh. "I'm tired of translating for those people. I wish they hadn't joined us." But he turned and waited for Doli and bel Bra to come up.

"She wants what?" Doli asked, shocked, when Plotniko translated.

"Her mistress wants your mistress to join her in the lead wagon." He spread his hands helplessly. "That's what she said."

Doli looked from one to the other, confusion on her face. "Uh, ah, there must be some error here, something lost in translation. I mean, she's speaking Dartmutter, which isn't your tongue, and you're translating into Frangerian, which is neither of our native tongues." Frangerian was the one language the two had in common. "I don't have a mistress, and everybody knows that." Suspecting that Plotniko's Frangerian wasn't very strong, she looked around for someone who spoke the Eikby dialect of Zobran and was strong in a language in common with her.

There, Alyline! *No*, not Alyline! She didn't really want anything to do with that brazen hussy. If it wasn't for Alyline, Spinner would be hers and would never have turned to that tavern whore. Well, Maid Primrose wasn't *really* a whore. Actually, she was a nice young lady Doli had made friends with. And Maid Primrose had rebuffed Spinner as soon as she knew what was going on between him and Doli—and that Golden Girl. Served him right, being unfaithful to two women at the same time!

But before Doli could call someone else, bel Bra spotted Alyline and scampered to her.

Plotniko groaned and reluctantly followed. No matter what Doli thought, he knew he'd translated right—and he knew who bel Yfir meant when she asked for Doli's "mistress."

When he reached them, Alyline was eyeing the handmaid who was clutching her hand. Bel Bra was barely restraining herself from tugging on Alyline's hand, aching to haul her by main force if necessary to bel Yfir—she didn't want to face her mistress's wrath if she failed to bring the noblewoman to her.

"Master Carpenter," the Golden Girl said with cool civility. "I almost think I understand the strange form of Zobran these people speak. Please tell me I'm mistaken that this one tells me the chief bed toy demands that I ride in her wagon with her."

Plotniko shook his head sadly. "I'm sorry, but that is what she wants. She was quite insistent." Behind him, he heard a gasp as Doli realized what bel Bra wanted.

"My mistress, indeed!" Doli sniffed.

"Whatever would make that trollop think I would want to ride with her?"

"*She* doesn't think she's a trollop. To her, being chief concubine makes her royalty—or close enough that there's no difference. And she believes you're a noblewoman."

Alyline barked a sharp, unamused laugh. "A djerwohl dancer a noble? *Pfagh!* The only thing nobles are good for is paying us to condescend to dance for them!"

Plotniko raised his hands helplessly.

"Well, she can—" Alyline cut off whatever she was going to say and jerked her hand from bel Bra's grasp. She made shooing motions with her fingers. "Go away. Tell your mistress I want nothing to do with her."

Bel Bra wailed and jabbered too rapidly for Alyline or Plotniko to understand. Her back was bowed and tears ran down her face as she futilely grabbed at Alyline's moving hands. The Golden Girl gave her a look of contempt and pity and walked away. Bel Bra cried louder and buried her face in her hands. Slowly, she sank to her knees.

Shocked by bel Bra's strong reaction, Plotniko and Doli didn't move for a moment. They knelt by her side, Doli taking the woman's head in her arms and pressing it to her breast, smoothing her hair and murmuring soothingly. Plotniko placed one hand on her shoulder and rubbed her back with the other comfortingly. Beneath the cloth of her blouse, he felt welts. But before he could ask about them, Haft rode up.

Haft was taking a break from the rear guard to check on the point. At Spinner's insistence, he reluctantly went forward on horseback rather than walking—even after the months he'd been riding, he still neither liked nor trusted horses. He had no idea what the problem was, but was more than glad for the excuse to dismount. He handed the reins to a passing Eikbyer and told him, "Keep going, I'll catch up with you," then asked, "What's wrong with her?"

Doli and Plotniko briefly explained what they knew. Before they were done, bel Bra opened her eyes and saw Haft. She cried out, broke away from her comforters, crawled to him and gripped the hem of his cloak. She jabbered away, kissing his boot every time she stopped to take a breath.

Haft tried unsuccessfully to pull away. It wasn't that he minded having a woman crawling at his feet, but a woman groveling at his feet and kissing his boots in so public a place was embarrassing—and would be much worse than embarrassing if Maid Marigold saw it. After a moment he bent over, grabbed her shoulders and stood her up. She ducked her head to the side, refusing to look at him. He took her chin in his hand and forced her face up, then cupped her cheek and brushed away a tear with his thumb.

"Such a pretty face shouldn't be covered with tears. Now, tell Uncle Haft what the problem is," he said softly, and brushed away another tear. Plotniko translated for him, though he changed the "Uncle" to "Lord."

"Lord, my mistress desires to see the gilded noblewoman, but the gilded noblewoman refused. My mistress will be angry with me for failing." Plotniko tactfully changed "gilded noblewoman" to "Alyline" in his translation.

"It's not your fault Alyline doesn't want to see her," Haft tried to reassure her. Plotniko again modified the translation.

"But it is!" bel Bra wailed, tears flowing anew. "My mistress greatly desires to talk with the gilded noblewoman, and instructed me things will go hard for me if I fail to bring her back."

Plotniko suspected the welts under her blouse had to do with "things will go hard" and was about to say something about them when Haft said, "Let's go and see what she wants." He put his arm around bel Bra's shoulders and

headed for the front of the caravan. Plotniko and Doli had little choice but to follow. After a few steps, Haft remembered
Maid Marigold and let go of the handmaid. He wouldn't want
word to get back to his lover that he was holding another
woman, she might misunderstand no matter how noble and
innocent his motive was. Women! A man could never predict
what a woman might think or do.

When they caught up with the man leading Haft's horse,
Plotniko urged him to remount. "Bel Yfir thinks highly of herself," he explained. "She'll receive you better if you're on
horseback than if you're on foot."

Grumbling about vacuous people to whom image meant
more than substance, Haft mounted.

Bel Yfir was pleasantly surprised to see her handmaid return with one of the nobles protecting the train and smiled at
him quite prettily. But she was *very* displeased to see Plotniko. She stuck an accusing finger at him and shrilled, "I demand that man be severely chastised!" which Plotniko
dutifully translated. Her teamster glanced at Haft and decided
he was better off keeping the wagon moving than stopping.

Haft blinked at her, then grinned at Plotniko. He looked
back at her, amused. "Why?" he asked.

Bel Yfir related how she had so reasonably asked Plotniko
to stop the train so she could relieve herself and take a rest,
and that he, with insufferable arrogance, had refused! She
couldn't help exaggerating the incident, any more than Plotniko could help underplaying it in his translation.

Haft roared with laughter when Plotniko finished. Doli tittered behind her hand when Haft repeated it in Frangerian
for her.

"We can't stop for something silly like that!" Haft told bel
Yfir. "If you have to make water, get off the wagon and find a
bush." He leaned toward her and put a hand on the side of the
wagon for balance. Plotniko took satisfaction in translating,
"You may have been someone very special and important
where you come from, but out here you're just another
refugee. Make the mental adjustment or you won't last long."

He grinned at Plotniko and Doli, then heeled his horse and continued forward to check on the point.

Bel Yfir gasped and sputtered, but Haft was beyond her by the time she could form a coherent word. She spun, looking for someone to take her affront out on. Her eyes settled on Plotniko for a second, then shifted to bel Bra. A wicked smile spread across her face and she crooked a finger at the handmaid.

Bel Bra blanched and reached for the wagon to climb on, but Plotniko stopped her and pulled her away. Wordlessly, he took Doli's hand and rubbed it down bel Bra's back.

Doli's eyes widened and she gasped, "What?" Not even when she was a slave had she been beaten to leave welts like that.

Eight miles from Dartmutt the southwest road intersected another that meandered roughly north-south. The train turned north and stopped for the night soon after the last wagon made the turn. The forest didn't have a clearing that could accommodate more than a few wagons or dog carts. They closed up more than when they were on the move, and most of the wagons stayed on the road with their horses or oxen tethered under the trees nearby. Spinner and Haft were busy making sure sentries were posted and that each unit had its sentry-duty rotation set. By the time they returned to their own rest area for the night, Zweepee, Maid Marigold, and Maid Primrose had the evening's meal ready for them. The mixed squad of Zobran Prince's Swords and Skraglander Bloody Axes that had accompanied them rejoined their own units, which were camped nearby.

Haft smiled at Maid Marigold when she offered him a bowl of stew, but took the spoon from her hand after she fed him a mouthful and insisted on feeding himself.

"Where's Alyline?" Spinner asked as he dug into the stew Zweepee ladled for him.

"She and Doli," she emphasized the second name, "are with that Dartmutter handmaid. Don't worry, they'll be back."

Spinner noticed an odd stress in Zweepee's voice. He knew

about the afternoon's incident between Plotniko and the earl's chief concubine, of course, and was vaguely aware that he and Doli had taken one of her handmaids away. But the stew was delicious and he was hungry, so he thought no more of it and concentrated on his dinner.

Fletcher, who kept track of such things, reported that another hundred or so refugees had accreted themselves to the caravan during the afternoon.

"Any soldiers?" Haft asked.

"Fifteen. All individuals from different units. I've already seen to assigning them to squads." Then he left.

Spinner had just finished eating, and Haft was snuggling with Maid Marigold, when Alyline and Doli entered the circle of light around the fire, bel Bra between them. Fletcher and Plotniko were directly to their rear. The way Fletcher handled his longbow, he looked like he wanted to string it.

"We have a problem that must be resolved before we move on," Alyline announced without preamble. "Preferably right now." The fire sparked flashes of light off the golden hilt and scabbard of the knife that angled across her belly.

That got Spinner's attention and he reached for his quarterstaff.

Doli looked stern. Bel Bra's loose black gown seemed to shimmer in the firelight as she trembled nervously. Uncertainty and fear flickered across her face and she didn't look at the men.

A corner of Haft's mouth twitched. When the Golden Girl announced there was a problem to be resolved, it was usually something a man wouldn't see as anything major, or would settle in a manner quite different from what she had in mind.

"What's the problem?" Spinner asked, standing.

Haft brushed his lips across Maid Marigold's cheek as he disengaged himself from her and stood. Her hand lingered on his hip for a moment; she had a good idea what was coming and didn't want him to act precipitously.

"This woman has been beaten," Alyline said, putting a hand on bel Bra's shoulder. "Repeatedly."

"Who did it?" Spinner growled. "He will pay."

Haft loosened his axe in its frog. "A man who beats a woman can't pay enough," he snarled. Maid Marigold lifted her hand to his and gently touched him. He gave her a grim look.

Alyline smiled wryly and shook her head. "She, not he."

Spinner blinked, confused. "What?"

Haft remembered bel Bra's fear that afternoon. "Bel Yfir," he growled.

Spinner glanced at him, looked at bel Bra, back at Alyline. "She's a servant. Sometimes servants are struck by their masters or mistresses." He didn't necessarily think that was right, it was simply the way things were.

"She wasn't struck," Alyline spat back. "She was beaten. Severely. It left scars. More than once."

"*What?* Show me!"

"*Pfagh!* You just want to see a naked woman," she said scornfully. "*I've* seen them, you don't need to."

"Bu-But—" He hadn't thought of looking at a naked woman, he just wanted confirmation.

"Bel Yfir uses a split cane to beat her handmaids on their bare backs and legs when they displease her."

"I've heard enough," Haft snarled. "That woman is gone." He started toward the head of the caravan where bel Yfir's wagon still led the way.

"*Stop!*"

He stopped and turned back to Alyline. Maid Marigold ran to him and threw her arms around his chest to hold him back.

"We have to decide what to do before we do it," Alyline said as though scolding a recalcitrant child.

"We banish her from the caravan, that's what we do," he snapped back. "We allow no one to mistreat women!"

Alyline raised an eyebrow at him. She refrained from reminding him that he and Spinner had kidnapped her—and kidnapping was surely mistreatment!—even though *they* didn't think they'd kidnapped her. "Throwing her into the wild on her own isn't mistreating a woman? Or do you propose sending her handmaids with her? Or perhaps send the

Earl's Guards to care for her? *Think*, Haft. Look for repercussions—what happens after you take the first step."

Haft opened his mouth to object, then snapped it shut when he realized she was right. He glowered rather than admit it. He covered Maid Marigold's hands with one of his where they clutched each other low on his chest.

"You told her she was important and someone special where she came from, isn't that right?" When he nodded, she continued, "And here she's just another refugee." He nodded again. "You were right then. Now we will make good on what you told her before."

"How?" Haft asked.

"We haven't been through those wagons yet, we don't know what they're carrying that others might have greater need of. And those pampered bed toys don't have the born right to ride when others are weary from always walking. We take the handmaids from her. Bel Yfir and the other concubines can walk beginning tomorrow. The handmaids are free to walk with whom they wish."

"Were they slaves?" Spinner asked, implicitly accepting that they were now free from the concubines.

Alyline shook her head. "We questioned bel Bra closely on that. The nearest we could interpret her status was that she was an indentured servant. Her parents sold her into service for a set period of time. It is the same for the others. If she were a slave, I would make it go hard on bel Yfir."

Haft snorted. Knowing her, "go hard" might well mean she'd use her dagger to radically alter bel Yfir's appearance. But he was careful not to say anything.

"Are we decided, then?" Spinner asked. When no one objected, he said, "Then let's do this thing."

CHAPTER
EIGHT

Alyline gave bel Bra over to Zweepee's care, then walked briskly to get ahead of Spinner and Haft. Fletcher, Plotniko, and Doli were close behind. The Prince's Swords and Bloody Axes had managed to follow enough of what had been said to know roughly what was happening, and they came along as well, since the Dartmutter Earl's Guards camped near the concubines' wagons might take offense to any treatment of the concubines that they considered to be less than properly respectful. A few Border Wardens saw the determined advance and joined them, stringing their bows as they went.

They were still fifty yards away when a woman's scream startled them. They sprinted the rest of the way.

Spinner's shout, *"What's going on here?"* was almost drowned out by Haft's bellow, "FREEZE!"

The Earl's Guards were camped next to the concubines' wagons. They were all on their feet and each of the soldiers held a woman or even two, most of whom were struggling. One woman lay crumpled at a soldier's feet.

"Bal Ofursti!" Spinner shouted, looking for the Dartmutter officer. "Control your men!" Then he saw him—the Earl's Guards commander stood in the midst of his men, holding a woman so firmly by her hair she was bent backward.

Haft drew his axe and advanced. "Let them go!" he roared. Plotniko shouted the translation, though it was hardly necessary.

The Prince's Swords and Bloody Axes deployed in a semicircle with their weapons ready, the Border Wardens joining them, nocked arrows to their bows. The Earl's Guards reached for their weapons.

"This is not your concern," bal Ofursti shouted back. "These women are ours!" As if in emphasis, he jerked on the hair of the woman he held, making her gasp in pain. Again, Plotniko translated.

"Release them," Spinner ordered. *"Now!"*

Bal Ofursti jerked the woman's hair again, hard enough to yank her from her feet, and put his hand to his sword. Most of his men released the women they held and several drew their swords. A number of the women, freed, ran into the shadows of the trees away from the campfires.

"What do you mean they are yours?" Haft demanded in an ominous growl.

"These women are the earl's concubines and their handmaids, given to our care," bal Ofursti said defiantly. "The earl is dead, we all know that. These women need protectors. *We* are their protectors now."

"You protect women by treating them roughly?" Spinner snapped.

"They need to learn who they belong to," bal Ofursti snapped back.

"Belong to?" Alyline shouted. "You think they are your property?"

"You women, anyone who doesn't want to be taken by them, come over here," Spinner said.

Some of the women darted away; others moved more slowly, looking fearfully at the men who'd tried to drag them away. At first, three or four stayed but then they also edged away. Several of the Earl's Guards grabbed at them, but most evaded the soldiers' hands, and only four, plus the one who was on the ground when they arrived, remained held.

Haft advanced another step and hefted his axe. "Unhand those women," he growled, looking at the soldiers who held them.

Two did and hefted their weapons—they licked their lips

nervously, looking at the armed men facing them. Another woman jerked her arm free of the soldier who still held her. They ran to the shelter of the soldiers who backed Spinner and Haft.

"You don't listen very well, do you?" Haft said, pointing his axe at the soldier who hadn't released the woman he held. "Plotniko, tell him carefully, make sure he understands. If he doesn't let her go in five seconds, he will die."

Plotniko said it twice to make sure the Earl's Guard understood. The soldier hefted his sword and looked quickly to his comrades. Every man now had his weapon in his hand, but only one looked at the one holding the woman—those nearest him shifted to increase their distance from him. The Earl's Guard who stood over the fallen woman stepped back from her.

"Four," Haft growled.

The soldier licked his lips.

"Three."

He looked wildly about, still saw no support.

"Two."

He shoved the woman from him and stepped back with his sword lowered.

"You believe in living dangerously, don't you? Be careful it doesn't kill you."

"You want our women for yourselves, is that it?" bal Ofursti sneered. "You already have women, but you think yourselves the equal of the earl that you need more?"

As soon as Plotniko translated, Haft stepped up to the Dartmutter officer and backhanded him across the face. "One woman is enough for any man," he snarled, "but she must be willing." He looked around. "I think none of these women are willing to be with you.

"Know this! In this company, any man who takes a woman against her will, will hang!"

Spinner stared at Haft, astonished. That had never been a rule. Neither had the situation arisen before. A quick glance at Alyline's approving expression told him it had become the law.

Haft disdainfully turned his back on bal Ofursti and walked to the sobbing woman who still lay crumpled where he'd first seen her. As soon as Haft's back was turned, bal Ofursti stepped toward him, but in unison the Border Warders shouted, "Don't!" and leveled their bows at him. Bal Ofursti slowly stepped back to where he'd been and lowered his sword.

Haft knelt next to the sobbing woman and asked gently, "Are you injured?" She flinched, but he spoke to her again without touching her. She didn't understand him but recognized his tone; she twisted around to grasp his leg. "Come," he said in the same gentle manner. "I'll take you away from him. You're safe now." He put a hand on her arm and stood, lifting her. She stood weakly and willingly went with him. Then two of the other handmaids took her from him and bore her behind the shield of Bloody Axes.

"Now, what do we do with you?" Spinner asked slowly.

"We will go," bal Ofursti replied coldly, and began to order his men to gather their gear and saddle their horses.

"Stop!" Haft ordered when he saw the Earl's Guards move to obey their commander. "The last time we let an armed man leave, he joined a bandit company and came back to attack us. If you want to leave, you may. But you leave your weapons and armor here." Spinner looked at him, surprised. When he thought about it, he realized what Haft must have in mind.

"What?" bal Ofursti yelled at the translation. "You can't send us away unarmed! The Jokapcul or the bandits will kill us if they catch us without weapons."

"We can't let you go armed so you can attack us later," Haft said firmly. "Leave without your weapons or stay with us and keep them. It's up to you."

Bal Ofursti stared at him, thinking. He glanced at Spinner and the others, but mostly stared at Haft. He and his men couldn't leave unarmed, but if they stayed, they would be suspect until he did something to demonstrate trustworthiness to these nobles—or gain position above them. Still, then he and his men could keep their weapons and remain together, which would allow him to do what he needed to do. It was an easy decision.

"We'll stay. What are your orders, Lord Haft?" he said with a bow.

"The first thing, Captain," Spinner answered, "is you're relieved of command." Bal Ofursti gasped, but Spinner continued before he could protest. "We'll decide what to do with you later, but before then we have to—"

Haft interrupted him. "Sergeant Phard!"

"Sir Haft!"

"Those aren't soldiers, they're a rabble—they wouldn't even stand up for one of their own when I threatened him. They need proper leadership if they're going to be of any use to us. Assign someone to take command of them, if you please." Plotniko continued translating.

"Yessir. Corporal Armana, front and center!"

A banty little man who looked too small to wield the axe that hung from his belt stepped smartly out of the rank and came to attention in front of the Bloody Axe commander. "Sergeant Phard!" he reported.

"Corporal Armana, do you think you can turn that undisciplined mob over there into proper soldiers?"

Armana clasped his hands behind his back and half turned to look over the Earl's Guards. When he turned back, he announced loud and clear, "If I can't, I don't believe it can be done, Sergeant!"

"They are yours, Corporal. Don't hurt any of them too badly."

"Thank you, Sergeant." Armana turned to face Haft. "Sir Haft, with your permission!"

"Permission granted." Haft grinned wickedly at the Dartmutters. He suspected they were about to encounter a level of military discipline most of them had never seen.

Plotniko quite happily translated the exchange.

As he ambled toward his newly assigned unit, Armana said in broken Zobran, "Master Plotniko, will you be so good as to translate for me? I can't understand a word of the doggerel these Dartmutters speak, and I doubt any of them understands a civilized tongue."

"Most happily, Corporal Armana. Do you want me to translate what you just said?"

"If you will." While Plotniko repeated Armana's statement, the corporal casually looked at each of the Earl's Guards and moved closer to them. He laced his fingers together in front of his chest, then extended his arms, palms out. He pushed, and the crack of his knuckles echoed sharply from the surrounding trees.

"Well, lads," Armana said when Plotniko finished. "We're going to get along fine, I just know it. All you have to do is remember that I'm God, and to do everything I tell you. I'll have you in proper fighting trim in no time." As he strolled among them, he didn't seem to pay more attention to any one individual more than another. He came within arm's length of the biggest of the Dartmutters. "Now, just in case any of you think that just because the smallest of you is bigger than me, you can simply not obey me whenever you feel lazy—" His hand flashed out, fingers folded so the knuckles formed a wedge, and slammed into the man's solar plexus hard enough to drive the air out of his lungs and bend him double. He clamped a hand on the back of the Earl's Guard's neck and drove him forward. The man let go of his stomach with one hand to break his fall but still landed heavily. Armana dropped one knee into the small of his back, snatched the wrist of the arm he'd tried to break his fall with and twisted it around behind his back.

"Now, lads," he said calmly, looking at the men as he seemed to push up on the big man's arm without effort, "understand this about me. I killed my first enemy soldier before most of you were weaned. I've forgotten more about being a fighting man than *all* of you have learned combined—and I remember most of what I've learned." He let go of the man's arm and patted him roughly on the back of his head.

"There there, lad. You'll be fine." He stood and began to step away. The downed man made a noise and swept a hand around to trip him, but Armana lifted his foot out of the way of the sweeping hand and smashed down on it. The Earl's Guard screamed and rolled away, clutching his hand.

Armana looked around, then spoke calmly. "There was your first lesson—take it to heart. We noncommissioned officers of the Bloody Axes really do have eyes in the backs of our heads." He took a step or two, then stopped and looked at his new command again. "One more thing. The next man who attempts to lay a hand on me won't get a little love tap. I'll hurt him.

"Now, tell me what your sentry rotation is, then everyone not on duty bed down."

The Earl's Guards gaped at him for a long moment before Sergeant Afi finally said, "Guardsman bal Graenn has first watch, sir."

"I'm not some privileged 'sir,' Sergeant, I'm a corporal, I work for a living."

"Yessi—ah, Corporal. Guardsman Graenn has first watch."

"You were the senior sergeant?"

If Afi noticed that Armana said "were" rather than "are," he gave no indication. "I am."

"Draw up a new watch rotation. Two man watches. Pick men who can stay awake together. Any sentry I catch asleep on duty will wish he'd never woken up."

Haft grinned at Phard. "You made a good choice, Sergeant Phard."

Phard nodded. "Corporal Armana should have had a command long ago."

Haft joined Spinner and Alyline. "It looks like everything's under control here. Except for what do we do with the captain." He glanced at Alyline. He was glad the venomous expression on her face was directed at Captain bal Ofursti and not at him.

"Sergeant Geatwe," Spinner called to the Prince's Swords sergeant.

"Yes, Lord Spinner."

Spinner shook his head and muttered, "Don't call me 'Lord,'" then more loudly, "Take Captain bal Ofursti into custody, please. Disarm him and keep him secured and under guard until tomorrow morning."

"My pleasure, Lord Spinner."

The Prince's Swords' leader signaled two of his men to accompany him and advanced on the former Earl's Guards commander, who looked dumbfounded at the proceedings.

"Your sword, please, sir." Geatwe said, holding out his hand to accept the weapon.

Bal Ofursti looked at him blankly, as though he didn't understand.

Geatwe made a gesture to one of his men, who stepped close to remove bal Ofursti's sword belt.

Bal Ofursti may not have understood Geatwe's words, but his intent was clear. He moved suddenly, punching the soldier in the chest, driving him back and jumping backward, meanwhile drawing his sword. "You can't *do* this to me!" he shrilled, swinging his sword defensively from man to man.

Geatwe slowly shook his head. "You shouldn't have done that, Captain." In a flash, he was inside the arc of bal Ofursti's sword and had him grasped around the chest. With a mighty twist, he yanked the man off his feet and threw him to the ground. He landed hard on bal Ofursti's stomach with one knee, driving the air out of his lungs, and stomped on his sword wrist with the other foot. One of his men quickly stepped in and snatched the sword away.

"Now we have to bind you," Geatwe said, and lifted his knee to flip bal Ofursti over.

The other soldier stripped the sword belt from the prisoner, yanked the scabbard from it, and used the belt to bind the man's hands tightly behind his back. Geatwe stood and nodded. His men jerked bal Ofursti to his feet and followed the sergeant as he led the way back to their campsite.

"My men aren't going to be very happy about this, you know," Geatwe said conversationally. "Your behavior means some of them will have to lose sleep tonight watching over you. We'll bind your legs anyway to make sure you can't cause mischief overnight."

"*No*! You can't do this to me!" bal Ofursti yelled.

"And if you don't keep quiet, we'll have to gag you," Geatwe continued calmly. He didn't understand any of bal Ofursti's words, but he knew quite well what he meant. "And not only *can* I do this to you, I *am* doing it to you."

Spinner, Haft, and the others watched as they went, then Spinner signaled the other Prince's Swords to follow. They turned to the Dartmutter women and saw that those who'd run into the trees earlier had rejoined them.

"And now for you," Alyline said. Something in her tone made some of them shrink away even before they heard Plotniko's translation.

Not bel Yfir, though. She stepped boldly forward, smiling conspiratorially at Alyline.

"Lady." She bowed at precisely the angle one bows to an equal. "I wish to thank you for the way the noblemen rescued us from those commoners." Her smile vanished. "Though I doubt they would have tried had you joined me this afternoon as I had asked. If we had stopped when I requested, those men probably wouldn't have been made so irritable that they desired to take vengeance on our person."

"Is she saying anything worth hearing?" Alyline curtly asked Plotniko.

"Well, she thanked you for the rescue, but I imagine you'd be angered by the other things she said."

Alyline's mouth twitched. "Don't tell me, then. She isn't worth breaking a fingernail on. Tell all the handmaids to go with Doli to our campsite. Doli, I want you and Zweepee to check them for scars like bel Bra has and report back to me. I will speak to the bed toys privately while you're gone."

"Pfagh!" She realized she couldn't speak to them in total privacy; they didn't have a common language. "Plotniko, you'll have to join us to translate."

Plotniko sighed, but said simply, "As you wish."

Alyline looked at Spinner and Haft. "You may as well go back. Corporal Armana seems to have the Earl's Guards well in hand, and I won't need any help with these four lilies." She looked down at the knife that angled across her belly. "Before you go, someone cut a sapling I can trim for a switch."

Spinner and Haft exchanged a wide-eyed glance, suddenly glad the Golden Girl wanted them gone. Haft drew his axe and sliced down a four-foot-tall treeling. He handed it to her without stripping any of its branches. Spinner and Haft left the Bloody Axes following close behind.

Bel Yfir exulted. She'd known the gilded noblewoman held high rank in this company, but the height of her rank came as a surprise. The noblemen were in charge when they had to deal with the soldiers, but once that was done, *she* was the obvious leader. Now she would get matters straightened out properly, ranking lady to ranking lady. She gazed scornfully at Plotniko and wished there was someone else who could translate for them. Well, the gilded noblewoman knew Zobran, she could easily enough learn Dartmutter.

Not all of the concubines reacted the way bel Yfir did. Bel Kyssa and bel Kyn saw how deliberately the gilded lady trimmed the sapling with her gold-handled knife. They well knew how a switch was made and what one was used for.

Alyline sheathed her knife and said, "Come with me." She gave her switch a flick and nodded in satisfaction at its spring. She went directly to bel Yfir's wagon and stood a couple of yards from its back, looking expectantly at the trailing concubines in their thin, flowing gowns. She shook her head at their moonlight-dappled shoulders and thought how impractical the gowns were as travel garments, even covered by the travel cloaks they often wore over them during the day.

When the four reached her, she pointed the switch at the wagon and ordered, "Unload it."

Three of the concubines immediately realized what she intended and gasped. Bal Yfir, on the other hand, was oblivious—that translator needed to be chastised, she thought, and she wasn't going to listen to him until he was.

"Gilded noblewoman," she began with another precisely measured dip, "as the ranking people present, we have much to discuss about the conduct of this caravan."

Plotniko started to translate, but Alyline cut him off. "Don't bother translating. I'm not interested in anything the chief bed toy has to say unless it's an apology." She pointed at the back of the wagon with her switch, and the other three concubines began hauling chests and bundles out of it.

Bel Yfir was so enrapt with what she was saying she didn't notice for several seconds. When she did, she spun on them and screamed, "*Stop that!* That is *my* wagon, *my* property! You do not touch anything of mine without my leave!" And she shoved at them to make them reload the items they'd removed. She screamed again when fire lanced across the backs of her thighs. She spun about, looking for the source of the pain, and crouched to rub her injured thighs. The others, not wanting to be switched as well, began pulling things out of the wagon as fast as possible, with no concern for order or neatness.

"I told you to unload the wagon," Alyline said coldly.

Bel Yfir drew herself up, ignoring the pain in her thighs, and began to protest. But only a scream came out of her mouth as Alyline flashed her switch again and struck the chief concubine on the side of her right thigh.

"But—" bel Yfir wailed, tears running down her face.

The switch flashed again, to the side of her left thigh, then Alyline pointed it at the back of the wagon.

"You can't—"

Alyline grabbed her shoulder and spun her around. She swung her switch twice, once across bel Yfir's buttocks, once across her back. Bel Yfir crumbled to the ground, bawling.

"Tell her," Alyline said slowly to Plotniko, "that I despise men who beat women, but I truly hate women who do." She waited for the translation, then said, "Tell her as long as she lays there, I will continue to switch her. As soon as she stands and begins unloading the wagon, I will stop."

With cries and yelps of pain, bel Yfir scrambled to her feet and began to help the others.

After a moment, Alyline said, "Tell the others to stop, let her finish the unloading by herself."

The other three stepped aside when Plotniko translated and stood fearfully watching Alyline and her switch. Bel Yfir's commands for them to help ended abruptly when Alyline's switch cut across the front of her thighs.

Doli returned well before the wagon was empty; she gaped at bel Yfir for a moment before she noticed a fraying in the woman's gown and realized that Alyline had struck her with the switch. Then her eyes narrowed and a thin smile crossed her face. She smiled briefly at the other three, spoke to Alyline quietly, then left to fetch torches. The wagon was almost empty by the time Doli returned with three burning brands. Alyline took one from her and had Plotniko take another.

"Open them," Alyline commanded, waving her switch at the concubines. "Not you!" to bel Yfir. "You finish unloading."

There were eight chests of various sizes, from small enough to sit atop a table and hold sheaves of documents to large enough for two people to sit comfortably atop, along with more than a dozen bundles wrapped in cloth bound with stout cord. The chests were made of rich woods, reinforced at their corners with bronze knuckles, and all but the smallest banded with bronze and iron. The smallest and the largest were closed with locks, the middle six with simple clasps. Two of the middle-size chests opened to reveal women's clothing; mostly thin gowns, diaphanous robes, or other exotic wear, though there were more practical garments as well. The other four contained foodstuffs in bottles or otherwise preserved.

"How many of the women only have the clothes they wore when we left Eikby?" Alyline asked.

"Most of them, I think," Doli replied.

Alyline nodded. "We'll put these garments aside until we can work out a fair distribution." Plotniko didn't translate.

Doli nodded in agreement. "The same with the foodstuffs, I think." She looked at the concubines—bel Yfir had dumped the last cloth-wrapped bundle and joined the other three concubines. The labor of unloading the wagon had caused her to sweat through her gown in places, and it was obvious she wore nothing underneath. Doli looked at Plotniko and hid a smile; he was obvious about not looking at the former chief concubine's charms—and just as obviously wanted to.

"Unbind the bundles," Alyline ordered. The four women

fell to the task, fumbling at the knots; more than once one or another yelped and sucked on a fingertip after breaking a nail on a recalcitrant knot. The bundles, all but two of them three or four feet long and a foot in diameter, contained more clothing and preserved foods, and one opened to disclose a recurved bow, arrows, and bladed weapons. The two largest held tents.

"My my," Alyline said to bel Kyn, who stepped briskly back from the weapons bundle after she opened it. "Who do you suppose those are for?" Plotniko rephrased the question in his translation.

Bel Kyn shook her head and stammered, "I don't know, lady. This isn't mine."

Alyline nodded, then tapped the locked chests with her switch. "Unlock these." The three all looked at bel Yfir, who hesitated, then came reluctantly forward and drew a chain from around her neck. She withdrew two keys from one of several lockets on the chain and used one to open the larger chest. It contained a man's finery fit for a prince—or an earl. Alyline laughed with delight. "We have men who need clothing too." She tapped the small chest with her switch.

Bel Yfir dropped to her knees and begged to not be made to open it.

Alyline tapped the small chest again, then lashed out and whacked bel Yfir on the shoulder. "Don't snivel," she ordered when the woman cried in pain. "I imagine you struck your handmaids even more quickly when they didn't obey immediately, so you're getting nothing you haven't given many times already."

Bel Yfir sobbed as she spoke. Alyline looked to Plotniko for a translation. "She says the earl will beat her, maybe kill her, when he joins us and discovers she opened that chest."

"Only if he's still alive, if he can find us, and if we allow him to," Alyline said patiently. She waited for the translation, then added harshly, "And I don't allow men to beat or kill women."

When Alyline lifted the switch again, bel Yfir bent and unlocked the chest with trembling fingers.

"No wonder," Alyline said, smiling at Doli once she saw the chest's contents—jewelry too massive and heavy for a woman. "He sent his jewelry out with his women in case he had to leave too fast to bring it himself." She looked back at bel Yfir. "Did the Earl's Guards know you carried this?"

She shook her head.

Alyline nodded. "Too much temptation. He must have been afraid the soldiers would take the jewels and leave the women to their fates."

"Or take the jewels *and* the women for themselves," Doli added.

"All right," Alyline said briskly. "Pile the women's clothing here, the men's clothing here, the food there. Bring the small chest, and we'll see what the next wagon holds.

The other wagons, none quite as large as bel Yfir's, held correspondingly fewer chests and bundles filled with clothing and foodstuffs. One bundle in each was half filled with bladed weapons and another a tent. Each wagon had a very small chest filled with gold coins. The Earl's Guards didn't know about the coins either.

Once everything was separated for distribution, Alyline had the four sweaty women line up facing her. She smiled at Plotniko's profile; the temptation of four women clad in thin, wet garments was too strong, and he was openly gazing at them. They blushed at his attention.

"We have many people, women, children, oldsters, who have been walking since Eikby. Some have walked even farther. Tomorrow, as many of them as can will ride in your wagons. You may spend the rest of the night sleeping in your wagons, but tomorrow you will walk. Now turn around."

The four women moaned, knowing what must be coming, but meekly turned anyway. Alyline lashed each of them across the back of the shoulders, above the tops of their gowns—except for bel Yfir, who she left trembling in anticipation of a blow that didn't come. She saw Doli flinch with each blow that landed, so she told her softly, "I haven't hit anyone hard enough to break the skin, just hard enough to get their attention . . . and leave a mark for a day or two." Then to the concubines, "Now get some sleep, you have a long walk tomorrow."

When she and Doli left, Plotniko followed closely, but let space grow between them as soon as they were away from the concubines, until he completely angled away to find his own campsite. On the morrow, he resolved, he would find other people who spoke the Dartmutt dialect so he wouldn't have to be the only translator.

CHAPTER
NINE

Braving the hazards of the dark, a few dozen or so stragglers from the rape of Dartmutt stumbled across the caravan overnight and were taken in. None of them were soldiers, and only two were men who could be trained to arms—if there ever was time to stop and train them.

It was dangerous for the wagon train to stay on the meandering north-south road, they needed to get off it as soon as they could. But before the caravan set out, there was a piece of unfinished business from the previous evening that had to be dealt with.

What to do about Captain bal Ofursti.

"We can't trust him," Haft insisted. Nobody disagreed, yet . . .

"We can't take him with us as a prisoner either," Spinner insisted, just as firmly. "We have to send him away."

Haft shook his head. "Have you forgotten Captain Dumant?" They'd encountered Dumant and a squad of Skraglander Bloody Swords in the forest in the southeast corner of the Princedon Peninsula before they reached Eikby. In fact, Haft and some Zobran Border Warders broke up a bandit ambush the Bloody Swords were walking into. Dumant had refused to join them in any capacity other than commander. They'd let him go—though his men elected to remain with the Frangerians and their larger party. Dumant later returned as a leader of the Rockhold bandits.

"I haven't forgotten," Spinner said. "But have you actually *looked* at bal Ofursti?"

"Of course I've looked at that arrogant popinjay!" Haft said scornfully. "I think he's worthless as a soldier."

"And those Earl's Guards of his?"

"They're Corporal Armana's now," Fletcher reminded him.

"Yes, Corporal Armana's. Have you?"

Haft snorted. "A bunch of tavern bully boys. They'll fight anybody smaller than themselves, anybody unarmed, and anybody too drunk to fight back. Armana told me they were ceremonial troops." He snorted "He's got his work cut out for him, trying to turn *them* into a proper platoon of fighting men."

Spinner nodded. "That's why we can turn Captain bal Ofursti loose, banish him from the caravan. Captain Dumant was a real soldier, even if he was too proud of his rank. This one is a courtier. Like you said, he got his commission because of *who* he knows, not *what* he knows. If he runs into bandits, he won't take over, he'll get killed."

"So you're saying instead of us hanging him, we let him go for bandits to kill?"

Spinner flinched. "Maybe he'll manage to evade bandits and get to someplace safe. There's always that chance."

"Right," Haft said dryly. "Someplace safe from bandits. And where's that?" He snorted again. "Someplace where the Jokapcul are, that's where. They'll take him prisoner and either kill him or turn him into a slave. Either way, he'll suffer less if we hang him now."

"I'm not going to hang him."

"You're firm about that, aren't you?"

Spinner nodded.

Haft looked at the others. Fletcher and Alyline were clearly aligned with Spinner. So was Zweepee.

Silent did his best to look neutral. Among the Tangonine, his tribe, someone like bal Ofursti would be slathered with honey and staked out over an anthill.

Sergeants Phard and Geatwe, the senior enlisted men among the Skraglanders and Zobrans, were nearby. "Let him go," they both agreed.

Maid Marigold, though not a member of the council,

leaned close against Haft and whispered into his ear, "Don't be a murderer."

Haft looked at her quizzically. He was a sea soldier, a Frangerian Marine; killing people was his job. He sighed deeply: killing in battle; hanging was different. "All right," he agreed. He looked at Phard. "Get him."

Phard went away and returned in a few minutes with bal Ofursti. He'd unbound the officer's legs, but his men had had to gag him overnight to still his yelling. The gag was still in his mouth. Phard carried bal Ofursti's fine saber in its belted scabbard.

"Captain bal Ofursti," Spinner announced after looking at the disheveled Dartmutter officer for a long moment, "we have decided. You are banished from the caravan. We will unbind you and you will leave. You will not return, under pain of death." Then to Phard, "Release him."

"You can't do this!" bal Ofursti said, or croaked, as soon as the gag was removed. "You can't send me out there alone and unarmed. That's the same as a death sentence!"

"We narrowly decided against hanging you here and now," Haft snapped. "Would you rather we did that?"

Bal Ofursti worked his jaw and throat to get them in better order before he replied. "At least give me my sword and knife, and some food."

"We cannot spare food," Haft said before Spinner could order food for him.

Spinner held back the retort he wanted to make; it wouldn't do to show dissension. Instead he asked, "Does anybody have an old sword to give him?"

"I do," Fletcher said. "I'll fetch it." He was back in a couple of minutes with a straight sword in a worn scabbard; its belt had a knife in a sheath. At Spinner's nod, he handed it to bal Ofursti.

The officer looked at the sword, appalled. It was far inferior to his saber. He began to draw it to check for rust on the blade, but Phard's hand suddenly clamped on his neck.

"Don't do it, laddie," the grizzled sergeant rumbled.

He let go of the sword hilt and it slid back into the scabbard.

"Now leave," Haft ordered, pointing west. "If we see you again, you are dead."

Bal Ofursti took two slow steps backward, looking anxiously at the impassive faces that stared back at him. Then he spun around and ran.

They continued along the meandering northerly road. Refugees still headed more or less west, wandering, lost in their flight from the Jokapcul who were pillaging Dartmutt. Most of them had learned by now that there was no safety in numbers, and so made their way through the caravan once they saw its westerly direction. Others accreted to the caravan. No one told them nay, nor did many say yea to the new arrivals—the caravan was moving too fast for anyone to take the time and energy to pass judgment on them, and it wasn't going to stop until the end of the day.

They were a sorry bunch, these newest additions. More than half of them had gotten away from Dartmutt with nothing but what they wore, or what small goods they could snatch up as they ran. Some who had fled with nothing had the presence of mind to pick up what others had dropped as they made their way through the forest west of the city. Many of the men and a few women bore weapons of one sort or another, mainly knives and hunting bows. Many of the refugees who had been camped farthest from the harbor managed to make their escape with enough to survive for a time in the wilderness. Only a few, who were just arriving in the environs of Dartmutt when the Jokapcul attacked, had wagons.

They saw oddities in the caravan, these newly accreted additions. Here and there along its length was a man wearing a richly brocaded jacket, an extravagantly embroidered shirt, fine, snug trousers, and soft, glowing boots. A far larger number of women were clad in loose gowns of silk or cotton, some of which were finely embroidered in gold and silver thread, or shod in fawn-skin shoes, or protected from the dirt and dust by linen travel cloaks, or resplendent in velvet capes. These were the people to whom Alyline and Doli had meted out, one garment per person, the wardrobes from the chests in the concubines' wagons. Not many of the new arrivals saw the four foot-sore women who whined as they trod the road, dressed in thin flowing robes that hung from their shoulders by thin, satin straps and turned nearly transparent where they clung to sweaty flesh. Not all who did see them wondered about the red welt that slashed across the shoulders of three of those women, or the frayed stripes across the gown of the fourth unhappy woman. None saw all four of those women as they were spaced out along the column. Few saw the platoon of twenty soldiers, most of whom cast occasional wary glances at the banty little soldier who chivvied them through their paces in the trees west of the road.

Hardly any of the new people noticed the soldiers or other armed men who fell in behind them as they walked or rode with the caravan. And most who did notice were soldiers, or had been, and understood why soldiers stayed close behind newcomers—and they made sure to keep their hands clear of their weapons.

All saw the taller than average, dusky-skinned young man who rode from one end of the caravan to the other, and the respectful way nearly all greeted his passage. A very few recognized his uniform and wondered how it happened that a Frangerian Marine was in charge of the refugee caravan. Did that mean a counterattacking army was nearby, or at least a large force to rescue the refugees? Whichever, it gave them hope.

Veduci, the bandit leader, had stayed with his own people since the day they'd joined the caravan, and they'd had as little contact with the Frangerians leading it as possible—especially Haft, who Veduci believed would as soon as not cut him and his people down. So he hadn't seen what happened with the Dartmutt Prince's Guards, though he knew about it. In fact, though remaining close to his own people, Veduci made sure he knew as much as possible about what was happening along the caravan's length. At all times while it was moving during the day, and as long as movement was safe at night, he had no fewer than four and often as many as eight of his people scouting. They didn't appear to be scouting, of course, since that would draw attention, and such attention wouldn't do. But the scouts wandered up and down the column, eavesdropping on conversations, engaging other refugees in conversation, picking up all manner of rumors. During the day, Veduci's scouts were more often women than men—women were seldom perceived as potential threats. At night his men most skilled at stealthy movement went about quietly listening in on campfire talk.

So, not only did Veduci know about the Earl of Dartmutt's caravan before they reached it, he knew who was in it before Spinner and Haft did. He knew bel Yfir was acting the spoiled pet before she sent for that Golden Girl. He had a more graphically detailed report of the tracery of welts and scars on the back and legs of the handmaid bel Bra than did Spinner and Haft. He knew all about the confrontation with the Earl's Guards and its subsequent change of command. He knew almost as soon as the Golden Girl did that all of the handmaids' backs bore marks from being switched by the concubines. He knew about bal Ofursti's expulsion from the caravan. And he knew what was in the smallest chest carried in each wagon of the Dartmutter caravan.

Disaffected soldiers, royal playthings accustomed to far better treatment than they were being afforded, a group of handmaids who had good cause for anger and resentment. A banished, angry officer who was likely pacing the caravan. And royal riches.

These things required thought. One well-placed arrow at the right time could ally the Earl's Guards with him. And that captain could possibly be used as a diversion. Use the royal playthings to create more distraction. What about the handmaids? Other than the scars and welts, they were—every one of them—fine-looking women. Did his band have use for more women? Of course, men could *always* find use for more women, especially attractive women. Then, while everyone's attention was elsewhere, snatch the royal riches.

But no matter what plan he might come up with to gain the royal riches, at this time there was nowhere to go with them.

Besides, thought and planning take time, and with the Jokapcul so close in Dartmutt and likely already extending their perimeter, and the caravan making haste to gain distance from them, there was no time for such thinking. And there were more immediate concerns—the growing number of refugees attaching themselves to the caravan. Who were they, and what might they have that was worth taking?

No, any banditry would have to wait.

"Hello, friend," the bandit leader said to a red-faced, puffing man who stumbled out of a forest trail onto the road. Zlokinech, one of his men stopped with him.

The sleeves of the man's linen coat were tied around his neck so he could wear it like a cape. Under the dirt and wear of long travel, the coat itself was dyed in bands of color from top to bottom so each band blended into the next in the Bostian manner, and was piped in royal purple. The sweat-stained cotton shirt that would have been mostly hidden by the coat sagged off the man, and his trousers were bunched and bloused around his waist, held up by a belt that drooped a very long tongue—the clothes belonged to a much larger man. But the redness of this man's face and the shortness of his breath told Veduci they were indeed his; their looseness was because he'd lost a great deal of weight recently. He looked like he had been a well-off merchant.

Veduci stopped while the man paused to catch his breath. He knew some Frangerian, which was the trading language, though he hadn't admitted it to Spinner and Haft. If this man was a merchant, he probably did as well. Veduci talked calmingly to him in that language. "We've been on the road since Eikby, running from the Jokapcul in Penston. We'd hoped to find succor in Dartmutt, but got there just as the barbarians invaded. Now we go farther north. Where do you head?"

"My wagons—I don't know." *Pant.* "I'd thought to find passage on a ship in Dartmutt." *Puff*, and a shake of his head. "But—my wagons! You saw?"

Veduci nodded. "We arrived just in time to see."

The caravan chugged and jerked by, mostly unnoticed by

the merchant. The refugees paid them little attention. The soldiers who passed gave them a quick once-over and kept going.

"My wagons—they're lost!" *Pant.* "Now I don't know where to go."

"Where is your family, your retainers?"

"My—" *Gasp.* He looked about madly. "They were—" *Puff.* "They were right," *pant,* "behind me."

"We're here," a reedy voice said.

The merchant turned to the voice and scurried to it, arms spread wide. "I was afraid I'd lost you!" *Pant.* He flung his arms around the beardless youth who followed him from the forest trail.

"Mother comes on the cart," the youth said, pushing to free himself from his father's smothering grasp; he was an age where a boy no longer wants to be hugged by a parent.

"The cart—" *Sob.* "My wagons!" He spun to Veduci. "My wagons! I emptied an entire wagon's worth of cloth bolts and metal household items crossing Skragland, all in exchange for food for my family and people!" *Pant.* "I still had four wagons when we reached Dartmutt." *Heave.* "I tried to bring them when we fled the city, but the Jokapcul were too fast." He buried his face in his hands. "They came and slaughtered two of my drivers." *Cry.* "The other drivers cut horses free and rode away, leaving my wagons behind." He lifted his face and his voice rose as well. "They could have continued driving. The Jokapcul who killed the two drivers stopped to plunder those wagons—my other two wagons were safe, we could have left with them!" He ended with a wail.

A pony cart emerged from the trail, led by a young man who walked next to the pony's head. A stout woman as finely—and dustily—dressed in clothes too large sat on the cart's small bench. A lass of not quite marriageable age sat on top of chests in the back of the cart, and another in full flower walked behind. The pony strained under the load it hauled.

Now more of the refugees looked at the newcomers. Some didn't recognize them as such and wondered idly why the pony cart had stopped. A few slowed to make space for them in the column, resuming their pace when the newcomers didn't join the caravan.

"Who are these?" the cart driver asked, awed by the steady stream of people moving along the road.

"We're refugees from Eikby, near Penston," Veduci quickly replied. "We are protected by many heavily armed soldiers led by Frangerian Marines who are leading us to safety."

The young man breathed in evident relief. "*That's* who they were. I saw some soldiers moving north in the forest. I didn't know who they were, and they made me afraid for my mother and sisters. But they just looked us over then continued on without speaking to us."

Veduci nodded. "A flanking patrol, to screen us from surprise attack or ambush." He noticed a small team of soldiers approaching, curiously eyeing him and the merchant, and gestured at the passing caravan. "Join us. You are safer with us than anywhere else. Please."

"Thank you, good sir," the merchant said, and told his son to guide the pony cart into the next opening. The driver of an approaching wagon saw and slowed enough for them to move in.

A thin smile was on Veduci's face as he made note of where the merchant and his family were in the column—he had noticed the telltale bulges of money pouches under the merchant's coat. And he knew the most precious goods the merchant carried had to be in the cart his son drove. He let them get a short distance ahead, then stepped out to follow before the approaching soldiers reached him.

Zlokinech made sure they were far enough ahead of the soldiers that he wouldn't be overheard before quietly asking, "Tonight?" He smiled as he tapped his fingers on the hilt of his short sword.

"No. If anyone is killed and robbed, suspicion will immediately fall on us. We don't do anything until we are someplace where it's safe to leave this caravan. I will say when; do nothing until then. Make sure all know that."

Zlokinech nodded. "Do nothing until you say." He went off to make sure the others knew.

Spinner watched refugees in ones and twos and fives pass through the caravan and continue their aimless flight as he rode toward its van, where Alyline and Fletcher led the way, a hundred yards behind a squad of Zobran Royal Lancers.

"Nearly as many join us as not," he said when he reached the van.

"We're orderly," Fletcher observed. "And they pass through our flankers on the right. They see we know what we're doing, so they see safety with us." He shrugged as he watched a trio of refugees race across the road a few yards ahead, with no more than a worried glance their way. "Those who bother to look," he added.

"They *think* we know what we're doing," Alyline said with a sniff.

"Oh, we know what we're doing, all right," Fletcher said. "We're doing our very best to get ahead of the Jokapcul and stay there."

"Pfagh!" Had she been a man, or a cruder woman, the Golden Girl would have spat. "What we are doing is the same as them, running for our lives without a safe destination."

"We're heading north of the Gulf," Spinner corrected her. "The entire Jokapcul strategy is to make landings at cities and large towns. There are no towns on the north coast for them to conquer, only small fishing settlements—"

"You know this?" Alyline challenged.

He nodded. "Frangerian Marines don't only defend ships at sea, we guard them in port. We have to know what is where on all seacoasts. I've made the Princedon Gulf passage twice."

She sniffed again, thinking Spinner's knowledge of the north shore of Princedon Gulf—and Haft's as well—was probably learned from tavern tales told by seamen and sea soldiers, rather than from visiting it. She didn't ask him, but Spinner being Spinner, and mindlessly in love with her, would have had to admit the truth of her suspicion.

Instead she demanded, "And then?"

Spinner repressed a shrug. "We follow the coast to Handor's Bay."

"Pfagh! And you think the Jokapcul ships can't get there faster than these refugees can walk?"

"They have to stop and consolidate sometime. Besides, they're still moving north from the southern coast, fighting in Skragland. They'll soon enough run out of the soldiers they need to continue around the coast and will have to stop."

She opened her mouth to give a retort, but Fletcher cut her off.

"He's right. The Jokapcul Islands are said to be densely populated, but they don't have an unlimited population of military-age men. Either they pull back from the interior or they stop their advance along the coast. They have to." There was a note of uncertain hope in his last three words.

"We have only the word of panicked refugees that the Jokapcul are continuing inland," Alyline said, but quietly, not argumentive.

Neither man responded, and they rode on in silence for a piece, before Spinner turned back to ride the length of the growing caravan once more. There were more than three thousand souls in the caravan by the time Haft sent word back from the advance scouts that they'd found a good place to stop for the night.

Half squads of four or five soldiers, woodsmen, hunters, and half-trained fighters flanked the colum   couple of hundred yards to each side during its march. Silent, the giant nomad from the steppes, wandered with Wolf at his side, patrolling close enough to the cleared land surrounding Dartmutt to keep an eye on the Jokapcul. His primary purpose was to give the earliest warning possible if the invaders began moving west or northwest. Secondarily, he would kill any enemy soldiers he could without endangering himself—or take a prisoner if the opportunity arose. He shuddered at the thought of handing a prisoner, even a Jokapcul, over to the untender mercies of Alyline and the other women as they had once before, but the women could get information from a prisoner when the men failed. That thought brought another: Did anyone in the caravan of refugees speak Jokapcul?

Before this war, the Jokapcul had some trading with the western nations of Matilda and Oskul, so some merchants and others were likely to speak the language. He shook his head, certain there were no refugees from the far west among those who traveled with them. Surely there were others elsewhere in the world who spoke Jokapcul. Not likely very many, though. Still, one of them might have joined the caravan. They needed to find out. Perhaps a Scholar? He knew there were Scholars who devoted their lives to the study of the Far West, including the Jokapcul Islands. But he didn't know of a Scholar who had joined them. That was something else they needed to find out. Even if he didn't speak Jokapcul, the Scholar might have other arcane knowledge that could be useful. He had learned during his travels that Scholars were to the soft people of the southern lands what the venerated elders were to the nomadic peoples of the steppes—fonts of vast and valuable information.

When the setting sun cast the forest's shadow all the way to the walls of Dartmutt, Silent turned west and headed back to the road the caravan was on. Wolf padded at his heel. Many refugees had passed him during the day, wandering aimlessly, lost in the forest. Some of them had fled in terror at sight of the giant and his wolf, or kept a wary distance. Those who didn't, he directed to the refugee caravan and told them it was the safest place for them to be—at least, he told those with whom he could find a common language. But he had killed no Jokapcul, nor taken a prisoner. He did, though, have new questions that needed answers, and observations about the Jokapcul to pass on.

INTERLUDE
THE DESERTS

High-Low, High-Low, to Desert Lands We Go

(Part 1, Low)
by
Scholar Munch Mu'sk
(Reprinted with permission from
It's a Geographical World!
without the illustrations,
on which someone else holds right-to-copy)

STEPPING-STONES

A vast tableland, a humongous two-tiered plateau, fills much of the southeastern quadrant of the Continent of Nunimar. On the north, it stretches from the Princedon Gulf to Elfwood Between the Rivers and the Easterlies, and is bounded on the west by the Eastern Waste. The plateau begins abruptly with an escarpment that juts up a day's wagon journey north of the city state of Dartmutt and travels east until it rises into the barrier wall of the Sentinel Mountains, which continue onto and around the bend of the Inner Ocean. A third of the way to its northmost reaches, the plateau is cut across its entire width by another, much higher escarpment. That southern portion is called the "Low Desert." The larger, northern portion is the "High Desert."

Little is known about the Low Desert, and less about the High, though much is speculated about both. Indeed, only the Dwarven Mountains and the eerie Land of the Night Dwellers are less known and more speculated about. It is likely safe to say that the more outrageous the speculations, the less factual they are.

Other than in its several-hundred-league length, the southern escarpment of the Low Desert isn't much as escarpments go. For most of its length, it is a mere twenty or thirty feet in height, though it does jut out nearly a hundred feet in a few isolated spots; never, though, in its entire length does it flatten to nothingness. As one can easily see, the Low Desert's escarpment is dwarfed by the hundred-mile-long escarpment that borders part of the Great Rift on Arpalonia and towers one or two thousand feet for its entire length. Even more spectacular, though markedly less lengthy, is the so-called "Dwarven Giant" that girds a portion of the west side of the Dwarven Mountains. Although a mere fifty miles in length, the Dwarven Giant is a mile and more of sheer drop. So insignificant in appearance, despite its length, is the Low Desert's escarpment that some travelers have called it "tedious."

PROVISIONS FOR LIFE

The vegetation of the Low Desert has likewise been described as dulling to the senses. Most of the Low Desert is covered with patches, some many acres in size, of hardy grasses that are able to find root in its extremely sandy soil. A number of breeds of low-lying, succulent bushes also eke out a living there.

Only in widely scattered oases centered on perennial ponds so large they might better be called small lakes can trees be found. Unlike the forests that abut the lands to its west and southwest, the Low Desert itself only supports two types of trees; though, as the reader shall see shortly, one of the trees has variants. One kind of tree, without noticeable variants unless size is a variable rather than a function of age, is broad and flat and spreads out in a wide cone from its base, like a fan. Obviously enough, it is called the fan tree. The fan tree (*tarehe umti*) has a central trunk, or stem, that goes from the ground to the tree's topmost tip, but branches sprout from it beginning mere inches above its roots. Long, slender leafs grow both up and down from the branches, and are long enough that each upward growing leaf nearly interlinks with the downward growing leafs from the branch above it, so that the entire appearance of the tree seen from a modest distance is that of a gossamer fan. The fan tree grows to a height of about twenty feet. The other tree, called, for unknown reasons, the "bumber" tree (*refu umti*), is even more curious in appearance. It sports a tall trunk bare of branches and leafs until its apex is reached. There, it sprouts long, broad leafs that spread out, caplike, and looks like nothing so much as a fat-handled, small-capped parasol. One variant of the bumber tree grows as high as forty feet and bears large, hard-shelled fruits that dangle from just below its crown of leafs. The other, which seldom reaches thirty feet, bears beneath its crown large bunches of succulent fruits the size of a large strawberry.

Curiously enough for a desert, the Low Desert is spotted with numerous pools of potable water, and veined with many small streams. Many of the streams emerge from or empty into pools, but not all the pools have associated streams, nor do all streams have understandable sources or mouths. In most instances, geographers don't know where the water comes from; certainly not from rain, as little rain falls on the Low Desert.

Despite the evident barrenness of the Low Desert, the resourceful traveler needn't carry provisions for an entire journey. Indeed, there is a far more generous larder of foodstuffs available than one might normally expect to find in a desert, albeit some of it must be approached with caution. The plenteous grasses (*majani majani*) are too hardy for human consumption without the flour ground from its seeds first being immersed in liquid for extended periods of time. As the inhabitants of the Low Desert generally use the fermented milk of their domestic riding and burden beasts as that liquid, the bread and pasties of their diet are the only such known that will inebriate the unaware who partake of them too plentifully. Some of the bushes found around pools have edible berries, nuts, or seeds. Most of the berries can be eaten as plucked, though it is wise to first brush (or better, wash) the sand off them. The berries of the quaintly named crawl'em bush (*tukio baya*), on the other hand, are extremely toxic if eaten raw. The name of the crawl'em bush is said to come from the reaction of a person who eats a handful of the berries; he falls to the ground and crawls in circles until he dies. Yet if the berries are first crushed, then boiled in copious amounts of water, they yield a highly nutritious and tasty porridge. Most of the nuts and seeds from the bushes must be roasted before they can be consumed by humans, though lesser animals seem to have little problem deriving sustenance from them. The fruits of the bumber trees need no particular preparation prior to use in repast.

Meat is also available in the form of three different breeds of gazelle and two of antelope. In the vicinity of the northern slopes of the Sentinel Mountains, there is also a large-horned sheep, the meat of which tastes like mutton that's been left in the sun too long. Small, ground-dwelling mammals and lizards are also to be found, mostly near pools of potable water. If one is truly desperate for meat and unable to catch other game, it is claimed that the riding and burden beast of the inhabitants of the Low Desert, the "comite," can be eaten without too deleterious consequences.

The chief animal of the Low Desert is the above named comite (*en gamia*). Some, with too little knowledge of philology, claim the name is a corruption of the word "committee," as the beasts are said to look like something designed by a committee. More likely, *comite* is a corruption of the Desert Men's words *kumi* and *tajiri*, which, together, mean "ten rich," as a Desert Man is considered rich if he has ownership of ten comites. The comite is capable of living for extended periods on the thick ridge of fat that grows along its back and makes it look as if it wears a long pack.

PEOPLE

Of the many strange and wondrous curiosities of the Low Desert, the strangest may be its nomadic Desert Men. No one knows their genesis. Although they claim to have origin myths, they refuse to tell them to Scholars. Neither does anyone know the source of their language, which is replete with sharp consonants and twice as many vowels (which are copiously used) as any other language.

The Desert Men are fierce, ready to fight and kill any persons they encounter in or adjacent to their desert. They sometimes prey on travelers along the coastal road that runs the length of the north side of Princedon Gulf, or in the eastern-most stretches of the Eastern Waste. It appears that every Desert Man is constantly armed with a broad-bladed, curved sword, bow and arrows, and several knives. Some also bear a spear. It is well worth noting that should the traveler avoid being attacked while traveling the Low Desert and reach one of the Desert Men's enlodgments, he is treated as an honored guest, is inviolate from assault, and is required to partake generously of their bread and pasties.

Desert Man garb consists of voluminous robing and scarfing in the colors of sand flecked with the greens of grass and bushes. It is said that they are masters of camouflage, able to hide totally invisible anywhere within their territories. A few geographers believe they accomplish this by using Lalla Mkouma; Scholars of demonology strongly disagree, insisting that there are not enough Lalla Mkouma in existence to accommodate all the Desert Men. Nothing is known about the garb of the Desert Men women, as they are kept carefully hidden from view of the infrequent guests. Even though women are never seen by guests, it is reasonable to surmise that the Desert Men do have women: no Desert Man has ever been observed cooking or laundering, and they must procreate somehow.

The housing of the Desert Men, such as it is, consists of low-lying tents carpeted with rugs crudely manufactured from the hair of comites. The tents, sand-colored and green-flecked in the same manner as their robes and scarfs, are difficult to see in the middle distance, and impossible to discern in the far distance. They encamp in one location until need for forage for their beasts compels them to move to new grass.

The Desert Men have no metallurgy, which forces them to occasionally descend from their plateau to the city state of Dartmutt, where they trade skins, meats, bread, and pasties for swords, knives, cooking utensils, and other metal objects they require. It is also said they trade gems discovered in the vastness of the Low Desert. If that is true, the trade in gems is done quietly and outside normal trading venues where taxes would be imposed. This is likely true, as the swords and knives they acquire are of the highest quality, and it would take far more skins and exotic foodstuffs to pay for them than the Desert Men are likely to have.

ROADS

Traces of ancient roads crisscross the Low Desert. Scholars are so uncertain as to who built the roads, or why, that there are numerous theories advanced about them. Indeed, there are so many theories about the origin of the roads, all acrimoniously attacked and defended, that describing any of them in this paper would serve no purpose other than to cause heated discussion in the "Letters" section of this journal. Alas, no cartographer has ever mapped the roads. That is not to say none have *attempted* to do so. Unfortunately, those cartographers who have journeyed into the Low Desert for the purpose of mapping the roads have never returned, so how much mapping they may have accomplished is moot.

(Coming soon: Part 2; The High Desert)

It's a Geographical World! is pleased to present this first of two articles by Scholar Munch Mu'sk, the renowned professor of Far Western Studies at the University of the Great Rift.

III
THE ESCARPMENT

CHAPTER
TEN

The sun had long set by the time Silent and Wolf returned to the command group. A cocked eyebrow was the only remark Silent made at his first sight of the large tent with vertical walls and a peaked roof that had been set up for Spinner and Haft. Similar though somewhat smaller tents were erected around it. Wolf made a more emphatic comment on the tent—he circumnavigated it until he found a proper place and made his mark. Now no matter where the people moved the tent, he'd be able to find it again. He trotted into the tent behind Silent.

The giant didn't even try to hold back the laughter that boomed out of him at what met his eyes inside. The interior of the tent was lit by glass-globed lamps hanging from the roof supports; the barely flickering light splashed the woven rugs that covered the ground with richly colored scenes. A cot complete with sheets and a thin mattress lay against each side of the tent. Against the back wall were two small field desks with folding camp stools. Spinner sat scowling on one camp stool; on the other, grinning, Haft lounged as easily as possible on a stool that didn't have a back to lean against. Alyline, Fletcher, and Xundoe sat on other camp stools in front of the desks, Doli perched on the cot nearer Spinner. The sextet had obviously been in deep discussion.

Haft waved welcome at Silent and snapped his fingers at Wolf, who cocked his head and eyed him curiously, then came to him, sniffing for a treat. Spinner closed his eyes and looked embarrassed. Fletcher grinned and shook his head. Alyline snapped, "It's about time you showed up." Only

Xundoe looked as though everything was exactly as it should be.

"Interesting things happen when I'm gone," Silent said when he stopped laughing. "Tell me about this." He waved a hand at the tent and its furnishings as he sat cross-legged in the space the others made for him. He was so tall that even seated on the rug-cushioned ground, his head was nearly level with the others.

Alyline was the first to answer. "We are no longer a small band," she said. "We aren't even a large band in flight from immediate danger like we were when we left Eikby. Our *leaders* need to look more like leaders than like a couple of self-important refugees." Spinner looked embarrassed; Haft grinned more widely. "Now if only they'd do something about their uniforms, look like officers instead of just a couple of common soldiers—"

Looking deeply offended, Haft snapped erect. "Now just wait a min—"

"Dartmutt is only a few miles away," Silent interrupted. "Many thousands of Jokapcul are there, with more pouring in hourly. We're still in considerable danger."

"But not in immediate danger," Alyline said. "If we were, you would have come back much sooner and sped us on instead of this casual late arrival. But as I was saying, we now have the population of a large village, or even a small town. Our 'leaders,'" she nodded condescendingly at Spinner and Haft, "must show symbols of authority and power. These tents are such symbols. Fletcher and Zweepee have one, Xundoe has one, so do I. There's even one for you." She looked at him closely. "It was designed to accommodate a concubine with her handmaids sheltered under its surrounding awning. I think you'll fit inside without too much trouble."

Silent chuckled and looked about. "Me, live in a soft city man's cloth tent? I'll never again be able to show my face in the lands of the Tangonine people."

"A soft *city woman's* tent," Haft said with a guffaw, that quickly overcame the offense he'd taken at Alyline's "common soldiers" remark. Silent laughed with him.

Xundoe brushed his fingertips across the cabalistic markings on his robe. "Don't laugh. Symbols are extremely important to people." He gave Spinner a sidewise glance. "Most people. I fully agree with Alyline about the importance of the tents." He gave a contented sigh. "And look forward to nights on a goose-down mattress, no matter how thin." He looked dreamily into nowhere and murmured, "Imagine." In the Zobran army, a mage as low ranking as he never slept in a tent or on a mattress in the field. In garrison they had cots, but their mattresses were stuffed with straw, not goose down.

"What did you find?" Spinner asked, anxious to get the conversation off the subject of the comfortable tents and bedding.

Silent grunted. "Anybody got some food? I haven't eaten since this morning."

"I'll apologize for all of us," Doli said, jumping to her feet with embarrassment flushing her face. "We should have thought of that. I'll get a meal for you. Wait here." She was on her way out of the tent as she finished.

Silent smiled after her and cast a mildly disapproving glance at the others. They had the grace to look away—Doli was right, they should have thought of food for him.

Doli was back in moments bearing a bowl of stew on a trencher. Two women stopped in the entrance; one carried another bowl of stew, the other had two loaves of bread and a cup of rancid butter. Just outside, a man Silent didn't recognize stood with a bowl of half-roasted meat still on the bone—there wasn't room in the tent for all the food bearers. After placing Silent's other trenchers on the cot she'd been sitting on, Doli set down the bowl with the meaty bones for Wolf. Wolf stood, walked stiff-legged to the bowl and chomped a nice chunk of venison.

Silent pulled a spoon from somewhere in his fur garments and dug in. "Did anything else interesting happen here today?" he asked between spoonfuls.

"More refugees joined us," Spinner replied.

"'Ow 'any?" Silent asked with his mouth full.

"More than a thousand," Alyline answered.

The giant's eyebrows popped up and dropped back down.

He nodded, but didn't stop eating. The caravan had increased by more than a third, maybe close to half, during the day. He wondered if any of the new people had any experience in feeding a large number of people on the move. That was a skill few people had. He doubted the sea soldiers did either.

A slight, unhumorous smile crossed Alyline's face. "The royal bed toys finally stopped crying and saved their energy for walking." Her smile widened but became no more friendly. "One of them sat by the side of the road for a while; she expected someone to stop and give her a ride. Nobody did."

"Zweepee tells me the concubine's feet are too badly blistered for them to walk tomorrow," Fletcher said quietly.

"We have to let them ride until their feet heal," Spinner said.

"Let them suffer!" the Golden Girl snapped, glaring at him. "Their handmaids were as much as slaves, and they beat them. They left scars! When I was beaten, at least they knew enough not to leave marks." She had been a slave, dancing for the entertainment of the clients of the Burnt Man Inn, a slaver's inn, when Spinner and Haft found and freed her and the other slaves.

Doli had also been a slave at the Burnt Man Inn. She nodded almost imperceptibly at Alyline. She felt herself fortunate no one had left marks on her, other slaves at the Burnt Man had been scarred for life.

"I saw the blisters on bel Bra," Haft said casually. "Don't worry, she'll be in pain tomorrow." Then sotto voce, he said to Spinner, "Even if she doesn't walk, blisters like those will hurt every time she moves her feet or something touches them."

Silent had eaten rapidly and was wiping up the last of the rancid butter with the heel of his second loaf of bread when Haft spoke. He didn't care to hear any more about making the concubines suffer—pain was part of war, but it didn't have to be inflicted for casual punishment, which Alyline's attitude toward the concubines seemed to be—so he resumed talking with his mouth full. When he had everyone's attention, he paused to swallow and began again.

"In mid-morning, a large force of Jokaps headed south on the Eikby road. My guess is they're looking for us or they expect to join up with the Jokap troops that were following us." He grinned. "They'll be disappointed either way.

"They didn't send anybody west or southwest, and only a couple of troops headed north—I saw them head toward the north shore of the Gulf, though I'm not positive that's where they went. Tomorrow we need more scouts ahead in case they went to interdict this road. All day long their cavalry rode in small groups through the farms, looking for refugees hiding in the corn. They found some and used them for sport before killing them." He grimaced and shook his head at the memory. "Interestingly, they didn't bother anyone who was fleeing. Those were the people who joined us." He looked at the others questioningly. "But I saw far more than a thousand unmolested refugees headed west."

"More than half of those who came on us kept going," Fletcher explained.

Silent nodded. "There are still more people wandering lost in the forest between here and Dartmutt. Maybe tomorrow we should have flankers search for them and direct them to the road?"

They all looked at Spinner and Haft for a decision; the two Marines looked at each other.

"We'll decide later," they said simultaneously.

"Not too much later," Doli said, one of the few times she made a contribution without being directly asked.

"She's right," Fletcher murmured.

Rather than getting mired down on that point, Silent asked one of the major questions he'd come up with during his day wandering the forest edge with Wolf. "Do we have anyone who speaks Jokap?" He watched the consternation on everyone's faces, then said, "I would have brought back a prisoner if I'd had a chance, but no lone Jokap wandered into the forest. A prisoner will be easier to question if we have someone who speaks his language. We need to find out." The others nodded and murmured agreement.

"Is there a Scholar anywhere in the caravan?" That question was met with blank expressions. Not only did none of them have any idea what they might need a Scholar for, they couldn't imagine why a giant of the steppe nomads would even think of one. "Some of them speak Jokap," Silent explained. "And all of them have arcane knowledge. There's no telling when some arcane knowledge might be important."

"That's right!" Xundoe said excitedly. "Many Scholars even know about magic. If there is a Scholar with us, he might have knowledge I can use!"

Haft nodded at him, then looked at Fletcher and Doli. "Can you two and Zweepee find out?"

"Yes," Fletcher answered. Doli nodded.

"Speaking of Zweepee," Silent said to Fletcher, "where *is* your wife?" Zweepee was normally with the group when Silent returned from a day-long reconnaissance.

"She's going through the caravan with her helpers, making an inventory of what the new people have and what they need."

"Is she asking about their trades and skills?"

Fletcher barked a short laugh. "Knowing my wife, she probably is."

"Now, there's one more thing we need, or people will start dying." Silent's serious tone made everyone look intently at him. "We've got, how many, three and a half thousand people now? All those people on the move, and you know more will join us in the coming days. How are we going to feed them?" He held up a massive hand to block the questions and statements that immediately came at him. "I know, we've got enough food on hand to last several days, and game is still ready enough while we're in this forest. Foraging is plentiful as well, so we aren't going to run out any time soon. But there's the problem of distribution so everybody gets a fair store of food, and we need a central store of food to make sure nobody's hoarding more than their fair share.

"These are things the nomads know well. Among the Tangonine people, we have honored people who control the food supply. If they fail in their duty, there is fighting among the people. Eventually people begin to die from starvation, and some leave the horde to wander tribeless."

"Can you . . . ?" Spinner asked hesitantly.

Silent shook his shaggy head. "I hunted for game, and when I was a youngster I foraged, but I wasn't a provisioner. I know what they did and why, but not how they did it."

Fletcher reached for a sheaf of parchment on Spinner's desk and began paging through it. "We have butchers and sausage makers, millers and bakers, but do we have a food distributor?"

"Do we even have a complete roster of the Eikby people?" Spinner asked rhetorically.

Haft snorted. "Where's Plotniko? He'd probably know."

"The last time I saw him he said he was looking for other people who spoke Dartmutter," Xundoe answered.

Silent again shook his head. "Distributing food in a town isn't the same as provisioning people on the move. A town has warehouses and granaries, nomads don't."

"But nomads have wagons," Fletcher said.

Silent opened his mouth to say the Tangonine people didn't have wagons, then closed it without speaking; his people had pack animals, of which the caravan had some, and captured warriors from other hordes who they used as porters. They did the same job as the wagons in this caravan could. He nodded and asked, "Do we have enough wagons to use as food warehouses?"

Fletcher exchanged the sheaf of parchment for one on Haft's desk and paged through it until he found the listing of wagons and their contents.

"This is yesterday's," he muttered, then louder, "Food is scattered with no order throughout the caravan. I imagine we could consolidate it, but that would take time, and I don't think we have the time to stop right now."

"So we do a little bit each night," said Haft.

They agreed. More immediately important, Spinner and Haft insisted and nobody greatly disagreed, were soldiers.

"Twenty or thirty stragglers in uniform joined us during the day," Spinner said. "I don't have an exact count because I didn't get to meet all of them. They are from almost as many armies and units."

"No full squads?" Silent asked. He'd seen a few squads moving westward during the day.

Spinner shook his head. "They came singly or in pairs. They were pretty demoralized. I managed to assign all of those to whom I talked to various squads. Nearly all of our soldiers have been in at least one battle where they beat the Jokapcul, so I hope they can raise the morale of the new men I gave them." He looked thoughtful for a moment, then added, "It's probable that many of the men who joined today are also soldiers, but they threw their uniforms away."

Silent nodded agreement at that. "I'm sure there are still a few squads that haven't passed through us yet," he said. "I'll try to get some of them to join us tomorrow."

"Most of the Zobran Border Warders speak Skraglandish," Haft said. "Take one of them with you to translate if you meet Zobran soldiers."

Silent started to object that he didn't need a Border Warder to accompany him because he spoke some Zobran, then realized the Border Warders were more fluent in Skraglandish than he was in their tongue. Besides, it would give him an opportunity to improve his Zobran. He nodded.

"Do any of the Skragland Borderers speak the Dartmutter dialect?" he asked. "There are Dartmutter refugees and soldiers out there. I don't think any of the Zobrans can understand that dialect."

"I'll find out," Haft replied.

"Our flankers on the left reported seeing soldiers out there, walking parallel to us," Fletcher said. "There may be a hundred or more, if I interpreted their reports right."

Spinner grimaced. "Sergeant Geatwe of the Zobran Prince's Swords told me he thought he saw bal Ofursti skulking along out there."

Haft grinned. "Well, if he wants to come back in . . ." He cracked his knuckles.

There was nothing more they could accomplish that night, so shortly after, they said their good-nights and everybody but Spinner and Haft headed for their tents.

Spinner began readying himself for the night, but Haft stood in the middle of the tent, lightly drumming his fingertips on his thigh. He looked at his cot as though mentally measuring it, then toed the rug as though checking its softness. He gripped the tent's center pole and looked from it to the front and the back of the tent, again as though measuring, and moved his hands as though feeling a wall under it. Once more he toed the rug. Not once did he look at Spinner. But Spinner finally looked at him.

"You don't sleep alone anymore, do you?"

Haft grinned broadly. "Not when I can avoid it."

"And you're trying to figure out how to bring her in here and have privacy."

Haft nodded brightly.

Spinner groaned and picked up the blanket from his cot. "It's all yours," he said, and pushed through the tent's door flap.

Haft looked around the now empty tent, wiping his hands together gleefully, eyes glowing. "Now where are you, Maid Marigold?" he murmured.

"Here I am," she replied, poking in through the door flap.

He turned and smiled at her. "So you are." He held out his arms and she darted into them. "Were you huddled outside the tent all this time, waiting?"

She answered him with a kiss.

From elsewhere came the sharp report of a slap, and Alyline's voice exclaimed, "Get out of my tent!"

Then Doli's voice said, "My tent is big enough for two."

By then Haft and Maid Marigold were so involved they didn't hear Spinner's muttered, "I'm sleeping in the open, where I can be immediately ready if there's an attack overnight."

* * *

In the morning, the Zobran Border Warder called Tracker and the Skragland Borderer named Meszaros went into the forest between the road and Dartmutt with Silent and Wolf. The caravan was near the northern edge of the city's surrounding farms, so they went far back as a rear flanking guard. Tracker and Meszaros stayed fairly close to Silent and were just as glad Wolf ranged on his own. It wasn't that the two border soldiers feared the animal—Meszaros spoke for both of them when he said, "Wolves aren't good, and they aren't bad, they're just wolves is all. Just when you think you've got them figured out and you know what they're going to do, they go and do something different and you realize you don't understand them at all."

Silent didn't respond to that, he was confident that he knew Wolf very well—and that Wolf would do pretty much exactly what any free-ranging member of his own tribe back on the steppes would do in a given situation.

The best part of an hour and a couple of miles behind the caravan, Wolf led them to the first of what Silent expected to find a lot of—a dispirited squad of a dozen soldiers.

These were Skraglander Kingsmen, the innermost guards of the King of Skragland—which gave truth to the rumors that the king was dead or in hiding. The black bear pelts the Kingsmen wore as cloaks identified their regiment, but other emblems worn on the cloaks suggested they came from different elements of the regiment, that they hadn't started their journey into the Princedons as a squad. Half had double-bladed axes, the others two-handed swords. They sat around a fire; a quick look around by the border soldiers told them the Kingsmen didn't have anyone on watch. Yes, Silent concluded, dispirited and close to giving up. He signed the two men with him to stay in place, then moved so silently and slowly that he was seated in the circle before the Kingsmen realized they had company.

Silent's hands were empty and in clear view, with his wrists draped over his crossed legs. He didn't flinch when one Kingsman grabbed his axe, ready to fight. Silent's only movement was to rotate his hands palm up, emphasizing their emptiness. The other men scrabbled for their weapons, twisting around to peer fearfully into the trees.

"Where did you come from?" the axe wielder demanded with a tremor in his voice. Silent recognized the tab on the collar of his cloak as the insignia of a senior sergeant of some sort.

"I come from your best chance of survival," the steppe giant said in gravelly softness. He kept his expression friendly.

"What do you know of survival?" the axe man demanded.

Silent rolled his shoulders in a half shrug. "Enough to know the people I'm with have fought the Jokaps many times and beaten them every time."

The sergeant snorted. "Nobody beats the Jokapcul."

Silent looked at him levelly. "Then it's too bad I don't collect trophies from the dead. I could impress you with them."

"You lie!"

He slowly raised his right hand to point his thumb over his shoulder. "A couple of miles back that way is a caravan with near three and a half thousand people. 'Bout four hundred are soldiers, including some Skraglanders. All of them have fought the Jokaps. Most of them—the ones who've been with us for more than a few days—have beaten the Jokaps in battle. We also have a war wizard. I don't see a war wizard here, but we could use more soldiers."

"Why should I believe anything you say?"

Silent's face went hard. He gave the senior sergeant the kind of look a fighter gives an enemy he's about to defeat. "Because my companions and I could have killed you instead of me sitting down to talk."

"You don't have any companions!"

Silent slowly raised his left hand and pointed a finger straight up. An arrow zipped past the sergeant and thunked into a tree just to his rear.

"Yes I do," Silent said softly, his expression again friendly. He flicked his eyes at the leader's axe, still hefted and ready to use. "The Jokaps beat you. We beat the Jokaps. You don't scare us, so how about you put that down and let's talk.

"I am Silent, a wanderer from the Tangonine People of the

northern steppes. What is your name?" He reached out a hand.

The Kingsman looked at the hand for a long moment. He couldn't help but see how big it was, how much strength it had. It took no stretch for him to envision that hand yanking him across the fire if he took it. He took a steadying breath, lay down his axe, and reached for the hand.

"I'm Upper Sergeant Han, Second Company, Skragland Kingsmen." He attempted to squeeze exactly as hard as Silent did, but the hand he grasped was so much bigger than his, he couldn't get the leverage to squeeze.

Silent smiled, shook Han's hand, and let go without applying undue pressure. He raised two fingers of his right hand and flipped them forward. Tracker and Meszaros came to sit flanking him at the fire. Wolf stayed out of sight, prowling in case anyone should come up.

"How do you come to be here?" Han asked. "The Northern Steppes are far from the Princedons."

Briefly, Silent explained how he had gone wandering to see the sights of the world. He told them of being at the border post between Skragland and Bostia when two Frangerian Marines showed up, then encountering them again when they were fighting the Jokapcul. He didn't mention that he was still at the border post when the Jokapcul invaded Skragland. He skipped over the aborted journey up the Eastern Waste, but told briefly about Eikby and the successful battle there and skipped other parts of the journey. He gave a rough outline of the plan they had for reaching safety. The telling only took a few minutes.

Upper Sergeant Han didn't believe everything Silent said, and the plan, as the giant related it, was spare, but it was better than a dozen soldiers wandering alone, waiting for the Jokapcul to catch and kill them.

"We will join you," Han said at last, and looked at his men. None objected, and some nodded eagerly, glad of the chance to join a larger group instead of being so few among the enemy.

Silent gave the Kingsmen directions to the caravan and

watched them leave, then said to Tracker and Meszaros, "Let's see if we can find any more."

By the end of the day's march, the caravan was growing to five thousand people, more than half of whom were women and children and a liberal sprinkling of oldsters. At least half of the day's new men were soldiers, former soldiers or other armed, partly trained men. Somewhere, somehow, they had to find time and a place to train the rest of the men to arms.

There was some good news: Plotniko had located a Dartmutter trader who spoke fluent Zobran and another who was reasonably conversant in Skraglandish. And Zweepee had found a caravan master who understood feeding people on the move. Although his largest caravan had been fewer than a thousand people and their animals, he knew more than anybody else with them about how to handle storage and distribution of provisions.

CHAPTER
ELEVEN

On the second day after the Skragland Kingsmen joined the refugee caravan, Haft sat in a high crook of a tree near the edge of the forest three miles east of where the road past Dartmutt turned to follow the north shore of the Princedon Gulf. The forest ended abruptly there, almost as though a mad gardener had decreed that on *this* side of a line there would be trees and undergrowth in all their wild profusion, and on *that* side there would be nothing higher than a man's waist. The mad gardener hadn't been totally successful; in the middle and far distance Haft noted a few trees. They all looked stunted and thin. The road that made its way across the gently rolling landscape to the east showed some sign of recent use, but the only people visible consisted of two troops of Jokapcul light horse that had just merged onto it from another road that followed the western shore of the Gulf a couple of miles to the east. In the far distance thin tendrils of smoke rose from just beyond the horizon. Haft had seen such tendrils before—they were from a burning village.

Haft looked to the southeast. More troops of Jokapcul horsemen were headed north along the coast road; troops of marching infantry stepped off the road to make way for the horsemen. Beyond them he saw coast huggers beating their way between Dartmutt and the north coast, where they disappeared over the horizon. He couldn't see Dartmutt; it was far enough south that the entire city would have to be burning for him to even see smoke rising from it. He might be only a one-day wagon ride north of the city, but that one day ride was for a single horse-drawn wagon with mounted escort, not for a caravan that was now over six thousand strong.

He unseated himself and carefully climbed down. His perch had been high enough that the trip took several minutes.

When he reached the ground, he shook his head at the two Zobran Border Warders and the Skragland Borderer who had accompanied him.

"The Jokapcul are taking the north coast of the Gulf," he said redundantly. "We need to go back and take a closer look at that other road."

The border soldiers nodded and immediately headed west, paralleling the road at ambush depth—if someone had set an ambush on the road, they'd come onto its flank instead of walking into its killing zone.

Once they were away from the forest's edge, the canopy was thick enough that few bushes and treelings grew to impede their way; they covered the distance quickly but carefully. It took them a little over an hour to cover the three miles to where the road turned to the east. Kovasch, the Skragland Borderer, had slashed blazes into a tree to tell the column's point squad they'd gone east and to wait here; they were as clear and easy to see as they remembered. Kovasch cut a sign over the "wait here" mark to indicate it no longer held. They unhobbled the horses to ride back east a hundred yards to where a narrower road ran into the main road from the north. Their horses' tackle made little noise.

Haft dismounted and plucked the hobbles off the back of his saddle. The other three remained mounted.

"Lord Haft," said Kovasch, the Skraglander, "we can cover more ground if we ride." They spoke in Skraglandish, though it was the native tongue of only one of them. It was Haft's weakest language but the only one they had in common.

"We'll spot an ambush more easily on foot." Haft bent over to wrap the hobbles around his mare's fetlocks.

"Ambush? From whom?" Birdwhistle, one of the Zobrans, asked. "You said yourself the Jokapcul are headed east. And none of our flankers have reported any of them moving into the forest."

Haft warily ducked under the mare's neck to its other side. The mare snorted and stomped its hobbled hoof, almost yanking the other end from his hand. He hopped nervously back.

Hunter, the other Zobran, hid a laugh behind his hand. The Border Warders, like the Borderers, mainly went about on foot, but all of them were comfortable with horses. Haft shot them a glare.

"There could still be bandits," he said.

"The only bandits we've seen since we left Eikby are the ones who joined us before we reached Dartmutt." That was Hunter, when he got over his laugh.

"That doesn't mean—"

Birdwhistle pointed. "What's that slung on your saddle?"

Haft straightened up and looked. He saw nothing out of order. "What?"

"That big tube, that's what."

He looked curiously at Birdwhistle. "It's a demon spitter, as you well know."

"That's right, a demon spitter. And the little demon who lives in it seems to like you. Do you really think a demon that likes you will let you walk into an ambush without a warning?"

Haft blinked, turned his head and studied the demon spitter for a long moment. It had never occurred to him that the demon in it might be able to give warnings. He'd ambushed Jokapcul with demon spitters a few times—even hid by a trail a few yards from a stopped Jokapcul horseman who carried a demon spitter—and he'd never seen a demon give any warning to the Jokapcul.

"No, they can't do that," he finally said.

"How do you know?" Hunter asked.

"Well, they've never warned the Jokapcul."

"Maybe they don't like the Jokapcul," Kovasch said. "Ask him."

Haft looked at his three men, all still on their horses. "You just want me to look stupid, that's why you want me to ask the demon."

Kovasch leaned forward in his saddle. "Trying to learn something new is never stupid."

Haft studied the three and finally sighed. "All right, if it'll get you off those horses so we can get on with the recon."

He lifted the demon spitter tube from his saddle and cradled it in his arm so the small door on its side faced up and rapped lightly on it. The door popped open and the demon poked its head out.

"Wazzu whanns!" the diminutive demon demanded.

"We're going up that road," Haft said, feeling foolish. "Can you give me a warning if there's an ambush ahead?"

The demon put its gnarly hands on the sides of the door opening and levered itself up to where it could look at the smaller road. *"Naw ambutz. Goam'up."* It dropped back inside and slammed the door firmly behind itself.

"That sounded clear enough," Birdwhistle said.

"It didn't say it could give a warning!" Haft objected.

"It said there's no ambush," Hunter declared.

"It sure did," Kovasch agreed. He kneed his horse close to a broad-boled tree next to the road and blazed a mark on it to show the point squad which way they'd gone, and another to tell them to wait there. After a few seconds thought, he added two more marks that meant there was danger to the east.

The three turned their horses and set onto the side road.

"Are you coming?" Birdwhistle called back over his shoulder.

Grumbling, Haft replaced the demon spitter and removed the hobble from his mare. *He* was the commander, it wasn't right that his men should outmaneuver him that way in deciding what they were doing. Mounted again, he trotted to the head of the short column. A few minutes later, grumbling again, he was in second place in the column. He would have been in the lead but his mare didn't like leading, she always wanted to follow another horse. He grumbled, but didn't do anything about it. As uncomfortable as he was with horses, even after months of riding, his docile mare was the only horse he could abide riding for any length of time.

The forest to the north didn't end abruptly, as it did to the east. Instead it petered out, as though it had become tired and slowly decided it didn't want to go any farther. The first change, a mile or so north, was in the canopy, which thinned out enough to let sunlight reach the ground and allow undergrowth to flourish. Within another mile or so the canopy had thinned further, and undergrowth almost totally covered the ground. They noticed that the trees had thinner trunks, were shorter and more widely spaced. In a few more miles, they were so much smaller and more widely spread out that the landscape resembled parkland more than forest. The ground rose gently and, through the trees, they could see a horizon that looked too close. They rode toward it.

The ground leveled off at the too-close horizon and the road forked. One fork went straight north, and the landscape in that direction rapidly became barren and sere. The other fork wandered east just inside the parkland, but within view of the sere ground to the north. In the distance they could make out the beginning of an escarpment.

Haft took in a deep breath and forced it out. The landscape resembled another road forking, where one fork led to the arid Low Desert and the other into the lush forest at the root of the Princedon Peninsula. It wasn't identical, though. Here, the lush forest was to the rear.

"We go that way," Haft said, pointing east. "Let's go back and get our people." The quartet turned their horses and trotted back, once more at ambush depth from the road for as long as the undergrowth allowed.

Captain bal Ofursti bore a fury that wouldn't allow him to head west. He was an *officer*! Not only an officer, but the third ranking officer of the Earl's Guards! Those two Frangerians had no *right* to banish him from the caravan. How was he to eat out here alone? He was no commoner who could be expected to hunt and forage for himself, he was an *officer* to be *served* by commoners! *He* should be in command of the caravan. And the Dartmutter women—the earl's concubines and their handmaids—rightfully belonged to *him* and whomever he gave them to, not to those insubordinate *enlisted* Frangerians!

He had no idea by what magic those two had drawn the others under the spell that made them commanders. Why, they even had *sergeants* obeying them! Why, even an officer of the Penston Conquestors obeyed them! That was intolerable. Absolutely intolerable! It *had* to be magic that gave them command. It was simply not *possible* for two such lowborns to have command over so many—including an *officer*, even if the officer was only a Penston lieutenant.

Bal Ofursti knew nothing of how to use magic, other than to place orders with magicians, and he'd never even done that. But he did know how to *defeat* magic. One defeated magic by killing those who used it. So the solution to his problem was obvious—he would kill those two insufferable Frangerians! And then assume his rightful place—in command of the refugee caravan. He would reclaim possession of the Dartmutter women, and bel Hrofa-Upp would be his, as she should be. And he'd take that golden woman for himself as well—and any other woman of the caravan he wished!

But how to kill the Frangerians? Spinner might be difficult, since he rarely left the caravan. A direct confrontation in the caravan wouldn't meet with success; bal Ofursti knew Spinner's magic would probably bring soldiers to his aid before he could get close enough to kill the enlisted scum. Haft, though, spent most of the day outside the caravan, leading the scouts in the van or tarrying with the screening force to the rear. It should be easy to get to him before his magic had time to work and bring soldiers to assist him—and no axe man could defeat a good swordsman unless he caught the swordsman by surprise. And then he, bal Ofursti, would take Haft's crossbow and use it to ambush Spinner before word of Haft's death got back to him.

Captain bal Ofursti had no doubt he could make short work of either Frangerian in single combat. He was the best swordsman in the Dartmutter army. And the Dartmutter sword master said he was the best student he'd ever trained.

Staying carefully out of sight, he followed Haft and waited for his chance.

* * *

Halfway back to the main road, Haft's mare suddenly shied. Her unexpected movement, lifting her forelegs and twisting to the side, knocked him off balance and he threw his arms around her neck to keep from falling off. She screamed and bucked to the left when something *thunked* into the right side of her saddle, and this time Haft did fall, spilling over her left side. He rolled and skittered to get away from her scrabbling hooves and hopped to his feet, only to face a strange apparition—a madman charging at him with raised sword.

The man's hair and beard were matted tangles, his eyes were darkened with heavy pouches, spittle flew from between his lips, and his clothing was dirty and festooned with bits of leafs and twigs. He looked crazed. Haft had no idea why the poor man attacked—he was probably driven mad by running from the Jokapcul—and wanted to disarm him without killing him.

Wait! His clothing! Under the dirt and debris, he wore a red cloak and cerulean-blue jerkin and trousers.

Haft spun away from the man's overhead sword chop and took another look at him as he drew his axe.

"Bal Ofursti!" he exclaimed.

"Your death!" bal Ofursti shrilled, and ran at him again, swinging his sword in a roundhouse blow at his neck.

Haft half twisted out of the way and half ducked under the blade. He swung his axe up in a backhand arc to catch the sword, but barely tapped the fast-moving blade.

Bal Ofursti let his momentum carry him all the way around in a pirouette, spinning on his left foot. He stuck his right foot out and slammed it down when he faced front again and thrust, turning his angular momentum into a forward strike.

Haft twisted to the side and parried, barely avoiding the stab. Bal Ofursti danced to the side and jabbed again and again. Haft backpedaled to stay out of range, swinging his axe back and forth to slap the blade aside, but never making firm contact with it.

"Get out of the way, Lord Haft," Kovasch shouted. "I'll put an arrow in him!"

Haft sidestepped, but bal Ofursti went with him and bore in once more with a series of thrusts and slices.

"A touch!" bal Ofursti shrilled as one of his slices cut along Haft's left shoulder, drawing blood.

Haft bounded backward, then brought his axe down in an overhead arc that caught the blade and drove its point into the ground. "By the gods, we should have hung you when we had the chance," he snarled, then punched bal Ofursti's straining shoulder with a knuckled fist and jerked his axe away from the trapped sword. He bent his arm back and thrust forward with the upper point of the head of his axe, but bal Ofursti fell backward when his sword was released and the strike went above him.

An arrow thunked into the dirt where the Dartmutter officer landed, but he'd already rolled away.

"He's mine!" Haft roared, filled with realization that this was his man to kill, not some poor soul driven mad by the invasion.

Now it was bal Ofursti who had to go on the defensive as Haft swung his axe in diagonal arcs, each followed by a backhand with the spike that backed the half-moon blade.

Suddenly it was the captain who was backpedaling and attempting to parry blows—but Haft's axe was heavier than his sword, and harder to parry even when he got good metal on it. Back and back and back, through the bushes and between trees, stepping high to avoid tripping over roots or trailing vines. And always Haft came on relentlessly. Until it happened. A parry went awry and the axehead slammed the edge of bal Ofursti's blade into his own thigh. He screamed from the pain and instinctively bent forward to clutch at his injury, putting his head directly in the path of the following backhanded spike. The axe's momentum yanked him completely off his feet.

Haft reached the end of his axe's swing and pivoted his wrist. The dead man's head slid off the spike and he crumpled to the ground, where Haft stared at him for a long moment before reaching down for the red cloak to wipe the blood off his axe. The three scouts with him gathered around, looking down at bal Ofursti's husk.

"Now why do you suppose he did that?" Haft asked as he dropped the cloak on the corpse.

None of them had any idea why Captain bal Ofursti had attacked Haft. Neither did they understand how a man could get so dirty and tangled in such a short time in the forest.

It was dusk when they got back to where the road north split off from the other road and they found the caravan waiting for them.

During the day's march, the caravan had grown by some 250 people, nearly half of whom were soldiers. They now had about eight hundred soldiers, former soldiers, and partly trained men under arms. An equal number of able-bodied men had neither military experience nor weapons training.

"I have a mixed squad of Borderers and Border Wardens watching along the edge of the forest," Spinner told Haft after hearing what the reconnaissance patrol had found. "The rest of the soldiers and fighting men who came with us from Eikby are in a picket line east of us."

Haft nodded. He understood the reasoning. The men who came with them from Eikby had all fought and beaten the Jokapcul at least once, and could presumably be relied on not to desert during the night. But still . . .

"If the Jokapcul are still moving in the numbers I saw earlier, if they turn this way they'll overwhelm our people."

It was Spinner's turn to nod, he was painfully aware of that. "But they can slow them down enough to give some of the others a chance to escape."

Haft harrumphed. "I think there should have been a couple of 'maybes' and 'ifs' in what you just said." He shook himself, but couldn't think of anything different Spinner could have done. "Who's watching the other sides?"

Spinner looked at Haft quizzically; it wasn't that long ago Haft wouldn't have thought to ask that question without prompting. "Corporal Armana has a squad of the Earl's Guards to the south and Upper Sergeant Han has his men on the west side." He gave a wry grin. "And I was relying on you to the north."

Haft slowly let out a deep breath. "We need to get moving. What I saw east of here has me pretty nervous."

Spinner smiled. *That* was more like the Haft he'd served with for so long. "We can't go at night. Wagons will lose the road and people will wander off and get lost. A night movement with people who don't know how to make one will be too much of a mess. We have to wait until daybreak."

Haft made a face. As much as he didn't like it, Spinner was right—again. "Then let's get an early start. I don't like being here."

"We'll move out as early as possible. I climbed a lookout tree too—I don't like sitting here any more than you do."

What with one thing and another, they didn't get moving at the break of dawn. When you have more than six thousand people, some with wagons or carts, most without, some healthy and strong and able to cover distance quickly, others not so fit, and from many different cities, regions, and even countries, speaking a multitude of languages and dialects, then add in a distribution of food still so chaotic nobody could know whether anybody has to begin the day's march hungry—well, it takes time to get them organized and moving. They began preparations an hour before sunrise but the sun had been up for a good two hours or more before the point— a squad of Zobran Lancers guided by the Border Warder called Hunter—cantered off along the north road. Impatient to be off, Haft had already gone ahead with half a squad of mounted Bloody Axes to scout the way beyond where he'd gone the day before. The caravan didn't stop at midday, and the day wasn't hot enough to make anyone suffer, so the entire caravan was on the eastbound road along the border between the forest and the desert by the time Spinner called a halt for the night. Even though he thought they were still far too close to where he'd seen the Jokapcul marching along the Gulf coast, Haft didn't object—other than some mild grumbling that he wasn't serious about.

They reached the escarpment on the second day of eastern travel. They didn't camp on the road or next to it that night.

The escarpment rose above the scrub half a mile north of the road. Flankers investigated the escarpment and reported back that it was largely unscalable and had many shallow caves at its base. So Spinner, with Haft, Alyline, Fletcher, and Zweepee concurring, had the caravan move to the foot of the escarpment for the night.

There was one split in the cliff wall, though, that the scouts dismissed as shallow without actually entering.

Seife the Merchant, from far off Bostia, had lost his wagons and goods and barely managed to hang onto his wife and three of their four children during their flight across the continent. Now, he wasn't happy about leaving the road for the foot of the escarpment. Had he thought the cliffs were sound, he would have been content to tramp the extra half mile to their base for whatever protection they would afford from the elements. But the sedimentary rock, with its unevenly eroded layers, reminded him far too much of improperly stocked shelves whose contents would come tumbling down the instant the wrong item was dislodged.

He found the crack in the rock face a few paces from where his family was settling in for the night particularly bothersome. The people camped directly in front of it had gone in thinking it was a narrow entrance to a shallow cave, only to come out and announce it didn't widen out enough for them to spread their bedding, and didn't seem to offer much in the way of protection from the elements. Besides, the wind whistled through it too much.

Seife the Merchant brooded over that crack in the wall for a time. He pictured it as a shelving aisle. Sometimes, if the goods improperly stacked in a shelving aisle collapsed toward each other, they eased the dangerous imbalance from adjoining shelves, and he wondered about the condition of the walls inside the split.

After they'd eaten their spartan dinner, when his son and younger daughter had fallen asleep, and his wife and older daughter whispered with their heads together the way women do when they don't want men to know what they're talking about, he decided to investigate. Lighting a brand in their small cookfire, he said, "I need to take care of something, I'll be back soon. Don't wait up."

His elder daughter flashed him a quick smile and his wife cocked her head at him; she'd caught the contradiction in "I'll be back soon, don't wait up" but decided that in the wilderness it meant nothing, and the two resumed their heads-together whispering.

Seife had no problem entering the crack—he was able to walk straight into it with his shoulders barely brushing its sides. Before he became a refugee, he wouldn't have been able to squeeze through it at all, but with the unaccustomed exertion and lean meals of their flight, he'd lost a great deal of bulk. His wife now looked at him in ways she hadn't looked at him in many years, and their lovemaking, when they had the energy for it, was much more vigorous and satisfying than it had been in just as many years. A smile flickered across his face. Beneath the dirt and wear of the long trek, his wife had also lost a great deal of bulk and looked much better than *she* had in years, which greatly contributed to the increased vigor and satisfaction of their lovemaking as well.

The walls of the crack leaned toward each other as they rose. Seife didn't notice during the day whether they met, and the small torch he carried didn't cast its light high enough for him to tell. He entered the crack and looked from one wall to the other. The dancing shadows deceived his eyes so he couldn't tell if the walls were smooth or as tumbled as the outer face of the cliffs. He held the brand high and ahead of him with one hand while brushing the palm of the other hand up and down the walls. He silently chided himself for not having felt the outside walls; he couldn't tell by touch if these surfaces were as uneven as the outside wall, more uneven, or smoother.

He went in five feet, then ten, then twenty, and the split remained roughly as wide as at its entrance. He thought the smoothness of the shifting sand on the floor of the split meant the walls were sound, that they never tumbled. If he'd been able to read the signs, he would have known that large masses of water sometimes shussed through the split and washed out the gravel and boulders that tumbled from the walls. But he was a town merchant, not any kind of outdoorsman, so he didn't even realize there *were* signs, much less know how to read them. He kept going until he could no longer guess how far he'd gone. The whistling of the wind through the crack annoyed his ears almost as much as the grit that peck-pecked at his face, made his eyes water, and threatened to fill his ears.

Then, suddenly, his torch no longer made shadows dance on the walls and his brushing hand met air rather than layers of stone. He stopped abruptly and spun about, swinging the torch before him. He breathed a sigh of relief when he saw a stone face with a crack in it. On the ground he saw his own footprints leading directly into the crack. He thrust the torch up, but it blinded his night vision so he couldn't see whether there was a roof above his head or stars in the night sky. Slowly, he turned in a circle, holding the torch out at arm's length. The space he was in was so large his light didn't reach its sides except by the crack he'd emerged from.

He took two steps forward, lowered the torch and closed his eyes to listen. He knew what an empty warehouse sounded like. Perhaps a large cave would sound the same and he could estimate its size. But, no, all he got was quiet, though not the quiet of an empty space. Maybe if he made a noise and saw how long it took the echo to come back . . .

"Hello?" *There,* an echo!

Wait a minute, that wasn't an echo, not quite. It was more like a footstep.

"Hel-Hello? Is someone there?" He heard something from over *there* this time, it sounded like slow breathing. *No!* The breathing came from over *there*! No, it came from . . . In half a panic, imagining bandits or ravening beasts closing on him, he opened his eyes and spun about to flee.

And ran smack into something very hard—the chest of a very large, very strong man.

CHAPTER
TWELVE

"Lord Spinner, Lord Haft," said Wudu, one of the Prince's Swords guarding the commanders' tent, as he ducked his head under the closed door flap. "Mr. Fletcher and Sergeant Mearh are here with someone who wants to see you."

Sergeant Mearh was the leader of the squads of Zobran Light Horse who were pulling perimeter guard duty.

Spinner and Haft looked at Wudu. They had just been discussing sleeping arrangements; Haft wanted privacy for himself and Maid Marigold, but Alyline and Doli had been giving Spinner a very hard time about giving up the tent every night for Haft's "dalliance." "It looks bad," they told him, "for you to sleep under the sky every night while *he* plays with his bedmate." Spinner didn't care that much, but he was tired of having Alyline and Doli berate him over the issue. There wasn't an extra tent for either of them to move into, and Alyline wouldn't allow Spinner into hers, and even if he was willing to spend his nights in Doli's—she'd made clear her willingness to welcome him—Maid Primrose, who shared Doli's tent, would have no part of him.

Needless to say, Spinner and Haft were annoyed by the interruption.

"Can't it wait until morning?" Haft snarled.

"Sergeant Mearh says it's very important, sir."

Spinner snarled in disgust.

"Let them in."

"Yes, Lord Spinner." Wudu quickly glanced at Haft to make sure he wasn't going to countermand the order, then ducked back out and pulled the door flap aside for the three men to enter.

Fletcher came in first and graced the two Frangerian Marines with a look that seemed to ask, *How are you going to deal with this?* He took a place standing between Haft's desk and cot and folded his arms across his chest. Sergeant Mearh came next, sword in hand, and stood between Spinner's desk and yet-to-be-slept-on cot.

The third man stepped in and gave a deep, sweeping—but mostly mocking—bow, then stood with arms akimbo, his feet spread as if he were balancing on the deck of a ship at sea. He was very large and wore a familiar double-reversible cloak, tan side out, with three stripes on the shoulder and a merman clasp holding it together at the throat. "*Lord* Spinner? *Lord* Haft?" he questioned with a broad grin. "The last time I saw you two, you were just a couple of frightened pea ons trying to evade and escape."

There was a moment of stunned silence from the two before they leaped to their feet and rushed around their desks, jostling each other in their haste to be the first to reach and embrace him.

"Rammer! We thought you were dead! How did you get away?"

Sergeant Rammer had been the Marine detail commander on the *Sea Horse*, the Frangerian merchantman they'd been on when the Jokapcul invaded New Bally. The last time they saw him was in New Bally, where he was a prisoner; he'd seen them hiding in the shadows near where he was being held and signaled them to take off on their own.

By the time they finished greeting each other, Alyline, Doli, and Zweepee had crowded into the tent behind them, along with Sergeant Phard of the Bloody Axes and Sergeant Geatwe of the Prince's Swords. Spinner and Haft were forced back behind their desks and Rammer against the desk fronts. The Marine sergeant turned about and looked at the faces crowding him. His gaze lingered longest on Alyline, openly taking in the vest that didn't quite close between her breasts, and the pantaloons held low on her hips by a girdle of gold coins.

"Mistress," Rammer said, and essayed a cramped bow. "Is your Sothar player near?"

Spinner goggled at him. Sergeant *Rammer* knew about the Sothar player? He wasn't even Apianghian! Spinner, who was, hadn't known, even though Alyline was from the highlands of his home country!

"No, he is not," Alyline replied sourly. At Rammer's disappointed look, she added, "Thanks to the ignorance of two of your fellows."

"Spinner! How could you not know?"

"Well . . ." Spinner spread his hands helplessly.

"Would somebody please get a stool for Sergeant Rammer?" Haft interjected. He realized he and Spinner had just lost points with their detachment commander, and he didn't want to lose any more. "And everybody, please sit." He gestured at the cots.

Doli squeezed past Sergeant Mearh and perched on the end of Spinner's cot nearest the desk. Fletcher and Zweepee waited for the camp stool to be produced and opened before they sat on Haft's cot. Once Rammer was seated, Sergeant Mearh took the place next to Doli—if Spinner didn't want her, maybe she could become interested in someone else. Sergeants Phard and Geatwe chose to remain standing. Spinner and Haft introduced everyone.

"All sergeants?" Rammer said with a chuckle. "No officers?" He paused, waiting for an explanation.

"One captain refused to join us and went over to the bandits," Spinner said.

"We had to strip another captain of command when he thought his men could have their way with women without the women's consent," Alyline said. "Haft killed him," she added with a hint of approval in her voice.

"Well . . ." Haft spread his hands. "It was self-defense." He quickly moved on. "There was a good officer in Eikby," he allowed. "But he got killed in the defense of the town."

"He'd been a sergeant in the Easterlies before he retired to become captain of guards at Eikby," Phard explained with a touch of pride in his voice.

"We do have a lieutenant from Penston, but he's too demoralized to be of use as an officer," Geatwe added.

"Very interesting," Rammer said after the explanation. He chuckled again. "It is sergeants, after all, who really run armies." Then: "This is quite a large following you two have. How did it happen?"

"They've sort of accreted," Spinner said, not wanting to admit that so many people had chosen him and Haft to protect them and lead them to safety.

"It's a long story, Sergeant," Haft said. "But tell us, how did you escape?"

Rammer shook his head. "I still don't quite understand what happened," he said solemnly, then looked like he was considering a question. "Does everybody here speak Frangerian?"

"I think so," Haft answered. He *thought* that he sometimes talked to everyone in the tent in the common trading language. But Alyline didn't, and neither did Mearh.

"I think everyone's stronger in Zobran," Spinner said, looking around for confirmation. He nodded at the replies, then said, "Zobran."

"All right, Zobran it is, then," Rammer said in that language. "We Marines and sea soldiers were all separated, spread out among the sailors so there weren't two of us in any group." He chuckled. "I guess the Jokapcul were afraid if they left us together we'd find a way to fight and defeat them.

"Anyway, my group—a score of sailors who spoke half a dozen different languages, in not all of which I knew the basics—"

"What are the basics?" Doli interrupted.

Rammer looked at her carefully before answering. "The basics any soldier or sailor needs in a port of call are enough of the local language to find food, drink, lodging, and a woman for the night." He watched her for a moment until he was satisfied she wasn't too flustered by his answer, then continued.

"My group, twenty squids and a ship's supercargo who spoke some strange Kondive Island dialect, was being transferred at night from a town square to a guarded warehouse. There were no guards outside the warehouse, which the soldiers transporting us evidently thought was strange. They stopped us in the street while two of them went inside. When they didn't come back out right away, another went in to look for them. That left only two guards on us. Suddenly, they were dropped by arrows, and three civilians ran out of a nearby alley and barred the warehouse door, locking the Jokapcul inside. Then they led us into the alley and away to a smithy, where the blacksmith and his apprentice broke our manacles. A doddery old man and a girl of maybe twelve were there. They led us by back ways to a dry channel under the city wall. The old man took one look and decided I was the leader. He told me there was a dry canal on the other side that would lead us to the forest. 'Come back soon,' he said. He also said more prisoners would be freed by the night's end."

Spinner and Haft looked at each other when Rammer mentioned the old man and the girl. *Tiger*, they both mouthed, the old man and young girl who had helped them escape from New Bally.

"We waited inside the forest until two hours before dawn. Three more groups joined us, but none were Frangerian Marines. Nigh on half of the sailors didn't want to wait, or preferred striking out on their own. There were near fifty of us when we set out east. A Ewsarkan sea soldier," he nodded at Haft, who he knew was Ewsarkan, "a Kondivan, a Matildan, and the rest were squids.

"It was quite a job avoiding the Jokapcul, they were all over Bostia. We lost the Matildan and a dozen sailors by the time we reached Skragland." He paused, remembering the men they'd lost crossing Bostia. "By then we were all armed. In Skragland we seemed to always be just ahead of Jokapcul who were moving inland, and there were times we had to go to ground for a week or two.

"I saw right away that trying to cross the Eastern Waste in

winter was a bad idea, so we headed south through eastern Skragland and Zobra to the root of the Princedon Peninsula. There, we cut across, straight to Dartmutt." Spinner and Haft looked at each other again; it hadn't been so obvious to them that crossing the Eastern Waste in winter was such a bad idea, they'd had to find out the hard way. "We got there in time to see the Jokapcul invasion. So we went north, then east."

Rammer grinned. "And then who should we run into?" During his telling, Silent and Wolf quietly crowded into the tent. When Phard and Geatwe shifted to make room for the new arrivals, Rammer turned his head to see who had come in. To his credit, he didn't pause in his narrative while he looked appraisingly at the giant for a moment and calmly let Wolf sniff him.

"How many of you are there now?" Fletcher asked.

"About a hundred and fifty fighting men, most of whom have their families with them." He quirked a smile. "Some of the squids who came from New Bally with me were pretty unhappy about becoming soldiers." He shrugged. "It balanced out. They now have women of their own, and some have adopted families.

"So tell me about you," Rammer said.

Spinner and Haft made short work of their narrative—or they tried to. Except for Xundoe as many as could fit of the members of the company who had been with them since before Eikby were crammed into the tent. They took turns filling in whenever they thought the telling was too short.

Rammer raised his eyebrows at the coincidence that the old man and young girl who had led him and his sailors to the channel under the New Bally walls had done the same for these two, then nodded and murmured, "That explains a lot," when they told him the old man had been a Frangerian sea soldier in the days before Lord Gunny. Fletcher and Zweepee supplied far more detail about the Burnt Man Inn than either Spinner or Haft was comfortable with—the details made them sound like some kind of heroes, which they knew they weren't. He whistled when Silent told how the two had fought the trio of Jokapcul swordsmen and three lancers at the border, and Spinner defeated the Jokapcul officer even though he was weak from loss of blood. "I finally believe in that stick of yours," he said, when Silent was through. When they told about the battle against the Jokapcul troop, where they'd first met Xundoe, he said, "I want to meet this war wizard of yours." The Eikby story, which was mostly told by Fletcher, Zweepee, and the sergeants, impressed him. "I've always maintained that a nineteen-year-old junior Marine is the most dangerous person in the world. I think you two proved that in Eikby."

At that, Spinner hoped the blush in his dusky face didn't show clearly in the lamplight. Haft grinned, blew on his fingernails, and buffed them on his shirt.

When the telling was done, Rammer became all business. "We're together again now, we'll join forces. Between us, we have close to a thousand soldiers and fighting men. If we pretend that's a regiment, we can call both of you battalion commanders—you'll both pull double duty on my staff— What?" He looked around. The atmosphere in the tent had suddenly turned tense. His eyes barely widened when he saw Sergeants Phard, Geatwe, and Mearh with their hands on their weapons, ready to draw them.

Fletcher cleared his throat and spoke politely but firmly. "Sergeant Rammer, we all understand that you were formerly Spinner and Haft's commander. And you have gathered your own force, so I assume those men are loyal to you. There are most certainly strong personal loyalties on this side. We have more than four times as many soldiers and other fighters as you do. Nearly all of them have fought the Jokapcul and lost under their previous commanders. Many of them have fought the Jokapcul under the leadership of these two," he nodded toward Spinner and Haft, "and won. They know they can win fights with the commanders they have. But they have no idea who you are.

"It's much the same with the people. Everyone who joined us before we reached Dartmutt knows that these men protect them better than anybody else has. They don't know that you can protect them.

"What do you think will happen to morale if the commanders who have led them to victory in battle, and provided security from the invaders, are abruptly replaced by a stranger?"

"I like these two," Silent rumbled. "I don't know you."

"My men and I follow Sir Haft," Sergeant Phard said menacingly. "All the Bloody Axes do. And where the Bloody Axes lead, the other Skraglanders follow."

"The Prince's Swords have sworn allegiance to Lord Spinner," said Sergeant Geatwe. "The Royal Lancers go with us."

"The Border Warders and Borderers also follow Haft," Zweepee put in.

The others also spoke for one or another unit, all saying they followed Spinner and Haft, not Rammer. Wolf lowered his head and growled.

All but Alyline.

"These two kidnapped me and sent my sothar player away," she said bitterly, referring to Spinner and Haft. "I should look on you as a savior, rescuing me from my kidnappers." Her hair swirled in a golden cloud when she shook her head. "But I don't. If Mudjwohl still lives, I know I can get these two to find him and restore my life. Can you do that for me? I doubt it."

"So we don't join forces," Rammer said coldly. "How are you going to explain that when you get back to Frangeria? You are going back, aren't you?"

Spinner grimaced and Haft looked aside.

"Yes, we're going back," Spinner said softly. He sighed. "I think it's a mistake if we don't join forces."

"I'm glad you see that much. But I'm your commander."

"I'm sorry, Sergeant Rammer," Haft said sadly, "but not many of our people will go along with that. The three of us would have to leave and go on our own."

"You go nowhere without the Bloody Axes," Phard said sharply.

"And no one else commands us." Geatwe echoed him for the Prince's Swords.

Haft turned his hands out helplessly.

"We're going to the same place, we need to go together," Spinner insisted.

"I agree with you," Rammer said seriously. "But me being under your command will be awkward. And what effect will that have on discipline when we get back to Frangeria?"

"Oh, no, Sergeant Rammer, it won't be any problem when we get back. There we're just a couple of pea ons, and you're our detachment commander," they hurried to reassure him.

"It's just that here," Haft said, grinning, "everybody wants us to be in command."

Rammer stood up, jammed his fists onto his hips, and dropped his chin to his chest, lost in thought. After a long moment he raised his head. His face was steely and his eyes harsh as he looked from Spinner to Haft and back. "All right," he said slowly, deliberately, the voice of a very dangerous man who was attempting to avoid conflict but wasn't going to accept less than his due, "I understand. These are your people. They are here because of you, they follow your lead and none other. That's the way they want it." He paused to give them an opportunity to speak.

Haft shot a quick glance at Spinner, who nibbled at his lower lip. Neither spoke.

"I am the most experienced military man here," Rammer continued when he saw neither had anything to say. Neither did the other sergeants, who may in fact have been in their armies longer than he'd been a Frangerian Marine. "What job do you have for me? Commander of an autonomous unit moving with you is not a good idea, we need unified command."

"Oh, well!" Haft sat more erect, relieved that conflict was avoided, his mind abuzz in an attempt to come up with a better job for their former detachment commander.

"Well?" Rammer asked stiffly. "Captain of archers?"

Spinner sighed. Rammer was a most excellent crossbowman, but . . . "Our archers mostly use longbows," he said. "Fletcher is the best longbowman I've ever seen. If we had an archer company, he'd be its captain."

Fletcher cocked an eyebrow—this was the first he'd heard of that.

"I see," Rammer said flatly. "I have far more shore experience than you do. And I was a hunter before I joined the Frangerian Marines. Captain of scouts, then?"

"Jatke was a hunter too," Spinner said, a touch of uncertainty in his voice, "right up to when he joined us. His experience is more recent than yours. He's captain of scouts."

Rammer laughed harshly. "I evaded Jokapcul columns and patrols all the way across a continent until a few hours ago. Jatke's experience is more recent than mine?"

Spinner grimaced. Haft looked away.

Rammer leaned forward and planted a fist on each of the field desks of his two former men. With his face close to them, he said softly, ominously, "I'm the most valuable soldier you have in this camp. Even more than you. What job do you have for me?"

Spinner and Haft looked at each other. They knew how important Rammer could be to them and their ragtag army. But what position could they give him that wouldn't threaten their command and sow discontent among the troops?

Spinner dropped his eyes as he thought and his gaze fell on his copy of *Lord Gunny Says*. Ragtag, that was it!

"Training commander," he said, looking up. "Sergeant Rammer, it's what you said, you're the most experienced man here. You know more about fighting and war than anybody else. Certainly more than us." He gestured to include himself and Haft. "Most of our men have experience in one or another army, and we have some very experienced sergeants. But nobody has anywhere near the experience you do. What we most need is someone who can train them to be good soldiers."

"Right!" Haft's eyes lit up as soon as Spinner said "training commander." He was almost bouncing with excitement on his stool. "We don't expect you to turn them into Marines, of course, that would be asking too much of any one man. But, yes, training commander! That's what we need, and you could really do it. Why, I remember how you drilled us on the *Sea Horse*."

Rammer removed his fists from the desks and straightened. "Training commander." He turned and looked at the others. The sergeants were grinning. They agreed that training commander was a serious need, and they thought a Frangerian Marine sergeant was an excellent choice to fill it. Fletcher looked relieved and Silent amused. Wolf sat on his haunches with his tongue lolling out of his mouth. "Yes, I can see proper training is needed here." He nodded. "I did a tour on the training field at Camp Gray," the Frangerian Marine recruit training base. He looked at them sharply. "What makes you think I can't turn these—these men into Marines?"

"Can you?" Haft did jump this time. "Is it possible to turn regular soldiers and half-trained fighting men into Marines?"

Spinner closed his eyes, but managed not to shake his head. "If anyone can, Sergeant Rammer can," he muttered.

Haft turned to him. "I do believe you're right!" he said.

Rammer laughed at Haft's enthusiasm. "Not while we're on the move, I can't." He shook his head. "I'll be hard pressed to do any training at all."

"But if anybody can do it, you can," Haft said.

"I glory in your confidence," Rammer said dryly. Sitting again, he leaned forward and folded his arms on the desks. "Now, how are you organized? Who needs training the most?"

"We've mostly got squads and some platoons. We're keeping the soldiers together according to the type of unit they came from. For example, all the Bloody Axes are under Sergeant Phard, and the Prince's Swords under Sergeant Geatwe." Spinner shook his head. "We use the veterans and half-trained men to fill in where needed."

"*What!* You don't have companies organized? Gods, you've got more than enough to make a full battalion, almost enough for a paper regiment, and you don't even have companies?" He looked at them, astonished.

"Ah, well . . ." Spinner stammered.

"We didn't think of that," Haft said weakly. The sergeants started laughing, which they hid behind their hands when he flashed an angry glance at them.

Rammer snorted. "And you're the commanders. I'm not so sure I want to put my men under you. Look, get me a roster—you *do* have a roster, don't you?—and I'll start getting a battalion organized. What's this," he asked when Zweepee pushed a sheaf of paper into his hands. "Oh, thank you," he said when he saw it was a roster. He looked around at Fletcher and the three sergeants. "We'll do this together—you know these people, I don't."

Moments later Rammer, Fletcher, and the three sergeants had gone outside and runners were dispatched to summon all the squad and platoon leaders.

Haft and Spinner looked at each other.

"Is he taking over?" Haft asked, stunned by the way Rammer had taken charge of organizing their makeshift army.

Alyline burst out laughing. Doli and Zweepee immediately joined in. A noise that might have been laughter rumbled out from somewhere deep in Silent's chest. Wolf huffed; they could swear he was laughing too.

"Tell us about him," Fletcher said to Spinner and Haft when he and the sergeants returned a bit later.

So they did. Rammer listened, and pitched in a couple of times himself.

Sergeant Rammer was a grizzled veteran of a decade and a half as a Frangerian Marine. The men who served under him may have loved him or hated him, but they all believed he knew everything there was to know about fighting and being a Marine. Rammer could have been an officer if he'd wanted, but he didn't want to be an officer.

"I'm a sergeant, so no officer expects me to kowtow to him in proper courtly manner," he said about it. "If I was an officer, *every* officer of higher rank would expect me to kowtow in proper courtly manner. I know more about leading Marines and fighting than any lieutenant or captain who never served in the ranks, and more than most field grade officers." He paused in reflection, then continued, "I know more about fighting and handling junior Marines than *any* officer who never served in the ranks. What officers know that I don't won't help them get a frightened Marine to go over the side or win fights. Officers have to put too much time and effort into courtly matters. It doesn't matter how courtly you are, there's nothing courtly about fighting."

Most of the junior men who served under Rammer in ship's detachments believed the officers gave him command of those small units that went far away from Frangeria for long periods of time just so he wouldn't be in any of their units, where it would be obvious to everybody that this sergeant knew more than they did about the important things. Privately, though he'd never admit it, Rammer thought the same thing. He didn't mind. He got extra pay for being a detachment commander—and he hadn't had to put up with officers when he was in command of a detachment on a cruise.

CHAPTER
THIRTEEN

Spinner and Haft tried to make it look like the decisions had been theirs, but in reality all they did was sign off on the decisions the sergeants made. By morning Captain—formerly Sergeant—Phard, was in command of Company A, which consisted of most of the Skraglander units, and Captain—formerly Sergeant—Geatwe commanded most of the Zobrans in Company B. Company C consisted of the soldiers, formerly sailors, who had escaped from New Bally with Rammer, the half-trained fighting men, and the rustiest of the veterans, under the command of Captain—formerly Sergeant—Mearh. Sergeant Rammer—he refused to accept an officer's rank—had Company D, the training company. Veduci and his surviving men were also placed in Company D, where they would be secure under Rammer's watchful eye. The sea soldiers who had escaped New Bally with Rammer were the company's other officers, though they didn't call themselves officers—they called themselves drill instructors. As soon as Rammer thought his men were trained well enough, he and his officers would hand command to someone else and form a new company of untrained men. The Border Warders and Borderers were combined into a reconnaissance/sniper platoon commanded by Lieutenant—formerly civilian hunter—Jatke. Each company had a lancer platoon, although most of the Skraglander lancers were variously armed with swords, axes, and spears rather than proper lances. Lieutenant—formerly Corporal—Armana retained command of the Dartmutter Earl's Guards platoon, which was placed in Company A. The Earl's Guardsmen appeared to seriously dislike the arrangement, but were wise enough not to object loudly. The odds and ends of other sea soldiers in the caravan were appointed lieutenants, commanding platoons in the newly formed companies. The Bostians who came with Rammer became a platoon within Company B, while the Penston Conquestors went into Company C.

Sergeant Rammer somehow became the battalion Chief of Staff as well as training company commander. Captain—formerly civilian—Zweepee was in charge of logistics; Lieutenant—formerly civilian—Doli was personnel; and Captain—formerly veteran—Fletcher had intelligence, which meant Jatke reported to him.

Silent flatly refused to accept any rank or formal position within the battalion. And Alyline considered herself above such things.

Spinner and Haft didn't adopt new ranks. Neither felt comfortable about calling themselves "General," or even "Colonel." Besides, nearly everybody in the caravan called them "Lord"—except for the Bloody Axes, who continued to call Haft "sir."

The caravan, by now nearly seven thousand strong—of whom more than a thousand were men under arms—got moving an hour after sunrise, more quickly than the previous two mornings. The effect the new military organization had on the time it took to begin moving wasn't lost on Spinner and Haft.

"Do you think he's trying to take over?" Haft asked softly as he sat astride his mare next to Spinner before heading out with the point squad.

"The better question is," Spinner replied, just as quietly, "do you think they're letting him take over?" Spinner asked his question with relief; he always felt on the verge of being overwhelmed by being commander.

Haft looked back at where Sergeant Rammer was, in the best tradition of Marine sergeants, barking and berating a group of untrained men into something that could generously be called a military route-march formation. His and Spinner's former detail commander certainly gave every impression he was taking command of their small army, unit by unit. While

Haft liked having someone who truly knew what he was doing handling the training, he himself *liked* being called
"Lord," and was uncomfortable with the possibility that he
was losing his position to Rammer.

Instead of expressing his misgivings, though, he shook his
head to the question about whether the men were letting Rammer take over and said, "I don't know." Then he heeled the
mare and led a squad of Zobran Royal Lancers from Company B east to scout the way. As soon as he was gone, Spinner
signaled Lieutenant Jatke to send out the designated squad of
Border Warders to make sure the right front of the caravan's
movement was clear of ambush or approaching Jokapcul.

The caravan covered a dozen uneventful miles that day.
The escarpment the road roughly paralleled continued the entire distance, with nowhere a break that allowed passage to
the north. They stopped an hour before sunset, and Rammer
used the last of the daylight to put the men of Company D
through sword drills.

"They're worse than a platoon of recruits," Rammer complained when he joined Spinner, Haft, and the other leaders
when the sun finally set and they sat down to an evening meal
of stew and stale bread. "The recruits who come to Frangeria
to join the Marines come willingly. Most of them want to
prove something, or have some other reason for wanting to be
Marines. These people?" He shook his head. "They're trapped
in a situation not of their own making, that they don't want to
be in—and most of them don't want to become soldiers."

He complained, but Spinner and Haft couldn't miss a glint in
his eye that they recognized—Rammer was enjoying himself.

And so it went for a week. Each day the caravan set out a
few minutes faster than the morning before. Every day the
men under training marched in better formations under Rammer's unrelenting guidance. At the end of each day's march,
Rammer put his "recruits" of Company D through fighting
drills. And every evening Rammer complained about their
unwillingness to learn and their poor quality as would-be soldiers. Alyline, Zweepee, Doli, and Maid Marigold listened to
his complaints with varying degrees of belief, ranging from

disbelief from the Golden Girl to naive and fearful acceptance from Maid Marigold. The men—Spinner, Haft, Fletcher, and Xundoe, along with the other company commanders—kept their peace. This was nothing they hadn't heard from every drill sergeant they'd ever encountered in whatever army.

Until the evening Haft leaned toward Spinner and whispered, sotto voce, "You know, Spinner, he sounds exactly like Sergeant Thunder did when I was in Boot Camp."

Spinner nodded and replied equally softly "Sergeant Blunt was always saying the same things to my recruit platoon too. I think that's a required part of the training regimen."

Rammer scowled at them for a moment, then burst out in laughter. When he got himself under control, he told them, "All right. From now on I'll only complain about how poorly the recruits are doing when I'm yelling at them." He laughed again, then looked over his shoulder in the direction of his company's bivouac before adding calmly, "Most of them are in good shape from their long march, so I don't have to put them through physical conditioning. Maybe they don't want to be here, and maybe they don't want to be soldiers, but they understand that they need to be able to fight and that what I teach them can keep them and their families alive." He nodded to himself. "They're learning fast—a lot faster than any platoon I put through the drill field in Frangeria."

Dust rose from the passage of the near seven thousand people who trundled along the road. Wheels rumbled and axles squeaked on tired wagons and carts. Oxen lowed their displeasure at hauling their loads for so long, men cursed at having to heave stuck wagons out of ruts or soft dirt, women shrilled at straying children, dogs barked at strange or interesting things they passed. Pigs grumbled and snorted, chickens and geese cackled in their cages, not aware of their fate as dinner.

With all that, the caravan was strangely, almost eerily, quiet. Missing from the other sounds of travel was the casual conversation of a multitude on the move, and no one got into heated arguments when a wagon lost way and slowed its followers. The soldiers who walked along the column saw to the quiet, their sergeants and officers—all just promoted and taking their new ranks and responsibilities seriously—saw to it that they did. And Spinner, in his endless ride from the van of the caravan to its tail and back, constantly checked on the officers and sergeants.

Even Sergeant Rammer, marching and drilling his recruit company along the northern flank of the caravan, marched and drilled them with less bellowing and roaring than a Marine drill instructor was want to use.

Still, some people managed to quietly converse.

Veduci had seen her before, of course, that woman who limped along on newly callused and still bleeding feet some yards in front of him. He'd seen her first when she was beautiful and haughty, and knew that beauty was still there under the dirt and dust of lengthy foot travel on an unimproved road. The haughtiness, if it was still there waiting its chance to resurface, didn't bother him—he knew how to handle haughty, and turn it to his advantage. Now her face was streaked with the tracks of tears, her formerly well-coiffed hair bedraggled. Her once translucent gown was clotted enough with dirt to be opaque.

He knew that the former favorite concubine of the Earl of Dartmutt was accustomed to pampering. Accustomed to having her every whim attended, to having people kowtow, to the finest clothing, to being clean. But she was dirty and footsore and humiliated. Her garment displayed more of her flesh than any other than her master and fellows on his bed should see. No one gave her succor; she received no more respect than a common ragamuffin. If she dropped down to sit in the dirt beside the road and wail out her need for aid, the people passing by would pay her no more attention than she had paid beggars in the streets of Dartmutt—Veduci knew this, he had seen her squat next to the north-south road on the first day she was made to walk, and had seen everyone ignore her pleas—those who hadn't, pointed and laughed at her.

She was now dirtier and more footsore than on that first day and, though the tracks of tears still stained her face, she no longer cried. Now her face was set in grim lines. When her eyes darted about, they weren't furtive, but in search of advantage. Her face was reddened, but not much from the sun. She might not be accustomed to walking great distances, but she knew how to use patches of shade to avoid sunburn. In the first couple of days after that golden woman had made bel Yfir walk like a common refugee, her face had been red mostly from humiliation. Now it was red mostly from the fury that simmered within her.

Yes, Veduci mused, she was ripe to ally with him. It wouldn't take much effort to convince her that helping him attain his ends would be to her advantage. Then, when he left the caravan with the earl's jewels and coins, he could take bel Yfir as well, and then truly live the life of an earl! He picked up his pace until he fell in step with her.

"It is a shame, lady," Veduci said sympathetically.

She turned her head and looked him up and down. He dressed more roguishly than most in the caravan; an unbleached homespun shirt gathered by a fine leather belt, ill-fitting but well-made deep green trousers, a dandy's tooled leather boots on his feet. The scabbarded sword and knife on his belt looked to be both quality and well-used.

She sniffed and looked away without replying; she had little use for vagabond adventurers.

"They think themselves too high and mighty," he continued. "They don't know how to treat people of quality, they think you're no better than anybody else." He gave out a gentle snort. "They are ignorant commoners who don't realize that some people, such as yourself, really *are* of a higher quality and deserve better treatment. It's a disgrace, an absolute disgrace that people such as they," he waved a hand in a vague manner that could indicate any of a number of wagons in the caravan, "should ride while you are made to walk."

"Then I shall ride in your wagon," she said with a trace of her former haughtiness.

"Alas! I am but a humble man, a proper man, who recognizes my betters—I have no wagon. I do, however, have a horse on the back of which you might ease your delicate feet."

Now she looked full at him. "Where?" she asked breathily.

"Stand a moment and it will join us," he said. His bow concealed a smile that stopped just short of a smirk.

True to Veduci's word, Zlokinech shortly reached them, leading a saddled horse.

"I fear I do not have a sidesaddle," Veduci told her, "but you may ride straddling this saddle, or I can have my man strip it off and you can ride directly on the horse's blanket."

Bel Yfir was tired and her feet hurt. "I'll ride astraddle." She faced the horse's side and gripped the saddle fore and aft. She lifted one foot, put it down, lifted the other, and put it down. She looked uncertain at the single stirrup on her side of the horse and murmured meekly, "I don't know how to mount a saddle with only one stirrup on the side." The red that suffused her face from her neck now was embarrassment.

"My most abject apologies, lady," Veduci said, evidently abashed, though he was no such thing. "I should have realized! He had known full well she probably didn't know how to mount a man's saddle, he wanted her to feel a weakness from which he could easily and gracefully extract her—to her gratitude. "Allow me." He placed his hands firmly on her slim waist and savored for a moment the feel of the smooth, soft flesh through her thin gown. "When I lift, raise your left foot to the stirrup. I will help you erect, then—I hesitate to say it— you must swing your right leg back and over the horse. Are you ready?"

"Yes." She sounded almost eager.

He lifted her effortlessly and held her steady while she fit her foot into the stirrup. He didn't let go while she clumsily maneuvered her right leg over the horse's back, and still held on while she settled herself in the saddle. When he let go he let his left hand casually brush down her thigh and his right briefly caress the small of her back.

She looked down at him as though thinking, You did that deliberately, you took liberties with my person. But I allow it—this time.

The escarpment bowed inward and receded three or four miles from the road. A light forest grew between the highway and the heights. The scouts continued to find no break giving passage north through the cliffs. The road angled slightly north of east, so the shore of the Princedon Gulf, which also angled slightly north, came no closer. Not that it seemed to matter—the Border Warders scouting toward the coast reported that the Jokapcul seen moving east more than a week earlier didn't appear to have reached so far—either that or they'd gone farther, maybe all the way out of the Gulf. So far as anyone could tell, the coast was clear all the way to the Inner Ocean, where the caravan would turn north toward Handor's Bay, or another open port.

In mid-morning, Guma—the lieutenant of Lancers—raised his hand and reined in his horse when he saw Lyft cantering through the main body of the point squad; Lyft and Naedre had ridden ahead to the left front to inspect the forest. Haft, who'd been telling Guma to assign three more lancers to scout the edge of the distant cliffs, halted to hear what Lyft had to say.

Lyft snapped off a salute when he skidded his mount to a halt. "Strange men are camped ahead," he reported. "About a mile off the road. Not Jokapcul. We saw about two hundred before I came back to report. Naedre is watching them."

"If they aren't Jokapcul, are they refugees?" Haft asked.

Lyft again shook his head. "They didn't look like refugees. I think they're the Desert Men I've heard about. They wore sand-colored robes and, instead of horses, had strange-looking beasts such as I have also heard live in the desert."

"What were they doing?" Guma asked.

"What did the beasts look like?" Haft added. He'd seen Desert Men and their beasts once when the *Sea Horse* stopped on the desert coast to catch game for the ship's galley.

Lyft answered Haft first. "They are taller than a horse and have very long necks that hold their heads up high. They look as fat as an unshorn sheep, but their coats seem to be short-haired. Their color was mottled white and gray and tan. I think they can hide easily in the desert."

Haft and Guma nodded; the description matched what they'd both seen.

Guma repeated his question. "What were they doing?"

"Nothing. They looked like they were resting in camp."

"What kind of security did they have out?" Haft asked.

"None that we saw."

Haft looked into the trees in the direction Lyft had come from. No security? That didn't sound right. "What about women and children? Wagons?"

Lyft shook his head. "Only the men and their riding beasts."

"I don't think they use wagons," Guma said.

Haft nodded absently. A couple hundred men with no women, no children, no wagons, and no security—just sitting calmly in the forest outside their desert. Next to the road. It seemed ominous, or at least very strange. "How were they armed?"

"Swords, lances, bows."

"What about demon weapons?"

Lyft shook his head. "I didn't see any." He shrugged, not that he would have necessarily recognized any demon weapons other than the couple he already knew.

"Send someone back to tell Spinner," Haft told Guma. "And send someone to make contact with the Border Warders, tell them what we found and find out if they've seen anyone."

"Right, Lord Haft," Guma replied. He twisted around on his saddle to signal two men to come up. They cantered away in opposite directions as soon as he gave them their orders.

"Now," Haft said to Lyft, "I want to see what you and Nae-dre found."

The forest between the road and the cliffs still had the leafy trees the caravan had traversed since Eikby, but in far lesser profusion. There were no towering lookout trees or dense canopy.

Some of those trees sent bare trunks twenty or thirty feet up before they sprouted thin branches with long, thin leafs. The leafs met each other, so each branch looked almost like a single, long, broad leaf. The branches came out in a circle from the same place and bent gracefully groundward after first climbing up a short distance. Altogether the trees gave the impression of being tall, thin mushrooms with green caps. The refugees, native to Dartmutt, called them "bumber trees."

Other trees weren't nearly as tall, ranging from knee high to a child to thrice a tall man's height, and were even stranger than the bumber trees. The fronds of these trees branched out fanlike just above the ground, in such profusion and equality of thickness that Haft couldn't discern which was the main trunk and which were branches. Maybe none was the main trunk; Haft couldn't tell without examining them closer than he had time to spare. Each shaft sprouted leafs its entire length, and when Haft looked closely, he saw each leaf sprouted more leafs—and that each of the branchings from the base of the tree to the smallest branching off a leaf was fanlike, so that no leaf or branch blocked another from the sun. He thought these were very strange trees. Seen from east or west, they were mere inches wide, from north or south they fanned nearly as broad as they were tall.

The little undergrowth that took root in the sandy soil was mostly sproutlings of the larger trees, though there were scattered low-creeping bushes with purple berries. Here and there wind and blown sand fought an unending war to polish or pit rock spires that poked up more than twice the height of a man or were piled in jumbles.

Small birds flitted low over the ground, from berry bush to berry bush, snatching fruit on the wing. Lizards basked in the sun, or took shelter from it behind the fanning trees. Some, larger than others, lay unmoving alongside or under the berry bushes, heads tilted up, mouths slightly agape, long tongues rolled up inside. A feeding bird flitted too near to one of the larger lizards, whose head moved almost too fast to see before its tongue shot out to snag the bird and whip it back to the lizard's mouth. *Crunch!* Feathers, a foot or two, and a long-beaked head, protruded from the lizard's mouth. After a moment the lizard swallowed and all evidence of the bird was gone.

Lines of insects crawled here and there, bearing gifts of detritus from there to here. Long-legged hoppers munched on fan leafs before hopping to a more succulent leaf to munch some more. Low slung, small crawlers made their ponderous way from one lizardly leaving to another, nearly indistinguishable from the sandy soil.

The only sounds in this strange forest other than the rhythmic plopping of the hooves of their horses were the shrill pipings of the flitting fliers, the occasional crunches of feeding lizards, and the rustling of leaves moved against each other by the breeze.

More than half a mile from where he'd returned to the point, Lyft held up his hand and dismounted. "We go on foot from here, Lord Haft," he said quietly.

Wordlessly, grateful to get down from the mare, Haft dismounted. He looped his reins around a branch of one of the fan trees and looked around, wondering how he'd be able to find his way back to this spot if he had to leave quickly—the ground was sandy, but firm enough so it didn't easily take a man's footprints.

Lyft slid his lance into its saddle loops and drew his sword. "Ready?" he asked.

Haft loosened his axe in its holder but didn't draw it. He nodded. Lyft easily loped deeper into the forest, Haft following just as quietly. Little more than a hundred yards farther, Lyft turned abruptly where a fan tree shaded the south side of a jumble of rocks and disappeared from sight. Haft started, then drew his axe as he darted to the place where the lancer had vanished. He found no mystery to the disappearance; instead, he found that the rocks were piled in a U large enough to shelter several men from the wind and blowing sand. Lyft and Naedre looked to him to join them.

Before Haft could ask how Lyft had managed to find this place so easily, or why Naedre was here instead of where he could watch the Desert Men, Naedre held a finger to his lips and signaled for Haft to follow him.

To Haft's surprise, Naedre didn't leave the shelter of the rocks, but slithered into a gap in the rocks that his body had blocked from Haft's sight. The gap was a tunnel barely wider than a man's shoulders, just high enough for Haft to hold his head upright to see where he was going. Haft didn't go far; not much more than five yards, before he emerged from the rocks and found himself shoulder-to-shoulder with Naedre in a hollow blocked in all directions by a thicket of fan trees. He heard the burble of water.

Haft looked along the ground below the fan tree directly in front of him. A sparkling stream about fifteen feet wide flowed under the trees—it was wider by two or three times than any other waterway they'd crossed on the north side of the Gulf. Men in desert garb lounged along both sides of the stream, their mounts on tether lines behind them. The mounts, yes, the strange beasts of the Desert Men. Tall as a man at the shoulder, with long necks that allowed them to eat high leafs or graze ground growth; their backs bulged up so they were far taller than their legs said they should be—Haft wondered if what he'd heard was true, that the beasts stored food and water on their backs so they could go for long times without food or drink. There were weapons aplenty; bows and quivers, lances, swords—always more than one per man—and each man had at least two knives visible about him. Haft looked closely but saw no demon weapons, or anything that resembled a spell chest in which demon weapons might be stored. He saw many sleeping blankets laid out, but no tents were pitched; there were cooking pits with small fires flickering in their bottoms. One area away from the bedding and fire pits seemed to be designated for latrine use, which surprised Haft. The men were quiet. What little they said to each other they only said to men close enough to hear a whisper.

And there were no women or children.

They watched for fifteen minutes and then a little longer. Haft couldn't think of a peaceful reason for so many armed men to gather without their women and children—and so quietly. Yet he was puzzled by the evident lack of purposeful activity in the encampment or the reported lack of watchers around it. When he'd seen enough, he tapped Naedre and the two slithered back into the tunnel through the rocks and returned to where Lyft waited for them. Once out of the tunnel, Haft looked at it and wondered if it would carry voices. He remembered that neither Lyft nor Naedre had spoken before he and Naedre entered the tunnel. He dipped his head to the side and they nodded in reply. The three loped back to where the horses were. Haft was surprised at how close Naedre's horse was to his and Lyft's.

"Did you check around for sentries or other groups?" Haft asked when they stopped.

Lyft gave him the kind of look a junior man gives an officer who asks a question so dumb it doesn't deserve an answer and said, "Of course, Lord Haft. We searched from the road to five hundred yards away from it, and found no one, nor did we find sign of anyone other than those who we already knew had been there."

Haft nodded. He was sure the two men had done exactly as they said. He was also sure they weren't as skilled at spotting sign as the Border Warders and Borderers were. He was almost sorry he'd used the Royal Lancers for the point squad. But the Royal Lancers were stronger fighters than the others, and the point squad was more likely to have to fight than the border soldiers with whom he'd run the reconnaissance before they turned onto this eastbound road.

A passage from *Lord Gunny Says* came to him. *You never have exactly the men or weapons you need in exactly the balance you need. Neither does the enemy. That's why we train in as many different ways as we do: So that when we need someone or something that we don't have, we can do a better job of covering the lack than our enemy can. Our superior ability to substitute who and what we do have for what we don't have is a major part of why we win all of our battles.*

Well, Haft didn't think he and Spinner had done the best possible job of substituting in this case. He looked to the south. There were Border Warders there. Some of them probably accompanied the man Guma had sent to alert them when he returned. They could search the area for sign of more.

"Go back and keep an eye on them," he told Lyft and Naedre, "while we decide what to do."

He watched where they ran as the two loped back to their observation post and shook his head. He knew the only reason he could see the sign they left was that he'd seen them lay it. But he was confident the Border Warders would see it when they came. He climbed onto his mare and trotted back to the point squad.

CHAPTER
FOURTEEN

Birdwhistle and Tracker were two of the original Zobran Border Warders to join the band, long weeks before it grew large enough to become a refugee caravan. Like most of the Border Warders, they'd both been poachers before accepting the prince's pardon in exchange for putting their skills to the warding of Zobra's borders. Like their brethren in mottled green surcoats, they were highly adept at stealthy movement in forest and glen, though more so in forest than glen. Their tracking abilities, of both game and man, were superlative— if they didn't see a sign of man or beast, that sign probably didn't exist. And they were excellent marksmen with their bows—longbow for both, now that Birdwhistle had demonstrated its value in combat to Tracker, who had previously used the short bow.

The land they traversed between the north shore of the Princedon Gulf and the road the caravan followed was different from the forests and glens of Zobra that were so familiar to them. The forest had fewer trees, and those were nearly all bumber trees whose mushroom-cap branches cast little shadow and fan trees that light filtered through. In short, more light reached the ground, which left fewer shadows for them to move through unseen. The very ground was different. In the forests of Zobra they had spent their lives moving. through, the ground was soft underfoot, covered with centuries of fallen leafs and twigs, mulch that returned life to earth to make fresh life. Here, the decaying cover was thin and spotty, the dirt was coarser, almost sandy, filled with pebbles, and stippled with stone. The hardness of the ground, and its pebbles and stones, didn't take sign as well as the forests of Zobra.

Still, they could see sign. Here, a deer had passed, nibbling on the leafs of low branches. There, a boar had rooted for succulents hidden beneath rocks. They exchanged a glance and a grin when they spotted pug of cat—they knew Haft was afraid of big cats. And they found they could move unseen even with the lack of shadows; had they not been unwilling to ease their watch for Jokapcul or other threats, they could easily have taken that deer when they passed unnoticed within thirty feet of it.

It wasn't until they found improperly buried scat and dirtied leafs that they found sign of man. They cast around in overlapping spirals, looking for more sign, before Birdwhistle found a carelessly tripped rock. Flat and as big as a man's palm, it had been moved from its earlier resting place, exposing the lichen that grew on the pebbles on which it had sat. They followed a line from the incompletely buried scat through the disturbed rock, and twenty paces farther found a glob of sputum spattered on some pebbles. Two paces farther still, they came across an almost imperceptible indentation in a stretch of coarse dirt; though it didn't show clear shape, they knew it was a human footprint. On closer examination they found the rounded end went toward the scat, the broader end to the east—the direction they'd followed the other signs to reach the footprint. It was hard to tell in the sandy soil, but they were certain it was recent. The sign they'd seen gave no evidence of who left it, but they doubted it was an innocent fisherman or local hunter. They nocked arrows and continued.

Birdwhistle kept his eyes up, watching for men; Tracker bent his neck, searching the ground for sign. They cast from side to side as they went—and both listened intently for sounds not made by wind or animal.

They didn't pay particular attention to the smells that wafted on the sea breeze from the Gulf, since the salt tang in the air would interfere with anything they might smell at a distance, though scents came to them before sounds or visual signs. But ignoring that smell was almost a mistake. They dismissed the unpleasant odor of rotting fish until they smelled it mixed with burned wood. Then they recognized the scent as an unpalatable sauce much relished by the Jokapcul, who made it from the juices of fish they baked in the sun. The two scouts exchanged a glance and a nod and changed their course gulfward, flickering from shadow to shadow through the thickening trees nearer the Gulf.

Birdwhistle clacked his tongue in the call of a red-throated nutberry bird. Tracker stopped and moved only his head to look at him, then where Birdwhistle looked. Two Jokapcul soldiers in metal-studded leather jerkins lounged under a bumber tree, one leaning his back against its trunk, the other laying on his side. Neither wore his helmet nor held his sword in hand. Both Border Warders clenched their fists on their bows—these two would be easy to kill.

But they weren't here to fight, they were here to find danger before danger found the refugee caravan.

At a barely discernible signal from Birdwhistle, the two scouts eased back until they were out of sight of the two enemy sentries.

You go that way, I'll go this, Birdwhistle said, using hand signals. Tracker nodded and they parted.

They passed the unwary sentries at a great enough distance to be unseen even if they walked erect in the open. But they walked neither erect nor in the open—they were wraiths, invisibly slipping through what shadows there were.

More than fifty yards beyond the sentries, growing noises came from the other side of a thicket of oddly segmented, reedlike trees that would bar passage to most men. But Birdwhistle wasn't most men, he was a Zobran Border Warder, a former poacher, a man whose life had always depended on never being detected as he moved about patrolled royal preserves. He edged into the thicket, leaving almost no sign of his passage. The thicket wasn't large, barely more than twenty yards wide and half that deep—and it was hollow. Two yards inside, the ground was almost clear, with reasonable shade cast by a canopy of slender leafs that sprouted from the upper portions of the reedlike trees. He darted to the far side of the hollow and flattened himself on the ground to slither between the close-packed trunks that made the thicket unpassable to most men. His body lengthed into it, he stopped and looked at a sight that froze his blood.

Three Jokapcul magicians sat in a semicircle facing the thicket. Between them and it hunkered several demons. One of the demons was a bedraggled Lalla Mkouma, another was a troll. Birdwhistle didn't recognize the others. He couldn't understand the words the magicians barked and growled at the demons but, curiously, he was able to make out what the demons said in reply. The magicians also seemed to understand the demons, though they didn't speak in the barks and growls of the Jokapcul tongue.

"Why zhud ee?" demanded a slight, man-shaped demon with ebon skin when a magician finished speaking.

"Naw likuu!" the Lalla Mkouma piped, with a flounce of her hair.

A large demon with massive shoulders, wearing a cloth wrapped around its head and a vest stretched to bursting by the bulging muscles of its back, growled threateningly when one of the magicians made to strike at the Lalla Mkouma. The magician swallowed and put his hands down.

Another magician barked and growled, flicking an oxtail whisk in time with his words.

A very large, shaggy, black dog morphed into human shape when that magician finished and snarled, *"Ziz naw ooze vorst. Oo naw tellum ee doo ere!"* then briefly morphed into a low-lying cloud before returning to its shaggy dog shape.

"Naw likuu!" the Lalla Mkouma piped again. The magician who had made to strike her before glanced at the very large demon that had threatened him and satisfied himself with glaring at her.

The first magician spoke again, then listened intently to the slender, black, little-man demon.

"Ee ead whatch ee whanns!" the smallish demon declared haughtily.

The second magician then spoke at fair length. The demons looked at each other when he finished and seemed to sag.

The black dog resumed human shape long enough to say, *"Ee gottum boint,"* then rotated through cloud back to dog.

The third magician, silent until now, grinned wickedly and held up an open tin of pellets. He doled them out to the demons. All but the Lalla Mkouma bolted them down and held their hands out for more. The Lalla Mkouma turned her back on the magicians after receiving her one pellet and said, *"Ztill naw likuu."*

Birdwhistle did not dare even to breathe; the miniature woman seemed to be looking right at him. She smiled around the pellet she nibbled on and winked, then flipped her hair and turned her head away. He slithered back as quickly as he could without making a noise that would give him away.

Ten minutes later he found Tracker, who was looking for him. They hurried away, intending to move to a safe distance from the Jokapcul before exchanging what they'd found. Before they had a chance to tell each other what they'd seen, they ran into Geshio, the Royal Lancer that Lieutenant Guma had sent to find them. Geshio was on foot, having left his horse a quarter mile back. They sped back to the point squad with their report while the Royal Lancer continued looking for other members of the squad.

The caravan was stopped a half mile behind the point squad. Company A was arrayed in battle formation across the caravan's front. Company B was strung out along the south side. The less experienced and ready Company C screened the rear, while Sergeant Rammer drilled Company D to the north—the direction from which he and Spinner thought attack was least likely. Silent and Wolf patrolled the road and forest to the rear to give warning of anyone coming from behind.

Spinner waited with the point squad, along with Fletcher, Xundoe, and Alyline. Doli seemed to be closer to her old self and hovered near Spinner. When Birdwhistle and Tracker appeared, Captain Phard mounted his horse and rode forward to join the command group.

"Who did you leave in command?" Spinner asked when Phard reined in.

"Corp— Lieutenant Armana."

Spinner nodded. He'd thought as much. He nervously returned his attention to Birdwhistle and Tracker, who arrived just then. He thought the fact they came back to report personally boded ill.

Birdwhistle told Tracker to go first; he suspected if he gave his report first, it might be deemed so important Tracker's wouldn't be listened to. When he finally heard what Tracker saw, he wondered if he should have gone first.

"There are Jokapcul on the shore," Tracker said. "They looked like light and medium infantry. At any account, I didn't see any horses. I was nearer the west end of their force than the east, so I couldn't see all of them." He took a deep breath. "But I estimate I saw half a thousand of them. There are probably more I couldn't see from where I was."

"What about magicians?" Xundoe asked.

"I didn't see any," Tracker replied before Birdwhistle could speak. "All I saw was the infantry, but I saw almost as many of them as we have proper soldiers, and there are probably more."

"What were they doing?"

Tracker chuckled sadly. "Guarding prisoners. Soldiers." He shook his head. "They didn't have a proper camp set up yet, except for cages to keep the prisoners in. Or maybe they think that's a proper camp." He grimaced and shook his head. "The cages weren't fit for dogs. They weren't high enough for a man inside one to sit erect, and only as wide as they were high. A man could stretch out lengthwise in the cages, but most held three men, and they weren't wide enough for three to lay side by side. There were rows of tents, but not enough for all the Jokapcul I saw. It seemed they were just beginning to pitch their own camp and taking their time about it. It looked almost like they were taking a rest from a long march before starting their work."

"What uniforms did the prisoners wear?" Spinner asked. "And how many were there?"

"No uniforms. They wore no more than loincloths; some were altogether naked. I saw nearly as many prisoners as there were Jokapcul." He shook his head. "It gets cold along the shore at night. I fear the cold will punish them severely."

"If they didn't have uniforms, how do you know the prisoners were soldiers?" Doli asked.

"There are signs. The way a man holds himself, how he shows the fear he feels. The way he examines his surroundings."

"So you're sure?" Alyline asked skeptically.

Tracker gave her an impatient look—of course he was sure. But before he could find the words to say so that wouldn't be insulting, Spinner interrupted him.

"Alyline, I can go into any city in the world where there are civilians and soldiers, all in civilian garb, and point out man by man which is a civilian, which a soldier, and be right ninety-nine times out of a hundred. More, nine times out of ten, I can tell what army they are from and what kind of unit. It's easy when you know how."

Alyline cocked an unbelieving eyebrow at him, but let it go when Phard nodded and said he could as well.

"What about weapons?" Spinner asked Tracker. "Did you see any cache or dump that might be the prisoners' weapons?"

Tracker shook his head. "No, lord. The only weapons I saw were those carried by the Jokapcul."

Spinner considered this for a long moment; that there were Jokapcul on the beach was very bad news. He thought the caravan should continue onward without doing anything to attract their attention. On the other hand, he felt they should free the prisoners. The addition of more than five hundred soldiers would be a great boon to the survival of the caravan.

But more than half a thousand Jokapcul . . . They didn't have the strength to attack that strong a force. Besides, there were those Desert Men north of the road. What would the Desert Men do when they heard the sounds of battle along the shore? So what were they to do?

"Did you also see Jokapcul and prisoners?" he asked Bird-whistle.

"No, Lord Spinner," Birdwhistle said solemnly, though he felt sheepish—Tracker's report made his seem insignificant in comparison. "I saw magicians and demons." He related the discussion, of which he'd heard one side—or at least as much of it as he could make sense of. He began, "There was a Lalla Mkouma—"

"You're sure it was a Lalla Mkouma?" Xundoe interrupted.

Birdwhistle held one hand about a foot above the other. "A voluptuous woman-creature with very long hair, wearing a diaphanous gown."

Xundoe nodded. "Continue."

"A Lalla Mkouma, a troll—"

"How do you know it was a troll?" the mage demanded.

"I've seen one." He held a hand just above elbow height. "It was gnarly and its skin looked like it could rasp the rust off iron."

Xundoe began to ask another question, but Spinner cut him off.

"Let him finish his report, then ask questions."

Xundoe nodded acquiescence, and Birdwhistle gave his report without further interruption.

"Describe the demons you didn't know," Xundoe asked the instant he thought Birdwhistle was finished. He nodded at the descriptions and asked questions about a few details. "The big one was a djinn, the small, ebon man-thing an exus, and the big dog was a Black Dog," he said, nodding when his questions were answered. He looked around at the others. "They are very bad. The only good thing is, it sounds like they don't want to work for the Jokapcul."

"But they have to, because there isn't food to support them in the forest north of the Gulf," Fletcher said.

Xundoe made a face. "That's what the Jokapcul *want* the demons to think."

"Is there food for them?" Spinner asked hopefully.

Xundoe spread his hands. "I don't know what Black Dogs

and exus eat, meat I imagine. Djinn can eat anything." He briefly lay a long finger against his cheek. "Or, actually I'm not sure djinn eat anything at *all*. The Elementary Demon Keeping course I took didn't cover djinn feeding habits. Lalla Mkouma can eat anything people can eat—at least for a short while. Trolls *will* eat anything, including rocks." He glanced at Spinner. "So there is food for them, or for most of them. Maybe they're new to this world and don't know what they can eat here?"

"Do you think that was all the demons?" Spinner asked.

"There probably weren't demons of other types, except for watchers and spitters. It's too bad Birdwhistle didn't see them from the front." He waved off Birdwhistle's correction. "Yes, yes, I know you saw the Lalla Mkouma from the front. But they're pretty independent. The others have a leader when they move in packs, and sometimes the leader wears an emblem of some sort. If you'd seen the other demons from the front, you might have seen something that would identify them as leaders. So we don't know if the Jokapcul only have one of each kind or several."

Tracker was watching east during Birdwhistle's report. He broke in to say, "Here comes Hunter," another of the Border Warders.

In moments, Hunter joined them, panting lightly from his long run. Geshio followed close behind on horseback.

"Archer and I found strangers south of the road, Lord Spinner," Hunter reported. "A war party, I believe." He went on to describe a band similar to the Desert Men they discovered north of the road.

"Were there women and children with them?" Alyline asked.

"No, lady. Only men, all armed and looking ready for a fight. That's why I think it's a war party."

Geshio's arrival headed off any other questions from the Golden Girl.

"Did any of the other Border Warders see anything?" Spinner asked the Royal Lancer.

"No, Lord Spinner."

"Did you find them all?"

"I did."

That was a relief, Spinner thought. But everything was so far beyond his experience and training, he barely had a hint of where to start making plans. He needed help.

"Guma, send runners to get the other company commanders," he said.

Guma immediately dispatched three lancers, one to get each of the company commanders.

Spinner next turned to Birdwhistle and Tracker. "Go back and keep an eye on the Jokapcul. Let me know if they move—and try to get a better count of both Jokapcul and prisoners." To Hunter, "Return to Archer, let me know if those Desert Men move or make any changes in their disposition." And finally to Geshio, "Find the other Border Warders and tell them to stay in place and to report back if they see anybody else." Not only did he need more information about the strangers, he was certain Rammer would also. He wished Silent and Wolf were near. They would be able to find out more about who else might be out there than anybody else, or find a route around the Jokapcul and the Desert Men. But they were ranging somewhere to the rear of the caravan, and nobody would be able to find them unless they wanted to be found. So he turned again to Guma. "Send someone to Lieutenant Jatke, tell him I need a squad of Borderers."

Spinner was so wrapped up in his thoughts that he didn't notice Phard's nod of approval. The grizzled veteran was now more certain than ever that he'd made the right choice when he put himself and his men under the command of the two Frangerians.

Shortly, Rammer, Geatwe, and Mearh arrived. Spinner quickly filled them in.

"We need to know more about what's to our north," Rammer said, looking suspiciously in that direction. "And we need to know more about the prisoners and their guards."

"I've already sent for a squad of Borderers, and instructed Birdwhistle and Tracker to learn more."

Rammer turned his head and eyed Spinner for a moment.

His look said that he realized he'd done a better job of training the young Marine than he had assumed. Finally, he said, "If I can think of anything you haven't already done, I'll let you know."

Spinner blanched. He didn't think he'd thought of everything; he knew there had to be more. But if Sergeant Rammer couldn't think of anything else . . . He looked to the other company commanders. None of them had any suggestions either. Rammer and the others—Phard, Geatwe, Mearh, Guma, all older men who had far more experience—seemed to think that he and Haft were doing well as commanders. He hoped they were.

Kovasch arrived at the head of a squad of Borderers and sketched a quick salute as he jumped off his horse. "What does Lord Spinner want us to do?" he asked. From the tone of his voice, the Royal Lancer sent to get the Borderers had already given him details of why the caravan had been stopped.

Spinner told him what they knew and what he wanted the Skraglander to find out. He looked around to see if anybody had anything to add. No one did, so he said, "Do it."

"Immediately, Lord Spinner." Kovasch turned to his squad and barked, "You heard the man. Let's go!" The Borderers would follow the tracks left by Haft and the two Royal Lancers. They'd leave their horses with theirs and head north and northeast on foot from there.

Now the rest of them had nothing to do but wait. Everyone else looked so calm, but to Spinner, waiting was the hardest part.

IV
FULL FRONTAL ASSAULT

CHAPTER
FIFTEEN

The scouts had made no attempt to avoid leaving tracks. To the Borderers, following them was almost like following a well-traveled road. They stopped and dismounted when they reached the three tethered horses.

"Tether mounts," Kovasch ordered as he looped his reins low around the trunk of a bumber tree with a knot he could undo with a simple yank. "Wait, I'll be back. Be alert." He followed the faint traces of men's footprints to where Haft had the Desert Men under observation. His men tethered their horses, mindful as Kovasch had been to leave them where they could reach grazing. They were well-trained and disciplined, they didn't need to be told to pair off and form a defensive perimeter once their horses were seen to.

When Kovasch reached the place where the footprints turned and disappeared behind the fan tree into the rocks, he stopped and chortled the call of an oriole common in both Skragland and Zobra, but foreign to the north coast of Princedon Gulf. He knew Border Warders would recognize the call and immediately know someone was signaling them; he didn't know that about Haft and the lancers. He positioned himself where someone who had gone beyond the fan tree could see him. After a moment he moved at an angle, so he could see partway around the fan tree without getting close to it, and chortled the call again.

He saw a flash of blue—the color of the Royal Lancers' surcoat—and an arm stuck out and waved him forward. He entered the U and found Naedre alone. The lancer touched finger to lips and, as soon as Kovasch nodded, disappeared into a hole in the eastern rock face. A moment later Haft came out of the hole and gave the same finger-to-lips signal before signaling him to follow. He went back into the hole. Kovasch followed.

The Borderer leader saw the Desert Men lounging along the stream, no women or children and no weapons ready, just as he'd heard. After a few minutes Haft tapped his shoulder and they left the observation point. Haft led the way out of the rocks to where they could speak quietly.

"You saw?" Haft asked. Kovasch nodded. "They've been like that since I first saw them. We haven't found any sentries."

"But those rocks are such an obvious place to watch from," Kovasch said in wonder.

Haft nodded. "Yes, it's very strange. Lyft and Naedre searched nearly half a mile from the road to the north and didn't find any sentries or signs of anyone but this group."

"There's another group like them south of the road," Kovasch said. "And the Border Warders found Jokapcul with magicians on the beach."

Haft grimaced and looked to the south, then back to the Borderer. "We need to find out if anyone is farther north."

"That's what Lord Spinner said. He agrees it's very strange. He wants to find a way around them." He nodded in the direction of the Desert Men.

"What does Sergeant Rammer say?" Haft asked.

"He agrees."

"How many of you are there?"

"I have ten men with me, all good forest men and trackers."

"Good. Split into pairs and scout to the north, cover as much ground as you can. Are your horses with ours?" When Kovasch nodded, he continued, "Leave one man with the horses."

"That was my plan also."

"Good. Go. Report back before sundown if you don't find anything. Or sooner if you do."

Kovasch nodded once more and grasped Haft's extended hand. He turned and hurried back to where he'd left his men.

Haft watched him for a few seconds, then returned to watch the Desert Men.

Five pairs of Skraglander Borderers, clad in homespun and the skins of shaggy animals that didn't live in this odd forest above Princedon Gulf, headed north and fanned out. One pair went to the escarpment to look for passage through it or to its top—either as a route for the caravan to take, or that by which the Desert Men had come to where they now waited. Another prowled an area half a mile wide by two miles long directly north of the Desert Men; they had to have left sign there. The third pair searched a similar area directly to the north, and the fourth a mile-wide strip reaching north from that area to half a mile south of the escarpment. The final pair headed west, in search of any Desert Men who might be closer to the caravan.

They didn't know if the Desert Men had enough skill to hide their tracks, but it didn't matter. The comites—the beasts the Desert Men rode—couldn't hide the soft marks of their feet, splayed wide to allow them to walk easily on sand. There was a clear trail along the side of the stream by which the Desert Men sat in such unnatural calmness. The Borderers examined the trail and pondered. The trail looked like the padding of several hundred of the beasts—but the way the prints went in both directions, southbound over north, it could have been the same couple of hundred making the round trip more than once, or maybe the Desert Men camped by the stream now had relieved an earlier band.

The stream itself came out of a wide gap in the escarpment. Kovasch and Dongolt cautiously entered the gap. Its walls were very steep but not sheer, and scree piled at their bottoms. The ground of the gap's bottom sloped gently down on both sides to the watercourse, which showed signs of frequent flooding and course change. Knee-high, hardy grasses and a few low-lying bushes grew between the scree and the water-course; it was barren of trees, but there were trees visible beyond the gap. Both men nocked arrows and ran crouched through the hundred yards of the gap. They knelt behind trees and examined their surroundings.

Beyond the broad gap in the escarpment's face was a huge bowl with sides that sloped up to the height of the south-facing cliffs. Inside the bowl they saw the same bumber and fan trees they'd seen between the escarpment and the road, mixed in with leafy trees that cast proper shadows. A wide swath on the south side of the bowl was clear of leafy and fan trees and only sparsely dotted with the bumbers. The north side, or as much of it as they could see from where they knelt, was modestly covered with leafy trees. In between, the trees were thick enough that it was hard to see all the way through in any direction other than to their rear or directly to the sides—and hard to estimate distances. They were pretty sure the bowl was more than a half mile in diameter, but less than a mile. It was probably deeper than it was wide. The undergrowth was thinner than they would have expected had it not been for the signs of flooding in the gap—frequent floods would kill undergrowth before it could flourish.

After several moments of observation, during which they spotted nothing more than a covey of quail skittering from underbrush patch to distant underbrush patch, they nodded at each other and sprinted to the cover of the nearest leafy trees. After a time, moving with swift caution from one cover to another, they moved with less speed.

They found the tick tracks of more quail, pads of several foxes and small cats, hop tracks of hares, and the skitter tracks of other small animals. But no sign of people or the Desert Men's beasts other than their tracks alongside the stream. The stream itself bubbled and rushed down a deep cut in the north wall of the bowl. On the east side, they found traces of a rutted road angling up the slope. They paralleled the roadway to the top and looked over a flat land coated with the same hardy grass that grew in the gap. The grassland seemed to extend to the horizon. They followed the road, overgrown with grass, for a quarter of a mile. It went straight northeast for as far as they walked and a short distance beyond where they could make it out without following. Here and there were small pools of water, not all of which were fed or drained by rivulets—none seemed to be pools left over from rainfall, so Kovasch and Dongolt knew they must be fed by underground streams.

From there they looped around to the northwest and found where the stream began its cut into the bowl. Trees grew along the banks, which were firmly packed from the back and forth padding of the Desert Men's comites. Here, they were able to see more clearly that the most recent tracks headed north, away from where the Desert Men camped near the road the caravan was on. Kovasch climbed a tree and saw that three or four miles away the trees thinned out to nothing and the stream meandered alone through grass that seemed to fade into sand before the horizon. He spotted a small herd of gazelles in the grassland, but nothing else other than a few carrion-birds drifting high in the sky. The two returned south of the escarpment and searched to the east of the stream, but found nothing more of interest.

The other pairs found nothing other than the stream side tracks. They reassembled where they'd left their horses. Kovasch reported back to Haft. Half of the Borderers stayed with the watchers. Kovasch led the others back to Spinner and the caravan.

It was a painful decision to make, but they weren't strong enough to attack the Jokapcul guarding the prisoners—Birdwhistle and Tracker had reported that there were seven hundred guards over more than five hundred soldier-prisoners. Another three hundred women and children were kept in pens farther east than Tracker could see from where he first watched. Even if they managed to catch the Jokapcul completely unaware and quickly beat them, there were the two groups of Desert Men bracketing the road to the north. Between the Jokapcul and the Desert Men, if they attempted to free the prisoners they would most probably be soundly defeated and the entire caravan lost. They had to go north, around the enemy forces in front of them.

"There wasn't sign of anybody else?" Spinner asked yet

again. He studied the map Kovasch had drawn as though, if he looked at it long enough, it would speak up and tell him things that weren't marked on it.

"Only alongside the stream," Kovasch replied, giving the same answer he'd given every time Spinner asked.

"Then maybe, just maybe . . ." Spinner murmured and let his words trail off. He traced the arrow-straight road that went northeast from the bowl.

"I'm bothered by all the tracks that go back and forth along the stream," Kovasch said, not for the first time. "There are far more than the Desert Men ahead of us could have made. And the last tracks went the other way."

"Could the tracks have been laid down by group after group going to that place and returning?" Spinner asked.

"Why would they do that?" Alyline asked. "If they keep a group near the road as an ambush force to catch unwary travelers, they'd more likely keep one there all the time instead of changing them frequently."

Kovasch nodded. "That's right. They'd have to change forces every couple of hours to make the tracks I saw. I couldn't tell for certain in that sandy soil, but I think none of them were more than a few days old. And Lord Haft says the group he's watching has been there since Lyft and Naedre first saw them." He pretended he didn't hear Spinner's muffled groan or the Golden Girl's amused sniff when he said, "Lord Haft." Spinner and Haft were the commanders he'd sworn to follow. In his eyes that made them lords, no matter how much Spinner insisted they weren't.

"But there was no sign of anyone else," Spinner asked one more time.

"None that we found."

"If they didn't find any sign, there must not be any to be found," Jatke said. He assumed the tracking abilities of the Skragland Borderers were as good as those of the Zobran Border Warders, and he knew the Border Warders were better trackers than he was.

"There are about two hundred Desert Men camped on each

side of the road," Spinner said. "All heavily armed and without women, children, or oldsters." He looked at Kovasch, the only one in this group who had actually seen the Desert Men, for confirmation. He wished Rammer were there to give him some guidance—or better yet, take command, if the others would only accept him as commander. But Rammer had agreed it was more important for him to spend his time training his company of recruits, drilling them in basic formations and weapons use. "That way," he'd said before he left to do it, "if we are attacked by a large force, they won't get slaughtered quite as quickly—and they might do some good before they die."

"Two hundred on each side of the road, and they don't have sentries," Kovasch said. "I don't understand why they don't have sentries."

Neither did Spinner or anybody else; they all found the lack of sentries bothersome.

"All right," Spinner said after thinking it over, "I want the stream, the gap, the bowl, and the road out of it watched overnight. If no more Desert Men come, and if those already near the road stay where they are, we'll go cross-country to the gap in the morning and take that old road.

"Fletcher, can you find a safe route for the wagons during the night?"

"If Jatke goes with me, between us I think we can." He looked at Jatke, who nodded. "But where does the old road lead?"

"Someplace where there aren't Jokapcul, and away from the Desert Men next to this road." Who else might be along the old road, Spinner had no idea. There might be danger along that route, but he knew for certain there was danger along the route they had been following.

Here and there during the night, near where Borderers and Border Warders set their observation posts, and along the route Fletcher and Jatke found for the wagons, scrub-covered sand drifts shifted unnoticed. Men in green-flecked, sand-colored robes emerged from the drifts and, drifting like small clouds of mist, made their way elsewhere. A few went to the two Desert Men camps that flanked the road. Most went to the escarpment and made their way to its top by openings and slopes that were less obvious than the broad gap the stream flowed through. None passed near enough to the sentries to be detected.

The caravan hadn't unloaded to make a proper camp, and the people didn't take time to properly break their fasts, so the lead wagons moved out onto the route scouted by Fletcher and Jatke less than half an hour after the sun's leading edge appeared above the eastern horizon. In under an hour the entire caravan was on the move, away from the coast-paralleling road. Mounted soldiers from Company B, the Zobrans, rode up and down the length of the caravan, enforcing the no-noise rule Spinner had imposed. Silence, or as much quiet as possible with so many people and wagons on the move, was essential if they were to avoid detection by either the Desert Men or the Jokapcul. The people ate cold rations as they went.

Along the coast, two pairs of Border Warders kept an eye on the Jokapcul. Two more watched the Desert Men lounging south of the road, and two Borderers watched the Desert Men north of the road. None of the groups gave any indication they were about to move, and the improvements the Jokapcul slowly made to their camp suggested that they planned to remain where they were for a long time. The Desert Men made no improvements, but no one knew enough about them to know whether that signified anything. The watchers were to stay in place until mid-morning the next day, then rejoin the caravan—unless the Jokapcul or Desert Men began to move. In that case, they were to observe long enough to be certain of the direction of movement, then report back.

The best case, or so Haft said, would be for the Desert Men to move south or the Jokapcul north. "Let them fight it out between themselves," he declared. "Then we won't have to worry about either."

* * *

Despite grumbling and complaining from the people, Spinner and Haft didn't allow the caravan to stop at midday. They wanted to put as much distance as possible between them and the bands of fighters between the escarpment and the Gulf. The other leaders concurred wholeheartedly. The caravan stretched out as the day went along, but the Zobran soldiers kept urging the slower movers to pick up their pace so the caravan wasn't as extended as it might have been. By nightfall, when Spinner and Haft finally allowed a halt, the end of the caravan was two miles north of the escarpment, to the northeast of the bowl they'd used to mount it. The steadily blowing wind, which had brought the scent of the sea from the south all during the day, changed and came steadily from the north.

In this open land, they gathered the caravan into a tight circle instead of leaving it strung out on a line, and broke that great circle into ten smaller circles of wagons. They parked the dog carts in lines connecting the wagon circles. Most of the horses and draft animals were tied on tether lines in the center of the great circle. Spinner didn't allow fires or tents that night, an unpopular rule that was enforced by the Skraglanders of Company A. Two rivulets, narrow enough for a man to step across without stretching his legs overmuch, ran through the great circle. A pond was fed and drained by one of the rivulets; a hundred yards downstream there was a larger pond, though it too was small. The other rivulet fed a third pond within the great circle.

Unhappy because of the grains of sand blown by the northerly wind—grains that lodged in eyes, peppered lips and open mouths, penetrated every opening of clothing, stuck to skin—the people settled down to eat cold meals. After eating, they put out bedrolls. The lucky ones lay out their bedrolls inside covered wagons where they weren't constantly buffeted by the wind and scoured by the blown sand. Others lay under wagons, where they were provided some slight shelter from the wind. The temperature began to drop sharply after the sun set, prompting some to believe their water jugs would be ice-rimmed come morning. Everyone who could found another body to cuddle with under covers for warmth.

Company B sent squads out half a mile and more in screening positions to give warning in the event Desert Men approached during the night. Sergeant Rammer drilled the recruits of Company D before he released them for dinner and sleep.

"An hour!" he spat when he joined the command group. "That's as bad as no training at all. They need *days* of training before they know basic formations and weaponry. Then they need *weeks* of drill before they can perform without having to stop and think about every move they make."

"It was more than an hour," Fletcher said. "Anyway, an hour here, an hour there. It adds up over time."

"Do we have the time?" Rammer asked, thrusting his face at him.

"We *don't* have the time to bicker among ourselves," Zweepee chided. Rammer had the grace to clear his throat and shut up. Fletcher simply smiled at his wife.

"Do what you can with them," Haft said grimly. "If we're lucky, they won't have to do any fighting before they know which end of their weapons to wave at the enemy."

Rammer grunted and made a sour face. He harbored no illusions about their chances of avoiding both the Jokapul and the Desert Men for that long—not to mention other dangers they might encounter along the way.

"Where's Silent?" Spinner fretted.

Nobody knew. The giant of the Northern Steppes and Wolf hadn't been seen since they went to check the back trail.

Then they decided that first thing in the morning they would send out a platoon of lancers to scout along the road, and a platoon of Zobran Light Horse along the escarpment to see if there was a safe route back to the coastal plain farther to the east. The caravan would ready itself and follow the lancers. If the Light Horse found another route, continuing northeast for a time before returning to the road might be a lengthy detour, but it had the benefit of increasing the distance between them and the Jokapul and Desert Men on the coast plain.

An hour before dawn a Zobran Light Horseman galloped into the center of the camp. "Lord Spinner, Lord Haft," he called out as he leaped off his horse.

"Here!" Haft said groggily, untangling himself from Maid Marigold and pulling out of the blankets they shared to stand before the horseman.

"What?" Spinner asked, joining them.

"Lords, a strong force of Desert Men is approaching from the northwest. We estimate nearly two hundred."

Before he finished his report a Royal Lancer galloped up. "Lords, more than a hundred Desert Men are approaching along the road."

In moments two more of the outriders reported in. More bands of Desert Men were moving toward them from the north and the west, all told about six hundred, perhaps a third of them mounted on comites, the rest on foot. By the time the scouts finished their reports, the middle of the camp was bustling with people rising to find out what the commotion was about. Most of the people in the circles to the north, east, and west were also up.

Then it got worse.

"Lord Spinner," Kocsakoz, a Borderer, reported out of breath following his run from north of the coast road, "the Desert Men we watched are coming this way!"

Several minutes later Takacs, another of the Borderers, showed up with the information that the Desert Men south of the road had moved north and joined up with the band from the road's north, and both bands were approaching. As many Desert Men warriors as the caravan had soldiers and half-trained fighting men combined were approaching from all directions!

"It could be worse," Haft ironically said to the shaken Spinner. "Slice and Hatchet"—the senior of the pairs of Border Warders watching the Jokapcul—"haven't shown up."

"They have farther to run," Spinner said glumly.

"There are about a thousand of them," Fletcher muttered, "and we have fewer than eight hundred soldiers and fighting men, plus Rammer's recruit company. They're attacking, we're defending. I was always told attackers need to outnumber defenders by at least three to one in order to win."

Rammer shook his head. "That's with the defenders in fortified positions. We're behind circled wagons, not fortifications." He looked into the distance. "We need a Manila John Basilone, or a Dan Daily."

Haft remembered the legendary heroes Lord Gunny had taught about. They didn't have the magical weapons those men had: *machine guns*. But, "We have these," he said, hefting his demon spitter. "They don't. Xundoe?" He looked at the mage.

"We have a dozen men who know how to use them," Xundoe said. "But I don't have time to set booby traps."

Rammer looked at Spinner and Haft for a beat or two. When they didn't start issuing orders, he did.

"Captain Geatwe, get your men ready to defend the circles from the west side to the northeast. I'll send most of Company C to reinforce you. Captain Phard, cover the approaches from southwest to east with Company A. I'll hold Company D in the middle to reinforce where needed. Magician Xundoe, see to the distribution of whatever magical weapons you can to the men who have been trained to use them. Questions?"

The only question went unspoken. Haft wanted to ask, *Who put you in command?* But he didn't say it. He knew his and Spinner's indecision had forced Rammer to give the orders.

"Do it," Rammer said, then to Spinner and Haft, "By your leave, sirs?"

"Do it," Spinner said.

With a nod, Rammer ran off, shouting for the men of Company C and D to assemble.

"I'll get Nightbird to assemble the healing witches and magicians," Zweepee said. "Doli and Maid Marigold, come with me, I'll need your help organizing litter-bearers. You too, Alyline."

The Golden Girl sniffed, but shook her hair and went along.

The night, which had been more quiet than most nights since the original band of refugees set out from Eikby weeks earlier, was suddenly filled with the cries of men preparing for battle. To the west they heard the drumming of comite feet as Desert Men galloped north to join in the coming battle. The ululations of Desert Men war cries pierced the cacophony in the caravan.

CHAPTER
SIXTEEN

The Zobran Royal Lancers were still forming up inside the circle of wagons astride the road on the northeast of the great circle when a flight of arrows rattled into it, thunking into wagons and the ground. There was a scream of agony, but only one person was hit. Then a hundred Desert Men swarmed in, those whose comites could squeeze between wagons or hop over wagon tongues, riding into the circle. A few of the beasts misjudged the jump and tripped, throwing their riders. Most of the thrown Desert Men quickly regained their feet, but a few stayed down, too badly injured to rise or trapped beneath their mounts. The rest scrambled through the circle of wagons on foot, their scimitars flashing in the moonlight.

"On them!" Lieutenant Guma roared over the screams of frightened women and terrified children. He thrust his lance at a dimly seen, screaming mounted Desert Man charging at him with raised scimitar. He twisted violently to dodge the man's chopping blade. Pierced through by the lance and unable to change the direction of his swing, the Desert Man was already dying. His falling body threw his aim off and the razor-sharp blade missed both Guma and his horse. Guma yanked and twisted his lance to free it, then spun about.

Despite the fierceness of the attack, his men were forming into teams. Here, a line of five horsemen lunged forward and crashed into a mass of dismounted Desert Men, bowling them over. One lost his lance, unable to wrest it from the body of the man he'd speared. Three others managed to free their weapons. The fifth lancer had missed. Their horses lashed out with flailing hooves, knocking Desert Men down, trampling downed men unable to roll out of their way.

Four lancers charged side by side into a knot of mounted Desert Men who were hacking away at two of their comrades. The Desert Men were caught by surprise and crumpled under the counterattack. Five of them and three comites died abruptly. The rest fled.

A Desert Man was briefly distracted by the screaming, clawing, kicking woman he'd just plucked out of a wagon and thrown over the front of his saddle. The distraction was enough that he never saw the lancer whose weapon pierced his neck. His fate was quickly shared by other Desert Men who were distracted by booty and captives.

But not all were distracted.

A screaming Desert Man, scimitar held high and back for a decapitating stroke, galloped at Guma. Guma saw him in time to kick his horse into jumping across the path of the oncoming comite. The two animals collided, Guma's horse thrown off its feet to land heavily on its side. Tripped, the comite flipped over it and crashed to the ground with the loud *snap!* of breaking bones. But Guma had been ready and threw himself out of the saddle just as the animals met. He landed away from the slashing hooves of his horse as it fought to right itself. The Desert Man who'd meant to unhead him wasn't ready and was flung forward like a stone from a catapult, landing on his own blade. He didn't regain consciousness before he bled out.

At the pounding of heavy feet, Guma spun again, lance ready to thrust or parry. He dropped to the ground, ducking under a flashing scimitar, and thrust upward. His lance went so deep into the comite's belly that it was yanked from his hands. The beast reared, screaming as its entrails spilled, and the rider struggled to maintain his seating.

Guma wasted no time in bounding to his feet and leaping at the beast and rider. He grappled the scimitar wielder around the waist, pulled him from his saddle and flung him to the ground. The man hit with a loud *whoomph!* of air being forced from his lungs. Guma, still on his feet, lifted a foot and slammed it down hard on the man's neck. The man's eyes popped and he let go of his scimitar to clutch at his throat. His chest struggled to draw air into his empty lungs, but his throat was crushed and his efforts failed. Guma swept up the dropped scimitar and turned about. The comite, with the lance still slicing through its guts, was on its knees, keening piteously. Guma stepped toward it and swung the scimitar into its throat, almost decapitating it. The animal's long neck and head flopped down from the cut and its body swayed for a moment before it toppled and shuddered one last time. Guma dropped the sword and gripped the lance. With a foot against the beast's side for leverage, he yanked his weapon free.

His horse was now back on its feet, but it was staggering, dazed from the collision with the comite. Guma looked about for another, but saw none standing free and sound. Instead he saw something more remarkable—the Desert Men were fleeing the circle of wagons, headed back into the darkness from which they'd come. Not nearly as many left as had come in the attack. The ground inside the circle was covered with dead, dying, and wounded. There were more comites down than Royal Lancers, and more Desert Men than their beasts.

Just then a platoon from Company C arrived to reinforce the Royal Lancers. In addition to swords, most of them carried bows and full quivers. Guma immediately lined the bowmen up on the outside of the circle and had them fire a few volleys after the fleeing Desert Men. Even though the fleeing enemy were almost impossible to see in the predawn light, screams told of arrows that found their mark.

It took long minutes for the wounded men and animals to stop their moaning and screaming. Only then could the frightened women get over their fear and screaming, to soothe away the children's crying.

Things didn't go so smoothly everywhere. Two circles around to the left, the Zobran Light Horse managed to get into formation before the Desert Men struck, but there were twice as many attackers than the Royal Lancers had faced. The Light Horse were at the inner arc of the circle when the Desert Men began storming through the outer arc.

"CHARGE!" roared Lieutenant Haes, sword held high.

The horsemen kicked their heels into their horses' flanks and bolted forward. The Desert Men who first broke into the circle were met by kicking, biting, war horses whose momentum slammed them back and threw them off balance so they couldn't swing their scimitars to full effect. The horsemen were prepared and had better control over their weapons. They swung and stabbed with their swords, and in a moment nearly every Desert Man in the first wave was down, clutching at red-gushing wounds—or lying still in death.

Then the second wave of mixed mounted and dismounted Desert Men reached the horsemen and a wild melee broke out. The force of the attack drove the Light Horse back into the center of the circle, where they were quickly surrounded by superior numbers.

Not all the Desert Men surrounded the Light Horse, however. A score or more rampaged through the wagons, flinging chests and baskets and storage bottles from them in search of coins and gems. They ignored the cowering children and oldsters they found, but shrieked when their questing hands fell on comely women. They threw the women from the wagons and roughly herded them into a guarded group to take away after they'd won this battle.

But not all the children and oldsters cowered, and not all the women allowed themselves to be taken easily. A Desert Man died ignominiously when an ignored boy of ten plunged a whittling knife into his throat and the child's aged grandma crashed a cast-iron cooking pot on his head. Another met his match when the woman he attempted to rape clawed his eyes out, then wrested a knife from his belt and plunged it into his lower jaw, through his pallet, and into his brain. Those and a couple of others were exceptions—most of the rampaging Desert Men festooned themselves with tawdry jewels, bulged their pouches with copper coins, and successfully herded women into a group that they gleefully jeered with taunts of what was to happen to them—and more than one woman, child, and oldster died attempting to fight back.

Perhaps it was a good thing for the Desert Men that the

captured women didn't understand their language, for the women might have attacked had they known what their captors had planned for them.

The fight in the middle of the circle was a stalemate. The Desert Men had the advantage of numbers and greater freedom of movement. They were wild and fought fiercely, but their battle tactic was individual combat, where the Light Horse were disciplined soldiers who fought as teams. It wasn't until some of the Desert Men broke contact and withdrew to where they could use their recurved bows and begin bringing horsemen down with arrows—a few of which hit their own men in the dark—that the tide of battle began to turn their way.

But it didn't stay their way for long. The former sailors who'd escaped New Bally with Rammer arrived to reinforce the Light Horse. They used their cutlasses to hew down the archers, then attacked the rear of the Desert Men who had surrounded the horsemen. With the circle surrounding them broken, the Light Horse were able to wheel out of their defensive posture and attack. The Desert Men broke and ran. One of them tried to drag a woman onto his saddle before he fled and was skewered by a sword in the hand of a horseman.

A platoon of veterans who'd managed to scrape off a little of their rust since being placed in Company C reached the circle to the right of the road on the northeast just before the Desert Men swarmed into it and reinforced the Zobran Pikers, who stood alternating pikemen and archers in a line. The pikers met the Desert Men head on. Half of the lead comites impaled themselves on the waiting pikes, which were firmly butted in the ground. The archers who stood between the pikemen made swift work of the riders. The Desert Men who avoided the axe-headed spears and broke through the line found themselves faced by veterans desperate to prove to themselves that they still knew how to fight, and more desperate to save themselves and the other refugees.

The entire first wave went down. The second wave's numbers were severely depleted by the archers before they reached the questing spear points and axe heads of the waiting pikes. The veterans moved forward to stand side by side with the archers between the pikemen, protecting the bowmen, freeing them to keep shooting their ranged weapons when Desert Men made it through the deadly screen of pikes and flying arrows. The Desert Men's charge broke apart at the circle's edge and the survivors fled. The few who had gone around to enter the circle from other directions were met and cut down by veterans who hadn't moved into the line to protect the archers.

The many troops of Desert Men, who outnumbered the defending Zobrans and their reinforcements, fought the same way they fought within the groups—as individuals. They had made no provision for any group of them to reinforce another in order to exploit a breakthrough. Twenty minutes after the first group hit the not-yet-prepared Royal Lancers, the last of them was beaten off and pursued by arrows and jeers.

Nor did they coordinate their attacks well. It wasn't until several minutes after the last of the attackers from the north and east were thrown back that Desert Men attacked the Skraglanders who manned the west defenses.

Heartened by the victories of the Zobrans and determined not to be outdone by them, the Skraglanders fought with a ferocity that exceeded that of the Desert Men. The battles on the west side didn't last quite as long as those on the north and northeast before the survivors fled after their tribesmen.

In the center of the circle of circles, the recruits of Company D, who hadn't been needed in the battle, heard the battles and knew all were victories for their side. Every man of Company D had seen close-up the effects of war, all of them had lost friends, relatives, or property to war. They were all refugees from war. Yet rather than feeling grateful that they hadn't had to fight, they felt left out. Their comrades—they already mistakenly thought of themselves as soldiers—had achieved victory while they had done nothing to contribute to it. Instead they were huddled away from the fighting like sheep.

One man cried out that he wanted some of the glory of the victory. Another echoed him. A third yelled that the Desert Men weren't defeated, they were withdrawing. A fourth cried out, "Let's get them!"

They ran en masse out of the great circle in pursuit of the Desert Men fleeing to the north. Rammer tried to stop them, but he was only one man, and in their excitement the recruits ignored his commanding voice.

"Get them! Go after them!" the recruits cried as they sped through the circles of wagons. *"Kill them!"*

The soldiers in the northern circles, who had just fought off the Desert Men, were in high spirits and their adrenaline still pumped energy through their bodies and brains. They heard the cries to go after the fleeing Desert Men, cries and shouts that drowned out the roared orders of their commanders to stop and regroup, and joined the pursuit. The units on the west saw the units north of them rushing after the Desert Men and added their numbers to the pursuit. Many of the Skraglanders covering the great circle from southwest to east saw and heard as well. The Skraglanders were less well-disciplined, more individualistic, than the Zobrans. Many of them leaped on horses and raced north to be in on the kill.

Fewer than a hundred Skraglanders were left on the south to defend the caravan from the Desert Men who had watched over the coast road and were now coming their way.

"What happened?" Haft gaped at the rout of men streaming north, his voice breaking into a high register halfway through his question. "They're running after them!"

Spinner fish-mouthed wordlessly. He didn't understand what was happening either.

Rammer came running up. "Undisciplined rabble!" he roared. Even in the dim light of a false dawn his face shone red. "Those recruits, they wanted a piece of the glory. Glory! Can you imagine? *Glory!* There was no stopping them. And everybody else followed. Even troops who should have known better!"

"We need to get them back here before they get themselves killed!" Spinner said, finally finding his voice.

Xundoe stumbled up to them, his arms filled with demon spitters, and a sack of Phoenix Eggs dangling from his shoulder. "The men, they ran away before I could—" he stammered. "What am I— How— They'll get *killed* out—"

Spinner tried to calm the mage while Haft looked around to see which commanders might still be in sight. He saw none.

"We need to go after them," Haft said, "and bring them back. But we need to have someone in command here while we're gone."

Spinner was carefully taking demon spitters from the shaken mage. "I know," he agreed. "We need Rammer to go with us. Phard? Geatwe?"

"I don't see them."

Spinner cursed under his breath. "None of the officers?"

"None."

"Where's Fletcher?"

"I don't know."

"I saw him near the horses," Rammer said.

"I'll get him," Haft said. "He can command until we get back." He ran off before Spinner or Rammer could say anything.

"What do you want us to do?" Alyline asked.

Spinner paused in the middle of mounting his gelding and looked at her. Doli, Zweepee, and Maid Marigold stood with her. All looked at him expectantly.

"See to the wounded. Organize parties to collect the bodies." He finished swinging his right leg over the gelding's back and looked for Haft as he settled into the saddle. He saw him running back.

"Fletcher will see to the defenses," Haft shouted as he neared. He barely paused before clambering onto his mare's saddle. The three Frangerian Marines and the Zobran mage raced off after their troops. Each with a demon spitter slung on one shoulder. Xundoe also carried a small sack of Phoenix Eggs.

* * *

The tip of Veduci's tongue poked between his lips as he watched and listened to the hubbub and clash of arms about the camp. For a time, from when word that the Desert Men were coming first reached him until the end of the fight, he'd been afraid. He'd never encountered the Desert Men on their own territory, had only ever met their trade caravans in the root of the Princedons and the northeastern corner of Zobra. His band had met the caravans in peace and traded small goods with them—the caravans were far too strongly defended; an attack by a band the size of his would have been nothing but suicide. But like everyone who lived or moved about the fringes of the Low Desert, he knew their reputation as fearsome warriors. He was certain they wouldn't attack this caravan other than with vastly superior numbers, and he had a fair idea of how few soldiers accompanied them and how little prepared the other men of the train were for battle.

Veduci stayed away from the fighting. Now that Rammer no longer commanded Company C, it was easy for Veduci to signal the remaining men of his band and lead them to the southeast side of the great circle, away from the defenses they had been assigned to. Still, it had seemed to him that this night could well be his last.

But something happened. By means he couldn't begin to understand, the soldiers and half-trained men had beaten off the Desert Men. And now nearly all of them were chasing the Desert Men deeper into the desert!

Out there, he was sure, away from what little protection the wagon circles provided, the Desert Men would turn the tables on the soldiers and reverse their initial defeat. Then they would come back and ravage the caravan, killing wantonly and taking as slaves those they didn't bother to kill.

Veduci had no more desire to become a slave than he had to be killed.

This wasn't a rich caravan. Everyone in it was a refugee, and too many of them had left nearly everything behind when they fled the Jokapcul invaders. Much, if not most, of what they'd carried from their homes they'd had to spend along the way to buy what they needed to keep themselves alive. Still, it was a large caravan. Even though there wasn't much wealth concentrated in any one location, there was more than a modicum of wealth scattered throughout it, especially in the small chests that had been carried by the Earl of Dartmutt's concubines—and he'd made sure to know where those chests were kept. He and his band should quickly take those chests and whatever else they wished and head back west, he decided, along the top of the escarpment to another place where they could safely descend to the coastal plain, away from the Jokapcul along the coast. Then back into the Princedons and Zobra, or north into Skragland, where there still had to be refugees in flight, ripe for the plucking of whatever wealth they had.

"Yes!" The tip of his tongue snapped back inside his mouth and he nodded decisively. "Zlokinech!"

"Yes, Veduci?" His eyes were barely visible in the growing light and his teeth showed in his smile.

"You know where our women are?"

"Yes." His teeth seemed to glitter.

"And you know where bel Yfir is camped?"

"Yes."

"Take half of the men, go get our women, and meet me at bel Yfir's circle."

"Yes!" Zlokinech cackled. "Right away, boss! Can we take any of the lovelies?"

"If any will come quietly."

Zlokinech darted away, calling the names of the men he wanted to join him.

Veduci called the remaining men close. "We are going. First we are going to get riches. Follow me." He led them into the center of the great circle, toward the place the leaders of the caravan had picked for their own night's sleep.

Of all the soldiers to the north, northeast, and west, the Dartmutter Earl's Guards were the only ones who didn't chase the Desert Men. Lieutenant Armana hadn't even had to raise his voice to keep them in place. The Prince's Guards were street ruffians and ceremonial troops, not real fighting men. They hadn't been at all anxious to head toward a real battle. They were ready enough to engage in tavern brawls or to fight over the favors of a woman, but in this case, their innate fight-or-flight reaction was heavily weighted toward flight. As it was, throughout the battles, in none of which they'd participated, the only thing that kept them from running away was Armana's calm, cool voice saying, "Steady, lads, stand steady," and the severe threat they heard in that calm, cool voice.

Every one of the Earl's Guards was absolutely convinced that if they ran, what Corp—*Lieutenant* Armana would do to them would make the worst tortures inflicted by the Desert Men seem mere love taps in comparison.

So they stood their formation in a western circle of the great circle, under the fatherly—though they saw baleful—gaze of their commander.

Fletcher's heart sank as he walked the length of the southern defenses. There were so few Skraglanders left in place. Only enough soldiers to defend one circle, and not well against a determined assault. Worse, the soldiers seemed chagrined that they weren't haring off after the Desert Men with the others. The only man he found who wasn't yearning to go north was Captain Phard—and Phard had his hands full keeping any of his remaining men from joining the chase. When he reminded them that the Desert Men had left their positions alongside the road, they steadied and got ready to greet them when they attacked.

The two stood side by side, looking southwest along the road when they weren't looking at the soldiers to prevent any more of them from leaving. Neither spoke of it, but they were both aware of the Jokapcul on the beach. Seven hundred soldiers were far too many to guard five hundred prisoners; that had to be a staging area. But where were the troops headed who must be assembling there? Whether they moved west or mounted the escarpment into the Low Desert, they presented a threat to the caravan.

They hadn't heard from the Border Warders watching the Jokapcul, so they were still in place, which was to the good. Unless the Jokapcul had somehow discovered the watchers and killed them. The Border Warders were good enough at concealment to avoid detection by the invaders, but what about the Jokapcul's demons? Could the demons find the Zobrans? Birdwhistle had reported that the demons seemed unwilling to stay with the Jokapcul, but would their belief that they would starve if the Jokapcul didn't feed them overcome their reluctance and get them to tell if they discovered the watchers?

The wondering was a frustrating exercise in futility.

"I'm going to check the rest of the circle," Fletcher finally said. "See how much damage there is, and how the casualties are."

Phard grunted. He wished he could go along, but knew that as soon as he left, most or even all of his remaining men might tire of waiting for the Desert Men from the road and head north.

Fletcher went clockwise around the circle.

The casualties were collected in the makeshift hospital that Nightbird and the other healers had set up in the central area. The Desert Men casualties were gathered separately from the caravan's. Those less severely wounded were bound as well as bandaged, and held under guard by a few women and a number of older boys, all armed. Some of the injured were going to die; neither the healing witches nor the healing mages had what they needed to keep all of the most severely wounded alive. More of the Desert Men's wounded than the caravan's would die—the healers treated their own first. Men untrained in arms bore litters, carrying the dead out of the circle of circles. Their own dead they lay in neat rows for burial in the morning. The Desert Men dead were dumped with far less ceremony. They could lay unburied until their tribesmen came for them—or until the desert's scavengers scattered their bones.

Among it all, women, children, and oldsters went from circle to circle and to the hospital areas, searching for their men who had been in the fighting, hoping against hope to find them alive and well. Some found their men wounded in the hospital. Others lay cold among the dead. Most looked in vain, for their men were out there somewhere in the desert, where the sounds of battle increased as the Desert Men stopped their flight and returned to the fight.

None of the litter bearers or searchers paid any attention to the people they saw rooting through belongings in the wagon in the commanders' area of the camp.

CHAPTER
SEVENTEEN

"How goes it?" Fletcher greeted Lieutenant Armana. He sighed in relief at finding a platoon that hadn't chased after the Desert Men with everybody else. He was aware of frightened people watching him from inside and under the surrounding wagons and knew he needed to do something to ease their fear.

"It goes quietly." Armana looked at his Earl's Guards, still standing in formation, weapons in their hands—but not really ready to use them. "They wanted to run, every man jack of them. But they're good lads, they stood their place when I told them to."

Fletcher looked at the ground, which was bare of battle sign. "Did they fight?"

Armana shook his head. "The Desert Men didn't attack here." He spat to the side. "Which is just as well. I wasn't all that keen on fighting them."

Fletcher chuckled. He knew Armana meant he didn't think his men would have fought well. "Do you think it would help if I address them, tell them how much we all appreciate what they do?"

Armana shrugged. As a longtime enlisted man, he knew commanders' pep talks didn't often do much to improve morale, but they were less likely to damage morale if given by someone who had the men's respect. He thought Fletcher, as much as anyone, had the Earl's Guards' respect.

"Why not?" he answered, and led the way to the formation's front.

Fletcher stood with his hands clasped behind him, rocking

back and forth on the balls of his feet, looking over the Earl's Guards. He had to admit to himself that he'd never seen such a sorry excuse for a platoon when he was under arms in the Bostian army. It wasn't that their ranks were crooked or their uniforms unkempt; after all, they were ceremonial troops and knew how to look sharp. It was their demeanor. They were terrified, these fancy bully boys, there was no other way to put it, and not doing a very good job of hiding their fear. He was sure they knew more about fighting now than when they had reluctantly joined the caravan—Armana would certainly have seen to that. But they were untested, and none of them had ever expected to be in a real battle. The only fighting they'd ever thought to be involved in as the Earl's Guards was beating on ruffians in the streets of Dartmutt, little more than a tavern brawl. And they had just missed being in a pitched battle against warriors with a fierce reputation, and faced the prospect of a battle they couldn't avoid against either the Desert Men or the even more fearsome Jokapcul. Yet they stood, more afraid of the banty former corporal than of battle.

"Men of the Earl's Guards," he finally said, ceasing his rocking, "you've done well. Nobody ever expected you to be fighting soldiers, but you stood ready to do your duty if the battle came to you. The fight didn't come to you tonight. Perhaps it will this morning. Whether it comes again today or not, it *will* come. It doesn't matter if you are here, farther to the east or to the north. It matters not if you are to the west of here. Or," he looked at them hard, "if you are with the army that is growing around you or on your own elsewhere—the battle will come to you. When it does, I know you will stand your ground and acquit yourselves well. Because the alternative to standing is a most ignominious death, cut down from behind while attempting to run away like cowards.

"These people all around you," he waved his arm to indicate the people in and under the wagons, "all depend on you, their very lives depend on you standing fast and fighting fiercely no matter who attacks. And you will stand fast and fight the enemy. Fight him and win, because you are brave men, though you are doing something you never expected to do.

"So, men of the Earl's Guards, I thank you. And rest assured, Lords Spinner and Haft thank you as well. We all know we will be able to depend on you when the worst comes to pass."

He stood erect and, even though he didn't wear a uniform, raised his fist to his chest in salute. He held the salute until one, then another, and finally all of them thumped their fists to their chests. Only then did he cut his salute and face about.

"We'll see if I did any good," he murmured to Armana just before he marched away.

"I think maybe you did," Armana murmured to his back. "They're standing straighter and look a touch more grim than bunnylike."

Fletcher looked around at the wagons, hoping he'd given some measure of heart and hope to the refugees who needed the Earl's Guards to defend them, then turned into the middle of the great circle, where he heard a large number of people moving, to offer what comfort and guidance he could—or issue orders if necessary.

The Earl's Guards were still standing straighter and looking a touch more grim than bunnylike, listening to the not-distant-enough sounds of battle punctuated by the explosions of demon spitters and flares of Phoenix Eggs, when they heard a woman's scream.

Veduci was in the lead when he and his men reached the circle where he knew bel Yfir huddled against the night's cold. He dimly saw the silhouettes of men standing in formation and stopped outside the circle.

"Wait," he whispered, and signaled his men to lay down so they wouldn't be seen. "You," he whispered to the nearest. "Intercept Zlokinech, tell him to stay until I give the all clear." The bandit scuttled away. Veduci looked carefully to be sure the three bandits carrying the small treasure chests lay with the rest, then crouched and darted to the corner of the nearest wagon in the circle. He peered cautiously around the corner and recognized the banty silhouette of Lieutenant Armana. The Earl's Guards, he thought, and mentally snorted. He

knew they weren't real fighting men. Even though they outnumbered his men by nearly two to one, his men were practiced killers, where the Earl's Guards were mere brawlers, so
he didn't fear them. But if he and his men entered the circle,
that Armana might challenge them and make the Earl's
Guards fight. The sound of the fight might then bring real soldiers. He didn't delude himself, he knew his men wouldn't
stand their ground to fight real soldiers. It would be best if he
could find bel Yfir and quietly spirit her away.

But exactly where was she? He knew she was in this part of
the caravan, but he hadn't managed to come by the evening
before to see where she lay whatever bedroll she'd been allowed. He doubted that any of the refugees would have let her
enter their wagons—unless she agreed to share the bedroll of
an unmarried man, which he doubted she would agree to. So
she must be under one of the wagons. But which one?

He began searching.

Bel Yfir listened to Fletcher speak to the Earl's Guards and
spat in a most unladylike manner. She knew they wouldn't
stand and fight, no matter what anybody said. Had they been
men enough to fight, she and the other concubines wouldn't
have been stripped of their dignity and forced to walk like
common *trollops*—and in naught but their *shifts*, for all those
commoners to gleefully gape and laugh at!

She drew her blanket closer around herself and shifted position again, up from curling babelike on the ground to huddled half upright against a wheel. Not that changing her
position did any good. When she lay down, the very ground
leached warmth from her body. When she sat propped against
a wagon wheel or tongue, more of her was exposed to the relentless, chilling wind and the grit it bore.

She didn't *have* to be out here, exposed to the elements
with nothing more than a blanket to shield her from the cold
and wind. And the blanket was but *one* layer of wool, instead
of two layers properly filled with goose down! She *could*
have been inside that wagon over there, where the tanner's

family lay snug and warm. But only if she lay with the tanner's beastly bachelor brother.

As if *she*, the favorite concubine of the *Earl* of Dartmutt, would lower herself to laying with a mere *commoner*—a smelly, uncouth *brute* of a *peasant* with a *wen* on his face!

Why, the tanner and his family should by all that was right have vacated their wagon and *given* it to her—and taken that brother with them!

Oooh, but she would exact vengeance on those impertinent Frangerians who did this to her. Them and that *insufferably* arrogant gilded lady!

She spat most unladylike again. Gilded *lady*, indeed. Painted *trollop* was more like it!

A touch! Stiffer than the wind, smoother than the blowing sand, the touch jolted a gasp from her and spun her about, flattening her shoulders to the ground, eyes staring startled beyond the circle.

"*Hush, lady!* Don't be afraid," whispered a half-familiar voice.

Bel Yfir's eyes refocused from the mid-distance to less than two feet from her nose. She could make out no details of the deeply shadowed face before her, but the shape of the head and the hat joined with the voice to bring a name to her lips: "Veduci?"

"The very," he whispered. "Quiet. The Desert Men will return, but come and I will rescue you." He wrapped a hand around her arm and pulled as he duck-walked backward. She resisted, but went with him.

"Where are you taking me?" she whispered.

"Away—to safety. Away before the Desert Men come back."

In the distance she heard the clangor of battle. It sounded closer than it had a short time earlier. She began to straighten, but Veduci tugged down on her arm and she returned to a crouch.

"Keep low, lady. We dare not be seen."

"Let go." She tugged to free her arm. "I will go back and

get the Earl's Guards. They will obey me and kill that corporal. They will come to escort us, we will be safer with armed men." Just that fast, she forgot her earlier thoughts of the Earl's Guards' worthlessness as soldiers.

Veduci easily held his grip on her arm. "I have armed men to escort you ladies, better fighters than the Earl's Guards." He couldn't keep the contempt he held for the Earl's Guards out of his voice.

"They are sworn to protect me and the other concubines. Do you already have them? We must all go. With our handmaids."

"Yes, yes," he said impatiently. "They're all there. Everyone's waiting. Let's go." He tugged hard enough to overtip her balance so she almost fell forward.

"I want my sworn guards."

"Your sworn guards are worthless," he snarled. Now that they were far enough away from the wagons, he turned about and rose almost to his full height, pulling hard enough on her arm that she fell forward and let out a shocked squeak.

"Quiet!" He turned back and lifted her bodily. "Come along or I'll carry you."

Stunned and bewildered, she scampered to keep up with his suddenly brisk pace. In moments they closed on a shadowy mass that resolved itself into a group of people recumbent or squatting. Two or three of them moved in small jerks. Looking closer, she saw they were women—bound and gagged!

Bel Yfir screamed.

"What?" Captain Phard exclaimed when he heard the clanging of steel on steel a couple of hundred yards to his northwest. He peered intently in the direction of the noise, but saw only shadows at that distance. Were the Desert Men attacking the caravan again? Had some Jokapcul slipped around and attacked? And which refugee troops were they fighting?

He looked back along the road and saw nothing he hadn't seen every other time he'd looked—no one was coming that way.

"First platoon, on me!" he barked.

A dozen Bloody Axes broke from their defensive positions and formed up in two ranks in front of him. He swore, most of his Bloody Axes were in the fight out on the desert.

"Second platoon, up!" he barked. Two squads worth of Kingsmen trotted over and formed next to the Bloody Axes.

"Lieutenant Krysler!"

"Sir!" came the voice of a former corporal promoted to platoon commander.

"Take command here while I check out what's happening up there."

"Yessir!"

"First and second platoons, let's go!" Phard began trotting toward the nearby battle. The Bloody Axes and Kingsmen matched pace with him, one group to either side.

The Earl's Guards recognized the voice that screamed— bel Yfir, the earl's favorite! The woman they'd most been charged to protect. Unthinking, they broke ranks and ran to her aid. Lieutenant Armana roared out in his best parade ground voice for them to hold, to stand fast, but they ignored him. They may have been little more than tavern brawlers as fighting men, but they had been drilled endlessly on coming to the aid of the concubines, so they didn't hesitate in running to the rescue when they heard bel Yfir scream in distress.

Armana cursed and raced after them. Maybe they'd follow his orders when the fighting started and not all of them would get killed.

They didn't have to go far. Veduci and his people were less than fifty yards away from the circle. They were on their feet and beginning to head west when the earl's men fell on them.

"ATTACK!" Veduci bellowed. He dropped bel Yfir, whom he had bound, gagged, and thrown over his shoulder, and drew his sword. He put words to action and charged. The other bandits dropped their burdens, screamed battle cries and followed.

"Steady, lads!" Armana had shouted as he forced his way into the middle of the Earl's Guards. "Ready, *arms*!"

Some of the Earl's Guards paused in their headlong rush to flash their swords up to the ready and got on a proper line.

"At a walk, *advance*!" Armana bellowed. The Earl's Guards who had obeyed his first command obeyed this one as well. An instant later the other Earl's Guards were within striking distance of the bandits, and the bandits met them with furious steel. Several of the Earl's Guards crumpled with gushing wounds, the rest stumbled back fearfully.

"CHARGE!" Armana roared. The Earl's Guards with him ran forward and stabbed as Armana and Sergeant Rammer had drilled them. Four of the bandits were thrown back by their momentum; the swords that stung them were withdrawn, leaving gaping wounds in their wake. Armana swung his axe in a downward arc from right to left. The bandit he hit screeched to a shuddering halt, as though he'd run into a wall, then dropped like a stone, with blood spurting from the gap where his left shoulder used to meet his neck.

The Earl's Guards who had run forward and been thrown, reeling back, reacted to Armana's continuing shouted orders and fell in with the rest of their platoon. They began to use their swords the way they'd been taught in the earl's fencing training, and four more bandits fell wounded. The few remaining jumped back to regroup.

"Steady, lads!" Armana shouted. "We've got them. On my mark, advance!" He stepped forward and the Earl's Guards went with him, in a disciplined formation.

"You've got *nothing*!" Veduci shrilled back, unwilling to recognize that a rabble of tavern brawlers was fighting as a disciplined platoon and had already defeated his men.

"Now!" Armana bellowed, and his men struck again with disciplined stabs and chops, taking down more of the bandits as they tried to flee.

By the time Captain Phard and his pickup platoon of Bloody Axes and Kingsmen pounded up to the melee, all of the bandit men and five of their women lay on the ground, bleeding or dead—some of the women had picked up weapons and attacked when they saw their men down. The Dartmutt treasure chests lay where they'd been dropped, and the women the bandits had attempted to kidnap were huddled together. Someone had unbound bel Yfir and they had untied the others. The rest of the bandit women were ready to flee with their children, but had nowhere to go.

And there was no longer anything bunnylike about the blooded Earl's Guards. It wasn't a pitched battle they'd fought, nor was it against fierce warriors or skilled soldiers. But it was a deadlier battle than any of them had ever expected to be in, and they'd come through it victorious—and those who had obeyed Armana's orders came through unscathed.

The Dartmutter Earl's Guards were now more than merely street brawlers decked out as ceremonial troops.

When she saw that the wounded and dead no longer needed her attention, Alyline, with Doli and Maid Primrose in tow, inspected the circles of wagons on the southern side of the great circle, making sure the women, children, and other non-combatants were all right. Men, mostly farmers and trades-men, nervously manned the makeshift barriers formed by the wagons. There were weapons about; a few swords, some bows with filled quivers, battle-axes. But these men weren't trained in their use, and most felt more comfortable holding implements they were accustomed to: axes, cleavers, ham-mers, knives, a few scythes. Poor tools to use against trained soldiers, but, the Golden Girl thought, perhaps better to use than something unfamiliar.

"Pick up that carving knife," she said to a young woman here, "Take that knife," to a young woman there, "Pick up that cleaver, it's not too big for you," to a mostly grown farm girl. If another attack came from the south, she knew every hand would be needed, and every hand had to be armed. She picked up a short sword and hefted it. No, she thought she was more comfortable with the gold-hilted dagger in its golden sheath that angled across her belly, and dropped the sword.

She saw to it that all boys at least half grown were also armed. She knew the Jokapcul would show youth no mercy if they came. She suspected the Desert Men wouldn't either. The men shook with fear, the women shuddered with sobs, the armed boys shivered with nervous pride at the trust and responsibility they bore and were determined to defeat any enemy who came their way.

Lieutenant Krysler raised a skeptical eyebrow when the Golden Girl armed the women in the circle that blocked the road, but complimented her on her good thinking. She nodded curtly in reply, and headed to the next circle to see to its defense.

Alyline, Doli, and Maid Marigold were midway to the next circle when excited voices drew their attention back.

"Wait for me," Alyline snapped, and ran back to find out what was happening.

The Border Warder called Slice had just finished his report when she reached Krysler.

"What's happening?" she demanded.

"The Jokapcul are in the bowl," Krysler snapped at her. He turned to one of the Bloody Swords. "Go find Captain Phard, tell him."

"Yes, Corp—sir!" the Bloody Sword said, and sprinted toward the circle where Phard had taken his makeshift platoon.

"We may have our chance to find out how well these women fight," Krysler snapped at Alyline, then went to check his men.

She glared after him, jaw, fists, and shoulders clenched in anger at his disparaging tone.

"Indeed, we may!" she snarled.

Nearby, two frightened young women hugged each other and stared at her with doe eyes. She unclenched herself and waved them close. "Attend me," she said softly.

"Yes, lady," they said, and huddled close behind her, clutching the large-bladed knives she'd bade them pick up.

A moment later Hatchet, the last of the Border Warders watching the Jokapcul, sprinted into the circle. Alyline hustled to be close enough to hear his report. The two young women hurried to stay close to her.

Hatchet was heaving to catch his breath and his face was strained from his speedy run from the bowl; still, wonder showed clear on his face.

"The Jokapcul officers were haranguing their men," he

gasped. "I couldn't tell what they were saying, but I over-heard two demons arguing! One said they should leave the Jokapcul, the other said that the Jokapcul were coming at us and if they wanted to eat they had to come with them and do their bidding!"

"They're coming here now?" Krysler demanded.

Hatchet bobbed his head. "That's what the demons said."

"But you didn't actually see them start out?"

"No. I heard what the demons said and immediately came to report."

"You understood the demons?" the former corporal asked incredulously.

Hatchet's posture said he agreed it sounded improbable. Nonetheless, "They talk funny, but I could understand them, yes."

Krysler peered along the road, then looked back to where he hoped to see Phard and the rest of the soldiers. "If only we could get the Jokapcul and the Desert Men to fight each other," he muttered.

Alyline closed her eyes, wanting to withdraw completely behind her eyelids as though that would remove her from the path of the oncoming Jokapcul. But no, she knew she couldn't withdraw to someplace safe. Somehow, it was up to her to save the caravan from the Jokapcul. If only we could get them to turn north and attack the Desert Men, she thought. How could women distract soldiers from their attack, cause them to turn their direction and go into a battle they hadn't planned? A plan beginning in her mind, she quietly withdrew from Krysler.

"You!" She clamped a hand on the shoulder of one of the women shadowing her. "Go to the next circle of wagons." She pointed southeast. "Tell the fit women to join me in the first circle north of here. Bring only women who can run. Go fast."

The woman nodded and took off in a sprint.

"You, go to the second wagon circle," she said to the re-maining woman. "Tell the fit women there the same. Hurry, we have no time to waste."

She sprinted away to deliver the message.

In the circle that held the road, the Golden Girl turned and gathered all the women who looked like they could run. Once they were assembled, she rushed them to where she'd left Doli and Maid Marigold. Krysler didn't notice them leave, he was too busy seeing to the placement of the two demon spitters he had.

"Come," she said sharply when they reached the women. "We must prepare." They all scampered after her.

Alyline looked to the north during the long minutes it took for the women she'd sent for to assemble. The battle still raged, but closer to the northern edge of the great circle. She couldn't tell how it fared, but it seemed there were fewer cracks of demon spitters than earlier, and the sight of the occasional Phoenix rising on fiery wings told her Xundoe was in the thick of it.

The plan she'd thought of was audacious—and horrifying. It would work, she knew it would! And the very thought of it made her stomach crawl.

Her mind worked furiously, trying to devise an alternative, but nothing that she thought of had the certainty of her first plan. She knew it would draw the Jokapcul from their planned attack on the understrength southern defensive line and pull them toward the Desert Men. She didn't want to do it. She wanted to cringe, but the gathering women were watching her, looking to her for direction, for leadership.

She steeled herself. This was going to be harder than that morning at Eikby when she lured the Jokapcul from their camp to their deaths in an ambush. It might be worse than when Master Yoel sold her body when she was a slave at the Burnt Man Inn.

If she didn't quail in the face of something so—so—distasteful gave only the barest hint of what it was—it might work. And if the other women went with her, and if they did what they needed to do, and if they were able to run, then it *would* work.

She remembered times when Spinner fretted over all the

"ifs" in a plan, all the things that had to go right for a plan to work. He and Haft always managed to pull things off. She straightened. *If they can do it, then I certainly can!*

In a few minutes three hundred women had assembled in the wagon circle. Alyline looked at them. Some were young and coltish; some were old enough to be mothers, others grandmothers. The three hundred women ran the gamut of age and size. Some looked frightened, some nervous, some grim. But everyone gripped a blade.

Don't think about it, Alyline told herself, just do it!

Her voice rang out. "There!" She pointed at the distant battle. "Our men are fighting. There," she pointed toward the unseen bowl, "the Jokapcul are coming at us. We need to turn the Jokapcul and make them turn north, get them to attack the Desert Men! We will have to run to there." She pointed north again, to where the battle was slowly getting closer. "If you cannot run that far, leave now!" She paused. No one left.

Then she took a deep breath to steady herself and told them how they were going to do it.

Jokapcul scouts had been active in the hours before dawn. They prowled the plateau for a distance of three miles around the encamped caravan, and came as close as fifty yards to its circles. The scouts frequently reported back to the Kamazai Commanding. He knew the numbers of the Desert Men who closed on the refugee caravan. He knew how brief had been the Desert Men's undisciplined attacks against the refugees, and how they had been thrown back. He knew the losses the Desert Men had suffered, and how their chiefs struggled to get them to regroup. He knew how many soldiers there were among the refugees, and how so many of them had gone in undisciplined pursuit of the fleeing Desert Men, despite the entreaties of their commanders. He knew the battle on the desert was stalemated despite the few demon weapons the refugee soldiers had and the fierceness of the Desert Men.

And he knew how few soldiers still defended the caravan.

He was a very junior kamazai; this prisoner-guarding and staging area along the coast was by far the largest command he had yet held. Despite the size of the command, guarding prisoners and building a staging area was a demeaning task to be assigned. Why, not only did he have no cavalry assigned to his command, neither he nor his subordinate knights had horses!

A kamazai, without a horse! Outrageous!

And magic, why, they'd only given him three magicians! And he suspected they were lowly mages rather than full magicians. The higher kamazai who assigned him to that demeaning duty believed there would be no fighting, so he hadn't even provided him with proper demon weapons! The only demon his magicians had that might be useful in a battle was a recalcitrant djinn. The rest were defensive. Even the troll was more a laborer than a fighter.

When two scouts using his only Lalla Mkouma to conceal themselves had reported that bands of Desert Men warriors were camped on both sides of the road, and that the refugee caravan had attempted to bypass them via the Low Desert, he saw a chance to prove himself worthy of a *combat* command.

He would leave a hundred fighters to guard the prisoners and take six hundred fighters to make short work of the few soldiers who guarded the road south of the refugee caravan. Then they would take positions at the northern end of the defenses and wait for the ultimate victor of the battle on the desert, bloodied, weakened, and tired, to come to him and be slaughtered. He would have little use for his worthless magicians and their defensive weapons on the expedition, so he took only one, with the Lalla Mkouma and the exus.

His men were anxious to close on the caravan and do battle. Not because of bloodlust, which they had in full measure, as proper for Jokapcul fighters. Nor were they eager to fight because he commanded them with brutality and fear, which he used in full measure as proper for a kamazai. His men were anxious to make battle because he had promised them all the women they could take once victory was theirs.

He would be mounted after this victory, as would his knights. And he could assemble his own cavalry troops. He could turn *all* of his soldiers into cavalry if he wished!

And all the wealth the caravan contained, as well as the great glory of the victory, would be his.

CHAPTER
EIGHTEEN

Doli *gasped* at Alyline's plan—so did most of the other women.

"I can't do that!" Doli squealed. Her face burned. "Even when we were slaves, I never exposed myself except when I was forced to. This is . . . it's wrong to expose ourselves!"

"You haven't hesitated to expose yourself for Spinner," Alyline snapped, her face just as red.

Doli flinched as though struck. That was different. Bending over in a scoop-necked blouse and showing her breasts to strangers as a matter of "service" in an inn's common room simply wasn't the same as showing her body to entice the man she loved, the hero who'd rescued her from slavery. And it certainly wasn't the same as *this*!

Doli wasn't the only one to object.

"You *cannot* mean me!" snapped a woman in a thin gown that rippled in the light breeze.

Alyline looked at her sharply. "Bel Kyn, isn't it?"

Bel Kyn held her head high, chin jutting arrogantly. "I am the earl's concubine. You *cannot* demand such a thing of me."

Alyline gave her a steady, cold look. "In Dartmutt you may have been the earl's bed toy. Out here, you're just another woman—or a common trollop. Your choice. You *will* do what is necessary to save the caravan. Or do you want to be caned again?"

Alyline paid her no more attention, but Doli had raised a point that she realized she must address.

"When the Jokapcul come here, they will rape and torture and kill," she said loudly to the assembled women. "You know that as well as I do. We have to stop them from coming here.

"They are men. We are women. We know what men want from women." She paused while a wave of nervous titters and shocked gasps made its way through the crowd. "Yes. So we let them think they are going to get it. I know the Jokapcul will follow a woman and not stop even when their officers order them to. I know that because I've led Jokapcul into an ambush before." She looked to the east, where the sun was just beginning to peek over the horizon.

"Now strip off your clothes and let's go!"

Maid Marigold was almost as fast as disrobing as Alyline was. As soon as she was naked she faced the crowd; few of the other women had begun undressing.

"I was a prisoner of the Jokapcul once," Maid Marigold called out. "I know how they treat their captives. I will not wait here for them to come, I'd rather go out to attack them and die if I must! If one of them gets close enough to you, kill him without hesitation. When Alyline says 'Run,' run as if your life depends on it, because your life and more does!"

"Strip or I will strip you," Alyline snarled at Doli.

Doli sobbed but she shucked off her clothes and the others began to as well. Bel Kyn was the last to drop her gown. She did it reluctantly and with great embarrassment, but she did it.

Alyline held her dagger up to catch the sun's first rays. "Now let's go!" she shouted.

Three hundred naked women turned and trotted southwest, parallel to the road. In the distance they could make out, as a deeper shadow in the predawn dark, the Jokapcul troops advancing along the road.

Dawn's first light sped along the desert surface; illuminating the caravan's eastern circles, it shot across the western circles of wagons, and cast harsh shadows on the battle just north of the caravan. It filled the grass and sandy ground beyond and seemed to pause when it reached the three hundred naked women running its way, as though it wanted to romp with them. But it couldn't linger; it had to move on to shoot

sparks off the weapons and armor of the Jokapcul marching
up the road. It seemed to run onward a little faster then, as
though it didn't want to associate with those armed men. It
reached the bowl from which the road emerged and dumped
shadows in its depths, then climbed the bowl's far side and
quickly filled the land ahead as far as the eye could see.

The Jokapcul shuffled forward rapidly, at a pace almost as
fast as a trot, but less tiring. There was no great need to rush.
They knew it would be better to arrive at the flimsy barricades
when the shadows cast by the wagons weren't quite so long.
Six troops shuffled along, two in column on the road, the others in column flanking them to either side. All eyes were fixed
on the nearing objective.

Almost all eyes.

The knight commanding the left-rear troop looked out over
the desert, a landscape he'd never before seen. It didn't look
like he'd always heard deserts looked like—rolling hills of
blowing sand, with plentiful sand devils dancing among
them. Neither were there any of the thorn-studded, leafless
trees he'd heard about. Instead, the land was flat and quiet,
and there were large swaths of grass that horses could graze
on. He saw the battle a couple of miles to the north, and
smiled to himself at the surprise his troop—and the others—
would make for the victors of that battle when they returned
to the caravan. He was just swinging his gaze forward again
when movement on the desert caught his eye. He saw people
running parallel to the road, headed southwest. They were far
enough off, more than half a mile, that he couldn't make out
any detail, but they didn't look like soldiers; they weren't in
formation, and their gait seemed somehow wrong.

He growled at his sergeant to keep the troop running forward in good order, then sprinted to the head of the central
column, where the Kamazai Commanding led the force.

The Kamazai Commanding looked to his left front and
agreed, the running people didn't look like soldiers, they
looked more like refugees running the wrong way. He barked
a laugh, then snarled a command. The knight growled his
obedience and slowed to a walk until his troop caught up.

The knight stopped his troop when they reached him and pointed to the running people. They were closer now and, while he still couldn't make out detail, he was more sure than before that they weren't soldiers attempting to come around behind the Jokapcul force. He barked out a short series of commands, then led his troop, spread out on line, to where they would intercept the runners.

"Some of them are coming at us!" Doli squealed.

"Good!" Alyline snapped. She raised her voice. "Stop! Everybody, stop where you are."

Three hundred women staggered to a halt, their strung out line telescoped closed until they were in danger of becoming too closely bunched.

"Spread out, spread out!" the Golden Girl shouted. She turned them to face the oncoming Jokapcul and trotted in front of her troop of naked women. "Spread out! Let them see all of us. Hide your weapons behind your backs!" She watched while the women did her bidding, pointing to some who stood too close together, trotting here and there to push someone into line or separate women who crowded too closely together. They weren't arrayed as well as she'd like, but she looked over her shoulder and saw the soldiers not much more than a hundred yards distant.

"Look alluring!" she shouted, and turned to face the enemy, one hand planted on a cocked hip. "Smile at them!" she called out. Behind her, she heard nervous titters and anxious laughs. No one was sobbing, at least not loud enough for her to hear.

Recognition rippled through the Jokapcul and excited cries broke out in their ranks. They slowed as they gaped at the heavenly vision before them.

The Kamazai Commanding had promised them all the women they could take—and here were women offering themselves! Tall women, short women, plump and thin, and all sizes and shapes in between—and all beautiful. And they were willing! They had to be willing, they were all *naked*!

"We outnumber them," Alyline called out. "We can lure them in and kill them all before they realize their danger!

Wave to them!" She lifted her hand from her hip and waved it in *come hither* circles. She glanced side to side and saw other women waving, some hesitantly, some invitingly, though some weren't waving at all. "Keep your weapons out of sight," she cried out a reminder.

"Come to me, big soldier!" someone abruptly called out. "You're so big and strong. Come to me!"

Others picked up the call and girlish laughter pealed over the voices. "Come to me!" "You're mine!" "I want you!" "I need you!"

The Jokapcul had slowed almost to a stop when the women started calling to them. Then the calls galvanized them and they took off. Most of them dropped their weapons and stripped off their armor as they ran. A man has no need for weapons and armor when he's about to be surrounded by such willing and eager beauty—does he?

"They're ours!" Alyline shouted gleefully when she saw the weapons and armor being tossed aside. "Surround them, two or three of you to each of them!"

She fixed her eyes on the officer who trailed his men, barking and growling at them; he kept his sword in his hand and his armor fixed in place. Rolling her hips just so, she began slinking toward him. An unarmed soldier already stripped down to his loincloth grabbed at her; she imperiously brushed his hands away. He saw where she was looking, saw his commander looking back at her, and turned in search of a beauty who didn't have her eyes set on the commander. Three women reached out to him and bore him to the ground. He never saw, and barely felt, the dagger that plunged beneath his skull into his brain from just behind his earlobe.

The Golden Girl reached the officer and lightly placed a hand on his armored chest. He started to knock her hand away, but made the mistake of looking into her eyes and stayed his hand. He looked down the length of her body and back into her smiling eyes. He swallowed. Never in his life had he been so near such a beautiful woman, so golden a woman, so great a treasure. He went weak in the knees when she leaned her magnificent body against him and slid her left

arm around his waist. She closed her face on his until all he
could see was her eyes, eyes such that if a man lost himself in
them and never found his way back out, he wouldn't mind.
She moved her left hand from his waist to his helmet and
tugged it off. He placed his hands on her hips and slid them up
her body to her breasts.

His hands never reached their goal. They were halfway
there when they shot to his throat, to quench the fire that
flared there.

The Golden Girl stepped back. Fresh, red blood dripped
from the blade of the golden dagger she gripped in her right
hand. Hot blood spurted from the officer's slit throat, spattered on her face and chest.

When she was sure he was dead, Alyline turned and looked
around. The only people she saw standing were some of the
women. Everyone else was on the ground. Some women were
on their hands and knees, throwing up, some were screaming
and crying and chopping and hacking at the corpses of the
soldiers they'd slain.

"Everyone, on your feet! Line up!" she screamed. "Everyone!" She strode to the nearest woman who was stabbing and
stabbing a corpse and yanked her to her feet. The blood-
covered, naked woman squealed and struggled in her grasp,
lashing with her knife at the mutilated body that was now out
of her reach. Alyline slapped her hard enough to stagger her.
She blinked wildly when she regained her balance, then her
eyes focused on Alyline and she panted, regaining her breath.

"He's dead, you can stop killing him."

"He is?" the woman squeaked, and looked down.

"He is. Now line up with the others."

Shaken, staggering a bit, the woman did as she was told.

Alyline looked around and saw other women doing the
same as she had just done, shocking the women who were
still chopping at corpses in their mania. She gave them a moment to get into line. "Are any of them still alive?" she called
out. When nobody said yes, she asked, "Are any of us injured?" All the women were spattered, even coated, with
blood, and she couldn't tell if any of it was theirs, but none

claimed injury, not even the woman who stood bent over, massaging her throat. She waved weakly that she was all right. Another stood precariously balanced on one leg. "I don't think it's broken," she replied, and coughed out a sob of pain.

Alyline looked back to the main body of Jokapcul. They had stopped their advance on the caravan and were looking at the women—but they weren't moving north.

"Gather swords, chop at the bodies!" she ordered. The women darted about, picked up dropped Jokapcul swords, and started hewing.

The Kamazai Commanding shot occasional glances to his left front, watching the troop he'd dispatched closing with the running refugees. When the troop slowed, he growled a curse. Were they cowardly to hesitate like that before refugees? They started running again and his jaw dropped. They were now far enough away that he couldn't see clearly, but it looked like his fighters were throwing away their weapons and stripping off their armor as they ran! He roared out for his force to halt and carefully watched what was happening. The troop closed with the refugees, and nearly everyone, fighters and refugees alike, tumbled to the ground. Were they engaged in hand-to-hand combat, grappling like a mob? Then they started rising, but not all of them. Some ran about doing— something. Then light flashed off blades as the standing people chopped at those on the ground. There were more people chopping than there were fighters in the troop!

The kamazai's observations were interrupted by the knight who commanded the left front troop, the troop nearest the— whatever it was that was happening out there. He had a fighter with him. The fighter dropped to his knees in front of the kamazai and bowed his head.

"Kamazai," he said when the commander acknowledged him, "this lowly fighter has the sharpest eyes in my troop." He nudged the fighter with his foot. "Tell the kamazai what you told me."

"Kamazai," the fighter said in a croaking voice, "those refugees are all women. I think they killed our fighters."

The Kamazai commanding looked at him in stunned disbelief for a few seconds, then lifted his gaze to the distance. Yes, they looked more like women than like men. And nowhere did he see a glint of sunlight on metal-studded armor. Suddenly he was both frightened and enraged. He roared a command, and his entire remaining force, all five troops, turned from the caravan and raced toward the people in the desert.

When the troop peeled off, the light was wrong for Captain Phard to make out where they were headed. He'd sped back to the road-blocking circle when the runner Lieutenant Krysler dispatched to him gave his report—but not before detailing people in the circle held by the Earl's Guards to guard the bandit women and take care of the Dartmutter women the bandits had attempted to abduct. He ordered Lieutenant Armana to come with him and bring his platoon. Armana had fixed his men with a steely look and told them they were heading into a fight. They had swallowed and jittered nervously, the exuberance from their victory over the bandits melting away, but they went with their commander.

Captain Phard wondered what was going on when the entire Jokapcul body stopped still more than half a mile distant; that was much too far away for them to deploy into assault formation. He was bewildered when the entire force took off to the north. He curled his hands around his eyes to sharpen his focus and scanned the landscape north of the road.

There! There were people running north! Where had they come from? Who were they? Then he noticed something much closer.

"Where are the women?"

Krysler looked about, surprised at the question. "Lady Alyline was here, she must have taken them."

"Were they armed?" Phard asked, feeling a bit sick.

Krysler didn't know, but one of his men said that he'd seen the women gathering knives and other bladed weapons.

Phard groaned. That must be it: Lady Alyline had gathered a troop of women and taken them out to maneuver around behind the Jokapcul and catch them from the rear when they launched their assault. Such foolishness! Now the Jokapcul had seen them and were in pursuit. The women must realize they were no match for trained soldiers who outnumbered them by—he looked carefully to estimate numbers—two to one. Then he blinked. Where was that first troop that had left the main Jokapcul force to go north?

He gasped. The Jokapcul paused where he estimated the women had been when the main force began its pursuit. *Damn the distance!* He couldn't make out much detail, but it looked like the Jokapcul were examining the ground at their feet. Could it be the women had wiped out an entire troop of Jokapcul? *No!* That was *impossible*! And if they had, how many of the caravan's women lay dead on the desert?

He watched, wracked with anguish as the women ran north, toward the battle between their soldiers and the Desert Men, with five hundred Jokapcul in hot pursuit. The distance was too great for him to attempt to catch up with the enemy and attack them from the rear. Even if it hadn't been, he knew there were so many of them his men would all die in the attempt to save the women.

The women were doomed!

Each chop of a sword sprayed blood into the air and splashed more red onto the naked women, until they almost seemed garbed in tight red shirts and leggings. Alyline hurried around the field, checking the bodies, and breathed deeply in great sighs of relief when she saw they were all men. None of the women had been killed! She'd hardly been certain her desperate plan would work. But it had, far better than she had dared hope, and she was giddy with joy.

But two of the women—*only two!*—were injured, and she had to see to them.

The throat of a widow from a Bostian farm was badly bruised. "I killed him," she croaked. "I sliced off his manhood

before he died." The smile on her face when she said that
would have frozen the heart of any man.

"Are you able to run?" Alyline asked, concerned.

"Nothing wrong with my legs." She swallowed, and it was
obvious her throat was painful.

"Yes, but can you run? It takes wind as well as legs to run."

"Talking hurts, but I can breathe all right."

"Good. Start now." Alyline pointed north. The widow nodded and took off.

Alyline found the woman with the injured leg sitting alone,
rubbing her ankle.

"Can you run?" she asked as she removed the woman's
hands from her ankle and gently probed it.

"I don't think so," the woman said nervously. She nibbled
her lower lip as she looked south to the watching Jokapcul.

"I don't feel any jagged edges, so it's probably a sprain rather
than a break," Alyline said calmly. "What is your name?"

"Cwen."

"Cwen, we have about a mile to go when they come after
us. If you can't run, they'll catch you before we reach safety.
So you have to stay here and play dead." She smiled wryly,
looking at the young woman. "You're covered with blood, so
if you lay still they'll believe you are dead.

"Now lay down, I'll put bodies on you. That way you'll
look like you were killed by whoever is on top of you."

"Do you think it will work?" Cwen asked fearfully.

"It will if you lay still."

"All right." She trembled violently.

When Cwen lay on her back, the blood made her look like
she'd been butchered. Alyline dragged two bodies on top of
her; one facedown along her length, the other across that
body's back. She studied the small tableau for a moment; it
needed something else. She looked around, wondering what
she could add to the display.

"Stop!" she shouted to a woman nearby who was hacking a
body to pieces. She went and wrested the sword from her. The
woman's breath came in gasps and her face had a greenish tint.

"That's enough, go sit down with your head between your knees." The woman looked at her vacantly. She slapped her, hard. "Did you hear what I said?"

"Wh-what?"

"Go over there. Sit down and put your head between your knees."

Dumbly, the woman did as she was told.

Alyline watched her for a moment, then went back to the tableau. "Don't move," she instructed the lame woman. Without warning, she lifted the sword and plunged it into the lower back of the top body.

Cwen screamed.

"Be quiet! I didn't even touch you." She studied what she'd done. The sword went all the way through the body, but not far enough. She gripped its hilt and leaned her weight on it. The blade slid all the way through and its point stuck into the ground.

"Remember," she said to the nearly panicked woman, "don't move when the Jokapcul come. They'll believe you're dead and leave you alone."

"I will," Cwen said, but her soft words went unheard.

"Alyline!" Doli screamed. "They're coming!"

The Golden Girl looked to the south. The Jokapcul were now running their way. "Let's go!" she shouted, pointing north. She waited until everyone was moving, then spoke to the injured woman.

"They're coming, they'll be here in a few minutes. Remember, *don't move!*"

"I-I'll try." But she spoke to empty air, Alyline was already running.

The women had nearly a mile to run, but they had a half mile lead on the Jokapcul. Many of them were frightened. Many? Nearly all. The Jokapcul chasing after them were terrifying enough by themselves. So were the Desert Men they were running toward. Most of them were still uncomfortable about running around naked, uncomfortable knowing that soon more men—including men they knew—were going to see them naked. And smeared with blood. Alyline had a hard time making them pace themselves; unchecked, most of them would sprint until they were exhausted, then be caught and slaughtered. She raced from sprinting woman to sprinting woman and grabbed them to slow them down.

"Slow down, they aren't going to catch us," she panted. "We want them close behind us when we get there." She had to slap a couple to get their attention.

Doli was near panic herself, but she calmed when saw what the Golden Girl was doing. After a moment she began doing the same herself. So did Maid Marigold. Shortly after, several more women were racing to catch and slow down the quickly tiring sprinters. She did her best. By the time they were halfway to the battle on the north, they were in a group running at an easy pace. Women with stronger legs or wind helped women whose exhaustion was slowing them down.

The Jokapcul, running faster, steadily narrowed the gap.

When the women were about seventy-five yards from the battle between their caravan forces and the Desert Men, they began yelling to attract their attention.

The Jokapcul paused when they reached the site where the women had slaughtered the men of an entire troop. The sight of their butchered comrades enraged them. Women had done this! *Women!* They needed no urging when the Kamazai Commanding urged them on. What they had been planning to do with the women of the caravan once they were theirs no longer mattered—now the women were going to suffer severely, then die painfully.

The Kamazai Commanding and his subordinate knights bullied the fighters to keep their formations instead of rushing forward the way they wanted to. Soon they were close enough to see the women clearly. Then the men's eyes opened wide and their pace increased, despite the roared commands of the Kamazai Commanding, and the lines of the troop formations grew ragged.

The women were *naked*! Oh, they would have fun with these women before they punished them!

Their attention was so fixed on the bouncing female flesh

they were gaining on that they didn't look beyond to see the other danger they approached.

The battle had raged since before dawn, and they were tired, all of them. Blood trickled from wounds on many of the fighters on both sides. Bodies—of the dead, the severely wounded, and those too weary to continue—were strewn about the battlefield, which had shifted south to barely a hundred yards from the nearest wagons. The Desert Men still had the advantage of numbers, but the soldiers from the caravan had the advantage of disciplined tactics. When they first clashed, the soldiers arriving piecemeal were cut down individually by the wild Desert Men. But once the soldiers arrived in force and got organized, they stopped losing.

The fighting in the predawn darkness was chaotic, groups of soldiers or Desert Men moving here and there in search of foes, or individual Desert Men running about looking for someone to kill. There were few casualties, since targets were hard to strike and most blows missed or caused only minor wounds. Still, the Desert Men were more familiar with melees, and all of them were experienced fighters; many of the soldiers weren't. Only the infrequent use of demon spitters or Xundoe's Phoenix Eggs prevented a Desert Men victory.

Since the rising of the sun, the fighting had slowed; the men were tiring. The Desert Men were too proud to run from a fight where numbers were in their favor, and wise enough to remain close to their foes so their enemy could not use its demon weapons effectively. And with the Desert Men staying so close, the soldiers couldn't easily withdraw to the relative safety of the wagon circles—unless they were willing to leave their dead and wounded behind, which Spinner, Haft, and Rammer refused to do.

So there wasn't enough din of battle to block the men's ears to the yelling and screaming of the women. Indeed, exclamations of surprise from the combatants who looked quickly became louder than the battle as more and more of the men turned toward the yelling and, for the moment, were distracted from the fight.

The Desert Men were so stunned by the sight of so many blood-covered, naked women running at them, yelling and waving their hands in the air, that they didn't notice how many of those waving hands held daggers, knives, and cleavers. The soldiers were equally stunned, though they were farther from the women. With the increased distance, and the Desert Men blocking their view, none of them recognized the women; they had no better idea than the Desert Men who they were or where they'd come from.

Alyline looked back and saw that the Jokapcul were only fifty yards behind, nearly as close as the Desert Men the women were approaching. The Desert Men hadn't seen the Jokapcul yet; they were too busy gawking at the women. She gasped for extra breath and began yelling to the women.

"Point backward, point at the Jokapcul!" She put action to her words and screamed "HELP!" as she flung a pointing hand back. To her sides, other women did the same.

A few of the Desert Men directly to her front shifted their eyes and saw the rapidly approaching Jokapcul. They cried out in alarm and readied their weapons to meet the new threat. Then the women were among them.

All around, Desert Men who hadn't yet noticed the Jokapcul grabbed at women and pulled them close, pawing at breasts and flanks and more intimate places. The women screamed and twisted and pointed. Then the Desert Men let the women go and braced for the assault. Anyone who didn't pay attention to the screaming and pointing was stabbed, if not by the woman he held, by others who came to her rescue.

When the women reached the back of the mass of Desert Men, some paused to slash or stab at backs, or hack at hamstrings. A dozen or more of the struck Desert Men dropped, but one spun about, wrenching the knife in his kidney out of the hand of a Zobran innkeeper's daughter. Swinging his sword backhanded, he split her head. Another staggered forward, jerking away from the cleaver blade that had chopped into his shoulder. He turned around, swinging his own sword. The wound in his shoulder was deep enough that he had no strength to put into the swing. His strike failed to take off the woman's arm, but his blow broke the bone and knocked her to the ground. Enraged at being struck from behind by a naked woman, he switched his sword to his left hand and plunged it into her chest. Three or four other women fell to avenging blades, but the rest made it safely away from the Desert Men, who were now fully engaged with the Jokapcul.

"Spinner, Haft! It's us!" Alyline screamed as she led women toward the soldiers.

So did Doli.

"Haft, where are you?" Maid Marigold screamed.

Other women took up the cry, calling out the names of husbands, lovers, fathers, brothers.

All about, male voices replied to feminine voices and exhausted women were reunited with their men, who were nearly as exhausted.

Rammer was the first to recover. "Get those women back to the wagons!" he shouted. "The rest of you, collect our dead and wounded. *Move!*" He looked around for Spinner and Haft, who should have given the orders, and snorted—Spinner was trying to dislodge Doli's arms from their death grip around his neck, and Haft seemed too interested in forcing breath into Maid Marigold's lungs to notice what was happening around him.

Alyline heaved a couple of times to regain her breath after the long run, then screamed, "Back to the wagons!" Her piercing voice caught almost everybody's attention, and women began running for safety.

"Dead and wounded!" Rammer bellowed again.

Spinner finally managed to free himself from Doli's arms and pushed her toward Alyline. "Take her," he yelled at the Golden Girl, then looked around the battlefield. "Gather the dead and wounded!" he roared.

Maid Marigold gave Haft a last, quick kiss and bolted. He slapped her bare bottom as she took off, then echoed Spinner and Rammer in calling for the soldiers to collect the casualties.

In a few minutes all but a few of the dead were behind the

barricade and the women were scrubbing the blood from their bodies. Other women and girls, who hadn't gone out to challenge the Jokapcul, scurried to shoo away staring men and to fetch clothes for the naked women as the rivulets ran red and the ponds pooled with blood.

CHAPTER
NINETEEN

At first the momentum of the Jokapcul gave them an advantage; the Jokapcul were tired from their long run, but not as exhausted as the Desert Men. But their advantage didn't last. As more Desert Men joined in the fray, the advantage shifted again. But that advantage didn't last either, as the Desert Men found themselves up against the same difficulty they'd had with the disciplined troops from the refugee train—their individual combat tactic wasn't sufficient to defeat the teamwork the Jokapcul employed against them. Men fell on both sides, but more of the fallen were Desert Men than Jokapcul.

Haft stood leaning forward with a foot propped on a wagon tongue, watching the battle a couple of hundred yards distant. He gnawed on his lower lip and his fingers twitched against the tube of the demon spitter that hung down his side by its shoulder strap.

"I think we should do something to even the odds," he growled.

"I think we should just let them fight it out between themselves," Spinner replied. He stood erect and more relaxed alongside Haft, relieved to be out of the fight and in the relative safety of the wagon circles.

"When the Jokapcul win," Haft said, "they'll come after us. You know that, don't you?"

Spinner reluctantly nodded. "Yes."

"The Desert Men will run from them soon. They didn't run

from us because of these." He slapped the tube of the demon splitter.

The small door on the side of the demon spitter popped open and a tiny, bald head poked out. *"Eh! Wazzu doon'?"* the diminutive demon demanded. *"Mak doo mush noiz! Zhakim doo mush!"*

"Oh, sorry," Haft said quickly, taking his offending hand from the tube. Quickly, he fingered a small container from a pouch on his belt, popped it open, and removed a grape-size pellet, which he offered to the demon.

"Vood!" the tiny demon piped, and clutched the pellet to its chest. *"Oo gud'ghie!"* It let go of the pellet with one hand and reached out a gnarly arm to pat Haft's hand, then popped back into the tube. The door slammed closed behind it with a sharp *snick*. A crunching, gurgling liquid noise, which Haft had no desire to investigate, came out of the tube.

Spinner shook his head at the proceedings. He didn't understand the affinity Haft and that tiny demon had for each other.

"That's it!" Haft exclaimed, looking at the tube and rubbing it. "We can do it with these!"

Spinner shook his head. "They're too far away."

Haft snorted. "That's no problem. I'll take three or four men with demon spitters. We'll get close enough, get off a few quick shots, then run back here." He began looking around for men with demon spitter tubes. "We'll be back before they know what's happening to them!"

Spinner studied the battle with a worried expression. "Then what?"

"What do you mean, 'Then what?' 'Then what' is the Desert Men wipe out the Jokapcul and run away—they'll be afraid we'll use the demon spitters on them if they attack us again, so they'll run." He pushed himself off the wagon tongue and darted toward two men he saw with demon spitters. As soon as Haft told them what he wanted, they took off in different directions. When he returned, Fletcher was heading for Spinner.

"It's bad, but it could be worse," Fletcher said, getting right to it. "We have more than a hundred casualties accounted for—half of them are dead. Most of the dead are from Company D"—Sergeant Rammer's recruit training company, the first to race after the Desert Men when their initial assaults were thrown back. "More than twenty men are still unaccounted for—and half a dozen of those crazy women seem to be missing."

Spinner and Haft both grimaced at the news, but, yes, it could have been worse. Those recruits had been fatally stupid when they ran in hot pursuit of the Desert Men—they were lucky they hadn't all been killed. Now, though, the survivors might forever be worthless as soldiers.

"What missing women?" Spinner asked. "Alyline told me they didn't lose anybody, or even have any serious injuries when they trapped that Jokapcul troop."

Fletcher shook his head; he didn't know. "Maybe some fell when they were running, maybe some lagged behind and got caught." He looked out at the battle and shuddered. "Maybe they're still out there."

"That settles it," Haft swore. He unslung his demon spitter. "I'm going to do it." He looked in the directions the men with the demon spitters had gone and saw them returning; one brought another man with a demon spitter, the other brought two. He twirled a hand above his shoulder, signaling them to join him, then stepped over the wagon tongue and walked briskly into the open desert.

"We're going a hundred yards," he said without slowing his pace when the armed men caught up. "Then we'll spit at the Jokapcul until the demons demand to be fed. Have a pellet ready for them. We'll shoot again. Have another pellet ready, I don't want the demons abandoning us because they didn't get fed promptly. Any questions?"

"Don't you want us to spit at the Desert Men?" one asked.

He shook his head. "Leave them alone. They'll run as soon as they can. It's the Jokapcul we have to kill. Let's go!" He began running; he knew he had to hurt the Jokapcul, and hurt them badly, before they defeated the Desert Men. Within a minute the six of them were in position.

The Desert Men used their normal tactics; whether they milled about on their own or were packed together in tight masses, they fought as individuals. The Jokapcul, four troops abreast with one troop back in reserve, formed up four ranks deep and fought as teams. If a man fell, the man behind him stepped forward to take his place. The Jokapcul were slowly but steadily pushing the Desert Men back.

"Now!" Haft ordered, and they aimed at the back ranks of the Jokapcul troops, squeezing the levers that told their demons to spit. They didn't wait to see where the spit struck, but immediately shifted their aim and shot again. After the third shot, they paused to feed the demons.

Haft took advantage of the brief pause to look over the battlefield. The fighting had stopped and everyone was staring in their direction. Small clouds of sand and dust, the remains of the explosive spit-strikes, drifted away from the Jokapcul. There were about a quarter fewer of them still standing. At this range, little more than a hundred yards, he could make out writhing bodies on the ground—and still bodies as well.

Then it was time to pummel the Jokapcul again.

Close to half of the Desert Men broke and ran when the demons' spit erupted among the rear ranks of the Jokapcul, but most soon realized that the demon spitters were only striking their foe, and they stepped back to give Haft and his men a clearer field of fire. The Jokapcul began fleeing before the second fusillade of the second barrage was spat, and its eruptions tore apart what had been their front ranks.

Because of the casualties they'd suffered at the hands of the caravan's women, the Desert Men, and the demon spitters, the Jokapcul fighters now consisted of fewer than three full troops.

When the Desert Men saw the men with the demon spitters retiring to the wagons, they let out ululating war cries and raced after the Jokapcul.

The Jokapcul had marched several hours before dawn, prepared to attack a weak foe. Then they had run at speed across a mile and a half of open desert into an unexpected battle, and along the way found a troop of their own men slaughtered. They had been close to winning their unexpected battle against the Desert Men, by now they should be chasing the survivors of the enemy they had fought. Instead, they had been set on by a different force with demon weapons that killed or wounded far too many of them. They were terrified and running for their lives, headed directly to where they thought the bowl was with its egress to the coastal plain and their camp. The entire day had been wearing, and many of them were weakened by wounds. The wear of the long day, the shock of finding an entire troop slaughtered by the naked women, the long running they had done, the battle they had fought, and the terror they now experienced, combined to exhaust them further. They weren't in formations now, and nobody helped anyone who couldn't keep up on his own. Those who lagged behind were caught by the Desert Men and summarily cut down.

For their part, the Desert Men were tired, probably more tired than the Jokapcul. But they didn't run in terror, they ran in jubilation. The fastest among them began to catch up with the slowest Jokapcul and cut them down.

Slowly, they became aware of a drumming behind them. A few Desert Men twisted their heads to see who was coming. It was more of their own—racing on comites.

Two hundred mounted Desert Men sped through their running tribesmen, arrowing at the Jokapcul, screaming bloodcurdling war cries. The running men did their best to echo the war cries, but they didn't have wind to spare.

The lead Jokapcul staggered to a stop—they were at the edge of the escarpment, not the bowl with its safe passage to the coastal plain. The rest shuddered into them, some with force enough to throw men over the lip of the cliffs. The fastest fighters hadn't been racing *toward* the bowl, they had been running *from* the demon spitters and Desert Men; their thought hadn't been a route off the plateau, it had been putting distance between themselves and the men who were killing them. Most of them had dropped their weapons along the way to lighten their loads and speed their feet; many had flung off their armor. They were easy kills for the mounted Desert Men, who left some alive for their running tribesmen to finish off. Some of the Jokapcul, seeing that kneeling with arms spread in surrender wouldn't save them, chose to jump over the escarpment or attempted to skitter down its face. They lived little longer than those of their companions who had died under the swords and arrows on the plateau.

When the Desert Men had begun chasing the fleeing Jokapcul, Spinner snapped to Fletcher, "Take men out there, retrieve the rest of our casualties!" Then he ran along the outside of the great circle, watching in astonishment. Haft's plan had been audacious, but Spinner knew that sometimes audacity achieved more than anybody could expect. He snorted when it flashed into his mind that Haft's plan wasn't even half as audacious as Alyline's—and it was the success of Alyline's plan that allowed Haft's plan to form and succeed.

Haft caught up with Spinner by the time he reached the wagon circle from which the women had gone into the desert. So did Rammer. Alyline, Doli, and Maid Marigold, all dressed again, joined them there along with Xundoe. The Jokapcul and pursuing Desert Men grew smaller in the distance.

"Cwen!" the Golden Girl suddenly remembered.

"What?"

"One of the women, she was injured and couldn't run, we left her out there!" She flew into the desert, the morning sun shooting golden sparks off her clothing. Spinner raced after her.

"You men," Haft called to a lancer squad, "come with us. Bring extra horses." He didn't wait for them, but began running after Spinner and Alyline. So grim was he with concern for the woman left where they'd slaughtered the Jokapcul troop that he didn't hesitate to mount the horse a lancer brought to him. Alyline and Spinner also leapt onto horses.

"Cwen! Cwen! Are you all right?" Alyline called as she neared the killing field. There was no reply.

The men pulled up short, looking at the gruesome ground. The grass and sand were splashed liberally with red; mangled, mutilated bodies, some naked, many nearly so, were strewn about. One of the lancers bent low over the side of his horse and retched. The horses shied from the gory battlefield, and the men struggled to hold their skittish mounts steady.

A body moved. Alyline leaped off her horse and ran to it, splashing through gore and unmentionable bits of flesh. "Cwen!" she cried as she tugged at the topmost Jokapcul corpse.

"I'm here, lady." Cwen's voice broke with sobs. "I'm here. Please help me!"

"Here," Spinner said, appearing next to her. He gripped the sword that pinned the body to the ground and yanked.

Haft shouldered his way in and threw the body aside. But when he bent to remove the next body, Alyline shoved him away. Then she spun and pushed at Spinner, who was also reaching to fling aside the dead Jokapcul.

"Get away, both of you. She's naked! You can't look at her."

"But—"

"No buts! You cannot look at her now, I won't allow you to see her like this! Give me your shirt, one of you."

Spinner gaped at her for a few seconds before tugging his shirt from under his belt.

Haft was faster and handed his over.

"Now go over by the horses and keep your backs turned until I say you can look. Your men too."

Spinner and Haft backed off a couple of steps before they turned around. They made their way back the same way they'd come.

"You men, turn around, don't look," Haft bellowed at the lancers. He scowled fiercely.

The lancers gladly complied, welcoming the opportunity to look away from the mangled bodies.

Alyline had to kneel at Cwen's side and push the second body off the hidden woman. As soon as she was freed, Cwen sat up, threw her arms around Alyline and cried into her neck.

"I was so afraid, lady, but they didn't see me," she burbled.

"Then I was here for so long and nobody came, and I thought you forgot about me or maybe the Jokapcul caught you and you were all dead and I'd lay here trapped until the Jokapcul came back and found me and—" her voice melted away into uncontrolled sobbing.

"It's all right, Cwen," Alyline said soothingly, brushing her hands comfortingly over the woman's head and shoulders. "You're safe now. You were very brave, and I came for you. The battle's over."

She stopped talking and just held the crying woman for a few minutes until her sobs eased a bit, then said softly, "We can't stay here, we have to go. Here, I have a shirt for you. Let me help you put it on." She gently pulled Cwen's arms away and pulled Haft's shirt over her head, helped her put her arms into the sleeves.

The massacre at the plateau's edge ended. From the wagon circles, those who watched could see the main body of the Desert Men heading north, angling away from them. At the same time, a small group rode comites toward the circle that sat astride the road—to parley, it seemed. In response, Spinner, Haft, and their companions trotted there as well. Captains Phard and Geatwe had already repositioned their men to meet an attack from the west and southwest and waited with their commanders.

There were six in the Desert Men party. They stopped more than a hundred yards from the wagons. Four of them sat in line behind the other two. The feathers of spread eagle wings on a staff, carried by one who stopped slightly to the rear of the leader, fluttered in the breeze. All kept their weapons sheathed or slung. The leader held his open right hand up, the fingers splayed.

"It looks like they just want to talk," Rammer said.

Spinner nodded. Haft grunted. Both were wary.

"I will take a squad of Prince's Swords and accompany you, Lord Spinner," Captain Geatwe said.

"No," Captain Phard interjected. "A squad of Bloody Axes must go with Sir Haft."

Spinner and Haft looked at the company commanders, who were glowering at each other.

"We'll take two Prince's Swords and two Bloody Axes," Spinner said.

Haft nodded.

Phard and Geatwe scowled, but they nodded and turned to order the escort.

"What language do they speak?" Haft asked.

Nobody knew for certain, but Rammer said, "Most likely they understand the Dartmutter dialect." They sent for Plotniko in case they needed him to translate.

In moments the seven were mounted and trotting toward the waiting Desert Men. They pulled up twenty yards away.

The desert chief's standard bearer called out something in a language none of them understood.

"I don't understand," Spinner called back in Zobran.

"Neither do I," Haft added in Bostian.

The standard bearer spoke again.

"That's Dartmutter," Plotniko said. "His accent's thick, but I can understand him."

"Tell him you will translate," Spinner said.

Plotniko called out in the same language.

The desert chief used his knees to move his comite forward, his standard bearer advancing with him.

Spinner and Haft also advanced, along with Plotniko.

"Who is your chief?" the standard bearer demanded in Dartmutter after the chief spoke in his own language.

Plotniko translated that into Zobran, and the reply, "We are," from Spinner and Haft.

The chief sneered, then spoke again.

The discussion, passing through three languages, was halting with only the desert chief speaking his native tongue.

"The Low Desert belongs to us," the chief said. "You do not belong here."

"We were in danger, we only wanted to go around the danger."

"What danger? I saw no danger to you."

"There was a strong Jokapcul force on the shore. They would have attacked us if they knew we were there. And we couldn't move inland, since there were strong bands of Desert Men along the road."

"You were too strong, we would have let you pass our ambush unharmed, that's why our men who you watched were relaxed instead of in position to attack the road."

"You *saw* our scouts?"

"Your scouts are good in their own forests, but these lands are ours and we are better here. We are also better on the adjacent lands. As I said, this is *our* land. You trespassed, that's why we attacked you this morning. But you helped us defeat the Jokapcul. For that, you may return unmolested to the road. Stay below the Low Desert and we will leave you alone."

"Thank you. Going on the coast road will be easier for us. We will stay here for a few days and then gladly leave."

"*No!* You will leave now!"

"But we have wounded. We must care for them, give them time to heal before they are strong enough to move."

"You should have thought of that before you trespassed. The sun is not yet halfway up the sky. You will begin leaving by the time it reaches zenith. You will be gone from the Low Desert by the time the sun is halfway down the western sky."

"And if we can't start moving that soon?"

"Then three times as many Desert Men as attacked you this morning will attack, and you will all die." He studied them for a moment, his gaze lingering on Haft's bloody shirt.

"What your women did to the Jokapcul," the desert chief continued, "is nothing to what *our* women will do to any of you we take alive." He gave them a last glare, turned his comite north, and galloped off with his retinue.

"Start moving by noon?" Haft asked, astonished. "Is he insane?" He plucked at his shirt, drawing it away from his body.

"No," said Plotniko. "I think he's just the chief of a warrior tribe that doesn't like strangers."

"I think we should go like he says," Spinner said. He shuddered in memory of what the Desert Man said about their women.

"But our casualties!"

"We'll cope."

Fletcher's party brought back the rest of the bodies and a few severely wounded who had been overlooked when the soldiers withdrew from the fighting between the Jokapcul and the Desert Men. Three of the dead were women from the band Alyline had led out, as were two of the severely wounded.

Nightbird and the other healers objected to the move since there were thirty men and two women too badly wounded to travel safely.

"Use the aralez and the land trow on them!" Spinner snapped. "Have Xundoe help you, he's got two of the aralez."

"The demons can heal the surface wounds well enough," said the Eikby healing magician, who had three aralez and a land trow. "But it takes time for the deeper injuries to heal. On the outside a man can look like he has nearly healed wounds, but inside he might still be severely injured."

"If we don't go now there will be many more people too badly wounded to move."

The healers grumbled but agreed. They did manage to extract one concession: they and the worst wounded would be the last to leave. They set the aralez to work. The tiny doglike demons went from wound to wound, licking them, and in minutes visible signs of wounding lessened. Then a healing magician went from severe wound to severe wound, carefully watching his land trow. The demon, resembling a half-size man, lifted bandages here and there. Occasionally it poked a hand into an uncovered wound and probed about inside the injured flesh, then removed it with an ethereal glowing green something that disappeared altogether when it flicked it from its fingers.

Round and round went the five aralez and the land trow, licking and probing, and the wounds improved each time, until the healing demons had done all they could do.

By then most of the caravan was in motion and the lead wagons almost at the bowl. The healers quickly but carefully loaded the worst of the wounded onto the wagons and prepared to leave. They were able to move without a gap growing between their wagons and those in front of them. Watching from a distance, the Desert Men sat ominously on comites.

SECOND INTERLUDE

GUARD DOGS OF HELL

University of the Great Rift

Department of Far Western Studies

The Editors,
Unnatural Skeptic
Dear Sirs or Mesdames,

Having perused several issues of your journal on the shelves of the bookstore newsstands in College Center, the town outside the campus, I have concluded that *Unnatural Skeptic* is indeed precisely the type of "popular journal" in which it would be advantageous to publish several of my papers which, for reasons of style or powerful academic disagreement, are not suitable for publication in *The Proceedings of the Association of Anthropological Scholars of Obscure Cultures*, in which scholarly journal more than three hundred of my papers have been published.

Therefore, I take pleasure in submitting for your consideration my most recent paper, *A Factual Analysis of Guardian Demons Known or Suspected to be Currently Called Upon by the Jokapcul Armies Engaged in Attempted Conquest of All the Lands of the Continent of Nunimar for the Purpose of Debunking Certain Common Misconceptions*.

As I do suspect it would be presumptuous of me to assume that you are fully aware of my identity, I offer the following *c.v.*:

I am a tenured professor of Far Western Studies, of which department I have twice had the onerous privilege of being chairman, at the University of the Great Rift, with which institution of higher learning I am quite certain you are more than familiar. Indeed, I suspect that more than one of your editors is a graduate of this esteemed University, as the brief biographies of several of the scholars whose papers you have published note that they have degrees from this University, though it appears that none are currently members of the faculty. As noted above, I am the author of more than three hundred papers published in *The Proceedings of the Association of Anthropological Scholars of Obscure Cultures*. In addition to those scholarly papers, I have in recent months had papers published in *James Military Review Quarterly* and *It's a Geographical World!* I hesitate to add—but as I have been informed that when approaching a journal for the first time one should name all those journals in which one has previously been published—that a horribly bowdlerized version of a paper of mine was published in *Swords and Arrows Monthly*; fortunately, they misspelled my name (their typesetter left out the apostrophe in my patronymic), so the bowdlerization has to date caused me no professional embarrassment.

I look forward with near unseemly anticipation to your acceptance of my submission. Might I inquire as to the size of the honorarium you offer?

> I am,
> Scholar Munch Mu'sk
> Professor

From the Desk of the Editor

Unnatural Skeptic

Mangle,

Hey, it's that Mu'sk guy again! He must never read mastheads, or he'd know *UnSkep* and *James* have the same publisher and editorial staff! Guess that would explain the "Dear Sirs or Mesdames" salutation.

There's some good crap in here, but you have to dig to find it. Give it a title that doesn't read like an abstract and an opening 'graph that people'll be willing to read, cut the redundancies, and knock out most of the superlatives. You'll have to do some cut-and-paste to put it in an order somebody other than an academic can follow. I trust your judgment—but you know that.

Send him a your-firstborn-child-is-ours contract, minimum rates, he'll be happy.

Thieph

Deadly Hauntings

By Munch Mu'sk, Professor

It was deepest night as the strongly armed, thousand-man raiding party approached the lines of the Jokapcul outpost. Not even starlight penetrated to the ground through the cloud cover. The commander stopped his force and called his officers and most senior sergeants together for a final review of the assault plan and to make sure everyone was in the proper place. When all declared their readiness, the commander dismissed them to return to their men and make ready. But before any of them made it back to their units, the night was rent with the bloodcurdling cries of men being most horrifically rent apart. The few who managed to escape, bloodied and bruised, told of being assaulted by trolls who used their inhuman strength to rip limbs and heads from bodies; huge Black Dogs with jaws able to rip flesh and bones from living bodies; mauth dhoog that lay in wait and tore feet and legs off unwary passersby; and sang-mun that drifted foglike among groups of men, killing immediately each one they touched; and all the while imps sped chittering through the raiders, nipping bits of flesh from their bodies. A thousand-man raiding party was thus rent to nothing.

The astute reader will certainly have noticed that the above paragraph gives neither place nor army nor approximate date of the action; three strong clues that it is apocryphal. Indeed, although that description of an imaginary action demonstrates popular misconceptions about the named demon types, anyone familiar with the reality of said demons knows it is all wrong. To the ordinary person who goes through life without benefit of higher education, or at least wide reading or extensive travel, such descriptions seem credible because they hear the word "demon" and are ready to ascribe any manner of attribute to the creatures, no matter how unlikely or, even, absurd.

The beings collectively known as "demons" are, in fact, not supernatural but rather natural creatures of uncertain origin, though granted not native to any known land in the world. (This scholar is currently engaged in intense study with other eminent scholars to determine just where in the cosmos, known or unknown, the "demons" are actually from.)

Indeed, many of the so-called demons are quite helpful, not in any way "demonic." The troll noted in the above description is such a case. While trolls are strong enough to tear a body to parts, they are mostly used for chores that require strength, stamina, and utter lack of imagination. The troll-generated lights that luminate certain palaces, mansions, and some of the better inns are an example. Imps make marvelous fence wardens and never—well, almost never—skitter about individually far from their houses, which are commonly mounted on fence posts for the purpose of warding the fences.

Which is not to say that *all* demons are beneficial. The sangmun in the apocryphal scenario that began this paper has no known function other than to kill trespassers, which it does through the expedient of inflicting on them a disease so severe that no medicinal demon this scholar is aware of can cure it. The mauth dhoog doesn't lie in wait, but rather scampers about looking not at all dangerous, but rather like a friendly, albeit scruffy-in-need-of-a-bath-and-combing cocker spaniel. When the unwary traveler comes upon a mauth dhoog as it guards its road or path at night and attempts to befriend it, the mauth dhoog attacks with fang and claw, with invariably disastrous results for the traveler. The mauth dhoog's cousin, the Black Dog, is in no way friendly looking, and one's first sight of this demon is commonly one's last sight of anything—the Black Dog does indeed run about chomping and rending flesh and bone.

In most places warded by such guardian demons, one finds warning signs placed for the benefit of friends of those who use those guardians, otherwise the guardians would kill friend and foe alike quite wantonly.

The most obvious warning signs are the well-known imp houses, domicile of imps warding fences. The imp house is prominently mounted on a fence post and wires trail from it to the primary strands of the fence, which in turn normally have lesser strands connecting one to another to expedite movement of the imps from one strand to another. Commonly, signs are hung to warn of the presence of guardian demons. Such signs may have painted on them a pictogram identifying the guardian demon in local residence. Illiterate persons who come upon a written sign lacking in pictograms should nonetheless take heed and assume that the sign is evidence of a nearby guardian demon. Passing such a sign is unwise. In warfare, which is where guardian demons are most likely to be used, the signs are often more subtle than painted signs. They can be a rock cairn, runelike markings on a stone, blazes on a tree, or other seemingly random, easily misunderstood signals. On occasion, parallel signs demark a safe passage through the warded area.

Some, or even many, demons are quite amenable to control by ordinary persons, but that is not true of most guardian demons. Guardian demons, as a class, are in their own way more dangerous than the demons that inhabit weapons. The weapons demons, in the normal course of events, only attack on a specific order given by the person wielding the weapon and only injure or damage that to which they are directed. Guardian demons, to the contrary, once set in place, make their own determinations as to what or whom to attack, and will generally cease only when the magician who emplaced them recalls them. There are exceptions to that rule, of course. There are documented instances in which a guardian demon simply disappeared from the area it warded. No one knows why that happens, but any demon may, upon occasion and without any obvious reason, depart from whomever it has been in service to. There are also reports of demons attacking the very magicians who emplaced them in their warding positions, but those reports currently lack confirmation from proper investigatory authorities.

There are certainly other guardian demons, including such exotica as the Green Woman and gytrash; watchers such as banshees, dryads, elves, and various sprites are not, in the sense used herein, guardians, since they do not attack, but rather merely give notice to their magicians or others. For a more exhaustive survey of guardian demons one might peruse the relevant chapters in the six volumes of Scholar M. V. H'one's masterful *An Encyclopaedic Overview of Well-Known Demon Types*.

Unnatural Skeptic is proud to welcome the eminent Scholar Munch Mu'sk to its stable of doubting Thomases. Scholar Mu'sk is the author of literally hundreds of scholarly papers in addition to articles on less arcane subjects. He is past chair of the Department of Far Western Studies at the University of the Great Rift.

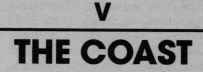

V
THE COAST

CHAPTER
TWENTY

Silent met them outside the entrance to the bowl.

"Where were you?" Haft snapped at him. "We could have used you this morning." He had bathed and put on a clean shirt. He was riding with the point squad, scouting a route for the train to follow that didn't take them too close to the road and the remaining Jokapcul on its other side. Borderers were scouting the flank to give warning in case the Jokapcul moved away from the shore—or if more showed up.

Silent grinned. "Nah, I was watching, you didn't need me. Where's Spinner?" He turned his massive horse—he called it a pony—to walk alongside Haft's.

"He wants to know where you were too," Haft retorted, hardly mollified.

"He most likely does. But I've got something to show you and him."

"So I'm here. Show me."

"No," Silent said with a shake of his shaggy head. "I want to show you both at the same time. You're going to love it."

"A surprise," Haft said sourly. "Just what I need, another surprise." He leaned over his horse's shoulder and spat. "I've had enough surprises in the last day, thank you very much!"

"But you'll love *this* surprise."

Haft shifted on his saddle to look around. "Where's that wolf?"

Silent grinned. "He's guarding the surprise."

It was near dusk by the time the end wagon was a mile from the entrance to the bowl. Even though they hadn't cleared the plateau by mid-afternoon, the Desert Men had merely watched from a distance and made no move toward the laggardly caravan. Spinner called a halt for the day. Again they circled the wagons for the night, though this time the wagon circles were strung out along the line of march rather than in a circle of circles. Haft, Spinner, and Rammer saw to the posting of sentries. They watched north as well as the other directions; Haft had half a dozen Border Warders scale the face of the escarpment to keep an eye on the plateau. The evening meal was the first chance Spinner and Haft had to get together. Silent was almost bouncing with excitement over the surprise he had, but held his secret while the others made their reports.

"None of them died today," Nightbird said of the severely wounded she and the other healers hadn't wanted to move. "But three are so weak they may not last this night."

"The others?"

She shook her head. "None of them are safe yet, they need days of rest. Even then, they might not all make it."

"But we're too near the Jokapcul on the shore to stay here," Spinner said plaintively.

Nightbird spread her hands in helpless resignation. The most severely wounded needed rest or they might die, but she understood that if they stopped, there was too great a chance that more people in the caravan would be killed or severely wounded.

Captain Phard said his Borderers scouting the right flank reported that the Jokapcul guarding the prisoners along the shore seemed agitated but didn't appear to be preparing to move. They hadn't been reinforced yet either.

Rammer reported that nearly half of Company D wanted out. Interestingly, most of the wounded understood why they had suffered as they did, and as a result, as soon as they were well enough, they wanted to stop and complete their training. He had begun recruiting more men into the training company, but there was greater reluctance among the untrained men after the debacle caused by Company D's pursuit of the Desert Men before dawn.

Other than that, food and water were in good supply and morale was improving now that most of the people thought they were out of any immediate danger.

"We aren't out of danger," Spinner said to that. "Not by a long way."

"I know," Zweepee replied. "I'm only reporting what the people in the caravan are saying."

"What are we going to do about the bandits?" Haft asked.

"The unwounded women have been scattered through the train and people are keeping an eye on them," Fletcher said. He looked at Nightbird for a report on the wounded bandit, but Alyline spoke first.

"That doesn't mean they aren't dangerous," she snapped.

"You showed that clearly enough this morning," Fletcher said with a sickly smile. "Women can be *more* dangerous than men. That's why *these* women are being watched *very* closely.

The Golden Girl nodded curtly.

When Alyline didn't say any more, Nightbird said, "Only three of the bandits survived the fight with the Earl's Guards. They aren't among the most seriously wounded, but their injuries are bad enough that they won't be able to cause mischief for some time. The wounded women are cowed. They seem eager to join with the rest of us and forget about their pasts."

Spinner snorted. "Can gray taburs change their stripes?"

Silent had slipped away during the reports. He came back as Spinner asked his question and interrupted. "Is it my turn yet?" he asked, bouncing on the balls of his feet.

"Yes," Haft said impatiently; he'd had enough of gray taburs. "It's your turn. Now what's your big surprise that had to wait?"

"Look what I found!" Silent said, raising his hand. It held the end of a rope that trailed into the shadows behind him. He gave the rope a very sharp yank. Three men tied to it tumbled into the fireglow.

They were Jokapcul magicians, bound and gagged. Wolf came with them and stood guard.

There was a moment of stunned silence as all gaped at the captured magicians. Then cacophony.

Silent grinned for a few moments before he held up his hands to stop them.

"Wolf and I ranged pretty far looking for Jokapcul following the caravan. All we saw was more refugees headed along the road, or trying to find routes into the Low Desert, or even headed for the Eastern Waste. When we got to where you stopped, I just had to wonder why. Then you turned off the road and I *really* wondered. So we took a look and found the Desert Men. I didn't think those two bands of them were enough to send you onto the Low Desert, so I looked farther." He shook his head. "Those Jokaps sure do treat their prisoners nasty. Their camp along the shore looked even worse than the camp they had in Eikby, so I figured you weren't sure of the Desert Men, and the Jokaps decided you.

"Something told me the Desert Men wouldn't let us cross their desert, not this many of us—especially when I saw the ones watching the road move after you. So you'd have to come back down after the fight. But we still had to be concerned about the Jokaps. I'll tell you true, *I* was concerned when I saw most of the Jokaps head for the Low Desert during the night. But then I thought the Desert Men were just as likely to fight them as fight you, so I put that concern out of my mind and took a closer look at what they'd left behind.

"What I found was a hundred bully boys who looked like they'd beat on anybody weaker than them but wouldn't stand and fight. And I saw these three arguing among themselves." He smiled benignly at the captured magicians at his feet and clucked his tongue at Wolf, who curled a lip to expose a rending fang.

The magicians shuddered; they were watching Wolf, not the people.

"I—" Wolf growled at him, and he nodded. "Sorry, Wolf. *We* watched for a time." Wolf nodded and returned his attention to the captive magicians. "We didn't see or smell any sign of demons." He shook his head and lightly nudged one of the prisoners with his toe. Silent was so big that the light nudge rolled the magician over. "These three were dumb enough to be outside the camp perimeter, with no soldiers nearby to protect them.

"So we walked in and took them into custody. Then I went to—"

"Wait!" Rammer, who didn't know the giant as well as the others, interrupted. "How could you just walk in without them raising an alarm? Why didn't they turn demon weapons on you?"

"Well, we didn't *exactly* just walk in. We sort of snuck up behind them. They were arguing so much they couldn't hear us." Wolf shot him a look and he quickly added, "Not that they would have heard Wolf anyway." Satisfied, Wolf went back to guard. "Anyway, Wolf jumped on one and held him down with his jaws on the Jokap's throat while I grabbed the other two and banged their heads together. While they were dizzy from that, I tied them up and gagged them. I gagged the other one before Wolf let him go, then I tied him too. They're just little bitty people, it wasn't any problem for me to carry them to where my horse was.

"Wolf stood guard over them while I went to see what was happening above the cliffs. I couldn't figure out *why* you were fighting the Desert Men in the open up there to the north." He held up a hand to stop their hurried explanations. "I know now. Haft told me this noontime."

He peered at Alyline. "At the time, I sure wished I was closer, so I could see just what it was you and those women did to that troop sent out to intercept you." He grinned. "Now that I know what you were doing, I *really* wish I'd been close enough to see clearly." He ignored the glare she gave him and looked appreciatively at Doli and Maid Marigold, causing both of them to blush deeply.

The men gaped at him, aghast, and Silent looked back at them with mock surprise. "I didn't see the bodies afterward, so I don't know what they did to the Jokaps." He turned very serious for a moment. "I will tell you something, though. Among the peoples of the Northern Steppes, there is one thing warriors are afraid of—and that is being taken alive and given to the women." He grinned. "That's partly the reason we're such fearless warriors—we'd rather die in battle than be captured and given to the women." He looked at Spinner, Haft, Fletcher, and Xundoe in turn before continuing. "Surely you remember what these three," he indicated Alyline, Zweepee, and Doli, "did to that Jokap we captured in our first battle together."

Nobody replied to that. The four men to whom Silent made his last remark looked uncomfortable; the three women stared stone-faced into the distance.

"We could have used you up there," Haft said, to change the subject.

"You did fine without me. Thanks to the Golden Girl and her brave women." He gave her a short bow. She nodded, but still looked disapproving. "Now, what do you want to do with your present?"

"That," said Spinner, looking sternly at the bound and gagged prisoners, "is a very good question. I wonder what languages they speak." They'd been making do with Zobran, with an occasional word or phrase in Skraglandish or Frangerian thrown in. None of the magicians had shown any sign they'd understood a word.

"Sit them up and ungag them," Spinner ordered. He gave the trio a moment to work their jaws, then asked in Frangerian, the universal trading language, "What are your names?"

They looked at him uncomprehendingly.

Haft asked the same in Ewsarkan, his native tongue, with the same result.

Zweepee asked in Bostian. Nothing. Spinner tried Apianghian, his native tongue. The response was blank looks and incomprehensible guttural jabbering in Jokapcul.

Rammer asked in Matigule, the language of the Kingdom of Matilda, the homeland of the Dark Prince who led the Jokapcul on their campaign of world conquest.

Understanding flared in the eyes of one and he opened his mouth as though to speak, but one of the others barked sharply and he kept still.

"Now we know what language they speak besides Jokapcul

dog-talk," Rammer said calmly. "Do any of you speak Matigule?" he asked the others. None did. He took a deep breath
and blew it out. "This is going to be a long night. By your
leave?" He nodded to Spinner and Haft. "Let's separate them,
I'll have to question them individually. Who's good at inter-
rogation?"

Spinner, Haft, Fletcher, Silent, Doli, Zweepee, and Xundoe
automatically glanced at Alyline, then away, and did their
best to look like they were pondering the question, some with
greater success than others.

"Looks like it's you then, Alyline," Rammer said.

"Give the prisoners to the women," Silent murmured
softly.

Alyline nodded slowly. "As you wish. May I suggest we go
someplace private?"

Rammer stood. He crooked a finger at the magician who
had stopped the one who showed recognition of Matigule and
said in that language, "You, come with me." Then to Spinner
in Frangerian, "Keep the other two apart, I don't want them to
agree to a story they'll both tell."

It wasn't as long a night as Rammer had thought it might
be. It made him queasy, but he let Alyline tease the magicians
with her golden dagger—and he stopped her before she did
any real damage.

They interrogated the first magician, then the one who'd almost spoken, then the third, and the second one again. The
first and third maintained the pretense of not understanding
Matigule. So well did they deny it even when Alyline played
on them with her dagger that Rammer came to think that
maybe they didn't know the language. The other magician
broke fairly quickly the first time he was questioned and admitted he spoke Matigule but denied knowledge of anything
else, saying only that they had been sent to help watch over
the caged prisoners on the shore. He also said he had no idea
why there were more fighters guarding the prisoners than
there were prisoners.

The first time through, Rammer told him he was lying, that

the first magician had already confessed they were going to kill the prisoners and then invade the Low Desert. The second magician denied it vociferously. The second time through, Rammer told him the third magician had said that the Low Desert invasion force was due to arrive in two days, and that it carried execution orders for the second magician, who the other two believed was unreliable. That, and a little bit of sharp-bladed encouragement from the Golden Girl, was all it took for him to talk freely.

"They don't have enough shipping to carry everything they need up the east coast," Rammer reported when the questioning was over. "So they're assembling thousands of people along the north coast of Princedon Gulf to use as porters, to haul supplies up the coast of the Inner Ocean to Handor's Bay. This force is the first of five or six guard battalions they plan to use to keep the slaves in line. He said he doesn't know where other prisoner camps are except along this coast, and I believe him.

"He said something else I found interesting. He said the soldiers who are still guarding the prisoners are upset that their commander took most of their strength, and they're afraid because he hasn't come back yet. I asked how he could know that when he was captured soon after the main force left, and he said the soldiers had been talking about deserting if their commander wasn't back by midday. He claimed the hundred that are left aren't combat soldiers, they're laborers who were given quick training in arms for this guard duty. He thinks if they desert, they'll kill the prisoners before they go. He also said they're waiting for azren, whatever they are."

Doli yelped at the mention of azren, and Zweepee covered her face. Even Alyline grimaced.

"What *are* azren?" Rammer asked.

"Demons that will kill slaves if they try to escape," Spinner said. "They," he nodded at the three women, "and Fletcher were guarded by an azren when they were slaves."

Rammer grimaced.

Haft ignored the remarks about the azren and studied Rammer solemnly for a moment when he finished his report. Then he looked at Spinner. "We couldn't have taken them before, not when all seven troops were there," he said. "We can certainly take one troop."

Spinner nodded. "Azren. Yes. We need a reconnaissance patrol. Silent?" He looked around; the giant was nowhere to be seen.

Spinner shook his head, then had Captain Phard send a squad of Borderers to recon the Jokapcul camp. When the patrol returned they made plans.

They didn't pitch the fancy tents for the command group that night; Spinner forbade the people to erect any tents at all. "We won't have time to break them down in the morning," he insisted. Nobody argued strongly. Those who didn't have wagons to sleep in made due with blankets on the ground or erected rude shelters.

Maid Marigold found two smallish fan trees that stood with their flat sides a few feet apart and used lengths of vine to lash their upper parts together, to make a sort of foliate tent that was open at both ends. She borrowed an unused blanket to close one of the ends. The shelter was big enough for two people to lie cozily together.

"I made us a shelter," she whispered to Haft when they finished making the plans for the morning. She leaned her chest into his shoulder, cradling his arm between her breasts.

He moved away from her. "I'm just going to wrap myself in my cloak and sleep next to Spinner," he said gruffly. "I have to go before dawn." He paused and swallowed. "I don't want to disturb you when I get up."

She reached for him and grasped his arm in both hands. "You won't disturb me. And it's all right even if you do."

"No. I won't be able to sleep with you beside me—I mean, I'll be thinking about what I have to do in the morning."

"I'll help you go to sleep, Haft."

"No. It's better—"

"Haft, I need you with me tonight." She sobbed and her voice broke. "After this morning, I really need you with me tonight."

He yanked his arm from her grip. "This morning," he spat. "That's why I can't sleep with you tonight."

She gasped and the back of her hand shot to her mouth. "Haft, *no*! What do you mean?"

"You took off your clothes and went out there where everybody could see you naked and you *killed* men, *that's* what I mean!" He remembered the gore on the desert where the women had slaughtered the Jokapcul just after dawn and shuddered.

Maid Marigold's shoulders started shaking. She covered her face with her hands and cried into them. "But that's *why* I need you tonight!"

"Don't do that!"

"What?" she wailed.

"Stop crying. I can't stand watching a woman cry."

"I—We—We *had* to do that. If we didn't we'd probably all be dead now!"

"You *killed men*! Women aren't supposed to kill. *Men* fight and kill, not women!"

"But we *had* to!" She wailed again and half turned away from him.

"Please don't cry." Her sobbing wrenched at his heart, but he still saw those butchered Jokapcul in his mind's eye.

"Why not? You don't care about me! I had to do something horrible to save us, and you don't want me anymore because of that. All you can think of is the horrible thing I had to do!"

"That's not true. It's just—it's just—"

"You don't care, you'd rather be dead than let me save you."

"But— Please, Maid Marigold, don't cry, please stop crying." He reached a hand to her, and she turned farther away from him.

"You don't care!"

"I care, I *do* care!" He stepped to her and folded his arms around her. She stiffened, but he drew her in closer. "I care. I care very much," he murmured into her hair. He rubbed her shoulders and caressed her head. "There there," he murmured. "There there."

They stood like that for another moment or so, then she relaxed and sagged into him.

"Where's the shelter you made for us?" he whispered.

"Over there," she said softly.

"Let's go."

She didn't let him take his arms from around her as she led the way to the shelter. He held her tenderly as they lay together in the snug confines of the makeshift tent and gently kissed her tears away. Eventually she stopped sobbing. But he didn't close his eyes until he was certain she was asleep. Just that morning she'd participated in a very vicious slaughter—she was a killer, he thought. How could he trust her now?

"You can't go," Rammer had said. "You're the commanders, you can't go."

That's right, Sergeant Rammer, Haft thought, *we* are the commanders! *We* decide who goes and who doesn't, not *you*! *You* don't tell *us* we can't go! Go ahead, let Spinner stay back if he wants to. This was *my* idea, I'm going! His problem with Maid Marigold from the previous night was driven completely from his mind by the job at hand.

Haft fingered a pellet out of his belt pouch and lifted it up to the Lalla Mkouma on his shoulder. She tittered into his ear as she daintily took it from his fingers. From the sound, it seemed she popped the pellet into her mouth and swallowed it whole. He was glad he didn't see that—the pellet was thicker than her throat. She burped delicately, made an "excuse me" noise, then licked his fingers clean; her tongue tickled. He lowered his hand and shook his fingers. Fingertips were supposed to *do* the tickling, not *be* tickled.

There was no point in looking to his sides to see if Balta, Farkas, and Acel were in position. Even if he could have made out silhouettes in the predawn dark, they carried Lalla Mkouma on their shoulders. The voluptuous little she-demons were spinning their gowns, rendering themselves and the men they rode invisible. He would rather have had three of the Skraglander Borderers—or even three of the Zobran Border Warders—with him on the mission, because they were better at stealthy movement, and better bowmen. But the Bloody Axes who claimed him as their leader had been furious at the idea that he'd go off and leave them behind, so he relented and brought them instead of three of the stealthy border soldiers.

He hoped they were in position there and hadn't gotten separated because of the invisibility. But they needed the invisibility. Though it was still full night when they left the encampment at the foot of the escarpment, the sun had just risen and the coastal forest wasn't dense enough to prevent them from being seen as they closed on their objectives.

He hoped they were as good with bows as they claimed. They were to silently take out the two observation posts the Borderers had found beyond the perimeter of the Jokapcul camp before the Jokapcul could give an alarm. There were four men in each post, hence four men on this mission.

To his left, the Jokapcul guards were barking harsh orders at their prisoners. Someone screamed. Perhaps a prisoner was being punished for some infraction.

There! He heard low voices arguing on the other side of a thin screen of stunted trees to the right front. "Shift left," he whispered uncertainly to his sides.

"Zhem wizz uzz," his Lalla Mkouma tinkled into his ear, reassuring him that the trio of Bloody Axes was with him.

The screen of trees may have been thin, but the observation post behind it was strong. A two-foot-tall wall of horizontal posts strong enough to stop arrows lay to the front and sides of a hip-deep, twenty-foot-long trench. Embrasures left in the wall allowed the soldiers in the observation post to look through the tree-screen—and to shoot arrows or demon spitters if necessary. The only direction from which to safely approach the post was the rear, the direction of the Jokapcul camp. But the post was three hundred yards from the camp, barely shoreward of the road, and they didn't need to circle nearly so far behind it.

Haft placed his feet carefully so he wouldn't step on any of the dry, fallen branches from the trees, and softly, so they wouldn't slip or crunch on the loose, sandy soil. His fingers lay alongside the firing lever of his crossbow, not on it—an accidental discharge would be catastrophic to the plan—but he still moved it as his head swiveled, kept it pointing where he looked. The bulk of the long demon spitter tube slung across his back was comforting.

When he had rounded the corner and was facing the back of the observation post, he clacked his tongue in imitation of the wingless harbird, then raised the crossbow to his shoulder.

"Zhem wizz uzz," his Lalla Mkouma chimed cheerfully.

As the Borderers had reported, there were four Jokapcul in the post—unless more were lying out of sight in the trench. None of them were looking through the embrasures. They were close together in heated, though muted, conversation.

Haft couldn't understand a single syllable of their growling speech, but he'd been a Marine long enough to know how soldiers talked and what they talked about. From their body language alone, he was pretty sure that two of them were arguing that they should simply take off—desert—"right now," and the other two were insisting that they wait a little longer to see if the rest of their unit returned from above the escarpment.

He took a deep breath to steady himself and aimed his crossbow. This was the tricky part. They'd only practiced it twice, and he wasn't fully confident of their ability to get it right.

"Now," he said softly.

Each man in the line he couldn't see had his assigned target. Balta shot an arrow from his short bow; arrows from the bows of Farkas and Acel followed before the first arrow was halfway to its target. Haft fired his crossbow. Farkas's target, the second man from the right, staggered when the arrow hit him in the neck. His mates only had an instant to look dumbly at him before the arrows shot by Farkas and Acel struck the men on either side. Haft's bolt punched into the helmet of the man on the left at almost the same instant.

The first falling man hadn't even made it to his knees when the last man to be hit sagged and began dropping.

Haft and the Bloody Axes were running as soon as Haft fired, lowering their bows and reaching for their knives as they went.

"Get visible," Haft ordered as they ran. Careful not to stab or poke their tiny woman-demons, they rubbed the thighs of the Lalla Mkouma, who stopped spinning their gowns and made them visible again.

They reached the trench and dropped in. Knives flashed as they made sure the sentries were dead.

Haft heaved in a deep breath and let it out in a whoosh. It had worked; no alarm was raised.

"Hide me, Lalla Mkouma," he said. She began spinning her robe again and he vanished.

An instant later the Bloody Axes also disappeared. There was a brief scrabbling noise as they scrambled out of the trench and headed west. Thirty yards away they stopped and listened. Nothing, just the usual sounds of the coastal plain, punctuated by normal camp noises from the Jokapcul along the shore. They continued west, toward the other observation post, half a mile distant.

The post was just visible through breaks in the fan trees when Haft's Lalla Mkouma flattened herself against his neck and hugged him tightly. He froze and braced himself for Farkas to bump him from behind, but Farkas had stopped as well, as had the other Bloody Axes at the Lalla Mkoumas' warnings.

On their left, a trail dotted with the hoof marks of deer and the tick marks of smaller animals angled toward them from the direction of the gravelly beach. Heavy footfalls and a throaty rumble came from the game trail. Haft cautiously backed up, probing behind himself with one hand. He felt Farkas, who also backed up. Five yards from the game trail, perhaps still within sight of a sharp-eyed watcher in the observation post, he stopped and squatted with his crossbow ready.

A troll appeared, lumbering along the game trail in a manner befitting a far larger creature. The throaty rumbling came from the troll's mouth—it looked for all the world like it was

softly singing to itself. A step or two beyond where Haft had
stopped, the troll abruptly stopped humming and moving. It
peered around at the ground, raised its head and sniffed the
air. It backed up and looked down where Haft had frozen,
bent far over and snuffled at the ground. Then it lifted its head
and looked directly at him.

"*Hoo zheer?*" the troll rumbled, peering suspiciously.
"*Wazzu whanns?*"

Haft didn't answer, didn't even dare breathe.

The troll took a lumbering step toward him. It somehow
seemed more curious than threatening. "*Hoo zheer? Wazzu
whanns?*" it asked again.

Haft swallowed and aimed his crossbow—not that he
thought a bolt would do any good against a troll. He'd heard
they had skin as tough as the hardest armor.

His Lalla Mkouma suddenly let go of his neck and bounded
off his shoulder, landing on his crossbow, bearing it down.
She flipped off it and scampered to the troll, squealing,
"*Vrend! Vrend!*" She leaped onto the troll and hauled herself
to its face. She grabbed its ears and held her face to its eyes.
"*Zhem vrendz!*" she insisted to it. "*Komm'ee, zee oozeph!
Vrendz!*"

"*Vrendz?*" the troll rumbled, crossing its eyes to focus on
the Lalla Mkouma's face.

"*Vrendz!*" she insisted again. "*Gud'ghiez.*" She let go of
the troll's ears and back-flipped to the ground. "*Komm'ee,
zee oozeph.*" She gripped the troll's hand in both of hers and
hauled. The troll followed, bent low to accommodate her
slight height. She tugged the troll to Haft's right side and
slapped the palm of a tiny hand against the blade of his axe.

The troll looked at the half-moon blade, then slowly lifted a
finger that seemed to have too many joints and traced the rampant eagle engraved into the face of the blade.

While it was doing that, the Lalla Mkouma clambered onto
its back and piped at Haft, "*Givvum han!*" He hesitantly extended his hand to her. She took it and placed it on top of the
troll's head. "*Skritz!*" she commanded.

Wide-eyed with wonder, Haft scratched behind the troll's

ear. The troll's skin was so raspy it wore at his fingertips. But the troll purred when he began scratching, so he kept it up. But if he had to do it again, he thought, he'd try to wear a chain-mail glove.

The troll removed its hand from the axe blade and reached up to take Haft's wrist. He pulled it from behind his ear and shifted his grip from wrist to hand. *"Vrend!"* it rumbled at him. *"Oo gud'ghie! Wazzu whanns?"*

The Lalla Mkouma chittered at the troll faster than Haft could follow. It twisted its head around to look at her while she talked. When she finished, it seemed to lose itself in thought for a moment.

"Tha' dru?" it finally asked.

"Dru!" she piped.

The troll looked up at Haft, down at his axe, back up to his face. *"Mee gittum eep,"* it finally rumbled. It reached around to lift the Lalla Mkouma from its back and placed her on Haft's shoulder. It ran off with far more grace than the ponderous lumbering Haft had first seen.

"What . . . ?" Haft asked around the sore fingertips he was sucking. He didn't understand what had just happened.

"Way'um," the Lalla Mkouma said. *"Oo zee zoon."*

Haft looked back and was surprised to find the Bloody Axes still invisible. "Don't ask me," he said softly. "All I know is we wait for developments. Look alert." He faced front again.

A few minutes later he saw two dark shapes barreling through the fan and bumber trees toward the observation post. He was pretty sure one of them was the troll. The other, in the quick glimpse he had, looked like a large, black dog. There were yips, a yell, and a scream from the observation post, all cut off almost before they could register on the ear. A moment later a huge black form leaped from the post and bounded toward them—it was the troll mounted on the back of a very large dog so black it was almost invisible even in the daylight.

"Dun!" the troll announced when the dog stopped a few feet short of Haft.

"Zhank oo!" the Lalla Mkouma on Haft's shoulder chimed.

The troll hopped off the dog's back; they both twisted about and sped westward.

"Where are they going?" Haft asked.

The Lalla Mkouma shrugged eloquently. *"Goam'aay,"* was all she said.

Haft took a moment to compose himself before ordering his patrol on to the observation post. The four sentries lay mangled at the bottom of the trench. They were quite dead.

"Let's get them," Haft said.

Two of the Bloody Axes took off toward where Spinner waited with the assault force. Haft and the third went to join the blocking force.

CHAPTER
TWENTY-ONE

The plan was simple. Spinner, with Company B, moved into place two hundred yards west of the beach encampment. Captain Phard led the Skraglanders and others of Company A into position a couple hundred yards east of the prison camp. As soon as he got word the observation posts were taken out, Spinner would lead the Zobran horse platoons of Company A in a cavalry charge through the Jokapcul camp. They wouldn't stop to engage any enemy who wanted to stand and fight, just hew their way through and try to set the Jokapcul to flight. At the west end of the camp they would spin about and head back east, engaging any enemy soldiers who hadn't run. While the horsemen were racing the length of the camp, the foot soldiers of Company B would charge into the camp and kill any Jokapcul they reached before they met the returning cavalry. The Jokapcul who ran west from the initial charge would disastrously encounter the infantry of Company A, which lay in wait for them to the west.

And just in case some Jokapcul fled north, Captain Mearh had Company C stretched out just south of the road. The re-constituted Company D was left to guard the caravan.

Simple plans have a better chance of success than complex plans do—there are fewer things that can go wrong.

That doesn't mean *nothing* can go wrong with a simple plan.

The knight left in command of the single troop guarding the prisoners had been much chagrined when the Kamazai Commanding ordered him to stay behind with his troop. He became even more unhappy when he learned the Kamazai Commanding had promised his fighters their surfeit of women from the caravan. Those common fighters were being given all the women they wanted while he—a *knight!*—was left behind guarding prisoners, and without even *one* woman for himself!

That was almost as bad as being a knight without a horse.

The Kamazai Commanding had taken the main force out well before dawn the previous day, and they hadn't yet returned. The knight knew his fighters were nervous, concerned that the main force had been defeated and an unknown force was about to descend on them. But, of course, that was nonsense! He knew the reason they hadn't yet returned: the Kamazai Commanding was giving his fighters time to sate their appetites with the captured women before coming down from the plateau.

And *he* didn't even have *one* woman to enjoy himself with!

Well, he'd see about that!

He carried his sheathed sword like a baton, the small demon spitter forgotten in its pouch on his belt, as he stomped from his tent in the center of the long, narrow camp toward the sun that was just peeking over the watery horizon. He barked sharp orders at his fighters as he went, whacking with his sheathed sword at any who didn't move quickly enough. He paused once to thrust the weapon through the bars of a cage at a prisoner who dared look at him, causing the man to scream out in pain when the metal-toed sheath jabbed hard into his ribs. It was only when he withdrew his sword that the knight remembered it was sheathed and did no more than bruise the ribs of the man he'd struck. He spat through the bars of the cage.

Snarling, he stomped on.

Most of the prisoners were captured soldiers. But the western end of the camp held other prisoners—three hundred women and children. The knight slowed down when he reached them and paced along the rows of cages, running the tip of his sword scabbard along the bars, making a rhythmic clacking. The women drew to the far sides of their cages and looked away from him. Children cowered behind the adults. He looked fiercely at the women, disgusted with how filthy they all were—how was he supposed to see if any of them were beautiful through all that dirt? He swore at them, as though it was their fault they couldn't keep themselves clean.

At length he stopped pacing and stared at a yellow-haired woman who huddled away from him. At least, he thought her hair was yellow under the dirt and oil that befouled it. He stomped to the side of the cage and jabbed his sword into it, slapped the woman's face with the tip of the scabbard to turn her face toward him. Her features were regular and he thought she might be comely.

Without looking around, he barked out an order. A fighter trotted up to him and saluted. He growled, and the fighter quickly drew a key ring from his belt and unlocked the cage. He reached in, grabbed the yellow-haired woman's ankle and dragged her out. She whimpered but didn't resist. She rose to her feet when the fighter grabbed her upper arm. She stood as she had been taught—head bowed, hands clasped behind her.

The knight stepped in front of her and stared for a moment. Her clothes were frayed in a place or two, but weren't torn anywhere. They weren't the best quality, but they were far better than homespun. At one time her dirty gray blouse had been lavender and her dirty gray skirt green; perhaps they would be again if they were properly cleaned. Likely this woman was from the family of a merchant, or perhaps that of a skilled craftsman. He took her chin roughly in his hand and forced her face upward, the better to see it. He spat on his fingers and rubbed dirt off her cheek. Yes, he thought, her skin is smooth. He brusquely poked her here, prodded her there, testing her softness, and was satisfied with what he felt.

He barked, and the fighter relocked the cage then stepped away. Then he took the woman's upper arm and led her away, toward the rising sun.

Once out of sight of the cages, the knight stopped. Using gestures, he ordered her to strip off her clothes and bathe in the surf. Just because he had to take what he hadn't been given didn't mean he had to settle for rutting in filth!

As the quietly sobbing woman reached for the hem of her blouse, the knight spun to his left and whipped his sword out of its scabbard. He'd heard the whicker of a horse. No one in the guard battalion had a horse! He darted to the treeline and, bent over, scuttled farther east and was shocked by what he saw through the trees.

Horsemen! Zobran Light Horse! Where had they come from? How had they gotten to the *east* of the prison camp?

It didn't matter, they were there. He spun about and dashed back to the camp. When he neared it he began roaring out commands to defend.

The woman, hands still on the hem of her blouse, stood frozen when the Jokapcul officer dashed away from her into the trees, moving only her eyes. She saw him speed back to the camp without even a glance in her direction. If whatever was to the east made him run, that was where she wanted to go. She let her blouse fall back in place and raced along the beach.

Spinner saw a flash of movement through the trees and wondered what it was—it could have been Jokapcul armor. "Did you see that?" he asked Company B's commander, Captain Geatwe.

"See what?" Geatwe asked. His angle was wrong, a fan tree had blocked his view.

Both men turned their heads toward a commotion in the direction of the beach. Neither made a move in that direction; it didn't sound like fighting, and they knew if it was anything they needed to know about, Lieutenant Haes of the Light Horse would inform them. They continued to wait for the two Bloody Axes to arrive and report that they'd taken out the observation posts. They turned their heads shoreward again at another, closer sound and saw a bedraggled woman riding in the arms of a Light Horseman.

"Lord Spinner," the man reported when he reached them, "Lieutenant Haes sends this woman to you. She came from the Jokapcul camp."

The woman was crying and not totally coherent, but Spinner could understand her Zobran without much difficulty. The important thing that came clear through her babbling was, "The Jokapcul commander saw you!"

"Put her down," Spinner ordered the horseman. "Go back, pass the word to wait for my signal to attack."

"Yes, Lord Spinner!" The horseman lowered the woman to the ground and turned his horse about. As he trotted back to his platoon he told everyone he passed to be ready for the signal. Geatwe sent a runner in the opposite direction with the same instruction.

"You stay here," Spinner told the woman. "You'll be safe until we come back for you."

She wailed in fear and clutched at his leg. "Don't leave me alone! Lord, I beg you, don't leave me alone."

With a great effort of will Spinner hardened his heart. He didn't want to leave the woman alone and frightened, but he'd need all of his fighters when they hit the camp, where he heard the sounds of men yelling. "You must stay here. We'll be back for you." He looked to both sides; everyone he could see looked back at him expectantly. He raised his right arm with his quarterstaff held erect and brought it forward sharply.

"At a walk!" he shouted.

"Walk!" Geatwe echoed.

The Light Horse, Royal Lancers, and Prince's Swords flicked their reins and moved out at a walk. The Zobran Pikers and Royal Foot followed.

"Trot" Spinner commanded, and the horsemen picked up their pace. *"Canter!"* and they speeded more. Then they broke into the clear. *"Charge!"*

Eighty horsemen, armed with lances and swords, broke into a gallop, charging the Jokapcul infantry, who stood in a thin line that bristled with pikes and spears. Beyond the thin line other Jokapcul were racing to join the formation. A few arrows flew at the charging horsemen, but most missed, and those that didn't were casually knocked aside by lances or bucklers.

More Jokapcul joined the line before the horsemen arrived.

More archers reached range and stopped to shoot at the charging mass.

The horses, crowded shoulder-to-shoulder, saw the hedgerow of pikes and spears facing them and drew up suddenly, short of getting impaled. Three riders were thrown over their mounts' necks and quickly dispatched by the Jokapcul.

The archers found the range and began picking off more riders.

"Pull back!" Spinner roared. There was a mad melee as the horsemen tried to turn their tightly packed horses around, and a couple more fell to arrows.

The Jokapcul jeered their withdrawing attackers—they'd suffered no losses of their own while beating off the charge and downing eight Zobran horsemen. The Jokapcul may not have been regular combat troops, but they firmly believed in their invincibility, and that was half of the battle.

The horsemen withdrew in chaotic order. The infantry following them had to weave and dodge to avoid being knocked down and trampled by their own cavalry, and even then a few were sent sprawling and some were stepped on, suffering broken bones or other injuries.

"Bows!" Spinner shouted. Everyone who carried a bow readied it and nocked an arrow, waiting for the command to fire.

"Volley, fire!" A volley of arrows flew from the edge of the thin forest at the Jokapcul line, but the volley was so ragged most of the Jokapcul easily avoided the arrows.

"Demon spitters!" Two of the swordsmen of the Zobran Pikers sheathed their swords and unlimbered the demon spitter tubes they wore on their backs. They took position and began to aim, but before they could fire, a crack of thunder came from the Jokapcul line and one of them flipped backward, sending his demon spitter tube spinning away.

The Jokapcul knight commanding the defense had finally remembered the small demon spitter he carried on his belt. It was the first time he'd used a demon weapon in combat, and he was impressed that it had done what it was supposed to do. He looked for and took aim at the second piker aiming a tube.

"Someone get that tube!" Spinner shouted. He didn't want to leave the demon spitter there, not knowing if the diminutive demon who lived in it might decide to leave if it was ignored. He saw one of the Prince's Swords snatch the weapon up and yelled at him, "Feed the demon!"

The swordsman looked uncertainly at Spinner. He'd never handled a demon spitter and didn't have any food for the demon, but Spinner was already directing the piker and archers to fire at the officer with the small demon spitter. So he darted to the downed piker and rifled through the pouches on his belt until he found the canister of demon food. He plucked a pellet from it and rapped his knuckles on the tube's tiny door. The demon popped its head out and snapped, *"Wazzu whanns?"* then gleefully snatched the food pellet and ducked back inside.

Arrows flew from side to side, and both lines were punctuated by the thunder of demon spitters. The Jokapcul commander was overconfident and missed his second shot. But by then the piker had already fired into the Jokapcul line and the eruption of demon spit had thrown down five broken, bleeding men. Others fell on both sides with arrows protruding from them. When the Jokapcul saw they were outnumbered and losing men, their line began to waver.

Spinner saw the Jokapcul pikes and spears wavering and men looking like they were ready to run. He gathered himself to call for another charge, but Geatwe's hand on his arm stopped him.

"Lord Spinner, we are too close, we can't get up momentum before we hit them."

"Why not?" The Jokapcul were only fifty yards away, but Spinner didn't understand that for a cavalry charge to be effective, everyone in it had to reach the enemy at the same time. They needed to come to speed together, and fifty yards wasn't enough distance for them to build the speed to gallop side by side.

"Send the foot, they can do it now," Geatwe said. "Have the horse cover them with arrows."

"All right," Spinner said, though he still didn't understand.

Geatwe began shouting commands, and the infantrymen with bows handed their bows and quivers to horsemen without. Then Geatwe gave the command and the swordsmen charged under an arc of arrows flying at the Jokapcul.

The Skraglander Borderer named Takacs shimmied down the bumber tree so fast he almost lost his grip on its ridged trunk and fell.

"Captain," Takacs said excitedly, "they are fighting at the far end of the camp!"

"What?" Phard looked to the west, but he didn't expect to see anything. He looked north of west, wondering where Sir Haft was, worried that something must have happened to him. The attack on the west end of the camp shouldn't have started yet; the Bloody Axes who carried the message to Lord Spinner should not have reached him before Sir Haft joined Company A—unless something had happened to Haft.

"Did you see any sign of—"

"Sir Haft comes!" Takacs interrupted, looking past his company commander.

Phard turned and blew his breath out in relief.

"Is everybody ready?" Haft asked without waiting for Phard to report.

"Yes, Sir Haft. And the fighting has already started."

"What?"

Phard gestured to Takacs, who said, "Sir Haft, I was up that tree. The Jokapcul have formed on the far end of the camp and are fighting Lord Spinner's force."

"They formed up?" Haft asked in surprise, to give himself a few seconds to think. "Have they broken?"

"They looked like they were holding."

Haft's mind spun. The Jokapcul should not have been able to get into formation; they should have been taken completely by surprise. Then he realized the two Bloody Axes who went

to tell Spinner hadn't had enough time to reach him yet—
somehow, the Jokapcul had discovered them.

"Are all of them there?"

"It looked like the entire troop, I didn't see any guards
among the prisoner cages."

Haft took a deep breath. "Infantry stay here in the blocking
position," he told Phard. "Cavalry charge west."

"Immediately, Sir Haft," Phard replied, and began giving
orders to his platoon commanders.

"Get my horse," Haft ordered Takacs before he had time to
dwell on it. The battle was several hundred yards away. As
much as he disliked horses, he could reach the fight a lot
faster on horseback than on foot.

The knight commanding the guard troop exalted when the
Zobran foot soldiers began their charge. It was exactly what
he wanted them to do. He roared out a sharp command and his
troop countercharged. The shield of arrows from the Zobran
horsemen passed harmlessly over the Jokapcul.

The Jokapcul were in fairly good order; they ran on a good
line, the archers dropping their bows in favor of swords and
spacing themselves to alternate with the pikemen and spearmen in the line. Just before the points of the extended pikes
and spears met the charging Zobrans, the Jokapcul stopped,
planted the butts of the long weapons on the ground, and
aimed their points at the onrushing bodies. The swordsmen
stopped as well and readied themselves to cut down anyone
who made it through the wall of points. Not every pike or
spear met its target, but enough did to seriously weaken the
charging Zobran infantry. The Zobran line broke up as soldiers swerved to avoid the pikes and spears, their solid line
fragmented into a series of short columns that attempted to
squeeze between the long handles.

The pikemen and spearmen dropped their long arms and
drew swords to strike at the sides of their attackers. Company
B's horsemen had to stop shooting arrows for fear of hitting
their own men when the Jokapcul charged. Now they raised

their bows again, but were able to loose only a few shafts before the infantry spread out and blocked their fire once more.

"Around behind them!" Spinner shouted, and heeled his gelding to race to the right and circle behind the Jokapcul. Then the world jerked and he flew from the saddle. The earth rushed up and slammed into him. Then blackness.

The Jokapcul knight saw the young man shouting orders and fired his demon spitter at him. He watched the young man's horse flip forward with blood flowing copiously from its shoulder, and saw its rider fly forward to land hard on the ground. The young man bounced once, then lay still and broken. The Zobran horsemen near enough to see froze at the sight of their fallen commander. The knight cried out in jubilation as awareness of the loss spread through the Zobran horsemen. He barked out more orders to his fighters, and they redoubled their efforts to drive back the swordsmen they were engaged with.

Captain Geatwe leaped from his saddle and used his sword to slice through the throats of the badly wounded, kicking the gelding to stop its thrashing so it wouldn't kick Spinner. Then he knelt at Spinner's side.

"Lord Spinner! Are you all right, Lord Spinner!"

Spinner didn't respond; he continued to lay limp. Moving quickly, Geatwe straightened Spinner's arms and legs and rolled him onto his back. Spinner was breathing, but his jaw hung slack and his eyelids almost closed over his eyes, showing only white.

Geatwe straightened and yelled, "Healer!"

"I'll fetch him," said Wudu, now the commander of the Prince's Swords. He ran to find the healing magician who accompanied Company B.

The Jokapcul fighters, seeing the Zobran leader down and his horsemen in growing disarray, shrilled out and fought harder, pressing the swordsmen back. The knight pointed his demon spitter at the Zobran officer kneeling over the body of the leader and pressed the lever again. The impact spun Geatwe around and threw him to the ground.

Seeing this the Jokapcul fighters pushed harder yet. The Zobrans had been about to win their battle but were now fighting, and losing, a desperate holding action. The only advantage the swordsmen now had over the Jokapcul was the clear footing behind them. In contrast, the Jokapcul had to step over or on the bodies of the fallen, and their feet slid and slipped on the bloody ground. The knight screamed a victory screech.

The Skraglander Bloody Axes and Kingsmen raced in a mob through the prison camp. They ignored the huddled prisoners, paid no attention to the beseeching hands thrust through the bars of cages, their entire attention focused on reaching the battle at the camp's far end. Bouncing and poorly balanced in his saddle, Haft slowly slipped from the front of the mass of horsemen to the rear. Frustration was added to his feeling of urgency to reach Spinner and the battle.

From his position in the lead, Captain Phard was the first to see the battle. The height of his horse allowed him to peer over the heads of the struggling men on foot. He saw the Zobran horsemen milling about, contributing nothing to the battle. He didn't see Spinner anywhere.

"ON LINE!" he roared, and reined his horse back to a canter.

Quickly, the Bloody Axes formed on him, and the Kingsmen spread out to the sides.

"CHARGE!" He aimed his horse at the knight, easily distinguished by the plume on his helmet.

The seventy-five horsemen slammed into the backs of the Jokapcul. They pulled their horses up and the horses kicked and bit at the Jokapcul as their riders swung swords and hacked with axes.

The knight heard the thunder of hooves behind him and spun about. His jaw dropped when he saw the Skraglanders. Where did they come from? he wondered. But he was well-trained, and automatically pointed his demon spitter and pressed the lever. A Bloody Axe flipped backward off his horse and landed with a thud. The knight started to aim at another horseman when he caught sight of the fearsome rider charging straight at him with a murderous axe held ready for a killing blow. He tried to swing his arm around to shoot at that threat, but was too late.

Captain Phard swung his axe and cleaved the knight from left shoulder to right hip. Then he almost fell from the saddle when his horse reared to kick at the backs of Jokapcul fighters. Phard quickly regained his balance and chopped into the back of an enemy soldier who had just become aware of the new threat.

Haft's mare continued galloping when the rest of the horsemen slowed to get on line, and he reached the Jokapcul a mere half length behind the Bloody Axes. His axe chopped down, rose, chopped again, sending out sprays of blood each time.

Then the battle was over; the Jokapcul were all down.

Haft stood in his stirrups, looking at the edge of the trees. "Spinner!" he shouted. Where was Spinner? He couldn't see him! And where was Captain Geatwe?

CHAPTER
TWENTY-TWO

"Spinner!" Haft shouted as he clumsily jumped off his mare. He dashed the few yards to where Spinner lay on his back, the healing mage who accompanied Company B kneeling over him. Behind the mage, where he could turn around to tend to him, lay Captain Geatwe. His surcoat and shirt had been removed and he was lying on them. An aralez stood on his chest, delicately licking at a gaping wound in his shoulder.

No aralez stood on or near Spinner. Instead, the healing mage worked his hands over the downed Frangerian, manipulating here, prodding there, rubbing in another place, lifting Spinner's eyelids and looking closely, as though peering into his soul.

"What's wrong?" Haft demanded, dropping to his knees at Spinner's side. "How bad is he hurt? Is he going to live?" He grabbed the magician's shoulders and shouted, "Tell me he's going to live!"

"Quiet!" the healing mage snapped without looking up. He continued his examination without pause.

"What happened to him? Where is he wounded?" Haft's eyes roamed Spinner from crown to toe and back. Spinner's chest slowly rose and fell with his breathing, but Haft saw neither wound nor blood. "Was it a magic attack? Is there a demon weapon that doesn't leave marks? Tell me! Speak up, what's wrong with him?" he babbled.

"Get him away!" the healer snapped into the air, still without looking up or pausing in what he was doing.

"Come, Sir Haft," Captain Phard said, clamping his hands on Haft's shoulder and lifting. "Let the healing mage do his job." Haft protested but was too shocked to strongly resist the bigger man who pulled him away.

"But—But, Spinner—"

"The healing mage is doing everything he can," Phard said. "Let us see to the others."

"The others?" Haft asked weakly, turning to Phard.

"The others." Phard nodded at the soldiers who were gathering bodies; wounded and dead, friend and enemy.

"The others!" Haft said strongly. He saw the injured being laid in the open and their wounds bandaged by other soldiers. There were so many.

But he wasn't just a junior Marine now, he was a *commander*—with Spinner down, he was *the* commander. The commander had responsibilities. He couldn't let his concern for individuals—not even for Spinner—distract him. And he had to take care of the things that Spinner would have been responsible for. He twisted his shoulders from Phard's hands, straightened himself, and marched to where the wounded were being gathered.

"Send to the caravan," Haft told Phard, who caught up with him. "I want all the healers here to tend our wounded."

There was no pavilion, just a swath of bare ground in the shade of the trees. Haft stopped and briefly spoke with each of the wounded, told them how well they had fought and that they had won a great victory over the Jokapcul. He tamped down the part of him that was glad all the wounded were Zobrans, Bostians, and Penston Conquestors from Company B—none of the Skraglanders from Company A whom he'd brought into the fight were among the wounded.

Three of the Skraglanders were among the dead, though, along with too many men of Company B. None of the Jokapcul had survived.

"Lord Haft," Lieutenant Krysler said, interrupting his inspection of the dead. "What do you want to do about the prisoners?"

"Prisoners?" Haft blinked and looked around. He didn't see any live Jokapcul.

"In the cages, Lord Haft."

Memory of why they had attacked the Jokapcul instead of passing them by jolted Haft with enough force to stagger him back a step. How could he have forgotten? "Free them," he ordered. "Wait, I'll come with you." He turned to look for one of the Zobran officers and saw Lieutenant Guma of the Royal Lancers.

"Guma!"

"Lord Haft." Guma marched over and thumped a fist to his chest in salute.

"See to security here," Haft told him. "Everything else looks under control." He kept himself from looking to where Spinner lay, to where he *didn't* know everything was under control. "I'm taking Company A to free the prisoners."

"Yes, lord."

Haft twisted about and marched away. Phard and Krysler were at his sides, shouting orders to the Skraglanders of Company A.

"Send a runner to the rest of the company, let them know what's happening and tell them to look alert to the west," Haft told Phard. "And another to the caravan. There are women, children, and oldsters here. We need women to help them." He looked at the cages. "They'll need food as well."

Phard turned away to hide his grin; yes, Sir Haft was turning into a fine commander. He might sometimes pretend that he didn't know what the rampant eagle on the blade of his axe meant, but he was truly one of them.

They freed the women, children, and oldsters first—their cages were nearest. Many of them were frightened and cowered in the back of their cages rather than crawl out into freedom. Others eagerly came out and fell upon their rescuers with hugs and kisses and cries of joy.

They were a pathetic group. They were filthy; they hadn't been allowed to bathe in a very long while. Nor had they been allowed access to privies; they'd been forced to void into buckets that were infrequently emptied by prisoners assigned to the so-called honey-bucket duty.

"It's a wonder they haven't had an epidemic," Haft snarled.

"How do you know they haven't?" Phard asked softly.

"Because there are too many of them still alive."

All the prisoners showed signs of starvation, with an almost exact correspondence between their degree of malnourishment and their dirtiness—some had been held captive longer than others. It wasn't clear through the dirt that covered them, but Haft was certain he saw bruises on many of them. He *knew* he saw scars and healing recent wounds—along with wounds that festered.

"Get healers here," he ordered. "See to their injuries."

The nearest caged soldiers saw the civilians being freed and began calling out to their liberators. Soldiers farther away took up the cry.

"Send the Kingsmen to begin freeing them," Haft told Phard. "Tell them to organize the first ones they free into squads and have them help uncage the rest. I want the Kingsmen to gather all of them into squads and platoons."

Haft turned at the sound of horses galloping from the north and saw a dozen mounted women rapidly approaching. Zweepee was in the lead. He waved at her and she veered toward him. She didn't object when Phard reached up and helped her off her horse.

"Gods," Zweepee murmured. "There are so many of them!"

"More than three hundred here," Haft agreed. "Half of them are afraid to come out of the cages. And many more soldiers to the west."

Zweepee looked at the other women, who had reined in and dismounted. "Tell them we have food coming, and healers to tend their injuries." She looked at Haft for confirmation.

He nodded and replied, "I already sent for them."

"Get them in groups and have them sit down," Zweepee told the women. "Do it now." She watched them hurry off, then looked into the cages at the people who hadn't come out.

"More women are coming in wagons, along with food for these poor souls." She said it so softly she might have been reassuring herself. Then, more loudly, "Where are the wells?"

Haft and Phard looked at each other; neither had thought of wells and neither remembered having seen any.

Zweepee punched her fists into her hips and leaned toward them. Somehow, she seemed to tower over the two men, though she stood half a head shorter than Haft and more than a full head shorter than Phard.

"How do you expect us to clean their injuries and cook their food without water?"

Spinning away from her, as much to hide his suddenly red face as to look toward the Bloody Axes who were still trying to coax the frightened people out of their cages. Haft yelled to the Bloody Axes, "Listen up! Has anybody seen a well? We need water for these people."

There was a long pause as the soldiers looked at each other and around for a well—none had seen one—before a newly freed woman cried out, "I saw them bring water from over there." She pointed into the trees to the north.

Suddenly, many people were pointing and yelling that they'd seen the Jokapcul carrying water buckets. They pointed in the general direction of the trees.

Haft hung his head for a few seconds, then looked up. "Send a few men to find the well, Captain."

"Yes, Sir Haft." Phard roared, and a squad's worth of Bloody Axes trotted into the trees. "If a well is there, they'll find it, lady," Phard said to Zweepee.

Zweepee looked at the number of people. "I hope they find more than one well."

"I'll have them keep looking," Haft assured her. But he spoke to her back, for she was heading toward a nearby group of seated people.

"Where are those healers?" she called back over her shoulder.

"Here we are," a mage answered. He and another, along with two healing witches, were coming from the east, where they'd been pulled away from the wounded soldiers they'd been tending. Assistants lugged chests bulging with herbs, potions, and healing demons.

"You take charge here," Haft said to Phard. "I'm going to

see how the Kingsmen are doing with the soldiers. Take care
of anything else Zweepee needs that we didn't think of."

"Yes, Sir Haft," Phard replied and saluted. He spent a few
seconds watching Haft walk away and thought, Commander's prerogative, leave someone else to deal with the diffi-
culties, then shook it off. Things might be even more difficult
in some ways with the soldiers.

They were.

As ill-treated as the civilians had been, at least they'd been
allowed to keep all of their clothes. None of the soldiers wore
more than an undergarment, and many not even that. Most of
the soldiers were scarred, and many had recent injuries. They
were as dirty as the freed civilians, and just as ripe for disease.
From their ribs and knobby joints, Haft suspected they'd been
fed even less than the civilians.

None of them had stayed in their cages. All had come out,
even though some didn't budge until ordered by Lieutenant
Han or his sergeants or corporals. They sat in ranks. None of
them resisted when the Kingsmen had gathered them into
squads and platoons—some even formed with men from like
units without being prompted. But despite their poor condition, not all of them looked defeated.

After Han related the relative ease with which the Kingsmen had organized the men, Haft told him to send a squad
into the trees to search for wells.

"I already had men check," Han replied. "A squad and the
strongest of these men are getting water now."

Haft nodded. "Good move, Lieutenant."

Han barely blinked at being addressed as "Lieutenant."
He'd been an upper sergeant when he and his men joined the
caravan, and he had made the adjustment to being an officer
quickly enough, though he thought that as an upper sergeant
he should have been made a captain over Phard or Geatwe,
who were lower ranking sergeants before the reorganization
that turned all of the sergeants and many of the corporals into
officers. But he understood the reasoning of Spinner and
Haft—the men they'd made captains had been with them for

a time and fought the Jokapcul alongside them; Spinner and Haft didn't know him.

"If you agree, Lord Haft," he said, "we will use the fresh water only for drinking and cleaning wounds. The men can bathe in the surf."

"Good thinking. Have swimmers stationed to rescue any of them who get in trouble in the water."

"I will."

"Have you started a roster yet? We'll need to know what units these men were from and find the best way to integrate them into the battalion."

"I thought I'd do that once they got cleaned up and we found some clothing for them."

Haft looked toward the tents of the defeated Jokapcul. "Have you had anybody check inside the tents?"

Han nodded. "They found enough clothing—including uniforms from many armies—for most of these men. Maybe enough for all of them. I planned to clothe them after they bathe."

"Good thinking again." Haft looked at Han, impressed by how much he'd thought of and taken care of on his own. "I'll be back to speak to these men once they've had time to get cleaned up and dressed. Tell them there's food coming. Carry on."

"Lord Haft." Han gave the fist-to-chest salute.

A Bloody Axe stopped Haft before he reached the area that held the cages of the civilians. "Sir Haft," he said hesitantly, "I can't allow you to pass."

"What?" Haft's eyes widened in surprise.

"The Golden Lady, Sir Haft," the Bloody Axe said with evident embarrassment. "The women are bathing. She said no men are allowed to come near."

"Surely she didn't mean me," Haft said, and began to step around him.

The Bloody Axe sidestepped to stay in front of him. "Ah, Sir Haft?" His voice squeaked. "The Golden Lady named you specifically." He paused to clear his throat. "Sir Haft, she said if I let you pass, she would roast my testicles over a fire." He cleared his throat again. "Without first removing them."

Haft blinked. Yes, he could believe Alyline had made such a threat. He could even imagine her carrying through on it. He cleared his own throat. "Well, we wouldn't want that to happen, would we?" He gazed in the direction he thought the women might be bathing and, remembering how pathetic the freed women looked, muttered, "Probably none of them are worth looking at right now anyway." Then, in a normal voice, "Did she say if I'm allowed to go anywhere?"

"Yes, Sir Haft," the Bloody Axe said with great relief. "A kitchen has been set up over there." He pointed into the trees. "She said you could go and inspect it."

"Inspect the kitchen." He shook his head. "All right, I'll inspect the kitchen. Carry on."

"Yessir! Thank you, Sir Haft," the Bloody Axe said brightly. He'd been very worried about having to stop his own commander.

Haft blinked his eyes and shook his head sharply when he reached the "kitchen." Men and older boys were busy digging a long row of shallow pits and building fires in them, or setting up a row of trestle tables along each side of the line of fire pits. Beyond the tables and fires the trees were filled with wagons. Women and girls, a hundred or more, were bustling back and forth between the wagons and the tables on that side of the fires, lugging foodstuffs and cooking utensils.

This is a kitchen? he thought. There were more than enough people and material to prepare food for two battalions! He dropped his head and thumped the heel of his hand against his forehead. Of course! They'd just freed more than two battalions worth of people, and they had their own soldiers to feed as well. They needed that many and that much to feed them.

He looked around to see who was in charge, who was there whom he knew, and a curious expression spread over his face. He didn't recognize any of them, men or women!

He shook his head. *We've gotten big.* The realization struck him hard. He'd spent most of his time either with the caravan's lead elements or with the small command group, rather than going from one end to the other of the growing caravan seeing people, meeting the new people who joined the caravan on its way around Dartmutt. He hadn't realized until now just how many people were traveling with him and Spinner. And this was only a small part of the caravan!

So who was in charge of this kitchen? Would that person know who *he* was?

"Haft!"

He turned his head to the familiar voice and saw Doli scurrying toward him.

"Haft, where have you been?" she said before she reached him. "Where's Spinner? We have so much to do here, so many people to feed—Alyline told me there are a thousand people out there who need feeding and then we have to feed our soldiers! I sent someone to find Zweepee because I know she's with the people Spinner and you freed from the Jokapcul this morning. She'll be able to tell me how many people there really are where's Spinner? How are we supposed to feed all of these people—that's going to take a lot of food—we need to send hunters out to find more meat are there any game animals in this forest, we need people foraging for fruits and vegetables and tubers does anybody know what is good to eat here where's Spinner?" She paused to take a breath and Haft broke in.

"Are you in charge here?"

"What? Yes, I'm in charge of the kitchen—I have to get all these people fed—are they hungry—now where's Spinner? I can arrange a serving line for the people to line up at the tables—"

"They're too weak to line up." Haft raised his voice to break through. "Doli, these people are very weak, they've been starved. Many of them are injured, some of them are sick. They aren't going to line up, you're going to have to serve them where they are."

"Oh," she said meekly.

"Do you have enough food for them? Is anyone getting water?"

"We have two wells right over there." She waved a hand absently. "Where's Spinner?"

"Is anybody out hunting? Is anybody gathering?"

"I—I don't know. Where's Spinner?"

Haft looked beyond her, into the trees, and saw people standing around among the wagons. "Put people to work gathering. Some of these people are Dartmutters, I'm sure some of them will know what to gather." He put his hands on her shoulders and turned her around. "Now go and do it." He gave her a little push.

"All right, I'll do it," she said as she started moving away. Over her shoulder she asked again, "Where's Spinner?"

Haft swallowed a sigh. "The last time I saw him he was over there." He pointed vaguely to the east. He hoped his voice didn't sound as thick as it felt. If it did, Doli would know something was wrong.

Evidently it didn't; she kept going.

It wasn't much longer before the rest of the healers were finished with the soldiers wounded in the morning's battle and moved west to aid the others in tending to the injuries of the former prisoners.

Most of the women, children, and oldsters had been able to bathe themselves in the surf. Alyline organized women from the caravan to gather fresh clothing for them from the wagons, and other women to sort the garments they'd stripped off to go into the water. Most of the garments they'd worn since they were captured were no longer good for any use but to be torn into rags, and many not even that. But some were still usable and were set aside to be washed. The people who were too weak or injured to take themselves into the water were carried to the water's edge and caringly laved by women from the caravan. There weren't many unable to bathe themselves; the Jokapcul had used anyone too weak or ill for weapons practice.

Alyline's eyes had a haunted look when Haft found her.

"I thought my slavery was bad," she said softly. "I thought the way the Jokapcul treated their prisoners in Eikby was worse. But this is the worst yet." Her eyes grimly swept from the west to the south, the directions where she knew the Jokapcul were to be found. "I want them defeated, Haft. I want them dead." She placed a hand on his chest and looked into his eyes. "Promise me," she said through gritted teeth. "Promise me, Haft. Promise me you will kill them every chance you get. Promise me you will defeat them, you will destroy them." Her voice grew harsher as she spoke.

Haft wanted to step back from the fury that radiated from her eyes, but he was the commander, he reminded himself, he couldn't back away from anybody. Not even from a woman who had led naked women to battle with the Jokapcul. With a great effort of will, he stilled the trembling that washed over him and lifted a hand to softly touch her cheek.

"By all that is holy and sacred to me, Alyline, I will do that. I promise."

"Thank you, Haft." She turned her face to fleetingly touch his hand with her lips, then stepped away. "Now I have to see to the soldiers. Where's Spinner?" She asked the last over her shoulder as she headed west.

"I'll check on him," Haft replied, but not loud enough for her to hear.

Yes, where was Spinner? Was he still with them, or had he gone on? Haft didn't know. Lord Gunny had said, *Marines don't die. They go to hell and regroup*. He didn't want to have to wait until he got to hell to regroup with Spinner. He really didn't.

CHAPTER
TWENTY-THREE

Haft didn't have to go to hell to regroup with Spinner.

"Nightbird said Lord Spinner suffered a concussion when he was thrown," Lieutenant Haes told Haft. "She gave him a draught for it, he's sleeping naturally now." He snorted. "Even the healing mages agreed that sleep is the best thing for him right now. They weren't too sure about the draught, but their demons could only do so much. The land trow couldn't do much, but it seemed to ease him."

"I don't trust those things," Haft mumbled as he knelt by Spinner's side. Spinner lay under a light blanket. His chest rose and fell with regular breath and his eyelids flickered with the movement of his dreaming eyes.

"Did Nightbird say how long it will take before he's well again?" he asked the Zobran.

"She said it could be tomorrow, or it could be a month before he's fully recovered. He'll sleep a lot for a day or two, she said."

Haft flinched. He knew injuries inside the head could be worse than serious wounds to the body, but a day or a *month*? "Where is she now?"

"She went with the others to tend the new people."

The new people. The Zobran officer assumed they were going to absorb the thousand former prisoners. Well, they had been taking in refugees all along. And he and Spinner had begun with just four freed slaves. So, yes, they would take these in as well.

"What did the healing mages say about how long it would be for Spinner to recover?"

"None of them were willing to speak to that."

Haft wondered what good the healing mages were if they couldn't heal Spinner. Then he took a deep breath and dismissed the thought. He laid a hand on Spinner's arm and leaned his head close to his ear.

"Get well fast, Spinner. I'll take care of everything until you're healed. But I need you. We all do. Oh, both Alyline and Doli asked about you. I think they both need you too. Get well, you need yourself too." He gave Spinner's arm a squeeze, then stood.

"How's Captain Geatwe?" he asked. The Company B commander was no longer laying next to Spinner.

"He's sleeping over there." Haes pointed toward the pavilion that had been hastily erected for the wounded. "His wound looks almost healed, but the healing magicians say his shoulder will be very sore for the next week or two."

Haft nodded. "And the other wounded?"

"They're doing better than I'm used to so soon after a battle. The healing witches are very good at what they do, and the healing demons the magicians control are, well, amazing."

"Good. I'm going to see how Captain Phard is doing with the freed soldiers now." He looked off into nowhere. "Have you seen Sergeant Rammer?"

"No. Nor the giant."

Haft found Sergeant Rammer with Phard and the freed soldiers. Rammer didn't know where Silent was either.

That was because Silent and Wolf had silently slipped away well before dawn, just after the forces that attacked the Jokapcul camp left to take up their positions. The giant nomad was on the plateau, beyond the escarpment's horizon, where he was welcomed as a guest in the Desert Men's encampment. They welcomed him partly because they were impressed by the courage of a man who fearlessly came alone into their land. They also recognized him as being, like them, a nomad, which alone might have granted him entrée.

But mostly they received him in a friendly manner because of Wolf. The Desert Men held the wolf sacred; they believed wolves were the companions of gods. Any man who traveled with a wolf must be blessed by the gods. And a man traveling with a wolf as his sole companion might be more than a mere man, and Silent's great size gave credence to that idea.

Communication was difficult. The closest most of them had to a common language was the Dartmutt dialect of Zobran, which Silent couldn't understand at all. But one of them was familiar with Skraglandish, and another, oddly enough, spoke passable Ewsarkan—in both of which languages Silent was fluent, or close enough.

Silent had become wistful when he first stood on the plateau in full daylight—it reminded him of home. Not in details, of course. The Northern Steppes had huge vistas of rich grass that stood waist high to a full-size man, and the plateau had only patches of grass, and that wasn't even calf-high to these stunted little people of the south. Combined, all of the tiny streams that laced the Low Desert didn't match any one of the great rivers that drained the steppes. There was a range of low mountains on the southeast corner of the plateau, but the Northern Steppes were bounded on the south by a mountain range so high that a people on the move could travel toward it for a week or more and it wouldn't seem to be any closer. There were no herds of wild horses here from which a boy could capture a mount to tame, and by taming prove himself worthy to become a man. And the Northern Steppes had lakes so big, a man could sit on his horse and not be able to see all the way across the water; here there were only occasional pools so small a man with good reach could jump across the biggest of them.

But the details aside, the lay of the land was familiar. There were vast areas of gently rolling land, others that were flat, and yet other vast areas that only appeared flat to those who couldn't read the land's lay.

After a few hours ride onto the plateau, Silent was in an area that only *looked* flat. But his vision, bred for and born into the steppes, saw the signs and read them, so he knew where the land fell and where it rose again. In no time he spotted the outriders who paced him, confident that he didn't have any idea he was being flanked. They were far enough away that he grinned openly and even laughed out loud at their error. He knew that had he wanted to, he could ride this land without those outriders knowing he was there. If he wanted, he could even disappear from their sight and by the time they found his trail be so far away they'd never catch up with him until he was ready for them to do so.

He did disappear from their sight for a time, but only so he could slip unnoticed upon a small herd of grazing gazelle and take two with his bow. He didn't kill them for himself, but because a guest should bring a present to his host. He resisted the temptation to wave to his escorts when he regained their sight.

Silent became momentarily wistful again when he first spied the Desert Man camp. He was sure they thought he hadn't spotted it yet, even though as soon as he did he angled his horse toward it. It was skillfully camouflaged, with its green-speckled sand-colored tents, but the shapes of the tents caught the eye that knew what the land looked like, and the camouflage fell away. The low tents were unlike the yurts of the Tangonine people, his own tribe. His people didn't try to hide their homes in their own land. The yurts stood tall and proud, each decorated with banners and hangings that proclaimed to the world who lived there and their accomplishments.

No matter how far away he was when he first saw them, Silent didn't realize how low the tents actually were until the chief invited him into his own. The giant nomad had to get down on his belly to crawl through the entrance. Back on the steppes, he could stand fully erect inside a yurt; here he sat cross-legged on a rug woven in richly colored patterns near the middle of the tent and still had to duck his head to keep from pressing it into the tenting.

The chief had accepted the gazelles with ceremony, and ordered a feast prepared in Silent's honor. Musicians played drums, flutes, and instruments with plucked strings. Singers—Silent quickly recognized that the torques around their necks marked them as slaves—set up a wailing that would have stung Silent's ears had he not during his travels grown accustomed to the strange and discordant sounds that other people found musical. Desert Men got up and danced when the music or spirits moved them to do so. At length the feast was served, copper platters laid out on low tables before the seated men, and everyone dug in with the fingers of his right hand. There were no women in sight, and Silent knew enough not to ask about them.

Silent was voluble in three language in praise of the food when it was served. In Skraglandish and Ewsarkan he extolled its virtues. In his own language he mocked its lack of color, how it looked the color of sand, dotted only lightly with reds and greens, totally lacking in the panoply of colors that rioted in a stew of the steppes; he laughed about its incredible blandness, only occasionally spiked with a dart of spice. The two Desert Men translated his compliments, and the chief beamed in pride. The other Desert Men roared their pleasure.

After eating, the chief ordered slaves to distribute ceremonial drinking cups, large receptacles with handles on both sides—large for the Desert Men, who needed both hands to lift them to their mouths. Silent was able to wrap one hand around the cup given him. The slaves then brought in goatskin bottles filled with fermented comite milk and bustled about keeping all the cups filled as everyone got boisterously drunk.

Rather, the Desert Men got drunk. Thanks to his great size, Silent could absorb a good deal more alcohol than they before he got drunk. Besides, the fermented comite milk wasn't anywhere near as potent as the fermented mare's milk he'd grown up with. By the time the Desert Men started keeling over, Silent was experiencing only a mild buzz.

It was a jolly buzz, to be sure, so jolly he felt like dancing. He jumped up from the place of honor, next to the chief, took a drum from the hands of a surprised musician and began to dance.

While he danced, springing here and there, spinning about, and kicking in ways that were a marvel to his hosts, his free hand beat out a rhythm on the drum none of the Desert Men recognized. He raised his voice in a joyful cacophony that thoroughly entranced his audience. Or perhaps they were thoroughly mystified how anybody could imagine that noise to be singing. But they were soon clapping to his drumbeat and keening a counterpoint to his singing. Some of the less drunk Desert Men leapt to their feet and joined in Silent's dance, and they greatly enjoyed aping his movements—even though they fell when they attempted the squatting kicks he executed flawlessly. A couple of the Desert Men who fell decided they'd rather sleep than get back up. Other dancers tripped over their sprawled bodies and they also decided they'd rather sleep than get back up. Soon enough too many bodies littered the tent floor for any of those still able to dance to be able to continue. Eventually, even Silent had to admit he was too drunk to dance around them, and he fell, laughing, alongside the inebriated chief.

The chief was laughing uproariously, more than ever pleased he'd welcomed the stranger as a guest. The stranger's odd dancing, drumming, and singing were even better than the gift of two gazelle that prompted the feast. Yes, this was a guest who would be allowed to move throughout his tribe's lands without being molested. He would remember to tell his men not to harm the stranger when he was found again in the desert.

The translator who spoke Skraglandish was snoring, but the one with Ewsarkan was still conscious and more or less able to speak. So Silent and the chief talked, and the giant told the desert chief why he'd gone there alone. Silent couldn't tell how well his words were conveyed by the drunk translator, but the gist of it must have reached through the alcoholic haze because the chief's mien turned serious, if not sober.

Finally the chief declared, "We will talk later. Now is time for sleep." He immediately fell over and started snoring.

Silent took the hint and got a blanket from his saddle. He curled up on the rug next to the chief. Before he fell asleep himself, he thought about the Desert Men's slaves. He knew how strongly Spinner and Haft reacted to slavery and was afraid that if they knew about it, they'd want to return to the Low Desert to free the slaves. He also knew they'd get slaughtered if they did. He resolved not to tell them.

*   *   *

Few of the injuries suffered by the freed soldiers were more serious than could be dealt with by the healing mages and their demons and the healing witches' potions and poultices. Mostly, those men were malnourished. Their spirits rose rapidly once they were fed and clothed and they realized they were free of the cages. Some of them asked for weapons even before they finished their first meal. Captain Phard, his officers, and NCOs started organizing them by unit type as soon as they'd been fed and looked over by the healers.

They were Bostians, Skraglanders, Zobrans, Easterlies, and sea soldiers of many seafaring nations, as well as soldiers from the captured city states of the Penston Peninsula, and even a handful of men from distant Oskul. There were border guards, lancers, pikers, light horse, light foot, heavy cavalry, heavy foot, swords, archers, and a variety of royal household troops. There were junior officers, grizzled senior sergeants, raw recruits, and everyone in between. None questioned the assumed ranks and authority of the officers and NCOs of the combined battalion that had freed them, and all were willing to accept their leadership and command. They didn't even question the right of the young Frangerian Marine with the huge axe to be the overall commander. There were no mages or magicians among them; the Jokapcul had summarily killed everyone they believed knew how to control a demon.

Sergeant Rammer took responsibility for organizing them.

The women, children, and oldsters were a bit different. Like the soldiers, most of their injuries were relatively easy to heal with proper care and cleanliness, and they all suffered from malnourishment. But some of them were ill, and some of the women—and even a few children—had infections because of the rough way the Jokapcul had handed them about and used their bodies. Those were more difficult to heal, and some of that healing would have to be on the march; the caravan could not risk staying long in that place.

Fortunately, there were large stores of food. It was the food preferred by the Jokapcul and not much to the taste of others, but it was food, and Fletcher and Zweepee were glad to add it to the caravan's storage wagons. There was likewise clothing taken from these prisoners or others the Jokapcul had raided and pillaged along the way, so every civilian—woman, child, and man alike—was able to have at least two complete sets of clothing. Many of the freed soldiers had to settle for Jokapcul armor, which they didn't much like; not only because it put them in the uniform of an enemy, but because the Jokapcul tended to be small and the armor was a proper fit only for the smallest among the former prisoners. However, they didn't object much to being armed with Jokapcul weapons. Doli and Maid Primrose found seamstresses and dyers who could take cloth and make surcoats for most of the soldiers so they would at least have a surface resemblance to the uniforms of the caravan soldiers and their units.

"Where's Spinner?"

As soon as all the former prisoners and the soldiers who freed them were fed and she had the "kitchen" crew cleaning up and preparing to fix another meal, Doli ran about asking everybody she knew.

"Where's Spinner?"

"The same place he's been all morning," said the Prince's Sword named Hyse, looking at her oddly. He pointed to the east, to the edge of the trees where Spinner still slept.

"He's not dead?" Doli exclaimed. "Oh, I was so worried, nobody would tell me where he was. I was afraid he might have been hurt, but he's just busy! Thank you!" she called back to Hyse as she scampered to the former battleground.

Hyse stood staring after her. She'd been *afraid* Lord Spinner was hurt? Nobody had *told* her? "But—" he called out, then stopped. If she didn't know, he was probably better off if he wasn't the one to tell her.

"Spinner! Spinner, where are you?" Doli cried out as she ran across the battleground, oblivious to the bloody sand under her racing feet. She looked anxiously at everyone, searching for Spinner, but didn't see him. She was inside the treeline before she realized everyone that she looked at looked away.

"Spinner!" she shrieked, suddenly terrified that he was dead after all. Bodies lay unmoving in the shade of the trees. Was Spinner one of them? No, they weren't unmoving, they were wounded and healers moved among them. She ran about aimlessly, looking at the wounded men, seeking Spinner.

"Doli!" Nightbird snapped, and the healing witch bustled to her. "Quiet, woman, you're disturbing the wounded! Have a care for them."

"But—But Spinner!" Doli's eyes were welling with tears. "Where's Spinner?"

"Come with me," Nightbird said, laying an arm over Doli's shoulders.

"Is he— Is he—"

"No, he's not dead," Nightbird said comfortingly. "He's sleeping quietly. I'll take you to him."

"He's sleeping?" Doli squealed joyfully, thinking he was merely resting after the strain of battle.

"Yes, sleeping. Now be calm and come with me." The healing witch gave her a hug.

Had Doli been thinking more clearly, she would have realized Spinner wasn't sleeping because he was merely tired. Spinner never lay down to sleep in the aftermath of a battle, he always saw to it that the wounded were cared for and the dead gathered for burial before he took any comfort for himself. "Yes, take me to him, please." She started walking at random, and Nightbird had to pull her back and point her in the right direction. The healing witch didn't let go of her.

"Spinner!" Doli cried when she saw him on a pallet of bumber leaves covered with a blanket. She wrenched out of Nightbird's grasp and ran to him. Kneeling at his side, she caressed his cheek, murmuring to him, then gasped and pulled back. Nightbird grabbed her shoulders and pulled her away before she could throw herself on Spinner.

"He's sleeping, that's all. He was thrown from his horse this morning and struck his head. But he's sleeping now, he'll be fine."

"But—But he's hurt!"

"Shush, shush." Nightbird gathered Doli in her arms and rocked her. "He'll be fine. He just needs to sleep. Don't disturb him now. Let him sleep."

Doli turned her face up to the older woman, tears running down her cheeks. "He'll be all right? You—You're sure?"

"He'll be fine," Nightbird said with more confidence than she felt. "Just let him sleep."

Doli fumbled a hand free and brushed at her tears. "All right," she said with a snuffle, "I'll let him sleep." Nightbird loosened her hold, and Doli broke through her arms to lean close over Spinner and hug him. She rained soft kisses all over his face, murmuring to him to get the rest he needed, promising to care for him when he woke. Then she sat up on her heels.

"You'll send for me when he wakes?"

"I will."

"Good." Doli rose to her feet and used her sleeve to wipe away the last of her tears. "I'm going to find Haft," she said sternly. "He knew Spinner was injured and he didn't tell me."

"Go gentle on him," Nightbird said to Doli's rapidly departing back. "He thought he was doing the right thing."

She found Haft with Sergeant Rammer, who had just finished organizing the new men into units and assigning them officers and NCOs.

"Haft!"

He turned, and groaned when he saw the way she was bearing down on him.

"Haft, we have to talk!"

"Not now, Doli, I'm about to address our new troops."

"*Yes* now! You come with me so we can talk."

"In a little while, Doli. There's something else I have to do right now."

"Fine. If you don't want to come with me where we can talk in privacy, we can do it right here."

Men in the ranks looked at each other. Their new commander was being addressed in a demanding way by someone who looked like a serving girl. Their officers and NCOs, most of whom had just been promoted from the caravan's existing units, signed them to be quiet, to keep their eyes straight ahead and ignore what was happening in front of them.

"But, Doli, this is important."

"Yes it is important, Haft. Spinner was hurt and you knew it and you wouldn't tell me."

"Doli, the last I heard, you were mad at him. Anyway, there was nothing you could do that the healers weren't doing better."

She froze, glaring at him, fists tightly clenched at her sides. "*Me*, mad at *Spinner*? Wherever did you get that idea?"

He made the mistake of shrugging and saying, "You know. After that night he spent with Maid Primrose in Eikby."

She reacted so fast he didn't even see the hand that slapped his face until it was on its way back to hit him again. He was barely fast enough to grab her wrist before she connected a second time.

"Ow! What was that for?"

"You—You—" she sputtered. She kicked him.

"Doli!" Haft hopped back, letting go of her wrist as he reached for his stinging shin.

She followed, pummeling both sides of his face with open palms. "You—You—"

Rammer sighed and shook his head. He stepped behind Doli and threw an arm around her waist. Ignoring her indignant squawk, he lifted her off her feet and turned around so she faced away from Haft.

"Put me down!" she shrieked. She flailed her arms and kicked her heels, but couldn't hit him with any force. "Let go of me, you—you—"

Rammer walked away with her struggling in his arms and protesting.

"Now now, Mistress Doli," he said calmly. "You're not behaving like the lady we all know you really are. Haft has important things to do now, and he didn't hurt anything by not telling you about Spinner."

"He—He had to bring up that—that—"

Rammer shook his head. "The way I heard it, you *were* mad at Spinner. But that's over now. We all have other things to do."

"Put me down, you—you—" She flailed and kicked more vigorously.

"Mistress Doli, I'll put you down as soon as you stop trying to hit and kick me," he said firmly.

"You—You—" She kicked and flailed even more violently, then sagged in his arms.

Rammer set her on her feet but didn't let go immediately. When she was still for a few seconds, he released her and took a step back. "Mistress Doli? Are you all right?"

She slowly turned and glared at him, her face flushed deep red. She pointed an accusing finger and gasped, "You—you—" Then she spotted Haft, both of whose cheeks were glowing bright red from her slaps, and flung her arm at him. "And you too!" she screamed. She spun about and flounced away, head high, fists once more clenched at her sides.

Rammer watched until he was certain she wouldn't turn back, then he rejoined Haft in front of the new battalion formation.

"Let that be a lesson to you," he said softly when he reached Haft. "Never, *ever*, remind a woman of her man's infidelity. Even when he's not her man and he wasn't unfaithful."

Spinner regained consciousness in the afternoon. Doli cooed over him and spoon-fed him broth. Then he went back to sleep. Though Doli stayed mad at Haft, she didn't go after him again.

Come morning, Silent was the only man in camp other than the slaves who didn't have an aching head and upset stomach. Which gave him a certain advantage.

He told the chief again what he'd said to him the night before. The chief nodded cautiously to indicate his understanding, and said something to the interpreters. When their translations agreed, Silent decided they weren't in too much postfeast pain to translate accurately and continued, advising the chief on what he should do.

Before the chief could compose a response, a slave brought a bowl of fermented comite milk for him and his face brightened. The chief eagerly emptied the bowl, then belched and sat quietly with his eyes closed for a few moments. When he opened them, he looked far less hung over. He sounded it too, when he spoke. The translators, who hadn't had a remedial libation, had trouble keeping up with him. He and Silent spoke back and forth.

By the time the sun was at its zenith, all the Desert Men were up, and most were no longer feeling the effects of the previous night—or near enough that it didn't affect their ability to move or speak. The chief ordered everybody to eat hearty. They did, though without music, singing, dancing, or more fermented comite milk than was needed for medicinal purposes. When they were all full, the chief dispatched riders deeper into the Low Desert. Silent and the chief made arrangements on how to meet again should they need to.

Soon afterward, the giant was back in the saddle, headed south, returning to the caravan.

The caravan stayed at the Jokapcul camp for three days. The eight hundred former prisoners, bathed, wearing clean clothes, and properly fed, regained strength quickly. The rest, combined with the ministrations of healing magicians and witches, had considerably moved their injuries and ills far along the path to health.

Spinner, however, was up and about the day after the battle. He wanted to move out immediately, or as soon as the new people could be fed into the caravan.

"You're a fool, Spinner," Haft snorted. "You had a concussion. They take time to heal. If you mount a horse now and try to do what you have done all along our journey, you will kill yourself."

"I'm all right, I just have a mild headache," Spinner replied.

"It's a small headache now," Alyline sniffed. "It won't be tonight if we go now."

"I'll be all right, really."

"Spinner, you're badly hurt," Doli told him, wrapping her

arms around his chest and pressing her body against his back. "You need rest."

Even Maid Primrose, who had barely spoken to him since she found out about Doli's love for him and his for Alyline when she first joined the flight from Eikby, stood before him and lay a gentle hand on his cheek. "You have to rest, Spinner," she insisted. If you don't . . ." She choked back a sob and turned away so he wouldn't see the tears slide down her cheeks.

Sergeant Rammer exchanged a grin with Captains Phard, Geatwe, and Mearh, then said sternly, "Marine, head injuries are treacherous. If any one of the healers says you need bed rest, you will have bed rest. And that's an order."

"But—"

"You shouldn't be standing up," Nightbird snapped, "you need to be in bed."

"Rest is the only cure for you," added one of the healing magicians.

"Lay down or I will put you down," Rammer growled.

"The Jokapcul—" Spinner objected.

"The Jokaps aren't coming now," Silent interrupted. "We have time for you to rest."

"How do you know that?" Spinner demanded.

Silent gave him a look that said he'd asked a dumb question. "We nomads of the Northern Steppes have our means."

"But—"

Haft, Rammer, and the company commanders closed on Spinner as Doli and Maid Primrose took his arms and pulled him to his pallet.

"But—"

Nobody paid any attention to his objections, and he didn't resist when the women lay him down and covered him with a light blanket.

"Haft," Rammer said when he was satisfied that Spinner was going to stay abed for at least a time, "come with me. We don't have much time, but we need to take full advantage of it. I want some help training the recruits of Company D. Have you seen to security?"

"Yes, Sergeant!" Haft said briskly in automatic response to his former detachment commander. "Lieutenant Jatke has the border soldiers screening to the west." Then he grimaced. *He* was the commander here, *not* Rammer! He was supposed to *give* the orders, not *take* them.

Rammer ignored the glare Haft gave him. The two headed for Company D. In fact, Haft knew Rammer was right about taking advantage of this time to train the recruits.

The shouts they heard as they approached the area assigned to the recruit company didn't prepare them for what they found when they got there. All the survivors of Company D's mistaken pursuit of the Desert Men stood in ranks with the men Rammer had recruited during the two days since—the survivors who had wanted to quit arms had instead decided to stay and get properly trained. Maybe it was simply due to encouragement or taunting from the other survivors, but they stayed.

Two hundred more men from the caravan were also gathered around—they all wanted to join the company and be trained in order to protect their families.

"We're going to need two training companies," Rammer said softly.

Haft simply nodded, he didn't trust his voice. Who would command the other company?

"Call a meeting of the officers," Rammer advised. "Find out who we've got who can properly train raw recruits."

"Right," Haft managed, and left to assemble the officers.

"We're going to have problems," Zweepee told Haft on the second day of the rest. It was a problem she would normally have taken to Spinner, but she didn't think he was well enough to deal with it, and she wasn't sure it could wait. Fletcher and Alyline, the only people she'd discussed it with, agreed with her.

Haft stifled a groan. "What problems?" He'd solved the problem of who would train the influx of recruits, but was still wrestling with who would replace the men assigned to that task from their positions as sergeants and corporals—and a lieutenant—in the other companies. He was also dealing with problems associated with the force suddenly growing from battalion-size to that of an understrength regiment. And, somehow, eight thousand people on the move had to be fed.

"The caravan had a few more than three hundred widows and other unmarried women," Zweepee said, either not knowing or not caring about Haft's other problems. "There are about a hundred and more among the prisoners we freed."

"Yes? We have 450 widows and other unmarried women. So?" Haft had no idea what she was driving at.

"We *had* about a hundred unattached men. Now we have about six hundred. There are too many men, not enough women. There will be fights."

Haft stared at her for a moment, not comprehending. There were always more men than women when a fleet put into port, and that seldom caused problems. Sure, a sea soldier or a sailor might get a little too attached to a whore and not want to share her and pull a knife on someone else who wanted to buy her for a time. But blood was seldom shed. All they had to do was . . .

He looked away from Zweepee and stared unfocused into nowhere. The caravan wasn't a fleet in port, it was a mobile town. Those women with their own wagon who had joined them before the company reached Eikby—and given intimate female company to the unmarried men—weren't available anymore. He was pretty sure all of them had paired off with one or another soldier. And, so far as he knew, no women had moved to take their place caring for the needs of the single men.

He'd heard of towns where there were more men than women, or more women than men. Whichever there were more of, enough left in search of mates that the balance was restored. People, especially men, particularly fighting men, couldn't leave the caravan, couldn't be allowed to.

He buried his face in his hands and wished Spinner was healthy so he didn't have to face this problem.

"How much time do you think we have before it becomes a problem?" he asked through his hands.

Zweepee shrugged. "If we're lucky, two weeks, a month."

"If we're lucky," Haft repeated. He made a quick calculation and muttered to himself, "If we're lucky, that's long enough to get more than halfway from here to Handor's Bay. "If we aren't lucky . . ."

Zweepee answered as though he'd spoken to her. "If we aren't lucky the problems are already starting."

"Let me think," Haft said. He briskly rubbed his face, then lowered his hands and walked away.

Zweepee watched him go. She also remembered the women with their own wagon and, unusual for a happily married woman, wished other women had taken their place. She shook her head. Not that four women would be enough. At least Haft knew there was a problem coming. Maybe there was some solution a soldier could think of that wouldn't occur to a woman. She hoped so. The thought of hundreds of soldiers without women deciding to take their way with whatever women came to hand frightened her.

On the afternoon of the third day, the healers decided Spinner was well enough to travel—as were the remaining severely wounded. The caravan set out soon after dawn the next morning, with Spinner under strict orders to spend most of the day in a wagon instead of on horseback, riding from one end of the caravan to the other. It wasn't as hard as it might have been to enforce the healers' orders—the gelding Spinner had ridden since they left the Burnt Man Inn in far off western Skragland was dead, killed by the demon's spit the Jokapcul officer had meant for him. He knew it would take time for him and a new horse to accustom themselves to each other. More important, he knew he wasn't up to learning a new horse just then.

They traveled out of sight of the shore and sea and made good time for a few days. Then the Zobran Border Warders roaming to the front brought back word of another Jokapcul prison camp.

CHAPTER
TWENTY-FOUR

Two days after the caravan resumed its eastward movement, the Dark Prince scuffed his soot-black boots through the sand, scattering the insects that feasted on the blood caked to the sand grains; here and there his hard leather soles crunched a shiny carapace. His hair was black, his shirt the color of hard coal, his trousers a moonless midnight, his cape a bottomless abyss. He held a black scabbard on one black-gloved hand and tapped it into his other black-gloved hand. His expression was as black as his garb. His stallion stood calmly nearby, munching on a patch of grass. The tackle seemed to merge seamlessly into the horse's ebon hide.

"Lord Lackland," said the Kamazai Commanding of the Jokapcul forces, coming to a halt in front of the Dark Prince, blocking his passage. The Kamazai Commanding's face was as heated as his expression was grim, lending it a color to match the bronze-dyed leather of his steel-rectangle-studded armor. His hands were wrapped so tightly around the hilts of the swords—one long, the other short—hanging from his belt that the knuckles were white.

The Dark Prince lifted his eyes from the sand and gifted the Kamazai Commanding with an expression equal in its grimness. Though in the case of the Dark Prince, fully half of the grimness was caused by the barbarian's use of the hated sobriquet. Someday, he thought, he would make this insufferable kamazai pay most painfully for use of the sobriquet "Lackland." For now, the Dark Prince said nothing. He waited for the Kamazai Commanding to speak.

"We have exhumed all the graves, the older ones as well as the fresh. The older held only the remains of slaves. The fresh ones held soldiers, more of ours than theirs."

The Dark Prince swept the bloodstained sand with his gaze. Why did this buffoon bother him with that detail? Buried soldiers were only to be expected, following a battle such as the one that had obviously been fought here. "Yes?"

"Ours were buried in shallow, mass graves," the Kamazai Commanding said through clenched teeth. "Theirs were put to better rest."

The Dark Prince struggled to control his impatience—shallow, mass graves were better treatment than *he* would allot a vanquished foe. He feigned disinterest.

"There are only the bodies of one troop's worth of our fighters," the kamazai said. "There were seven troops here. Where are the bodies of the other six troops?"

That information was so unexpected, the Dark Prince blinked in surprise. "Where indeed?" he snapped. "Look farther." It was impossible that six troops had mutinied and changed sides. Or . . . "Perhaps they pursue those bandits."

The Kamazai Commanding shook his head sharply. "I have scouts searching as far as a half day's march from here. The six troops will be found. They are not in pursuit. The bandits would not have had time to bury the dead if they had not killed the others." It was equally unthinkable that the six missing troops would have run in ignominious defeat.

Caws drew the Dark Prince's attention to the trees under which the dead had been buried. Carrion eaters were drifting down from the sky. Most of them alighted in the tops of the strange bumber trees; few attempted to perch on the branches of the fan trees, which were too springy to bear the weight of any but the smallest of them. Soldiers chased away the few birds bold enough to come to ground—chased them from the bodies of Jokapcul dead, allowed them to gorge on the bodies of the dead slaves and bandits. The Dark Prince imagined flies lighting on the corpses and laying their eggs, pictured the carapaced crawlers ponderously burrowing their way into the dead, and stifled a smile.

"Inform me immediately of your scouts' reports." He turned away to pace the battleground.

The Kamazai Commanding glared at the back of the arrogant foreigner who the High Shoton had seen fit to place in nominal command of his invasion force. A smile flickered across his face as he envisioned how he would make that insufferable princeling scream when he was finally given leave to dispatch him.

"Lord Lackland," the Kamazai Commanding reported that evening. "My scouts have returned from east and west. They have found no more graves, nor have they found signs of pursuit to the east nor signs of retreat to the west."

"And to the north?"

"None have yet returned from above the escarpment." He looked stonily in the direction of the line of cliffs that barred access to the Low Desert. "I have sent a troop to find them."

The Dark Prince followed his gaze and wondered.

The Kamazai Commanding thought and decided. "Some of the scouts who went west reported the bandit caravan left the road to climb the escarpment, then returned."

The Dark Prince flashed him a look mixed of hatred, disdain, and anger. "Why would they have gone above and then returned?"

"The Desert Men."

"They might have returned because of the Desert Men, but why would they have gone up in the first place?"

The kamazai only shook his head.

The two stood silent, side by side, for a few moments, each silently vowing death most hideous to the other, then looked to a sudden commotion in the forest and saw a young, mounted knight burst out of the trees.

The knight reined his horse mere yards from the duo and fell from the saddle as much as dismounted. The horse huffed and its eyes rolled wildly. Its hooves tap-tap-tapped nervously, as though it wanted to gallop farther. Blood mixed with the lather on its flanks. The young knight himself bled from multiple wounds. There was no control to his body when he dropped to his knees to give his report.

"Lord Kamazai," he barked, and added belatedly, "Dark Prince. Desert Men. They attacked. Killed all but me. We found—we found bodies. Scouts. Troops. All ours. Dead. Everyone." He hung his head, his body sagging and tilting to the side.

The Dark Prince and the Kamazai Commanding looked at each other, for once of one mind. The Dark Prince nodded curtly. The Kamazai Commanding returned the nod more thoughtfully, then marched off, barking and howling orders to his troops to prepare to move out, up to the plateau to punish the Desert Men. No one could be allowed to defeat a Jokapcul troop. *No one!*

The Dark Prince looked coldly at the knight who had brought the report from the near reaches of the Low Desert and coldly watched him fall to the side. He walked to his grazing horse and mounted to follow and observe the coming victory over the barbarous Desert Men.

The battle, when it came, was hardly one-sided. Yet it was a slaughter. Unlike when they attacked the refugee caravan, the Desert Men did not avoid the magicians and other users of demon weapons. They died in their scores and hundreds, but were relentless in their attacks on the magicians and other demon-weapon users. When the remnants of the Jokapcul force retreated, the Desert Men chief ululated orders to his surviving warriors to let them go. He wanted the word to spread among the invaders:

Mount the plateau of the Low Desert and die.

Don't miss the first two books
in the exciting Demontech
series!

DEMONTECH:
ONSLAUGHT
and
DEMONTECH:
RALLY POINT

When it comes to combating the
forces of evil,
all it takes is a few good men.

Published by Del Rey
www.delreydigital.com
Available wherever books are sold

Visit www.delreydigital.com—the portal to all the information and resources available from Del Rey Online.

- Read sample chapters of every new book, special features on selected authors and books, news and announcements, readers' reviews, browse Del Rey's complete online catalog, and more.

- Sign up for the Del Rey Internet Newsletter (DRIN), a free monthly publication e-mailed to subscribers, featuring descriptions of new and upcoming books, essays and interviews with authors and editors, announcements and news, special promotional offers, signing/convention calendar for our authors and editors, and much more.

To subscribe to the DRIN: send a blank e-mail to join-ibd-dist@list.randomhouse.com or sign up at www.delreydigital.com

The DRIN is also available at no charge for your PDA devices—go to www.randomhouse.com/partners/avantgo for more information, or visit www.avantgo.com and search for the Books@Random channel.

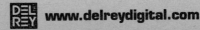 www.delreydigital.com